C000055955

The Perfect Match

The Perfect Match

Dandy Smith

embla books

First published in Great Britain in 2023 by

embla
books

Bonnier Books UK Limited
4th Floor, Victoria House, Bloomsbury Square, London, WC1B 4DA
Owned by Bonnier Books
Sveavägen 56, Stockholm, Sweden

Copyright © Dandy Smith, 2023

All rights reserved.
No part of this publication may be reproduced, stored or transmitted in any form
or by any means, electronic, mechanical, photocopying or otherwise, without the
prior written permission of the publisher.

The right of Dandy Smith to be identified as Author of this work has been
asserted by them in accordance with the Copyright, Designs and Patents
Act 1988

This is a work of fiction. Names, places, events and incidents are either the
products of the author's imagination or used fictitiously. Any resemblance to
actual persons, living or dead, is purely coincidental.

A CIP catalogue record for this book is available from the British Library.

ISBN: 9781471415364

This book is typeset using Atomik ePublisher

Embla Books is an imprint of Bonnier Books UK
www.bonnierbooks.co.uk

For Josh Butler-Smith. My familiar face. Always.

Chapter One

Now

Even though I've washed and rewashed my hands, there is still dried blood beneath my fingernails. Like rust on a bike chain. I sit in the eerie quiet of this room and stare at the magnolia walls, the little table which has been bolted to the carpet-tiled floor, the recorder tucked into the recess of the alcove, and try not to think about the cracked skull or the look on your face.

The chair creaks beneath my fidgeting weight. Getting comfortable after hours spent sitting is impossible; my back aches and my legs are stiff, and my tongue lies like a raisin in my mouth thanks to a night stretched thin answering questions.

Because of you.

I lift my hand to bite my nails – a habit I thought I'd left behind – and stop when I remember the blood and the ink staining my fingers. Then, the door to this magnolia hell swings open and another nondescript policeman strides in. The plastic cup of water looks too small in his large hand. He doesn't speak as he places it on the table, but the accusation in his eyes is clear: murderer.

He leaves and when the door closes behind him, it is gun-shot loud and makes me jump. My hand shakes as I pick up the cup, water sloshing over the sides and dripping onto the clothes I was given by the police when they brought me in. My own are somewhere in the station, carefully folded into a clear plastic bag labelled 'evidence'.

Even though I try not to think of you, I am swept along memory lane and the first pitstop is your university room; we were nineteen, huddled beneath the bedcovers, when you whispered those magic words for the first time, 'How much do you love me?'

'To the moon and round the stars.'

'Not enough,' you breathed. 'How much do you love me?'

'As much as you want me to and even more.'

Through the silky blackness, I could feel your smile.

But these words are the poisoned spell that brought me here. They are the reason for the body lying in the morgue.

My hand is wet. I've squeezed the neck of my cup until it has split, its watery insides gushing out. Dropping it onto the table, I stare down at the blood beneath my fingernails and then back at the closed door. They are waiting for an answer to a question that has been asked so many times in the last few hours, each word is seared into my skin. At the thought of blistering my tongue with the truth, of burning you, panic drags me down into the twisting dark, and I am wearing guilt like a pair of iron boots.

If screaming were a feeling, it would be this.

Chapter Two

Before

Pennard House is the perfect wedding venue. It has ivy-covered stone walls, a rose garden and a quaint footbridge over a large pond. A ceremony room with a chandelier and high, arched windows. I cast around for Ivy again but, predictably, she's late.

The bride and groom have been lucky with the weather, too, because June doesn't guarantee sunshine. At least, not in England. Today, though, the sun spills across the crayon-blue sky, and as I mill around outside, making pre-ceremony small talk with guests I don't really know, we inevitably seize upon this British conversational staple.

'Yes, absolutely gorgeous weather,' I tell the couple who saw me standing alone and decided to take me under their wing. I wonder again if they're siblings or if they're dating. They have the same thick, shiny, public-school hair and air of easy confidence that seems natural to the lucky few born into a family that can afford ski holidays in Verbier.

'Mummy was married in the spring of eighty-three,' the woman is telling me. 'And she said it was ghastly weather, didn't she, Talbot?'

Brother, then.

'Frightful,' he concludes before winding an arm around her waist. Lovers. Definitely lovers.

'Oh look,' she says, 'there's Auntie Morven.' Cousins, maybe?

A photographer appears and snaps some candid shots of me with these two strangers as I try to work out whether or not they've ever had sex.

As they chat, I check my phone, hoping for a message from Ivy explaining where she is or how late, exactly, she'll be. There isn't one. I'd thought, since this is *her* friend's wedding, she'd be on time. But then, Ivy Holt is the type of person that exciting, dramatic things just happen to. Adventures plucked from the air and gifted to her because she is beautiful and charismatic and educated. Just a couple of months ago she popped out to buy passata for dinner, and at the supermarket, she met a man she beguiled who promptly whisked her away for a weekend in Amsterdam. Naturally, she'd tired of him by the time they returned.

I decide not to check my phone again and to enjoy the wedding, especially since I'm not having to run around organising it. So, I sip my champagne and take it all in: the beautiful people in beautiful clothes, the raised spirits and raised glasses, the hum of expectation and cheer that ziplines through the crowd. As a wedding planner, I've been to dozens of these events and every single one is a perfectly formed bubble of happiness. At twenty-eight, I'm starting to attend just as many weddings as a guest. It's like a domino effect: once one friend from uni got engaged and married, the rest fell in line. Soon, I'll be the only one without an expensive piece of precious metal on her left hand. Ivy would snort at this, and tell me I'm being ridiculous, because what does it matter if I never get married? But she knows why, too. Because I don't want to end up like my mother. Just as she doesn't want to end up like hers.

I knock back the last of my drink, trying to swallow with it that panicky feeling of being left behind. Still, I *love* weddings. I love the rosy atmosphere and the gorgeous floral arrangements. I love the fashion and the music and the readings. I love the little anecdotes that are plucked from memory and scrawled onto pieces of paper, unfolded and read aloud. I love the food. I love—

'God, I hate weddings,' says Ivy as she appears by my side, a glass of wine in hand. I glance at my phone. As ever, she is unapologetically forty minutes late.

'You were meant to be here ages ago,' I say. 'This is *your* friend's wedding.'

She looks up at me from beneath long dark lashes. 'Zara Barton, don't be a snippy bitch.' In one smooth motion, she's taken my empty flute, popped it onto a passing server's tray and pressed a fresh drink into my hand, before turning her bright white smile on the two people who've been keeping me company. 'Talbot, Lollie, great to see you again.'

'I *adore* your dress,' says Lollie.

I feel a stab of disapproval when I realise it's the silk one from Wild and Fine that she can't afford. It costs the same as a week's rent. The thing is, these are all of Ivy's boarding-school friends from *before* and she has to keep up appearances. I just hope the tags are still attached, so she can return it later.

Once Talbot and Lollie move off, I ask her if they're relatives or lovers. 'Both,' she tells me. 'Well, kind of. First cousins. No. *Second* cousins. You know, whichever is legal.'

'Because that's not weird. It's like something from a Virginia Andrews novel.'

'Keeps the bloodlines pure,' Ivy sing-songs.

I shudder, picturing myself slipping into bed with my cousin Jamie. In my mind, he is still an awkward sixteen-year-old with acne, a Billy Talent T-shirt and too much eyeliner. 'Would you ever sleep with your cousins?'

'Cousin,' she corrects me. 'Theo was my aunt's stepson so he doesn't count, and even then he unironically wears socks with sliders, so absolutely not. As for Roman ... Let's just say, I'm glad he moved to New Zealand. Being an arsehole is his Olympic sport.'

I smile at her signature candour – it's impossible to stay annoyed with her for long, even when she's left me waiting on my own for forty minutes in a courtyard full of strangers. 'Dare I ask *why* you were so late?'

She smiles wickedly. 'I had to steal *this* –' she holds up her wrist so I can see the delicate gold charm bracelet '– back from my father, before it ended up in the hands of whoever he's currently bedding.'

A new dress she can't afford *and* a stolen bracelet to complete the ensemble? This wedding is more important to her than I realised. 'Did it belong to your mother?' I ask. It wouldn't be the first time Hugo had gifted his late wife's jewellery to another woman.

She nods, stroking a little leaf pendant.

'So you just broke in and took it?' I ask, not sure why I'm at all surprised.

She sighs. 'So dramatic, Zara. It's not like I smashed a window or kicked down a door. I used the spare key.'

'Much better,' I deadpan. 'Won't he notice it's gone?'

She lifts her chin. 'If he does, he'll have to come and get it back, won't he?'

I'm pretty sure the only way Ivy ever secured her father's undivided attention growing up was by getting into as much trouble as possible. Though she's older now, she isn't much wiser. It will take a lot more than a missing bracelet to make Hugo appear at our front door.

A waitress stops beside us with canapés, and we take two each.

'So Thea's the bride, but who's the groom?' I ask.

'Arlo.'

'Are they cousins?' I tease.

'Worse: they met at a farmers' market.' Ivy pulls a face: she's anti-meet cutes, and romance in general. 'I still can't believe Thea's getting married. I never thought she'd be a lemming. Sad.'

I scoff. 'Getting married is hardly the same as blindly following a crowd over a cliff.'

She arches one perfectly manicured brow. 'Isn't it?'

I sip my drink.

'Thea used to be a free spirit,' Ivy says. 'She was going to travel to India, buy a tuk-tuk and brew and sell her own chai tea.'

'She'd struggle to afford such a lavish wedding if she relied on chai-tea sales,' I offer dryly.

Ivy smiles, but continues in a sombre tone, as though we're at Thea's funeral and not her wedding. 'She never even wanted to get married. I mean, she read Carol Ann Duffy and started the feminist society at school, for God's sake.'

I bristle. 'You can get married and still be a feminist, Ivy.'

'How? Marriage is a patriarchal construct.'

'Feminism is about equality. You'd never tell a man not to get married because he's a man; telling a woman not to get married because she's a woman is, in itself, sexist.' I shrug. 'Besides, marriage and children are normal things to want.'

'Well, you're biased, you've always wanted to get married,' Ivy points out. 'Your whole bloody life is a blur of weddings. You're going to spend from now to eternity fishing sugared almonds in organza pouches out of every bag you own.'

I grin. 'You're so cynical.'

'I'm happy to be a cynic,' Ivy drawls. 'Leave me to my wine and my spite and my murder documentaries, thank you.'

Other friends, Amira especially, can't understand how we're so close when we have such drastically different life goals. But people are more than just what they want out of life. Ivy is candour and confidence. Snark and seduction. Freedom and fierce loyalty. And I'm never more myself than when I'm with her.

She waves to a couple across the patio then says to me, 'I hope Thea doesn't take his name. Your mum got it right when she gave you her surname and not Rupert's. Imagine having to share a name with your wicked little stepsister.'

'*Half*-sister, and anyway, Polly took Matthew's name when they married so she isn't an Ellery anymore either.'

'I'd never take a man's name. When my parents married, my father took my mother's,' Ivy says proudly, and I can't help but think Hugo did this more because the Holt family is powerful and esteemed, and less because he's a budding feminist. 'Besides, I like my name,' she continues, popping a canapé into her mouth. 'Why is it expected that I'd give up a piece of my identity, just because I have a vagina?'

I shrug. 'Is a name a piece of identity?'

She stares at me, dumbfounded. 'I don't know,' she says sarcastically. 'What if I started calling you Jasmine? Or Gertrude?'

I try not to laugh. 'Gertrude?'

She rolls her eyes with trademark impatience. 'Laura. Lauren. Whatever. Would you identify with that name? Or would you feel like I'd stolen something from you?'

'Yes, I suppose I would,' I relent.

'Forename, surname, they're both a part of who you are. Name and identity are interwoven.'

We fall quiet and I think about what she's saying. Ivy's family name is renowned, and thanks to Holt Hotels, it is synonymous with wealth and importance. While my family name – my mother's, because nothing she ever does is traditional – is renowned only to the people who live alongside her in Queen's Court, and for all the wrong reasons. Much to Ivy's disdain, I'm not sure I'd miss my surname if I gave it up for someone else's. In fact, I look forward to it. Eagerly.

'Be honest, Zara,' Ivy says, lowering her voice and leaning into me so I can smell her perfume. 'Do you want a husband and child because *you* want them, or because you've been conditioned to think you need those things to be happy?'

'And your endless one-night stands,' I counter, relishing our familiar game of verbal ping-pong. 'Do you have them because *you* want them, or because you know your father would disapprove?'

She hesitates, just for a second. 'I *really* like sex.'

'And I *really* like marriage.'

Ivy frowns, her catlike eyes narrowing. 'You can't know that, you've never *been* married.'

'You're impossible.'

She raises her glass. 'And right.'

I smile and shake my head. She's got that public-school confidence, too – lingering long after she was cut off from the family fortune by her grandfather, when overnight, she went from Gucci and summers spent in Mykonos, to Topshop and summers spent working two jobs just to pay rent.

'Remember when we used to debate things like: what gets you drunker faster, vodka or tequila?' Ivy asks wistfully, as though reading my mind.

'When we were students, and hangovers only lasted a day?'

I remember the night we met at university, in the bathroom of the SU. I was drunkenly reapplying my lipstick with one hand, while using the other to steady myself on the sink as the room cartwheeled around me. I was seven shots of tequila deep and nursing a broken heart, because my boyfriend, Luke, had moved miles away for university. I'd wanted to go with him, but, thanks to my mother, I was chained to Somerset.

Then *she* burst into the bathroom. Burst into my life. Took one look at my watery, bloodshot eyes, pointed a finger at me and started singing. After a couple of lines, I recognised the song from *Dirty*

Dancing. I joined in, and we sang the last line of 'Big Girls Don't Cry' at the top of our lungs.

She came close, so all I could see was the green of her eyes, which reminded me of light hitting water. 'You're beautiful,' she whispered, echoing my exact thoughts about her. 'If you were mine, I would never break your heart.'

And just like that, my inebriated pity party for one dissolved. Ivy, petite and dark and vibrant, was my knight in sequinned armour.

Then she was gone, leaving a trail of positive vibes and Jo Malone Wild Bluebell in her wake. I thought she was just another Drunk Girl in The Toilet; one I'd think about occasionally, and wonder. I didn't have to wonder for long, though, because I saw her again the following week. This time, *she* was the one bawling on the bathroom floor of the SU, and there wasn't a single classic 80s movie hit that could save her because she'd just been told her mother was dying.

I can hardly believe that was ten years ago. Sometimes, I can't remember what my life was like before her.

'Thea's become a personality void,' Ivy's now complaining, puncturing my recollections. 'I swear, all she's talked about for weeks is planning this "fairy-tale" wedding. I told her to just serve porridge, release three rabid bears onto the dance floor and call it a day.'

I wince, imagining doling out the same advice to one of my highly strung, neurotic brides. 'Was she impressed?'

'Absolutely not. Writing her own vows has pushed her so far over the edge, she's lost her sense of humour.'

'It's sweet.'

Ivy pulls another face. 'Yeah, because there's no better way to kick off eternity together than with a homework assignment.'

I laugh so hard, I almost choke on my drink.

'Also, since when do British people register for gifts? Like, what the fuck are you going to do with a crystal hippo, Thea?' I'm still laughing when she sighs and says, 'All weddings are the same.'

'They aren't,' I protest, though it sounds weak, even to my ears.

Ivy snorts. 'Wanna bet? Every time there's a wedding cliché, we have to do a shot. If I'm right, we'll have irreversible liver damage before the speeches.'

'Clichés such as . . .'

She ticks them off on her fingers. 'If we see a doughnut wall, a sweet cart, literally anything in a mason jar, drinks, flowers, fairy lights.'

I grin, because she's right and this is a game in which I will excel. I start thinking. 'If the bride stays silent during the wedding speeches,' I say.

Ivy's appalled. 'She'd better speak, she has two degrees, for Christ's sake.'

'If they serve chicken wrapped in ham at the wedding breakfast.'

'Perfect.'

'If they do the obligatory sparkler exit photograph,' I offer, on a roll now.

'Yes! Seriously, who thought it was a good idea for intoxicated people to handle actual fire?' A group of women eavesdropping on our conversation shoot us filthy looks. Ivy lowers her voice. 'Zara, I swear to God, if either of them says how lucky they are to be marrying their best friend, I'll fuck Arlo on the wedding cake.'

'Ivy!'

'He would, he's always had a thing for me.'

'Doesn't everyone?' I say because it's true. No one can deny Ivy Holt. 'This is such an evil game,' I tell her. '*We're* evil and we're going to hell.'

She smirks. 'Yeah, but I'll get us the best seats.'

Chapter Three

Eventually, we trickle into the ceremony room. On every available surface, there are pink and white peonies – my favourite flowers, ones I'll have at my wedding, if I can ever convince a man to stay in the same country long enough to propose. I'm thinking about Luke, even though I promised Ivy I wouldn't. I glance at her; she's watching me carefully. It's like she knows I've just let us both down. Before she can say anything, though, a hush falls over the crowd. Someone must've given the signal, because we instinctively rise for the bride.

The harpist starts playing Iron & Wine. We turn towards the candle-lined aisle and watch the bridesmaids walk self-consciously up it. Anticipation is thick in the air as we wait for Thea, twisting and craning to catch a glimpse. I've seen hundreds of brides in hundreds of dresses, but I still feel fizzy with excitement. I picture the dress I'd wear if I were getting married today: Italian lace, bardot neckline and long, flowing sleeves from Enzoani or Maggie Sottero. I sneak another look at Ivy. Her eyes are fixed resolutely forward, her expression unreadable.

If Ivy believed in marriage, I can't help but think – if her father hadn't taken the sanctity of it, screwed it into a ball and set it on fire in front of her – she'd choose something far less obvious than me to walk down the aisle in. Maybe a white jumpsuit, or even a dress in shocking scarlet.

Finally, Thea appears. She's beautiful. Demure. Serene. Everything I want to be on my big day. Her gown has a high neck and a low back. It's expensive, and so white it glows.

Ivy, who's finally deigned to turn around for Thea's entry, leans into me and whispers, 'White. *Really?* I mean, sure, who needs a hymen when you're wearing three grand's worth of Mulberry silk?'

I stifle a giggle. But sober up when I see Arlo's face. God, the way he looks at Thea. Like she's the centre of everything.

A memory of Luke sweeps me from the ceremony room and into the London hotel he'd taken me to as a surprise, a few months ago.

'Stay with me,' he'd whispered against my bare skin. 'I'm leaving for Bali in two days. Come with me. You'll be gone a month. Just one month.'

Going to London for a weekend was one thing, flying to Bali for a whole month was something else entirely. It wouldn't be just *one* trip. With Luke, there's always another flight to catch. I have my mother to think about. My job. Ivy. I have responsibilities. Abandoning everything would make me no better than my father. Besides, the nomadic lifestyle is Luke's dream, not mine. I want a nice house and a family to raise. I want stability. All the things I never had growing up, and globetrotting with Luke won't achieve that. So, I turned him down for the umpteenth time – and even though it was the right thing to do and I know I can never say yes, I dread the day he'll finally stop asking.

Ivy's hand on my wrist brings me back to myself. 'If Thea's predictable enough to take Arlo's name, I'm making us *inject* tequila into our veins.'

At the reception, Ivy knocks back champagne like it's water. I stand beside her and listen as she drunkenly makes plans with an old friend, Hattie, that there's no way she can afford to keep. 'Next month works for me,' she's saying breezily. 'But if we go to The Circle you have to get the squid. It's *the* dish.'

I know for a fact that Ivy's never even been to The Circle. She only knows about the squid through various food blogs, because she reads restaurant reviews like some people read the news. I'm sure The Circle is on the running list she keeps on her phone, of places she aspires to eat at someday. When she can afford to – if ever, because living in Bath on a PR assistant's salary, even in the tiny, damp flat that we rent, means Ivy doesn't have a lot of spare cash, in spite of what she's telling Hattie now.

Eventually, Hattie is whisked away by a group of thin women who all most definitely had a parent-funded gap year in Asia.

I want to tell Ivy, who's surveying the room strategically over the top of her drink, that she's wasting her time trying to impress these people. People who abandoned her after her mother died, and her father's affairs and embezzlement were slapped across page six. People who treated her as though bereavement and bankruptcy were contagious. People who didn't offer to help when, as punishment for her father's sins, her grandfather not only cut his son-in-law off, he deserted her, as well. But I don't. Because eating overpriced squid in coveted restaurants makes Ivy feel important: it tells people that, although she may be the estranged daughter of Hugo Holt and the granddaughter Alfred Holt tossed aside, she still has power, because she still has youth and beauty and money. Or, at least, the appearance of money. Now, admiring Ivy's dress, I think about all the unpaid credit-card bills I found in our flat, stuffed under the rust-coloured velvet sofa she just had to have. 'It's a bargain,' she'd said of that sofa, as the deliveryman, perspiring, maneuvered it into place. 'The salesman gave us a great discount. Truly, Zara, the secret to life is letting men believe they have a chance of fucking you.'

We speak to Thea only once. Ivy introduces me to her, and we both chorus that she is gorgeous, and moon over the dress, though I do it with much more sincerity than Ivy who is still seething that Thea did, in fact, take Arlo's name. Like all brides, Thea's mind is whirring, because this may be the happiest day of her life but it's also the busiest. She thanks us for coming, her eyes already scanning the room over our shoulders, looking for other guests she needs to talk to. I feel a sting of envy that I'm not getting married. That I'm not even close.

It's late. People are sunburnt and clumsy and drunk. I've lost sight of Ivy, who's off somewhere, bewitching men and making women hate her – because she may not have as much money as they do, but she's prettier and thinner, and always having more fun than anyone else in the room. Meanwhile, I've attracted the unwanted attention of a Cambridge alumnus, a man named Alfie, who is energetically regaling me with not-so-fascinating tales of his varsity rowing days.

He's somehow managed to back me into a quiet corner, away from everyone; and he's standing too close. I can smell his sweat and his beer-soaked breath. As he talks, he stares openly at my chest, and I wonder if he's disappointed that there isn't much to look at. Ivy once joked that if someone ever tried to motorboat me, they'd break their nose on my sternum.

So that I have something to do with my hands, I sip the drink I didn't ask for and don't want, but felt too churlish to turn down. Alfie moves closer still, and then his fingers are resting on my hip. Uncomfortable, I try to shift away but the drinks bar is pressed against my back.

'It was our "big win",' I hear him say as I tune back into the conversation.

'Wonderful.' I give him a polite smile. 'Anyway, it's been great talking to you but I'm sure my friend is probably wondering where I am, so . . .'

'She'll find you,' Alfie tells me. 'You haven't finished your drink yet.'

Is he one of those men who thinks buying a woman a drink is transactional: a G&T in exchange for sex? I'm not sure if it's my inherent British politeness that holds me here, or the fear that if I assert myself, he'll cause a scene and call me a cock-tease. I am tired of trying to find the perfect balance between being too friendly and not being friendly enough. I'm jealous that this is a concern that will rarely, if ever, cross the mind of our male counterparts. Still, I nod and smile and sip my drink again so as not to be *difficult*.

My disinterest in him isn't because he's unattractive: he's broad and bearded with sandy blond hair and dimples. In fact, he's objectively good-looking. But that bone-deep ache to touch him, to be touched *by* him, isn't there. Not like it is with Luke. But with Luke, as with all highs, it's followed by the inevitable comedown which leaves me exhausted and sick to my stomach.

I listen politely to his next story about a beer crawl in Bath before I try to excuse myself again. 'I really do need to find my friend. It was nice to meet you, though.'

Before I can move off, he steps into my path. I swing right, deciding to go around him, but he blocks my way, cutting me off from the music and the people beyond his broad shoulders. The barman's busy down the other end of the long bar; and the rest of the guests seem suddenly far away.

The frustration that's been building inside me for the last half an hour wells up and bursts from my lips, like water from a dam. 'Can you let me pass, please?'

Please. Polite or weak? Ivy would never have said 'please'.

He holds his palms up as if to calm a rabid animal. 'Whoa. Have I said something to offend you?'

He hasn't. What makes me uncomfortable is his bulk, his body language, the way he won't let me leave. I'm reluctant to explain this to him, though, because not only has he had a bit to drink but I'm not convinced he'll get it. I doubt he's ever felt trapped or intimidated by someone who is bigger and stronger and clearly wants sex from him.

'Well?' he says.

'No, you haven't said anything offensive, but—'

'Let's have another drink. Start over,' he says. Then he leans in too close. 'In fact, there's a minibar in my room.'

OK. I've had enough. I step forward to rejoin the party and find Ivy, but Alfie doesn't let me by. He may as well be a brick wall; there's no way I can get past him, and he knows it. Anger and fear swirl in the pit of my stomach. I'm about to tell him to back off when a tall man with dark hair and an expensive suit suddenly appears at my side. 'Ah, there you are, darling,' he says in warm, rich tones, sliding an arm around my waist. 'I've been looking all over for you.' I'm so stunned by this complete stranger, I don't know how to respond. No matter: he's already turning an icy smile Alfie's way and saying, 'Very good of you to keep my girlfriend company.'

Alfie frowns, his gaze roaming over the stranger, sizing him up. Where Alfie is bulky, built like a barn door, our latecomer is slender – a runner, maybe. If it comes down to a physical altercation, my money is on Alfie. Even so, he stays quiet. This stranger's presence embodies confidence and power. Beneath the relaxed way in which he holds himself, there is an undercurrent of menace. Of challenge.

Alfie, perhaps recognising this, makes up his mind. He clears his throat and mutters, 'No problem.'

The stranger holds Alfie's gaze. The silence stretches on for a few seconds longer than is comfortable, and suddenly, the tension is so thick, you could slice it up and serve it on toast. 'Enjoy the rest of your night,' says the stranger, releasing Alfie from whatever spell he'd cast.

Without so much as a grunt, Alfie slinks away.

'Are you alright?' asks the stranger, that warm, rich tone returning, like hot maple syrup poured over pancakes. I look up into his face; his dark brows are knitted in genuine concern. He's older than me, late thirties, maybe – there are fine lines branching around his dark eyes. 'I hope I didn't overstep. I was watching you for a while and it was . . . uncomfortable.'

'I'm fine,' I hear myself say, momentarily distracted by his smile; it's so white and straight. A Hollywood smile.

'It's a sad world we live in when some men can't take no for an answer.'

'Unless it's coming from another man,' I offer.

His expression is wry. 'I don't think we're that different from the lions you see in a David Attenborough documentary. Posturing for territory. Dominance. Sex.' Our eyes meet properly for the first time, and beneath the canopy of fairy lights strung above our heads, I realise his eyes aren't dark, they're hazel – moss and earth and autumn leaves. His hand is still on my waist, warm and reassuring. He notices, too, and clears his throat. Rather reluctantly, I think, he unwinds himself from me. 'Anyway, I want to apologise on behalf of our boorish friend.'

Boorish. I smile. How very public-school of him. 'Thank you for coming over,' I say, wishing I'd been more assertive myself.

'I hope he hasn't put you off the rest of us,' he says. 'It's not *all* men.' *Not all men.* Ivy would spit feathers at that, I know. She once said – after yet another news story of a woman being brutally raped and murdered by a man – that *not all men* is the equivalent to saying 'not all sharks'. Not all sharks bite, but they can if they choose to, because all sharks have teeth. You still wouldn't want to get in the water with one alone.

Although I agree with her, I'm not as acid-tongued, and don't spit my opinions in the faces of others like arsenic-laced bullets. Or maybe that's just how I justify my own cowardice.

'Alfie is probably off somewhere licking his wounds, but I'm not sure he's sorry for his *boorish* behaviour,' I say, with a smile.

His own mouth curves up at one corner. 'At least now he's being a twat elsewhere.'

Feeling that this is the verbal equivalent of him loosening his tie, unbuttoning his shirt and rolling his sleeves up to the elbow, my smile widens. The penned-in claustrophobia I felt with Alfie has dispersed, the threads of a bad dream being carried off into the night, and I realise I feel safe with his man, even though I don't know him. Ivy would scoff at this, of course, because men don't make her feel safe. Not since her father was caught shagging his PA behind her dying mother's back.

'So, how do you know the couple?' I ask, because I don't want him to leave. Not yet.

'We move in the same circles. Know the same people. End up at the same Christmas parties.'

I try to imagine him outside of this venue, certain he whiles away his time in dark wine bars, takes work lunches in expensive restaurants with crisp white table linen, and hosts exquisite dinner parties, the grown-up kind that boast a cheese course, with his thin, pretty wife. Involuntarily, my gaze drifts down towards his left hand. No wedding band. Interesting. He catches me looking and heat spreads across my cheeks.

'Maybe you know my friend,' I say to distract from my furious blushing. 'I'm her plus-one – Ivy Holt?'

There's a flash of recognition, I see it in his face; it's fleeting, like the glowing eyes of some small animal passing in the dark, then it's gone. 'Maybe,' he says vaguely.

'She's usually the life and soul at these events, I'm surprised you don't know her.'

He nods politely. 'And how are the two of you acquainted?'

'We live together.' His brow quirks ever so slightly, and I realise how that sounds. I rush to clarify. 'We're like sisters. Friends since university.'

I watch him carefully, but the recognition I thought I saw earlier is gone. Maybe it was never there at all. He's Ivy's type. Older. Charming. The kind of man that can fill a room all by himself. Like her father does. This man is almost the perfect match for her, I think. Except that for Ivy, a wedding ring, rather than acting as a deal-breaker, would be the cherry on the cake. Married men are safer because they're already attached. There's no chance of being hurt, like Ivy's mother was by her father. Like *she* was. Married men are inherently sinful: bad people for cheating on their wives. They reinforce her belief that men are uncaring bastards – and no one can argue because she has proof. Although, five years ago, after the mess she made of Quinn's life and the ultimatum I issued – stop wrecking families or you'll lose me – she promised she was done with married men.

While he's talking, I suddenly find myself picturing Ivy and this man together. All heat and bare skin and breathless excitement. It's her I see, tossing her dark curtain of hair over her shoulder as she rides him in one of those highbacked leather armchairs. He gazes up at her, enthralled by her impossibly long lashes, her tight, lithe body, her round, perfect breasts. He's bewitched by her, by the very essence of her. As all men are.

'It sounds as though Ivy would get along quite well with my plus-one,' my companion remarks, breaking in on my thoughts.

I flush; then my stomach sinks as I register what he's saying. Of course: a lack of wedding band doesn't mean a lack of partner.

'Jonty,' he adds. 'He's a close friend.'

I brighten.

'We're as thick as thieves,' he says, gaze skimming the crowd. 'He's around here somewhere, I'm sure.'

'Maybe they're already together. I hope he doesn't steal her away. Ivy's the only person at this wedding I know.'

'That's not true,' he twinkles. 'You know me.'

'We don't even know each other's names.' I look at him from beneath my lashes. I'm flirting, I realise. Even though I have no confirmation that Ivy's ever been with this man – that she's ever even met him – I've found myself in a secret, nonsensical little competition with her for his attention.

'Henry,' he offers. 'Henry Frith.'

I hold out my hand. A gesture intended to be playful, flirtatious. For a second, I'm worried he won't lean into it. But he does. His grip is firm and warm, his skin silk-soft. 'Zara,' I tell him, businesslike. 'Zara Barton.'

'Nice to meet you, Zara Barton.' The way he says my name is intimate, as though it's being whispered against my naked back. Another flush spreads across my cheeks.

'Likewise, Henry Frith,' I say, his name melting on my tongue, smooth like dark chocolate.

I buy him a drink – whisky and ice. There is something really sexy about a man who drinks whisky. It's debonair. A long way from the snakebites or the vodka and Cokes that the boys of my early twenties ordered, in the kinds of sticky bars that insisted on branding you with a near-permanent stamp upon entry.

Outside, we warm ourselves by the firepit, and he tells me about a whisky tasting he went to in Scotland last year. Even though I've never felt the burning desire to visit a distillery, I like hearing him talk. He's so charismatic. I could listen to his voice all night. It's the kind of smooth, full-bodied voice that commands attention, that could narrate an audiobook or host a podcast.

'Have you ever been to Scotland?' he asks me now.

'Never,' I tell him. 'But I've read about it.'

'Not the same.'

He swirls the last of his whisky in his tumbler. Then he meets my eyes. For a second, I wonder if he's going to invite me to join him in Edinburgh on his next trip. After the tasting, we'd tour the city's smoky, gothic buildings and wander hand in hand down winding, cobbled streets and into a cosy pub. We'd choose a table at the back, in front of the fire, and we'd remember the day we met, when we sat beside the firepit at a wedding, conversation spilling out into the night. He clears his throat, breaking my reverie, and the moment passes.

Disappointment pools in my stomach. It's completely ridiculous. I don't even know this man, yet I'm disappointed he isn't packing my bags and scooping me up for a weekend away? But I want to be like Ivy: the kind of person dramatic, exciting things just happen to.

Henry launches into another story. And even though I know I am tragic, while he talks, I turn the incident with Alfie into an anecdote to be told and retold in my imagined relationship with Henry. I would say: *I never considered myself a damsel in distress, but I'm glad I let you rescue me from that* boorish *man.* He'd smile and say: *Thank you for not asking me to don a cape and tights.* I would say: *Oh, but there's still time.* Then he'd kiss me and whisper: *You know I'm the happiest I've ever been. It's* you *who rescued* me.

The feminist in me cringes at imagining being married to a man I've only just met. But the strength of my feelings towards Henry surprises me. I haven't felt a connection this powerful, this quickly, since Luke. I imagine Ivy's scorn: I can hear her in my head, mocking me. The wild romantic in me has always aggravated the stern cynic in her. Even so, the bruised heart Luke's left me with, again, is looking for a distraction. A possibility. Something new.

'I want to know more about you,' says Henry. He leans back a little, taking me in. 'Tell me about yourself.'

'You want me to recite my CV?'

'Sorry. Did that sound like an interview question?'

I smile. 'A little.'

He winces. 'Not quite the mood I was aiming for.'

I want to lean in close and whisper, 'What mood *were* you aiming for?' but it's too bold. More Ivy's style than mine. Coming from her lips, this line would drip with sexual promise. Spoken by me, it would be clunky and awkward. An ill-fitting dress stolen from a big sister's wardrobe. Instead, I sip my wine and say mock-formally, 'I've been a wedding planner for six years, but before that I worked as an administrator at my university. My transferable skills include, but are not limited to, the following . . .'

Henry shakes his head, amused. But Ivy would have him eating out of the palm of her hand by now, I think despondently.

I watch the flames lick across the wood in the pit and feel his eyes on me, his gaze as hot as the fire warming my bare legs. 'So,' he says.

'A wedding planner? Does that make you a hopeless romantic or a bored observer?'

'A hopeless romantic, of course.'

'Did you used to watch your parents' wedding video like it was a Warner Brothers movie?'

I blink, taken by surprise. Though he doesn't realise it, his question stings, like being jabbed with the end of a lit cigarette. I choose my words carefully and keep my tone light so as not to bring down the conversation. 'No. My parents were never married.'

Apparently, my feigned carefreeness is too convincing because he pushes the burning end of the cigarette into me again. 'Are they still together?'

Reluctantly, I shake my head. I don't like admitting this to anyone if I can avoid it. It's the twenty-first century, split families aren't viewed through a lens of shame anymore; but Ivy is the only person I know who truly understands the weight of responsibility that can come from being the child of a broken home. She and I are the glue that failed to hold our parents' marriages together.

Henry, noticing my shift in mood, says, 'Well, I can assure you that a happy couple a long marriage doth not necessarily make.'

I'm not sure if he's talking about his own parents or himself. He's older, after all: maybe he's divorced. Our eyes meet for the hundredth time tonight, but this is different. It's intimate and sincere; I feel it all the way to my toes. We've started something. This is our first exchange of private information. We're no longer just strangers.

With the stars gleaming above us, and with the conversation flowing like warm water, I could kiss him. His bottom lip is full, and I imagine sinking my teeth into it. He leans in, so close, I'm breathing in the woody, spicy scent of his cologne. His gaze falls to my mouth and my pulse spikes. There's a swooping in my stomach, as though I am leaping off a cliff into the wild unknown.

Just as his mouth is about to come down on mine, I see Ivy over Henry's shoulder, hurrying out of the main doors. I know immediately that something is wrong, because Ivy never hurries. Usually, she takes her time, makes people wait – and if they don't, they were never worthy of her company. So when I see her now, stumbling through the dark, phone clutched in her hand, I know instinctively that something terrible has happened.

Henry forgotten, I get to my feet and walk fast towards her. 'Ivy!' I call, and she spins towards me. This close, I can see the white shock on her face, the dawning purple misery. 'What's wrong? What—'

'He's gone,' she breathes. 'He's dead.'

Chapter Four

It's been two weeks since her grandfather's death. The knowledge that it was quick – a heart attack while out walking the grounds of Holt House – is a relief. He didn't suffer slowly, like her mother did with cancer. And she lost her aunt young, too. Though I'm not sure how she died.

Ivy once told me that every Christmas, her grandparents threw a party at Holt House. They served champagne and canapés and Rococo chocolates, which, at her grandmother's insistence, the children weren't allowed – instead they were gifted velvet pouches stuffed with chocolate pennies. But Ivy's grandfather used to sneak her one anyway. The two of them would break away from the crowd and go to his study, where they'd sit and unwrap them together. Ivy had felt so grown-up, popping that chocolate into her mouth – it tasted of hazelnut and rebellion. A small act of defiance that made them as thick as thieves. Or so she'd thought. He pulled away from her the year we buried her mother.

'He avoids my calls,' she told me then, tears sliding down her cheeks. 'I don't know what I did wrong.'

'Maybe it's too hard for him. Maybe you remind him too much of his daughter.'

'I don't look much like her. Everyone says I look like my father.'

'You don't need her blonde hair and blue eyes to be like her. It's in a gesture. In the way you carry yourself.'

'I don't think that's it,' she'd said, and abruptly changed the subject.

The night Ivy found out her mother was stopping cancer treatment, she rang me, and I was on her doorstep within half an hour. We walked around Bath till the sun came up. 'I don't understand,' she'd told me. 'Why won't she fight? Why doesn't she love me enough to stay with me?' I didn't have an answer. Not then, and not now.

I remember the day of her mother's funeral: edging into her childhood room and seeing her curled up on the floor, a half-empty bottle of rum at her side. 'Ivy?' I'd called into the dimness. Her curtains were closed. The room was hot and musty. 'You need to get ready.'

She didn't answer. I'm not sure she heard. I scooped the rum bottle up and placed it carefully on the dresser. In the three years I'd known her, she was bolder and braver and always having more fun than anyone else in the room. Right then, she was just a girl who'd lost her mum. I opened the curtains. A shaft of warm summer light streamed in through the window, cutting through the dark. She'd recoiled and shielded her eyes.

'Have you eaten?' I asked, kneeling at her side.

She stared blankly back. We'd just graduated university. We were due to start our new jobs at the end of the summer and move into a an over-priced house share with two strangers. We were only weeks away from becoming fully-fledged, tax-paying adults, but I'd never felt so helpless.

'You need to eat.' Gently, I stroked her long hair back from her sweaty face. Then I went downstairs to the kitchen. Her childhood home was grand. Expensive. Undeniably beautiful. A four-bedroom detached old Victorian house in the heart of Bath. I grew up in a two-bed terrace in Trowbridge. Ivy could've fitted Mum's entire downstairs into her lounge.

When I returned to her room, she still hadn't moved. I set a bowl of yoghurt and fresh fruit on the floor and sat cross-legged opposite her. 'You *must* eat.'

She shook her head. 'Can't.'

'Can.' I took the spoon and heaped Greek yoghurt onto it, then brought it to her lips. She stared at me, eyes watering. 'Can,' I said again.

I fed her. When she'd finished, I helped her to her feet. She'd collapsed against me, her head on my shoulder. Her breaths were ragged, drawn through a crumpled straw of grief and rage. I held her up. 'Ivy, we need to get ready.'

'Can't.'

'Can.' I kissed the top of her head. Then pulled back and cradled her face. 'Let's get you in the shower. I'll be right beside you. I promise I won't leave.'

Slowly, she nodded.

She let me lead her to the en suite. I undressed her. She stood naked and shivering despite the summer heat. I washed her hair beneath warm jets of water, massaging eucalyptus shampoo into her wet locks.

Back in the bedroom, I helped her dress. Then I did her make-up. She sat perfectly still. A dark-haired doll. The black burn of rum was still in her bloodstream, so I went downstairs to make strong coffee – luckily for her, I had years of experience sobering up a drunk. I made her sip hot coffee until some of the colour returned to her cheeks. She'd stood in front of her full-length mirror. 'Fuck me, I look like a corpse,' she said.

My eyes had widened in surprise. It was the first time she'd sounded like herself since her mother died. 'A beautiful corpse,' I offered.

Her smile was weak. Her eyes drifted toward the window. 'I can't believe that in just a few hours my mother will fit into an ashtray.'

'Ivy!'

'I'm not wrong.' She'd turned to me and stood so close, I could feel her breath on my face. 'You'd make a beautiful corpse, too.' She ran her fingers through my hair. 'Like fire,' she said. 'Like the sun coming up.'

Eight years later, here we are, preparing for another funeral: her grandfather's. I button up my simple black dress. My mane of auburn hair is neatly pinned back in a clip, and I've painted my lips a peachy pink. I apply a final layer of waterproof mascara. In the mirror, Ivy appears behind me, leaning against my bedroom door. Her dress is black, too; long and sweeping. 'Still fits,' she says, wryly. It's the same one she wore to her mother's funeral.

'It's nearly time,' I tell her, still standing in front of the mirror. 'How're you doing?'

'The worst part is having to see Daddy Dearest,' says her reflection.

Though we both know she is secretly desperate to see him. She always is. It is *him* who is forever eager to avoid *her*.

25

'He's coming?' I can't keep the astonishment out of my voice. 'He hated your grandfather.'

'Not as much as my grandfather hated him,' Ivy says. 'But if you're going to fuck other people behind your wife's back, you should expect to be despised by her family.' She comes up behind me. 'I'm just glad my mother died before it all came out. She was so in love with him. She looked at him like . . . like . . .' She struggles to find the words.

'Like he was the answer to everything?' I offer.

In the mirror, she nods. 'Exactly.' She's watching me carefully. Sometimes I think she can see right into the very depths of me. 'I don't know why you're so desperate to fall in love, Zara,' she says. 'Loving someone just allows them to take the middle out of you like a sandwich and leave the crusts on a plate to rot.'

'That's not true.' I turn to face her.

'Isn't it?' She challenges me. 'What about Becky?'

'My mother did everything in the wrong order.'

Ivy rolls her eyes. 'You know your theory is bullshit. Your parents didn't break up because they had you out of wedlock, Zara. Following the right steps in the right order – meet, get married, have babies – doesn't bind people together forever. It isn't the secret key to happiness you seem to think it is. And anyway, it's a totally outmoded way of thinking.'

I don't say anything; there's no point, we've been here before, and we'll never agree. Though she mocks my theory, I know there's some truth in it. My mother fell pregnant with me a couple of years into dating my father. They never married. My mother claims he had affairs. I was only a few months old when he left her. Left *us*. Then he met Julia. Mum said she was sure he'd treat Julia the way he treated her. But he didn't. He'd fallen in love. A year after he and Julia married, they had Polly. This August, Julia and my father will celebrate their twenty-fifth anniversary. They're the picture-perfect family. Meeting the right person at the right time can transform your life. I've seen it. 'Anyway,' I say, changing the subject. 'We're going to be late if we don't leave now.'

She's watching me again in that careful, considered way that she has. 'So serious,' she says, with an annoyed pout. 'It's like someone died.' I don't entertain her morbid joke, which bothers her. 'Zara . . .' Her eyes narrow, cat-like, as she prowls closer. Without a word, she reaches behind me and gently tugs the clip from my hair, freeing a stream of auburn waves. She runs her fingers through it, sending tingles across my scalp. 'Like fire,' she says. 'Like the sun coming up.'

Wickerycombe is a beautiful, quaint village in the heart of Somerset, and straight out of the pages of an agricultural magazine. There are rolling hills and limestone buildings, little footpaths and dinky bridges, floral hanging baskets and a rustic pub. Even the cemetery is lovely: manicured and polished, with gravestones in perfect rows between ancient oaks.

As we sit in the church now, I return to the memory of her mother's funeral. I kept my promise: I didn't leave her. Not once. I held her hand through the service, where we sat on the hard pews of the cold, echoing church, staring at the lacquered box that held her mother's body. I didn't let go throughout the broken, beautiful speech she gave in her mother's memory. Or as we sat in the back of a hearse, driving slowly through the cemetery to the wake at her parents' home.

I hold her hand again now in that same church. Her gaze shifts towards the first pew, where we'd sat eight years before. She's remembering, too. I squeeze her hand and she squeezes mine back.

The wake is held at Holt House, her family's estate. The walls are ivy-covered – her namesake. The three-storey limestone period home has a turret and wide stone steps leading up to a gorgeous mahogany door with a stained-glass panel. Inside, it is full of original artwork, family photos, cashmere blankets, thick curtains, ivory paperweights, first edition tomes. Everywhere there are beautiful, unique trinkets collected by her grandparents on their worldly travels. Holt House is flanked by three acres of land – a huge pond, a walled garden, and a meadow. It is more than I could ever dream of having.

I try not to think of my mum's tiny terraced house, or of the cracked patio in our pint-sized garden that I played in alone as a girl.

Mourners move like a swell of ink across the reception room. I'm helping myself to a glass of wine when I feel his gaze. I could be in a crowd of millions and still feel it. Slowly, I look up. He is by the fireplace, tall and tanned and watching me: Luke Northman.

He crosses the room, not taking his eyes from mine. Then he's standing in front of me. It's the first time I've seen him in two months. He hesitates, only for a second, before pulling me into a hug. I wrap my arms around his waist and breathe him in; cedarwood and pepper, heat and skin. 'You're here,' I whisper against his white shirt.

He is so broad and strong and solid. In his arms, I feel dainty. 'How is she?' he asks, pulling back.

'She's Ivy. She'll be OK. She always is.'

'Because she has you.'

I want to tell him that *he* could have me, too, if he wasn't always leaving.

'Luke,' her voice rings out behind me. I glance over my shoulder and there she is, standing in the archway, flanked by floor-to-ceiling bookshelves housing first edition hardbacks and a rolling ladder – the kind I've only ever seen in period dramas. This setting, in all its grandeur and beauty, suits her perfectly. More so than our dinky damp flat ever has. She belongs here. Luke's arms fall away, and I stand to one side as he envelops her. He is so big, and she is so small. An exquisite, delicate ballet dancer, spinning in a jewellery box. The feeling of being dainty drains away and I am once again the galumphing giant to her ballerina. The two of them talk in hushed tones. It doesn't matter that I've known Luke since we were three. That we made nests out of freshly cut grass clippings on the verge of our neighbouring houses, that we've shared bathwater and chickenpox. First kisses and first love. It doesn't even matter that, at sixteen, I lost my virginity to him on my *Buffy* bed sheets. The two of them share a bond I can't touch. One of loss and grief and tragedy. I remember how Luke turned to Ivy after his brother, Edward, was killed in that car accident five years ago. Though I'm grateful I still have a mother and that I haven't had to bury a brother, my lack of trauma leaves me feeling as shallow as a shower, unable to truly comprehend the breadth and depth of their shared sorrow. The two of them grew very close after Edward's death. Like brother and sister. Ivy even confided in Luke about her affair with Quinn at the time, weeks before she finally confessed to me. She knows how highly I value family. How I'd feel about her meddling in someone else's the way other women meddled in mine.

'Sorry I missed the funeral,' Luke tells Ivy. 'I only landed in Gatwick a couple of hours ago.'

I want him to pull me into his arms again. To chase that feeling of being dainty and desirable.

Ivy's summoned away by another mourner, leaving Luke and me alone.

'So,' he says. 'How've you been?'

Most of the time, when someone asks how you are they don't actually want to know; but with Luke, it's always sincere. What he's actually asking is, how am I after the last time I saw him and told him we were done. Over. No more. That I couldn't keep waiting. Because I can't. We've been on and off for fifteen years. I must move forward; I can't keep glancing back. We want different things. I want to settle down. I want marriage and children, the nice house and a blonde cocker spaniel. He wants adventure and travel. He wants backpacking around Europe and swimming with turtles in Bali, to hop from city to city without ever stopping.

'Fine,' I tell him. 'How's the writing going? The blog?'

'Fine,' he echoes. 'I've partnered with a new hotel in Amsterdam. They're paying for the whole trip.' He clears his throat. 'I was thinking—'

But I never do find out what he's thinking, because Ivy reappears and says, 'Can we get out of here?'

The three of us end up back at our flat on the expensive velvet sofa we can't really afford. We drink the wine left over from the wake and scroll through Netflix.

'This looks good,' Ivy says.

I groan. 'When are we going to stop using the brutal murder of women as entertainment? It's just murder documentary after murder documentary.' I take the remote from her. 'How about this, instead?'

'A Christmas film in June?' She shakes her head and gets up. 'I might just go to bed.'

'It's getting late,' says Luke. 'I'll head off.'

'No, stay,' Ivy insists. 'I'm sure you guys have plenty to talk about.' She throws me a meaningful look, which I ignore. Luke, as well as being like a big brother to her, is also the only boyfriend I've ever had who's secured her seal of approval, and she'd be happy if we rekindled things. But it doesn't matter how much Ivy, or I, or even Luke might want that, I can't have the life I want with a man who is always leaving. Standing in the doorway, Ivy glances over her shoulder, eyes glittering, and adds, 'If the two of you have sex, *don't* do it on that sofa. It stains.'

'She's such a bitch,' I say fondly, when she's gone.

Luke is smiling. He reaches for the wine and tops up my glass.

'Do you remember when we were kids and we used to drink Ribena in your garden and pretend it was merlot?' I ask.

'Aged eight, I don't think I knew enough about wine to imagine it was merlot.' He grins. 'But yeah, I remember.'

'Aged twenty-eight, I *still* don't know enough about wine.' I take a sip. I am walking the fine line between tipsy and drunk. 'Except maybe that I should stop drinking now.'

'Ah, yes, the infamous Barton hangover,' he says with mock grandeur. 'How many hours of my life did I dedicate to driving into Bath to fetch you burritos? Or, worse, how many hours did I whittle away watching *Dirty Dancing* in a dark room, while you groaned into my lap?'

'It is not my fault that the only way to cure a hangover is with Mexican food and Patrick Swayze. I don't make up the rules.'

He smiles. Luke has always had the most beautiful smile: it's straight and white and lights up his grey eyes. 'I didn't have a chance to ask earlier, how's your mum?'

And just like that, the playful back and forth dries up. I stare down into my glass. 'Fine.'

'Zara . . .' There's reproach in his voice.

'She's fine,' I say again, as a wave of guilt and anxiety swells. 'Well, as fine as my mother can be. Fine for her.'

'When was the last time you saw her?'

The wave crests but doesn't break. 'When was the last time you saw *your* parents, Luke?'

He finishes his wine and sets his empty glass on the coffee table. *'Touché.'* Then he leans back against the sofa and closes his eyes.

I try very hard not to think about the dozen missed calls from my mother. That wave threatens to drown me. Instead, I banish her from my mind and concentrate on Luke. He has the longest, thickest lashes. It's criminal how amazing his lashes are. And his jawline. He has a great jawline; square and defined. I've kissed my way across it more times than I can count. I've traced the slopes and curves of his mouth with my tongue. I've explored the planes of his bare chest and run my fingers through his thick, tawny hair.

Luke opens his eyes and catches me staring. I try to look away, but I can't. His gaze searches my face, and he sits up. Heat pools low in my stomach; I want to kiss him. Sensing this, he shifts his weight and leans in a little. The wine glitters darkly in my veins, stripping me of my inhibitions. I could do it. I could, despite Ivy's instructions, have sex with Luke on this incredibly expensive sofa. The sex would be phenomenal. It always is. He knows my body better than anyone. First and last – that's what we promised – though since our teen years our lives have forked and led us down different paths, with different people. I always thought of the other men as detours, with Luke being the ultimate destination. But he isn't. He can't be.

'I've missed you,' he whispers against my mouth. 'You should come away with me.'

'Luke . . .'

'One trip.'

'It's never just one trip. You're in a different country every month. You're forever moving. There's always another trip.' I fall quiet and I know I should stay that way because we are just going over the same very old ground. Then I hear myself say, 'Stay here. With me.' And I hate the note of pleading in my voice.

'You know I can't. I'm a travel writer, Zara. I have to travel. It's my job.'

But it wasn't always because of his job. The summer his brother was killed in a car accident, Luke left to do the trip around Asia – *the one me and Edward planned*, he said. *The one we'll never do, now that he's gone*, he said. *I'll be away three months*, he said, *then I'll be back.*

That was five years ago now.

Luke's hands cup my face, and he presses his forehead to mine. I'm swimming in the grey of his eyes. They are stone and steel and winter skies. I love him. I've been in love with him for as long as I can remember. But loving him is pointless.

'I should go to bed,' I say. It's not an invitation. Luke knows it isn't. Reluctantly, he nods.

He pulls away, leaving me cold. Then he reaches into his satchel and hands me a bookmark. 'Prague,' he says as I take it. I have twenty-three bookmarks now. He picks them up from each new country he visits, and I slip them between the pages of my romance novels.

'Thank you.'

I get to my feet. 'I'd better check on Ivy.'

'It's great you have each other,' he says, and I can tell he means it. He isn't threatened by our bond like some of the other men I've dabbled with, to fill the empty spaces between my liaisons with Luke. 'Take care of her,' he adds, as I walk him into the hall. At the front door he pauses and looks over his shoulder. 'And call your mother back.'

Once he's gone, I climb into bed with Ivy. I'm wondering if she's asleep when she reaches out and laces her fingers through mine.

I'm tugged into a memory; the night her mother died. We were huddled together in her big bed then as well. Ivy didn't want to sit at her mother's side, clutching her clammy grey hand as Odette left her, motherless and mourning.

'It won't be like it is in the films,' she'd seethed. 'Mum won't pull me close and whisper words of inspiration. I will not sit there and watch her die. She *chose* this.'

So we didn't sit and watch. We listened instead. In some ways, I think that was worse. Her mother sounded like a broken boiler: gasping and hissing, her breath rattling painfully in her chest. She spat and babbled, enraged this was not the serene passing she'd hoped for. It took her all night to die. Her ragged, broken breath wheezing through cracked lips, loud and invasive in the quiet darkness of Ivy's room. Then, in the early hours of the morning, there was silence. Hideous, blessed silence.

She was gone.

Ivy squeezed my hand tight.

I remember thinking that cancer was an ugly way to die, and I'd much prefer something sudden; but nobody is safe from its clutches, rich or poor.

There was rage in Ivy's sobs. Rage and betrayal because she was right, her mother had chosen to leave her. She clung to me like I was the only person stopping her from going under. Maybe I was. With a note of painful desperation she whispered, 'If the silence ever takes you, I hope it takes me, too.'

Now, lying together side by side once more, she thanks me for coming to her grandfather's funeral.

I stroke her hair. 'Of course.'

'He was the very last piece of my mother.'

'I know.'

She curls in closer to me. 'I miss her.'

'I know.'

'I hate her, too.'

'I know.'

Silence.

'Love you, Ivy.'

It's dark, I can't see her gaze, but I feel it. 'How much do you love me?'

'To death.'

'And even then?'

I kiss her cheek. 'And even then.'

Chapter Five

'You need to go cold turkey,' Amira says into my ear. 'Cut Luke Northman out of your life. Or, at the very least, out of your vagina.' I'm standing in the bathroom, naked, letting the expensive, organic moisturiser Ivy bought me for Christmas sink into my skin before bed. 'He's been in my life for as long as I can remember, I can't just cut him out. It's impossible. Complicated.'

She sighs down the line. 'It isn't complicated, Zara. You make it complicated. You want marriage and a family of your own. Luke doesn't. It's actually quite simple.'

It's been just over a week since the funeral, since I was last alone with Luke, since I turned him down again, and I'm missing him so fiercely, it's a physical pain in my chest. I'm not feeling hardy enough to swallow the pragmatic, brusque advice that Amira doles out like one-penny sweets. I try to change the topic. 'How's Nathan?' But she doesn't relent.

'Zara, you *need* to move on. All this toing and froing isn't fair on you, and it isn't fair on him, either. It's actually pretty selfish. Do yourself and Luke a favour and meet someone new. Fall in love. Find your happily-ever-after.'

Which is easy for Amira to preach when she's already found hers. I've known her since primary school. For her, love was never the goal. She was career-driven, focused on becoming a commercial lawyer. She stumbled across Nathan, perfect, heart-surgeon Nathan, at a New Year's Eve party six years ago. They're married now, with a house and a ginger cat. According to The Plan, she'll be up for her long-awaited promotion this year and then two years after that, they will start trying for their first child. Amira's been in a happy, long-term relationship for so long, she's forgotten what it's like to date. The world of bland profiles and blander dates, dick pics and

WhatsApp messages with two ticks but no replies, are a distant memory. She's safe in the knowledge that at the end of every bad day, she has Nathan to come home to.

The last time Amira was dating, she was in her early twenties, when it was all about gin bars and lavish restaurants and sex. Finding The One wasn't a time-sensitive priority. I know that, objectively, twenty-eight is still young. It is. But twenty-eight is basically thirty, and who wants to still be swiping to find love at thirty?

'Look,' she says. 'Luke is like a drug you need to quit. For your health.'

'Don't cry over spilt milk. The early bird gets the worm. An apple a day keeps the doctor away.'

'What?'

I switch the phone to my other ear as I examine my face in the mirror, checking for fine lines. 'Oh, sorry, I thought we were talking in clichés now.'

She sighs. 'OK, get a couple of cats, then. Die alone. Let them eat your face. See if I care.'

I bite my lip, regretting my sarcasm. I mean, it's not like she and Nathan are only three months in and still smacked off their tits on serotonin. They're a serious, happy couple that are standing the test of time. I want that, too.

'I'm sorry,' I say. 'You were imparting wisdom. Continue.'

She pauses, and for a moment I worry she'll make an excuse and ring off, but she can't resist the plea of a willing student. 'The best way to quit a bad habit is to replace it with a good one. Every time you start yearning for Luke, go for a run or call a friend or just switch your focus. Think about something else. *Anything* else.'

'OK . . .' I agree, dubious.

There's a beat of silence, then, 'Zara . . . the reason I'm telling you to get yourself together now is because if you don't . . .' I can hear her thinking, weighing up whether she should say what it is she wants to say. This makes anxiety well in my chest, because Amira very rarely hesitates, which means this is going to be difficult to swallow. 'Because if you don't get yourself together,' she continues, 'Luke will. And that will be so much harder for you. I know you love him, and I know you know it will never work out because you both want such different things. But one day, and maybe one day soon, Luke will settle down with another woman.'

She was right. It *is* difficult to swallow. So difficult, I may as well be attempting to digest razor blades. Since Luke and I broke up in my first year of university, we've dated other people, but it's never been serious or lasted longer than a few months. No matter who we've welcomed into our beds, I've always felt they were just detours or pitstops because in between all those other people, we've found our way back to one another. I assumed we always would. That me and him, finally together, was the intended destination. But the thought that *I* was only ever a pitstop and that he will one day permanently settle down with someone else makes panic tighten my chest.

'I mean, we've dated other people but it's never serious. We've never moved in with anyone, or—'

'But we aren't twenty-two anymore. Or even twenty-five. You didn't really think the two of you would keep casually dating other people until you both suddenly end up on the same page?'

My answering silence says it all, because that's exactly what I thought. Even when we're apart, it feels like he's mine. Like I'm his, too. Like we belong to each other. I suppose I've always been waiting for Luke, expecting that one day he'll move back to the UK and want the same things I do. I suppose, at the same time, he's been waiting for me to abandon the idea of that white picket fence and join him on his travels.

Amira sighs. 'Zara, entering your thirties is like that last half-hour before closing time in a club. The music slows. The lights come up. You look around for someone to go home with . . . Don't be that last person lingering on the dance floor.'

When we ring off, I turn to settle down on the sofa in my pyjamas. Ivy is out at some work event, and I have the flat to myself, which would normally mean indulging in the things that I love but she loathes – like an upbeat romance and Indian food – but I can't watch two people falling in love without thinking about Luke and the woman he'll meet and marry who isn't me. She will be bohemian and full of wanderlust. She'll have beachy, blonde waves and a golden tan. She'll be young, younger than me, and have the kind of air-brushed, cellulite-free legs that look good in teeny shorts.

So, by nine thirty, I am in bed. And I am alone.

I take out my phone and scroll through social media, even though it very rarely makes me feel social and almost always makes me feel completely isolated. There's a litany of smug-couple photos; smug beach picnics and smug cinema trips and smug anniversary dinners. I get a pang of longing because I want to be the other half of a smug couple taking a smug photograph and smugly posting it online.

Then I scroll past all the wedding photos and the 'WE BOUGHT A HOUSE!' posts and the sonogram pictures. Ivy would roll her eyes heavenwards at those, and dryly tell me never to be that woman, please, the one who posts a black-and-white photograph of the inside of her uterus. But I envy them their elation. Then there are the never-ending pictures of babies. Babies in little socks and little hats and little jumpsuits with pink cheeks and tiny fists. 'All babies look like old men. Bald, wrinkly, red-faced,' Ivy always tells me. 'Having a baby is not an achievement, Zara. Anyone with a working uterus can do it.'

But I still want it. I want it all.

So I swallow my jealousy and my sadness, like spit before vomit, and I turn off my phone.

I'm woken by the sound of her. Ivy's low, wanton moan. I lie awake in the dark, in the sticky summer heat, listening to her chase an orgasm. Before I can question why, I'm creeping out of bed, across the cool, wooden floorboards. My door is already ajar. I skirt along the hall and there she is, framed through the open door of the living room, naked and riding a stranger on our sofa. Her legs are on either side of his thighs, tanned against the milky white of his skin. She sinks deeply against him, eyes closed, and tosses her head back. He grabs her hips and drives into her, but she takes back control, wrapping a hand around his throat and changing the rhythm. Deeper. Slower. But her breath comes harder and faster. My heart races in response. I don't move. I'm not sure why. Then her eyes open, and our gazes lock across this man's oblivious body. For a moment, it's like I'm beneath her; her skin against mine. I watch as sweet, self-indulgent ecstasy takes hold. Her orgasm is fierce as it surges through her. I feel the pale echo of it in my bones. And all the while, our eyes stay fixed on one another's.

Chapter Six

Mokoko coffee shop is a little gem. It's this tiny place right by Bath Abbey where the countertop is only a couple of metres from the entrance, but it's always quiet because the tourists don't realise that, behind the rush of coffee machines and the chink of porcelain, is a set of creaky stairs that lead up to a bright and spacious first floor. I'm sitting on a table by the window with my laptop. The milk-foam artwork decorating my coffee is so pretty I can't resist taking a photograph and posting it to Instagram, tagging Mokoko as I do. I forget to actually drink it, though, as I get swept up looking for the perfect shade of lemon and lavender tablecloths for the Monteath–Neville wedding. An hour later, swatches ordered, I'm composing an email to the florist. I'm so engrossed in my task, I don't notice him at first.

'Zara,' he says. 'Zara Barton?'

I look up.

Henry is standing over my table, a coffee in one hand. 'Are you stalking me, Miss Barton?'

I'm so surprised to see him here that words jam in my mouth. It's been almost a month since that wedding, but I've thought about him. That is, in the minutes my mind hasn't kept snagging on Luke.

'I'm not sure stalking skills were listed on my CV.'

He presses a closed fist to his heart and winces, as though I've dealt him a fatal blow. 'You're never going to let me live that down, are you?'

I grin.

He hovers, fishing for something to say because he doesn't want to leave. Ivy would let him suffer. She'd sit back and enjoy watching him sweat. But I'm not her, I want more than a meaningless fuck in the living room, so I smile and say, 'You work in Bath?'

He sips his takeaway coffee. 'Sometimes. Occasionally.' He nods towards my laptop. 'And you?'

'Sometimes,' I say. 'Occasionally.'

He smiles at my teasing. 'Sorry, was I being vague?'

'A little.'

I remember how ambiguous he was about whether he knew Ivy and how, even as we exchanged confidential information about broken homes and unhappy marriages, he never did say whether he was talking about himself or his parents. Henry, with all his charm and confidence, is both direct and evasive, whereas Luke is like a meadow that you can see across for miles. In the few interactions I've had with Henry, he is a forest with hidden dips and hollows. I find I want to explore each one.

A woman, who's trying to balance a plate of baked goods in one hand and wrangle her two children with the other, accidentally knocks into Henry, causing him to bump my table.

'You could sit down,' I suggest. 'If you want to join me?' We order two more drinks and split a carrot cake.

'Who woke up one day, held up a carrot and thought, this will be perfect with sugar, flour and egg?' muses Henry.

'Don't know. A mad genius. Probably the same person who knew that pineapple goes perfectly on pizza.'

He drops his fork and gets to his feet. 'Right. Didn't realise you were a certified psychopath.'

I'm still laughing when he sits back down.

'Funny. Interesting. Beautiful,' he says. 'I knew there had to be a flaw. Pineapple on pizza. Unexpected.'

'It's delicious!' I cry, delighted that he thinks I'm funny and interesting and beautiful.

He's just as handsome in the afternoon sun as he was in the soft light of the evening. He has glossy, dark hair and a strong profile, the kind you'd find on a Roman coin. I wonder again how old he is. It's a sad truth that society pedals the view that men age like whisky, while women plummet in value when our ovaries start to wilt. A view the beauty industry thrives on, spamming us with adverts about the effectiveness of retinol on wrinkles. I've never been in a relationship with anyone much older than me. I still get a jolt when friends mention celebrating their partners' thirtieth birthday and beyond, because when did we suddenly become old enough to date a thirty-something?

It's getting later. We are the last people in the coffee shop. A bored-looking barista is wiping down tables and piling chairs on top of them. 'It seems we've overstayed our welcome,' says Henry quietly. 'Are you hungry? We could grab an early dinner?'

Several thoughts race through my mind at once. Amira telling me to replace a bad habit with a good one. The idea that Luke is off somewhere right now, falling in love. Ivy indulging in hot, sweaty orgasms with a beautiful man on our velvet sofa. 'Sure,' I say. 'Let's do that.'

He takes me to a little restaurant overlooking the weir. It's all low ceilings and dimly lit, intimate corners, crystal glassware and leather chairs. It's pricey and striking, and must surely be on Ivy's list of coveted restaurants. The napkins are thick and stiff and luxurious. Self-consciously, I tug at the hem of my thin ASOS dress and wish I'd pulled something more expensive from my wardrobe this morning; it's a sorry situation to discover the restaurant napkins are better quality than the outfit I'm wearing.

I'm still browsing the menu when the waiter approaches.

'I'll have the steak . . . And my guest will have the duck,' he says. 'You can bring whichever wine the house recommends.'

The waiter takes our menus and retreats.

I've never had someone else order for me. I'm not sure if I find it rude or sexy. If I do find it sexy, does that make me a bad feminist? 'And what makes you think I like duck?' I ask lightly. 'For all you know, I'm vegetarian.'

'No one can be a vegetarian after trying this duck.' He smiles. 'Best I've ever had.'

I smooth the napkin in my lap, trying to decide how to feel about his overly confident nature. While attractive, it's not exactly what I'm used to. Sensing this, Henry's expression morphs from assured and playful to hesitant and abashed. 'I'm sorry,' he says to me and signals for the waiter. 'Order whatever you'd like. I shouldn't have assumed.'

He looks genuinely remorseful. Guilt washes over me. He's taken me to a beautiful restaurant, he's already said it's his treat, and I'm being a little ungrateful. 'It's fine,' I say quickly. 'The duck sounds great.'

'Certain?'

I nod. 'I probably would've ordered it anyway.'

Henry grins. 'Given your penchant for pineapple on pizza, I wasn't sure. It seems your palate needs an overhaul.'

'So, ordering for me is like a public service?'

'Exactly that, Miss Barton,' he says in a low, creamy voice that makes me think of lips and skin and heat. Gloria Steinem may not approve, but I decide that Henry ordering for me is supremely sexy. We've had two glasses of wine and not enough bread by the time the duck arrives. The fancy French red I can't pronounce swirls in my stomach, which is lined only with half a slice of carrot cake. I am tipsy. Maybe that is why, as I stare down at the pink duck on my plate, I think about my dad. My 'part-time father' as Mum calls him – he used to take me to the park for a couple of hours on a Saturday, where we'd sit on a hard bench and feed the ducks stale bread. A far cry from the rosemary-and-garlic sourdough they serve here at £8.50 a basket. I've gone from feeding ducks with a father I wanted so desperately to love me, to eating duck with a man I so desperately want to love.

Replace a bad habit with a good one.

The duck is exquisite. Henry ordered well. Having dinner with him is like browsing a booklet for the kind of couple we could be. We laugh loudly and a lot, we swap food and neither of us once looks at our phones. Whenever there is a lapse in conversation, it's natural and comfortable and doesn't last very long. Under the table, Henry's knees graze mine and our hands rest only millimetres apart.

For dessert, he orders us raspberry soufflé. I've never eaten one before. I don't think I've even been to a restaurant that serves it. In my mind, it is a pudding reserved for adults. Usually, I skim the menu and order whatever has the highest chocolate content.

We're still waiting for the desserts to arrive when my phone vibrates manically in my bag. I don't pick it up; I'm out, and everyone knows it's bad manners to answer a call when you're with company.

Henry smiles politely and I try to smile back, but my phone rings again. And again. And—

'Maybe you should get that,' he suggests.

'No, it's fine,' I say over the insistent, furious buzzing in my bag. Though, I'm starting to feel the first prickles of worry that someone is hurt. Other tables have noticed the noise and are shooting us looks. 'Actually, maybe I should . . .'

He waves a hand. 'Go ahead.'

My stomach plummets when I see it's my dad. He never calls, and when he does, it's usually for one reason.

'Zara, are you OK?' asks Henry.

I nod mutely. Not wanting to deal with my father and what I know he must be calling about, I consider turning off my phone. But then he'll be angry, and I don't need to add 'unreliable' to the list of reasons I am the subpar daughter. So, I get to my feet, weave awkwardly and clumsily between tables and answer his call.

I don't have a chance to speak before he starts ranting. 'I can't keep doing this, Zara. You need to go to her. Now. Right now.'

'I'm out,' I say weakly. 'I'm not sure I can—'

'You mother's not my bloody responsibility. Hasn't been for twenty-seven years. She's left me countless texts, voicemails. It *has* to stop.'

'Texts and voicemails about what?'

'I don't bloody know.' He's impatient and unimpressed. 'The same old nonsense. She's broken up with another bloke.'

My mother has a menu of men, and while she samples often, she can never quite finish a meal.

'I'm sick to death of this,' he hisses.

'I'm sorry,' I say, crumbling under the weight of his fury. I feel guilty, even though I haven't done anything wrong.

'Don't be sorry, just sort her out.' He sighs. 'It's not my responsibility to take care of her,' he reiterates, in case it wasn't clear the first time he said it, and I want to scream, *It shouldn't be mine either! But it is, because you left me all alone with her.*

I could refuse to cut my night short. I could switch off my phone and go back to Henry and pretend my father never called. But I don't have the heart, or lack thereof, to turn my back on my mum. With great effort, I swallow my resentment.

'She shouldn't be able to call me, anyway. I changed my number. How did she get it?' he snaps, the accusation clear in his tone.

'I don't know,' I tell him because I don't.

'I'm not dealing with this. I'm not. I'm with my family, Zara.'

It's as though I've just clasped a stinging nettle with both hands. He's with his family. His preferred family. His best family. His real family. I agree to go to the house. Then I ring off and dither on the pavement outside the restaurant. I don't want to go back in and see Henry, not when I'm feeling so morose, but my bag is in there and without his mobile number, I don't even have the option to text an apology and make my escape.

I take a few moments to compose myself. After an entire lifetime, you'd think my father's derision would feel more like being attacked by safety scissors than a butcher's knife. It doesn't. I take the fear that I am unlovable, and stuff it down into my gut. Then I paste on a smile and go back to Henry.

The soufflés have arrived, and I take a moment to mourn the evening we could've had. 'I'm so sorry, Henry,' I say quietly. 'I've got to go.'

He frowns. 'Everything alright?'

I try to sound breezy. 'Family . . .' I grapple for the words. 'Family emergency.' At the crease of concern between his brows, I backtrack. 'Not emergency . . . I meant . . . family situation.'

But it's too late. He's gesturing for the bill and asking the waiter to call us a taxi.

'Where are we headed?' he says.

'We? No, don't worry. I'll walk. Get the bus. I'll—'

'A taxi will be faster. I'm coming with you.'

'No. It's fine. I'll just—'

'Let's go.'

It all happens so quickly; he scoops me into a taxi where I mumble my mother's address, and then we're off. I stare out into the blurry amber glow of house lights as we race down residential streets, the creamy limestone buildings of Bath giving way to the red brick buildings of Trowbridge, Bath's less attractive, less affluent neighbouring cousin. As we near my mother's house, my stomach churns. I don't want Henry anywhere near this. The circle of people who know about my mother is small. And I want to keep it that way. I tell Henry to drop me off around the corner, but he insists on coming in with me. I try and fail to come up with a bulletproof reason why he can't. Beneath the anxiety, I feel a rush of affection for him that he's willing to stride into a situation he knows nothing about, just to help.

As we pull up outside, I see her. My mother is in the front garden on all fours, wailing into the lawn. After twenty-seven years of Becky Barton's hysterics, the neighbours pay her no attention. Except for the couple opposite, the new additions to Queen's Court, who stare open-mouthed from their living-room window. This must be their first viewing of the tragic production that is my mother's life. I slip seamlessly into my role of carer, of dutiful daughter, of animal tamer. This is a script I've been reading from for as long as I can remember, and I rub her back in rhythmic circles and whisper gentle, soothing words into her ear, as I sit on the ground beside her and wait.

Henry is standing beside the front garden gate. It's dark now and I'm glad I can't see his face because I know it will be a picture of disgust and regret. When he offered to help, he had no idea what he was getting into – and I'm angry with myself for not trying harder to stop him. Maybe some small, perverse part of me wanted him to come. Wanted to test him. To lay it all out, all the dark, ugly corners of myself, like some uninviting, potentially devastating coal mine and discover if, on seeing the danger signs, he is still willing to enter. Or perhaps I am trying to scare him away so I can throw my hands up and think, I did *try* to move on from Luke, to replace a bad habit with a good one, but it didn't work. It would be the perfect excuse to continue my fruitless on-again, off-again relationship with a man who'll never love me enough to stop leaving.

My mum's head lolls in my lap. I stroke her hair, a shade lighter than my own. She's lost weight again, she looks fragile, like a baby bird who's fallen from the nest. Her breath is warm and wine-soaked. But she's finally calmer and I want to get her inside. I start dragging her to her feet. We lurch to one side, almost tumbling into the shrubs. Then Henry rushes forward. 'Let me,' he says.

'It's OK. I've got her, you can go.'

He doesn't go. Instead, he scoops her up and carries her easily, moving past me and crossing the garden to the front door. I snatch my mother's bag from the ground and use her key to let us inside.

'Can you put her on the sofa?' I ask. 'First room on the right.'

The house smells of cheap alcohol and stale air. I walk down the little hall to the kitchen, flick on the light and wince. It's a mess. There's a teetering pile of dirty dishes in the sink and half-finished microwave meals strewn across the counter. On the dining table are empty cans and bottles. Jesus, how long has it been since I last visited my mother? I think there was snow on the ground.

I fetch water and tablets then hurry to the living room.

My mum is curled into the foetal position, her body wracked with sobs.

Henry hovers nearby, not knowing what to do, but he's still here. He looks relieved as I take over, sitting her up and trying to make her drink. She smacks my hand away, knocking the glass onto the floor. It bounces but doesn't break.

'Get off me,' she shrieks. 'Get away!'

'You're drunk. You need to go to bed and sleep it off.'

'Fuck off,' she spits. 'Just, fuck off.' Her eyes are bloodshot and full of hate. She starts to cry again, making noises like a wounded animal. I have a bone-deep ache to help but I'm powerless. I can't erase the past. I can't make my father love her. I lay a hand on her shoulder, but she bats it away just as she did the glass. She glowers up at me. 'You,' she slurs furiously. 'You were meant to save us, but you drove him away. You ruined *everything*. You ruined my fucking life.'

Even though I've heard this a thousand times, her words are still like sandpaper on sore skin. 'Come on,' I say, reaching for her.

She slaps my face. Hard. The sound echoes around the room. She stares at the hot, pink mark on my cheek. Just for a second, she looks remorseful but then her head lolls again as she's swept away beneath the undercurrent of cheap wine. She flops back onto the sofa cushions, gurgling like a baby.

'Zara . . .' Henry's voice rises from the darkness of the hallway, and I spin towards it. I'd forgotten he was here. My cheek stings. I'm mortified that Henry has seen the worst of us. Mortified even more that there are fat, hot tears in my eyes. He marches into the room, scoops up my now unconscious mother and carries her upstairs to bed. I thank him again and again, and tell him to go home, but he still doesn't leave.

Instead, he stays and helps me clean up. We work in silence, gathering up the many empty cans and bottles and putting them in the recycling. We do the washing-up and wipe down the countertops. It's soothing. It makes me feel more in control and even though I didn't want him here, I'm happy that, for once, I'm not doing it alone. On the dining table, I leave my mother a glass of water and some painkillers.

Henry and I don't speak until we're standing on the street. 'Is she often like that?' he asks.

'Blind drunk and raging?'

He nods.

I shrug. 'Often enough.'

'Zara . . .' He shakes his head. 'I'm so sorry.'

'It's fine.'

'It isn't.'

'Thank you for tonight. For the meal and for . . .' I glance up at the house. 'Everything.'

At the restaurant, the atmosphere had been flirtatious and fun, now it is strained and awkward. My guard is up because I really like Henry, but I know nothing can happen between us after tonight. No one wants to enter a relationship with a woman who comes with so much baggage. Especially when that baggage smells of vomit and acidic white wine.

'Is she getting help?'

I bristle at this. 'She's not an alcoholic. She doesn't go to meetings.' These are my mother's words, whispered fiercely to me throughout my life and regurgitated now. Ones I'm not sure I believe. She was convinced her drinking wasn't a problem because she didn't sit around in a circle with strangers, lamenting over her life with stale biscuits and weak tea. Unable to meet Henry's eye, I stare down at his leather shoes. 'She has a job. She copes.' Though I lie awake, sometimes, worrying she'll miss work and get fired and won't be able to pay her rent. How she manages it on her part-time school receptionist's wage is a mystery to me. Trowbridge isn't as extortionate as Bath, but it isn't cheap either. 'She copes and then she hits a blip, like tonight.' That blip is almost always another love lost which leads to her calling my father and him calling me and back around we go.

'Why won't you look at me?' asks Henry.

Because I don't want to see pity or loathing or revulsion. Because the knowledge that I am unlovable and not enough – not enough to win my father's affection, not enough to keep my mother from drinking herself into oblivion, not enough to make Luke stay – grows within me, like a dark, damp moss. I shake my head and say, 'Thank you again. It's late. I really must go.'

'Zara.' He steps closer, taking my chin between his thumb and forefinger, and forces me to meet his gaze. There's a softness to it that makes my insides ache. 'Everything will be OK.' He sounds so certain, I almost believe him. He closes his eyes briefly, and when he opens them again, I see something raw and vulnerable and honest. 'The night we met, when we sat by the firepit, I was going to ask you to come to Edinburgh with me.'

My pulse kicks and I shed the hideousness of this evening like a second skin, until it lies discarded at my feet. I'm remembering the warmth from the flames, the smokiness from the burning wood, and the electric anticipation, convinced he was going to ask. Then the irrational disappointment when he didn't. I've said no to going away with Luke a thousand times because he's in a different country every month. Committing to a nomadic lifestyle is one thing, but agreeing to a romantic, spontaneous weekend away is entirely different.

'I didn't know you,' says Henry, 'but I felt like I did. I feel like I know you.'

'I feel like I know you, too,' I whisper.

His hand moves from my chin to cup my face. 'I imagine your life hasn't been the easiest, Zara,' he tells me. 'But it's made you who you are, and I like who you are, very much.'

Chapter Seven

Ivy is manic. It is the eighth anniversary of her mother's death, and she's filling our house with noise to drown out her grief. But it's like trying to stem the flow of blood from a gunshot wound with a single piece of tissue paper. The grief keeps pouring out of her. She doesn't stop to examine it. She does the laundry, load after load, even though I am the only one of us who does the laundry. But she craves the white noise of the machine. She puts music on and turns up the volume so loud the bass pounds in the soles of my bare feet. She chats endlessly to me about nothing:

'Blondes get poor representation in the media. They're either bitches or bimbos. I mean, redheads get labelled, too. They're either raunchy or dull.

'Did you read about that girl who faked her own kidnapping and burned down a cottage?

'If I were a pigeon, I'd definitely live in the countryside. City pigeons are so scrawny and almost always have only one good foot.'

She fears the silence that took her mother. The silence that will one day take her, and take me, too. So she makes her life louder and bolder and won't let it touch her.

All morning, she smiles. It isn't *her* smile though. It isn't brilliance and perfection. It isn't the smile that makes men want her and women want to be her. It's waxy, and too wide, a smile distorted in a funhouse mirror. I sit in the living room so I can keep an eye on her, and I wait. I know how this plays out.

Eventually, she'll crumble beneath the weight of her sorrow. Maybe I don't understand the depths of that sorrow in the same way Luke does, but I'm here and I'm not leaving.

She makes us both peppermint tea and, over the edge of my book, I see her hands shaking as she pours the water. My steaming mug barely touches the coaster on the coffee table before she spins away, focused on the next task, the next distraction; but I catch her wrist.

'Ivy, come sit with me,' I say.

She hesitates, because when she's still it's easier for grief to find her. She scans the room for something to do, something to clean, but I can see from the shadows under her eyes that she's barely slept. She needs to stop. To relax.

'Please,' I say softly.

At first, she is rigid, spring-coiled. Then I pull her into a hug and eventually she softens, resting her head on my shoulder. I stroke her hair. It's silky between my fingers. 'Have you heard from your dad?'

She tenses. 'No.'

'Sorry.'

'Don't be. I'm not. He didn't even try to talk to me at Grandad's funeral. He hasn't bothered since I cut him out.'

This isn't strictly true. It is just something she tells herself to feel better. She invited him to the flat for Christmas last year. Cooked for hours. And he didn't turn up. Didn't even bother to call to say he wasn't coming. Just sent an email she didn't see until Boxing Day. His divorce from Wife Number 2 was finalised and he was celebrating with his mistress in Paris. Ivy has hissed at one too many of his girlfriends, each younger than the last, and it's easier for him to separate himself from her than it is for him to separate himself from his own carnal desires. She told me that he and her mother tried for years to have children before Odette sought help at a fertility clinic in Sweden and finally fell pregnant with Ivy. That her father went along with her mother despite never wanting children himself. Sometimes, I think Ivy is like a cat left to him by someone he loved, and he struggles to know what to do with her because he isn't, and never will be, an animal lover.

'You're better off without him,' I say. 'He's an adulterer and a crappy father.'

She shakes her head. 'What if I'm just like him – and that's why Grandad shunned me after my mother died?'

I shake my head. 'What happened with Quinn was five years ago. You promised me you'd never get involved with another woman's partner again, and you haven't. You aren't a homewrecker, which means you aren't like Hugo.' I give her a small smile. 'I wouldn't be friends with you if you were.'

She swallows thickly and goes back to staring out of the window. I've made things worse, though I'm not sure how. But then, reminding her of the only major row we've had in ten years when she's already feeling low is less than ideal.

'We could go out,' I suggest quickly. 'Anywhere. What do you want to do?'

She doesn't answer for so long, I wonder if she even heard me.

Then she says, 'Ice skating.'

'Ice skating?'

'I used to go with . . .' She trails off but I know she was going to say her mother. She clears her throat. 'It was fun.'

'Balancing on razor blades across a freezing, slippery surface is fun?'

'It's freedom. If you close your eyes while you skate, you feel weightless. Untouchable.' Her voice has taken on a rare, dreamy quality as she remembers. 'Every winter, we went to Lake Louise in Canada to skate. Mum was brilliant on the ice. Glowing in a hat and mittens, spinning and laughing in her midnight-blue skates. That's how I want to remember her. Not what she became in those last days, grey and rotting in her bed, struggling to breathe.' She inhales sharply. 'I just . . .'

'Let's go!' I say, desperate to take away her pain. 'There's a rink not too far away.'

'We can't. The rink here is closed for refurbishment and even if we drove to the one in Swindon, it's crowded, and I just can't *people* today.'

'I'm people.'

'Yes, but you're *my* people.' She meets my eyes and I feel it all the way to my stomach. 'Anyway, subject change,' she announces with fake cheer. She sits up and twists to face me. 'Tell me, who is your latest distraction?'

I blink. 'What?'

'You were still moping over Luke when I took you to that wedding six weeks ago, and now you're OK. Happier.'

I consider lying but she knows me too well. Still, I don't want to tell her about Henry. I've deliberately kept him to myself in the couple of weeks since he stood with me on the doorstep of my mother's house, because my happiness with him is new and delicate, and Ivy has a habit of closing her fist around my love interests and crushing whatever could've been before it's had a chance to unfurl.

'I'll take your silence to mean there *is* someone.' She says this lightly but there's an edge to her voice that tells me she's annoyed I've kept him from her. 'OK, who is he?' She raises a single dark brow. 'Or she?'

She's not going to let this go. I know she won't. Rather than string it out, I say simply, 'He's great.'

Her eyes narrow. 'Why won't you tell me who he is? Is he hideous? On a scale of one to the Elephant Man, how deformed is he?'

'He isn't *deformed*. And even if he was, it wouldn't matter – if he was a good person.'

She smiles then leans forward, wanting to know more. 'So, this man you're seeing, he's a good person?'

I nod.

'Is it Luke?'

I frown. 'Why do you think that?'

Ivy shrugs. 'He's the purest person I know. I mean, he's just good, isn't he?' Her fingers pull and twist at the cushion tassels. 'He's honest. Loyal. And he isn't exactly terrible to look at.'

When I introduced her to Luke during that first year of university, I worried he'd fall in love with her, like everyone else did. Ivy, the wild beauty, the sparkling, sizzling firework. She had a magic about her, the kind that made people burn for her attention. But Luke didn't fall in love with her. The two of them got on like brother and sister. I spent the next few years blissfully happy, between my two favourite people. Until Luke's brother passed away and Luke went on that first solo trip, never to anchor himself in the same country again.

'It's not Luke.' It won't ever be Luke, I think, it can't. 'It's someone new. I met him at the wedding.'

'At Pennard House?'

I nod. 'But you don't know him. I asked.'

She pulls a face and I think maybe she's offended he doesn't know her.

'I mean, he probably does know me,' she says. 'Bath is a small city. The people at that wedding attended like, one of four private schools in the area. They swim in very insular circles.'

She waits.

I don't want to give her his name. She'll do what she always does, find a flaw in him that, once she's pointed it out, I won't be able to ignore. But I know that refusing to talk about him will only hurt her, because we don't keep secrets. On today of all days, the last thing I want to do is hurt her.

'Henry,' I tell her. 'Henry Frith.'

She turns away quickly so I can't see her face, and tugs the throw onto her lap.

'What is it?' I ask.

When she looks at me again, her expression is carefully neutral. 'Henry Frith as in Frith & Sons?'

I shrug. 'No idea.'

'Henrietta's House?'

And of course, once she says it, I know exactly what she's talking about. Henrietta's House are those doll's houses with the little thatched roofs. Henrietta is an icon, with her strawberry-blonde hair and pleated skirt. So many of my friends had one when I was a child. I didn't. They were too expensive. Though my dad bought one for Polly on her sixth birthday.

'He's big money.'

'I don't care about his money. I didn't know anything about his money.'

She pulls another face. 'He's a bit old for you, isn't he?'

'Is he?'

'He's forty.'

OK, I'm a little bit surprised he's not in the thirties bracket, but it doesn't matter. 'You know a lot about someone you claim you've never met,' I say.

She shrugs. 'Like I said, insular circles. I was born in Bath, I work in PR, I know a lot of people. And if I don't know them personally, I at least know *of* them. It's literally my job to be aware of local CEOs, Zara. Frith & Sons is a household name. Frankly, I'm surprised *you* didn't know who he was when you met.'

'Well, I didn't.'

'You clearly didn't talk about his job,' she ventures. 'What do you even have in common? I mean, people like him don't usually . . .'

'What?'

We stare at each other. I am daring her to say what she's thinking. To finish her sentence. People like him don't usually date women like me. The tension mounts, and I dare her. I *dare* her.

'Like I said, insular circles.' She flashes me a quick smile. 'Anyway, I'm happy you're happy. And it's a fact that the best way to get over someone is to get under someone else.'

I feel a stab of irritation because this isn't just a fling. She has no idea.

'How's your mum?' she asks.

I can see the invisible dot-to-dot that joins her unfinished sentence to the question she's just asked. She's wondering why a man of sophistication and money and good breeding would get involved with the product of a broken home, especially as that home is a two-bedroom terrace in Trowbridge, funded by a part-time school receptionist and part-time drunk. But I am not my mother. I will not spend my life pining over a man who can't love me the way I need to be loved. I want Ivy to know I am not a one-night fuck. Someone disposable and easily forgotten. So I fling my words out there. 'Fine. She really liked Henry.'

I'm smug as I see the surprise register on her face. 'What? He's met your mum?'

I nod.

'But no one meets your mum. Only me and Luke. Why would you take Henry round to see your mum? When?'

And like pinging an elastic band against my own wrist, my words snap back, and I regret them instantly because now I have to admit this was not the conventional meeting of parents. 'Last week. Dad called because Mum called him. She was struggling.'

'You mean she was off her tits.'

'Yep.'

'Right. And Henry saw?'

'Yes.'

Silence.

'Why would you take him to her when she's like that?'

'I didn't exactly throw a parade with seventy-six trombones and stick her on a float,' I say, harsher than I mean to. 'Anyway, he was supportive. Totally accepting.'

'And you're seeing him again?'

'Yes, Ivy, I am.'

She presses her lips together and gives just the slightest hint of a head shake, as though in disbelief that he's even a little interested in me after seeing the horrid mess that is my family.

'OK, well.' Her eyes hold mine captive. 'As long as you don't love him more than you love me.' This is said lightly, but I see the uncertainty in her face, the apprehension as she waits for my reply.

'Impossible.'

Her smile is wide and brilliant; my answer is perfect. And true. When I'm with her, I belong somewhere.

'So,' she says. 'Is he good in bed?'

'Don't know. We haven't been together like that yet.'

I think about Henry and I sitting together beside the firepit, our lips only a breath apart, the air between us crackling; then the two of us standing outside my childhood home, his warm hands on my face. I think about him often and especially at night, when my thoughts grow stickier, darker.

'What does he have for breakfast?'

'How would I know?'

'It's important,' she insists. 'If he has bran flakes, then you know the sex will be boring. It'll be a set menu; no foreplay, missionary, skip the orgasm altogether. He'll fuck earnestly, like a gravedigger on duty.'

I shake my head. 'Where do you get this stuff from?'

'Have you ever heard of a woman having the night of her life then waking up to bran flakes the next morning? Because I haven't. I won't sleep with anyone who has bran flakes in their cupboard.'

I'm grinning as I think up another breakfast dish. 'What if he serves scrambled eggs?'

She pulls a face. 'Scrambled eggs aren't sexy. Nothing that resembles cat sick is sexy. Scrambled eggs are a red flag for messy intercourse. You'll be cleaning semen off the headboard for weeks.'

'Boiled eggs and dippy soldiers?'

'Run. He's a serial killer who has an extra-*special* relationship with his mum. He'll make you wear her floral nightgowns before he strangles you to death.' I'm still laughing when she adds, 'Poached eggs are sexy, though. They look vaguely like boobs. And they require an expert level of time management and finesse. It's basically an orgasm guarantee.'

I smile, glad her mood has lifted a little, if only for a few minutes. 'I'm going to make lunch,' she says.

'Poached eggs?' I tease.

She smiles. Then she's up and heading towards the kitchen. I'm picking up my book when she leans over the back of the sofa. I feel the warmth of her breath against the side of my neck.

'If things don't go well with Henry, you can always join me on the sofa next time,' she whispers. 'It doesn't have to be a spectator sport.'

Chapter Eight

It's a few hours later. Ivy's reorganising her wardrobe, music blaring, when Henry calls.

My pulse spikes, and I feel like a giddy teenager as I answer.

'Did you miss me?' he asks. This is how he always greets me. And though we haven't met up since that day we bumped into each other at Mokoko coffee shop two weeks ago – either he's been away on business, or I've been busy with a wedding – we talk nearly every night, long into the night, and sometimes into the early hours of the morning. I realise now, during all those conversations, he never asks after my work, but I volunteer the information, chatting away to him about my day, about delayed linen shipments and nightmare journeys travelling to pick up some obscure table decoration. Henry, on the other hand, doesn't discuss his work, referring to it vaguely as 'business'. Maybe he doesn't enquire about my career because he doesn't want to discuss his. Maybe he's had a slew of women after him because of his money.

I feel a pinch of annoyance at Ivy for telling me all that she did about him, because now I'll either have to feign ignorance or admit to gossiping about him to my friends.

'I always miss you,' I say.

He likes this. I feel his smile down the line. 'Let's go for dinner tonight.'

'I can't.' I glance in the direction of her bedroom. I know she can't hear me over the music, but I close the living-room door anyway. Just in case. 'My friend is . . . she's upset.'

'Invite your friend, or meet her afterwards. I can't stop thinking about you.'

'Me, too.'

'Then join me for dinner.'

We haven't even kissed yet, but I'm already thinking about having sex with him. The build-up has been slow and torturous. I think about meeting him for dinner, about the eye contact over the table, the sweet, sore anticipation at knowing I will be naked with him soon. A deep, lusty heat simmers through my veins. God, I want to. But I can't leave her. Not today.

'I'd love to . . .'

'What's wrong?'

I don't want him to think I've lost interest and I don't want to lie about why I can't see him either.

'It's the anniversary of her mother's death.' As soon as I've said it, I feel as though I've snuck him a stolen piece of her. Her pain is private. To avoid pity and questions, she doesn't volunteer that she's motherless to new friends or co-workers. She'd be angry if she knew I'd told him. 'She needs me.'

Silence.

'I understand,' he says and I'm grateful. 'Maybe we can meet for brunch tomorrow?'

'Can we make it a late lunch? I've got so much work to do.'

'You work too much.'

'So do you. You're always away on business.' The last word sounds accusatory or like a question, even though I didn't mean it to – should I be offended that he thinks I could be the type of woman to go after a man for his money? Is that why he hasn't told me about his work?

'*Touché.*' There's a muffled sound as he switches the phone to his other ear. 'So, what are your plans with your friend?'

'Well, I wanted to take her ice skating.'

'In July?'

I glance towards the closed living-room door, half expecting her to burst through it, livid that I have handed him yet another piece of her. I move towards the window. 'She used to go with her mum . . . before.' I look down at the steady stream of people moving on the street below. 'But it turns out the Bath rink is closed.'

There's a dark-haired woman staring directly up at our flat. She's standing still on the pavement as people surge around her. A rock in rushing water. Our eyes meet and my stomach drops. There's something familiar about her.

'Is this important to you?' he asks.

'Sorry?' I ask, distracted by the woman.

'To take your friend ice skating.'

'Well . . .' I glance over at the door again for any sign of her. Then lower my voice. 'Yes. But—'

'OK,' he says. I turn back to the window and look down. The woman is gone. 'I'll send a car for you around seven.'

'You'll send a car?' I give a disbelieving little laugh. 'What does that even mean? Send a car to take me where?'

'Just make sure you and your friend are ready and waiting at seven tonight.'

'OK, sure,' I say, a little giddy and very curious.

'And, Zara? Wear something warm.'

The car that arrives is slinky and black and pulls up outside the flat at seven exactly. We are in gym gear, though in my rucksack I have two jumpers and some gloves, which feels totally mad given the sweaty, July heat.

'Where're we going?' she asks again, like a sulky teenager being dragged to another garden centre.

'I told you, it's a surprise,' I say, even though I'm unsure myself. The driver opens the door for us, and we slide inside. I run my hand over the buttery leather of the seats, practically tasting the expense of it all.

She turns to me, eyebrows raised. 'Whose car is this?'

'Will you just shut up and let me take you out.'

The drive is short. We pull up outside the local ice rink. She's unsure as she stares up at the building. 'But it's closed . . .' she says.

I'm wondering why the hell Henry sent us here when the driver hands me a key and a note.

Zara,
Called in a favour. The place is yours for the night. If it's important to you, it's important to me, too.
Henry x

'What's going on?' she asks, moving closer so she can read the note. I fold the paper and stuff it in my back pocket.

'Let's go.'

The air in the rink is so crisp, you could snap it in half. I'm grateful for the jumpers and gloves I packed. We stand on the edge of the rink in the skates we took from behind the counter. Ivy's eager to get going. I stare apprehensively at the ice that glitters beneath the lights.

'I can barely rollerblade,' I admit. 'This is such a bad idea.'

'I'll teach you,' she tells me.

I pull a face.

She takes my hand and squeezes it. 'You trust me?'

'Until today, I didn't even know you could skate,' I exclaim in mock-horror. 'You're practically a stranger.'

She glares.

I smile. 'Of course I trust you.'

'With your life?' she whispers.

'With my life,' I say.

I let her lead me onto the ice. I stumble alongside her, and we shriek with laughter when my feet shoot out from beneath me.

'God, you're like a giraffe on ice,' she squeals.

'Or a rhino.'

She grins. 'Or that.'

'Shut up,' I say, clambering awkwardly to my feet.

She spends some time telling me to keep my chest up, shoulders square, knees bent, but her excitement to skate borders on desperation. It's selfish of me to hold her back. 'Go,' I say. 'I'm fine. I think I know what I'm doing.'

'Sure?'

I nod.

She kisses my cheek and then she's off. Fast. The blades of her skates cutting through the ice. I watch, stunned, as she spins and twirls effortlessly. She is poise and elegance and grace. So different to the girl who, two nights after her grandfather's funeral, was drowning her sorrows in shots of tequila at a sticky bar, before stumbling home barefoot and vomiting in the bushes outside the flat.

How have I never seen you on the ice? I think.

She fearlessly kicks out into another spin, hands drifting above her head while mine cling to the railing so hard they ache.

She's not just skating, she's dancing. She is a flame on ice – wild, twisting, burning. Heat and strength and power. She fills the space, branding the polished ice as she sweeps across it.

Under the lights, sweat glistens between her breasts. It's as though I'm seeing her body for the first time, the lithe, tight hardness of her. I wonder what it was like to grow up so beautiful.

Her skates barely kiss the floor as she glides across the rink. She throws her head back, exposing her throat, and I'm caught in the memory of her riding the stranger on our sofa, the smell of sex so thick in the air I could taste it, and the look on her face just before she came. It's how she looks now, swept up in something bigger than herself.

I'm hauled back to the present as she leaps. And I scream.

She is weightless. Soaring. Then she is falling. But she lands perfectly. Strong and composed.

She laughs. 'Why did you scream, Jamie Lee?'

'Jamie Lee?'

'Curtis,' she says. Then, at my blank expression she adds, '*Halloween*? The scream queen?'

'I thought you were going to break your ankle!'

'Oh, please. I've been skating since I could walk.'

She comes to a stop beside me. Breathless, she leans back against the rail. Sweat pools in the hollow between her collar bones.

'Ivy, why didn't I know you could skate?' I ask, stung that she's kept this part of herself from me.

She shrugs but avoids my gaze. 'I didn't see the point. I didn't think I'd ever skate again.'

'Why? You're brilliant, you're—'

'My mum taught me how. I haven't been on the ice since the summer I left for university.'

'Before your mum got the diagnosis?'

She nods. The silence that follows is weighted and mournful. 'Anyway,' she says with false brightness. 'Who arranged all this then?'

'Does it matter? We're here, aren't we?'

'Was it Luke?'

I frown. 'No.' Something flashes across her face, but it's gone before I can place it.

'Was it *him*?'

'Who?'

'Henry?'

I can't help the small smile that tugs at my lips, but I see her look of disapproval and my smile dissolves. 'What's wrong?'

She's uncharacteristically quiet. Then she says, 'Just don't get hurt.'

And she's so earnest, so intense, my heart races a little faster. 'I won't,' I promise.

'It's not serious between you two?'

'No,' I say, even though it feels like it could be. 'He just has a lot of money to burn, as you know. Besides, Ivy, I think the words you're looking for are "thank you".'

Her gaze flits to mine. 'Thank you.'

I shift a little closer so our shoulders touch. 'You were sensational out there.'

'I know.' She smiles and looks up at me from beneath her lashes. She's so close, I can count those little flecks of gold in her green eyes. 'Love you.'

I grin. 'How much do you love me?'

Her lips brush mine, soft and sweet. This is different from the drunken kisses we shared at university on a dare or on a whim. This is both surprising and expected. Impulsive and deliberate. Amiss and exactly right. I feel myself leaning closer but she pulls away and when she does, I can still feel the heat of her on my mouth.

We arrive back at the flat an hour later. She doesn't notice Henry, dressed in a dark blazer over a black T-shirt and blue jeans, standing a little way from the entrance to our building. 'I'll be up in a sec,' I say to her. 'Need to check the post.'

I wait until she's gone before I approach him. 'How was it?' he asks.

'Other-worldly. I can't thank you enough.'

'You're welcome,' he says. 'Seeing you happy is all the thanks I need.' He winces. 'Jesus Christ, that sounded less trite in my head.'

I like this about Henry, that he doesn't take himself too seriously. 'Sweet,' I correct. 'Not trite.'

We smile at each other, and in his eyes, there's excitement and anticipation. Like someone who knows he has the perfect present and can't wait to see it opened.

'Why're you here, Henry?'

Without taking his gaze from mine, he produces a silver lighter from his blazer pocket and flips it open. A flame springs to life, twisting and writhing. It makes me think of her, dancing on the ice tonight.

'What are you doing?' I ask, amused.

'I should've kissed you that first night by the firepit. Granted, it's not *quite* a firepit.' He nods towards the lighter in his hand. 'But it's the best I can do. For now.'

This gesture is the perfect cocktail of whimsy and charm, I think. It's one we'll regale our friends with at dinner parties. It's the kind of story that will make other women look at their partners and wonder why they've never been so sweepingly romantic. Most people won't admit it, but evoking jealousy in others is satisfying. It's a barometer by which you can measure how successful you are. 'So,' I say. 'Is this our do-over?'

He smiles. Then his mouth is on mine. He tastes of strong coffee and dark chocolate. Everything around me glitters and spins. The night sky and the earth and the blood in my veins. We kiss until our mouths are raw and I am drunk on him.

Chapter Nine

'I can't believe how *selfish* she's been,' I seethe, stabbing at the penne on my plate. I am too angry, too worried to eat it, so I drop my fork and reach for my water instead, wishing I'd just ordered Pinot.

'You've been friends for ten years and you're only now realising how selfish Ivy is?' asks Amira over the rim of her wine glass. We're in a little Italian restaurant close to her law firm, because even though it's a Friday evening, she's heading back into the office to work late. She wants to make partner in the next couple of years, as per The Plan, so she works every spare hour.

'She's not usually selfish,' I say, defending her even after what she's done. 'Not with me.'

'What did she do with the money?'

'Does it matter? It didn't go on the rent like it was supposed to.' I can't bring myself to tell Amira that she's blown it all on her friends from *before*, the ones she reconnected with at the wedding seven weeks ago, the ones she's been treating to extravagant dinners and afternoons at the Bath Priory Spa in a desperate bid to impress them, despite the final notice bills I found stuffed under her mattress.

'How did you find out?'

'The bank sent me a message to tell me we were in our overdraft on the joint house account, and then I got the call from the landlord to ask why the direct debit for our rent had failed.'

I'm furious all over again at the memory of confronting her, while she barely looked up to acknowledge my anger, dismissing me, when she did, with 'Zara, you're such a drama queen, I'm going to pay the money back,' before gifting me with an imperious spread of her lips.

'What are you going to do?' asks Amira.

'She says she's taking care of it.'

'And if she doesn't?'

'I'll dip into my savings.' Though I'm embarrassed to admit how very little I have. I love my job, but the wedding-planning company I work for is a small, family-owned affair and it doesn't pay well.

'Aren't her family rich? Can they help?'

'It's complicated.' At her raised, questioning eyebrow, I go on. 'After her mum died, all this stuff came out about Ivy's father having had multiple affairs, and then the Holts found out he'd been embezzling money from the family hotels, so Ivy's grandfather cut him off.'

'But he didn't take care of Ivy?'

I sip my water and shake my head, because even if she once had a trust fund I didn't know about, she burned through it long ago.

Amira frowns. 'Don't you think that's odd?'

'Alfred was grieving his daughter and incensed that his son-in-law had been shagging around and stealing from the family. It was probably painful for him to even *think* about Ivy after he lost Odette.'

'Have you considered *not* living with Ivy?'

'Why wouldn't I live with her?'

She looks at me like I've just admitted I don't know the alphabet. 'Because she's stolen the rent money.'

'She hasn't *stolen* it . . . She just—'

'Took it without asking?'

I can't say anything in Ivy's defence, so I shovel a forkful of pasta into my mouth. 'Sounds like Ivy and her father are two sides of the same coin. Don't give me that look, Zara, she's always been reckless.'

'If she says she'll sort it out, then she will.'

I add a shrug, downplaying it now because although *I* can rant about her, I don't like others joining in. It's my fault, though; talking negatively about her to Amira only adds fuel to the fire. Amira's never really liked Ivy, just as Ivy's never really liked Amira. They're too different. Where Amira is all lists and organisation and pulling her socks over her jeans to avoid tics in summer, Ivy is all spontaneity and wild abandon and skinny dipping.

'I'm probably just being dramatic,' I say.

'You shouldn't have to constantly clean up her messes,' says Amira. But it's not always me cleaning up after her. How many times has Ivy helped me pull my mum from a bar and get her home safely, or scraped me off the bathroom floor after Luke has come and gone again?

Then I catch sight of someone. The dark-haired woman who was watching our flat the other day is in the restaurant. She's by the entrance, talking to the hostess, probably making a reservation. Her hair is glossy and thick and tumbles down her back in black-coffee waves. From this angle, it's almost impossible to tell her age.

'I just don't understand your relationship,' Amira is saying. 'It seems claustrophobic.'

'Claustrophobic?' I echo, still distracted by the dark-haired woman. She's wearing a red polka-dot tea dress and a large straw hat that casts her face in shadow. I lean to the left for a better look because I am *sure* I recognise her. She feels so familiar.

Amira waves a hand in my face. 'Are you even listening?'

She glances over her shoulder to see what I've been staring at, but the woman has turned and is leaving. Was it the same woman who was outside our flat? I'm doubting myself now. And even if it was, does it matter?

'Zara?' Amira says, impatient now.

'Sorry, yes, I'm listening. You're claustrophobic.'

She sighs. 'No. Your relationship with Ivy is claustrophobic.'

My hackles rise. 'No, it isn't.'

'You're so entwined in one another, sometimes it's hard to know where one of you begins and the other ends.'

I take what she says with a pinch of salt because she's always been just a little bit jealous of how close we are, though she tries to disguise it with indifference or, like now, disdain. At twenty-eight, it's an unwritten expectation that you shake off the juvenile label of 'best friend' and replace it with a more mature, sophisticated label like 'close friend'. But the meaning is still the same. Closer means more important. Higher up the pecking order. The one you share *more* of yourself with. Before Ivy, that used to be Amira.

'Ivy doesn't date, you don't date,' she says. 'Most of the time it's just you and her.'

'That's not true. I date. OK, Ivy doesn't, but that's not who she is, she prefers to keep things . . .' I grope for the word and get a flash of her naked on top of the stranger on our sofa. 'Casual.'

Amira's smile is tight. She doesn't even know about Ivy's appetite for married men, but still secretly thinks she's a slut. She'd never admit it because she'd sound just like her mother, and it'd make her a bad feminist.

'But I date,' I say again.

'Not really. She tears apart every guy you bring home, and you inevitably lose interest.'

'Be fair, Amira, even you thought Ryan was boring. All he talked about was his work, which might have been interesting if he wasn't a tax inspector.'

'But it didn't bother you until Ivy pointed it out, like, two months into the relationship. No one will ever be good enough for *Ivy's Zara*,' she says, her words lemon-peel bitter.

'She likes Luke.'

'Have you ever thought that she only approves of Luke because she knows it will never work out between the two of you? He isn't a threat to her. To your friendship. How can he be, when he spends most of his time an entire ocean away?'

I look down at my plate because maybe there's a grain of truth in what she's saying, and I don't want her to know I recognise it. 'Well, I'm dating Henry and it's going really well.'

'And Ivy approves?'

'Yes, she does,' I say, not sure whether I'm lying. 'Not that I need her to.'

She doesn't though – I know she doesn't. How could she? She's never met him. *Refuses* to meet him, feeding me excuse after excuse. It's like she thinks if she doesn't meet him, he isn't real, and maybe he'll disappear before she has to.

'And even if she didn't approve, I like Henry. I see a future with him. I took your advice; I'm replacing a bad habit with a good one.' Though I don't actually believe Luke was ever a bad habit. He isn't a bad person. We've just never got the timing right, and I don't think we ever will, which is why things with Henry have to work out.

'I just want you to be happy and settled,' Amira says. What she doesn't add, but absolutely means, is 'like me and Nathan', and I wonder again what it's like to have your life so together. To be on the path you want to be on, travelling down it hand-in-hand with someone you've chosen, who has chosen you, too. 'You do still want children, don't you?'

'I do.'

'Does he?'

I sip my water, and just for a moment toy with the idea of smiling and nodding and exclaiming that, yes, we want at least three, because I always feel miles behind whenever I'm with Amira. It's not her fault. And life isn't a race but if it was, Amira is only a few yards from the finish line while I am still stumbling off the starting block.

'I think so . . . I mean, it's still new. Isn't it a little early to be pulling up baby-names websites?'

'But you need to know. You need a plan.'

Amira and Nathan have a strict life-schedule. Ivy hates this about them. But it makes them happy and, if I'm honest, it makes me feel better because it gives me time to catch up with her, to close the gap a little.

'If you don't have the marriage and children conversation with him now, you could spend a year, maybe two with this man. And if he doesn't want what you want, you'll be starting all over again, but you'll be in your thirties.'

The way she says 'thirties' is the verbal equivalent of picking up a pair of dirty knickers from your bedroom floor and holding them up to the light to inspect the stains.

'Then it could take another year to meet someone new, you want to date before you buy a house and get married. That takes you right up to thirty-five. Your fertility plummets after thirty-five.'

'Yes, I'm aware.' This fact is ingrained into all women. Most of us won't even know how we know it, we just do. At the thought of missing out, a cold bolt of anxiety shoots through me. 'Can we please stop talking about my withering eggs?'

'Sorry,' she says, reaching for the olives. 'I just want you to be happy.'

'So does Ivy.' I watch her reaction closely. She doesn't look up from her plate because she doesn't agree.

We leave the air-conditioned restaurant and step out into the scorching sun. Bath is rammed in the summer, teeming with university students and backpack-wearing tourists toting cameras, stopping suddenly in the middle of the street to take a picture of another limestone building, and locals who turn their noses up at both. The press of people makes it difficult to breathe. We break away from the crush and into Bath Abbey Square. I wipe sweat from my forehead.

While Amira grabs us two takeaway iced coffees from Mokoko's, I check my work emails. I try not to look on Friday evenings, but since Ivy boasted about me being a wedding-planner extraordinaire to all her *before* friends at Pennard House, I've gained a few new clients. One of them – Hazel – I've really warmed to. She's the kind of easy-going, organised bride every wedding planner dreams of.

Amira emerges from the coffee shop and hands me my drink. 'Here you go.'

'Thanks.'

She sips hers, looking sheepish.

'What?'

'I looked Henry up online,' she admits.

I wince. 'You didn't.'

'Just now. He has his own Wikipedia page. You didn't tell me he's *that* Henry Frith, as in Henrietta's House.'

'How did you even know . . .'

'Well, there aren't many Henry Friths in Somerset who have enough disposable income or connections to hand over an entire ice rink for the night.' She sips her coffee. 'I just . . . I'm surprised you're dating someone like that. He's not your usual type.'

'Isn't he?'

'I don't know,' she says sarcastically as we take a seat on a bench. 'Have you dated many millionaires?'

At her tone, I wonder if she's put out that Henry has more money than she and Nathan combined.

'I don't care about his money,' I say.

'Maybe you should. Money means power, Zara. Decisions cost money and if he has more of it than you do, that makes him the key decision-maker. Holidays, houses, weddings, where you're going for dinner on a Saturday night. There's an imbalance between you, right from the start.'

Her words grate; this is the second time a friend has implied my inadequate bank balance and lack of Oxbridge education makes me a less-than-suitable match for Henry. Why should I rethink my entire relationship with him because he has more?

'So you can only ever date someone within the same pay bracket as yourself?'

'No. Of course not,' she says, quickly, even though as a lawyer dating a surgeon, that's exactly what she's done. 'I just think it's something to be aware of. You want to build a future with someone whose world you feel comfortable in. You know, meeting their friends, their family. You want something that fits, not something you have to force together.'

I try to picture Henry introducing me to his rich friends, to politicians and West End performers, bankers and the children of the vaguely famous. The kind of crowd that Ivy hung out with *before*. But the truth is, I felt awkward and out of place at the wedding where I met him. I thought it was because I didn't know anyone, but maybe it was really because I was aware of the class difference; there's nothing impressive about my badly-paid job, my tiny, overpriced, rented apartment, or my broken two-person family. Henry was so kind and thoughtful when he met my mother. But maybe I'm naive to think that seeing her in a drunken stupor hasn't put him off having a serious relationship with me. Maybe, deep down, he is afraid I will turn out just like her. I am. I'm afraid. Clammy, cold panic spreads like a fog through my chest as I have visions of myself clutching a bottle of cheap vodka and crying into my lawn because I am unwanted and undesirable and too old and too drunk to do anything about it.

By the time I get home, I'm overseen by a stormy, grey cloud of misery. As soon as I open the front door, though, I can feel her good mood. It fills the flat like sunlight.

'What's going on?' I ask, stepping into the kitchen.

She takes two flutes out of the cupboard. 'I have amazing news.'

'Did you sort out the rent?'

She laughs. Then she goes to the fridge and takes out a chilled bottle that hadn't been there this morning. 'We'll never have to worry about rent again.'

'What do you mean?'

'I saw my grandfather's solicitor today.' This is not prosecco, it is champagne. And not the cheap kind from Tesco, the expensive kind from a fancy wine shop.

'And?' My heart is racing, because even though I don't know what's coming, I can feel that it is big. Her eyes are feverish and bright and dancing with a secret that I am desperate to hear.

While I spent my eighteenth drinking Apple Sourz from the corner shop, Ivy spent hers sipping Dom Pérignon in Paris. So even though she knows how to expertly open a bottle of champagne, holding it at an angle, keeping her thumb over the cork as she twists the base of the bottle until there's that gentle sigh of release, she doesn't because this moment is one of theatre; so she pops the cork and laughs as we are showered in champagne bubbles. We are celebrating and I still don't know why.

'What's happened?' I ask again, but she makes me wait.

She smiles at me; it is a smile that promises adventure and thrill and more champagne. 'Zara, it's mine.'

Silence. The air around us fizzes just like the bubbles in the champagne bottle. I don't know what she's talking about, so I raise both brows in a question. Her smile grows impossibly wide.

'Holt House is all mine.'

For a moment, my voice is lost to shock. '*What?*'

She's nodding. 'With Mum and Auntie Rosalind gone, it's just me.'

I have questions, so many questions. 'What about your cousins? I know you were your grandfather's favourite but—'

'The will said "blood-related grandchildren" which excludes Theo.'

'Is that fair?'

She shrugs. 'He was my auntie's stepson. He hasn't seen my grandfather since my aunt passed away, like, thirteen years ago. Why should he get anything?'

She twirls away from me, glass raised in the air, and drifts into the living room, leaving me to dumbly stumble after her.

'This is incredible, Zara. It's going to change everything. Imagine the parties I can throw at Holt House?' She giggles and I wonder how many celebratory drinks she's had since getting the call.

'But . . . how can it be all yours?' I ask. 'Don't you have another cousin? Rosalind's son?'

'Roman got a huge windfall after Auntie Rosalind died *and* we're splitting our grandfather's money *and* Roman's been in New Zealand for the last seven years, running his own pharmaceutical company. He's not going to trek all the way back to England for Holt House. He's not exactly struggling, Zara.'

'But—'

'Roman's company is probably worth more than the house, anyway. I really don't think he cares.'

I shake my head. It is inconceivable to me that someone wouldn't care about their claim to a stately home. 'Have you actually spoken to him?'

'We're having a call tomorrow,' she says, exasperated. 'Now, can you stop picking holes in this and just celebrate with me?'

'Of course. Yes!' I hug her, bashing my knee on the corner of the sofa. Even though this all seems wild and too fast, I'm happy for her. But I am sad for myself, too. In a heartbeat, everything has changed. 'We've lived together for nearly ten years, and now you'll be moving out into your own home,' I say. 'You're a homeowner . . . and I am not. I just . . . I can't believe it.'

'We can move into Holt House next week.'

I pull away. 'We?'

'Yes! Of course.' She tops up her glass. 'You're coming with me. Obviously.'

'Ivy, I can't afford to live in a stately manor.'

She is horrified. 'You thought I'd charge you rent? Don't be ridiculous. I won't charge you a penny.'

'I can't do that,' I say, even as tiny granules of hope filter through my sadness.

'Keep your money, save it, buy your own house one day. I'd offer to help with a deposit, but I know you won't take it. So let me do this for you instead.'

'Ivy, I can't,' I say blowing those little granules into the wind.

This gesture is too big. Too much. I can't accept it. The guilt won't let me. It was just a few hours ago that I was telling Amira how awful Ivy is.

'Can.'

'Can't,' I say anxiety fluttering in my chest at having to tell her the ugly truth. 'I spent this afternoon ranting to Amira about what a selfish bitch you are for squandering our rent money.'

Silence. I stare down at the cheap lino floor, shame spreading across my chest and cheeks.

And then she laughs. She puts a hand over her mouth, stifling her laughter to a giggle.

She throws her head back and yells to the ceiling, 'I *am* a selfish bitch.' She looks at me, eyes glittering. 'But now I'm a RICH selfish bitch.' She places her finger on the tip of my nose. 'And you're coming to live in my new stately home.'

I'm relieved that she's taken my confession so well, but still – I can't move into Holt House. What was it Amira was saying about money and power? For years, we've been on a pretty equal footing, splitting everything down the middle and complaining mid-way through the month that we're out of money. It won't be like that anymore.

'No one lives rent-free,' I say.

She shakes her head. 'You're always saying the only people you know our age that own a house got it because they lived with their parents for the last decade, or someone died. Isn't this better? We both know you can't afford to continue renting our horrid little flat alone. So that leaves you with two options: renting in Bath with strangers or going back to Trowbridge to live with your mother.'

She's right. I'd have to choose between a life of labelled fridge items and cleaning rotas and quiet sex so as not to disturb my flatmates, or clearing away wine bottles and scrubbing at vomit and sitting alone in my childhood bedroom. Or, I could come with her. Could live in a huge house with stone steps and turrets and a walled garden. Could have mimosas for breakfast and take my tea in the library room. Could rub elbows with the Talbots and Lollies and Henrys without feeling less than; without my friends or Henry questioning whether he and I are too many worlds removed, because I'd be part of his. Besides, it's her and me. Nothing can change our relationship.

I raise my glass. 'You get the boxes and I'll get the tape.'

Chapter Ten

The housewarming party is Pinterest-perfection. There are caterers and bartenders and balloons and fairy lights and little cakes with *Holt House* piped in swirly gold icing. Outside is a billowing milk-white tent with a live band and a black-and-white chequered dance floor – like a vast, glossy chess board. Waiters wander in and out with trays of champagne flutes and lobster canapés. Everywhere I look, there are beautiful, expensive people wearing beautiful, expensive things.

Everything glitters.

I'm standing on the fringes of the dance floor when she grabs me from behind, wrapping her arms around my waist. 'Zara,' she whispers into my ear, and I can smell her sweet champagne breath. 'The belle of the ball.' She turns me around and drinks in my dark green dress. The colour does nice things for my eyes, and the thick, clingy fabric does nice things for my body. 'How could anyone resist?'

'Thanks. You don't look too bad yourself.'

We smile because we know this is a grotesque understatement. In her black dress with its dramatic, thigh-high split, she is all legs and delicious temptation.

'Henry's a lucky man,' she tells me, before plucking two glasses of wine from a wandering waiter and handing one to me. 'So,' she says, surveying the crowd. 'Where is he?'

'At the bar. He put his housewarming gift on the table in the hall. That pile is huge by the way; we may need a second table.'

'What is it?'

'A solid-oak chopping board with HH carved into it. It's pretty. I didn't know chopping boards could be so expensive.'

She doesn't comment. He could have gift-wrapped a magic

lamp with a genie inside and it still wouldn't be right, because she is determined not to like him. 'I'm glad you're finally going to meet.'

She sips her drink without saying anything.

Henry has wanted us to get together for weeks, but she's turned him down repeatedly, claiming to be too busy with the house move. Which I struggle to believe since she's hired a removal company, decorators and an interior designer, who run around after us like we're endangered baby pandas. And though she hasn't found even one hour in the six weeks we've been living at Holt House to meet Henry, she's found entire evenings to devote to her old friends, who've welcomed her back into the fold with diamond bracelet-clad arms now that she has the money to keep up.

'It's like she doesn't want to share you,' said Henry one night over dinner when she failed, yet again, to join us, messaging me an excuse at the last possible second.

'There he is,' I say now, spotting Henry weaving between people to get to us. He's in a crisp white shirt and a pair of really good jeans, the kind that are exclusive to shops that only have a handful of items per rail.

My palms are clammy, and my breaths are coming harder. When I told Amira I didn't need Ivy's approval, I was lying. She's important to me. I want her to like him. I do. I do. I—

'Zara,' says Henry, pulling me close.

I grin up at him. 'Henry, this is Ivy. Ivy, this is—'

'Henry,' she finishes for me, smoothly.

She lets him kiss her cheeks.

'I've heard a lot about you,' he says.

The smile she gave me earlier is gone, replaced with something colder.

'The house is beautiful,' says Henry.

'One man's death is another woman's gain,' she says, and slowly sips her wine.

I flounder in the awkwardness of it all and wonder why she's playing this game; the 'be as cold and as crass and as blunt as possible to make people feel so uncomfortable, they turn and leave with their tail between their legs' game.

'Ivy has a great eye for interiors,' I gabble.

'Ada did most of it,' she corrects me, and she's just being obstinate because it is very unlike her to bat back a compliment.

'Well, yes, Ada's the interior designer, but it's your vision.' I turn to Henry. 'No matter how awful our student houses were, Ivy made them beautiful. Fairy lights, bunting, furniture from thrift markets.'

'You've come a long way since bunting and thrift markets,' says Henry.

She bristles at this. 'I do hope so. That was almost ten years ago. Zara and I have been together for over a decade now.'

'Together?'

'Friends,' I say. 'We met during our first year of university. It's a funny story actually—'

'Caitlin, Florence!' she calls, her focus on a gaggle of women across the dance floor. 'You'll have to excuse me; hosting is tireless work. Anyway, I hope you enjoy the party, Henry.'

Then she's gone. Silence.

Henry raises an eyebrow.

I clear my throat. 'We'll have to arrange another dinner.'

'And she'll have the time?'

'Yes. Of course she will. The house is pretty much unpacked now so . . .' I trail off into unbearable silence. I can tell he wants to say something but he's holding back. God, Ivy, I think, why do you have to be such a bitch sometimes?

'Well,' he says. 'If it's important to you, it's important to me, too.'

I feel a wave of affection for him. I love that this is the foundation on which we are building a life together.

'There's actually some people I'd like to introduce you to,' he says. Henry knows more people here than I do. I could've invited some of my own friends since I live here, too, but it didn't feel right because this place isn't mine. OK, so the flat wasn't, either, but it was ours, wasn't it? Whereas Holt House is all hers.

I recognise her work colleagues. *Ex*-work colleagues now, I suppose. I'm not sure exactly how much money her half of the inheritance amounted to, but even so, it must have been a lot for her to be able to hand in her notice at the PR company.

Henry leads me from the tent and across the garden. The late August heat is like a lover: close and leaving me breathless. As we reach the pond, he stops, and pulls me to him.

'I thought we were going to see your friends?' I ask.

He kisses me. It's unhurried and certain, just like him. His hands travel up my bare back, deliberately, slowly, and the need to have him is electric. Tonight, we will have sex. The thought is intoxicating, and I am giddy with it. I've wanted him since we met at the wedding three months ago and though we've been on several steamy dates since then, we haven't slept together. I wanted to wait until I was sure he wouldn't lose interest, or whether Luke would return and I'd lose interest, because I am twenty-eight and I want the next man I welcome into my bed to be the last. In just a few hours, Henry and I will be naked with each other. Sex with someone new usually makes me nervous, because what if the reality of me doesn't live up to the fantasy? What if I'm not as good in bed as his last partner? Isn't every woman worried about being the one he tells his friends was the worst fuck he'd ever had? But with Henry's hands on my body and his tongue in my mouth, there is only the sweet soreness of anticipation.

In the house, Henry introduces me to his friends. The women could all be clones of one another, with their glossy dark hair and midi dresses and Gucci belts. At one point or another, they have all either owned a horse or know someone who does. The men have white smiles and square chins and expensive watches.

Jonty is blond and blue-eyed with a slightly crooked nose, which seems to be the natural conclusion of playing rugby. He's the kind of broad build that could help you carry a large chest of drawers up the stairs. 'Good to finally meet you, Zara,' he says and kisses my cheeks. He grips Henry's shoulder. 'Our man here is pretty smitten.'

I smile. 'Glad I'm making an impression.'

'She's beautiful,' he says to Henry. 'You're beautiful,' he tells me. And even though I have a knee-jerk reaction to refute compliments, I smile and say, 'Thank you.'

Henry stands beside Jonty and both their gazes are on me. For just a moment, their attention feels like standing too close to an open fire and I have to look away.

'Willing to share, Frith?' jokes Jonty.

'Not this time,' Henry answers, stepping away from him and winding an arm around me. 'She's all mine.'

I look over my shoulder, searching for Ivy. She's standing in the doorway with a group of women I don't know. Her eyes find mine and a smile starts to curl her lips, then vanishes when her gaze drops to his hand on my waist. I resist the urge to slip out of his reach. The blonde girl beside her whispers something in her ear, stealing her focus. Then she leaves with her, and I feel suddenly, terribly alone.

Henry kisses me and tells me he's going to the bar again. I stand awkwardly with a group of strangers. Even though I live in the big house and I'm wearing the expensive dress and I'm drinking the expensive champagne, dipping my toe into the waters of a life that, only a few weeks ago, was so far out of reach it may as well have been on Mars, I can't fully submerge myself in it. I feel like a fraud as I nod and smile, listening to them talk about family skiing holidays and renovating their second homes and their days at Oxbridge. I do not mention the tiny two-bed terrace house I grew up in or the lost, drunk mother that raised me, or the father who abandoned us both before I could walk.

I am only ever truly myself when I'm with her.

A tidal wave of unhappiness washes over me, filling my ears and my eyes and my lungs.

Casting around for a distraction, I force myself to tune into the conversation.

'He's going to Amsterdam for his stag do,' says one woman. 'Three words: red light district.'

'Oh, God, I know. Obviously, I trust him, but I don't really want him in a strip club.'

Personally, I'd be less worried about my fiancé getting a private dance and more worried about how many sex workers are illegally trafficked and repeatedly raped by sweaty men with more money than morals, but I don't think my input would be welcome, so I sip my drink and keep my mouth shut. Ivy, on the other hand, would've just come out and said it.

Eventually, I go looking for her. Instead, to my shock, I find Luke. He's talking with a small group of men, his words coming on the back of a smile. There's an easiness to him that makes entire rooms loosen and exhale. I feel better just watching him. He pushes his fingers back through his hair. It's longer, long enough that it falls softly behind his ears, and the dark dusting of stubble across his jaw is new. He looks like he's just come in from cutting down trees in the forest. When he sees me, his face lights up. He excuses himself and makes his way over.

We hug. I breathe in the peppery cedarwood scent of him. When he pulls away, I can still feel the heat of him against my chest.

'Where's Ivy?' he asks.

'Around.'

'Rare that you two are apart.'

'It is?'

'Yeah. So why—'

'I didn't know you were coming,' I say by way of distraction, so he doesn't zero in on the unusual distance between me and her, and pick at it like a scab.

'Is it OK that I'm here?'

I pause, then start nodding like one of those bobble-headed toys.

'Of course it is. Yes,' I say, afraid to examine too closely how I feel about him. Usually, Luke is enough to make everything else fall away. Usually, he is enough to make me cast aside whoever I'm casually dating and fall back into bed with him, only to watch him pack a bag and leave for the airport a couple of weeks later. But though it's been four months since I ended things between us, even now, I can feel that *pull* to be with him, however briefly. So, I force myself to send these resurgent feelings scattering like marbles, losing them under the sofa where they will gather lint and dust.

'The house is . . . impressive,' he offers.

I smile and say nothing, because it isn't mine. It never will be.

'But it isn't where I pictured you living,' he says.

If this had been a comment from anyone else in this room, I'd have taken it as a dig. 'Where did you picture me living?'

'A cottage. Somewhere by the coast.'

I smile. 'What would I do in a cottage by the coast?'

'Whatever you wanted. You'd own your own wedding planning business and—'

'I could never own my own business.'

'Why not?'

'I just couldn't . . . I'm not that smart. You need to be smart to own a business.'

'You *are* smart.' He lowers his head, so I am caught in the grey of his eyes. 'You, Zara, can do anything.'

I'm trying to ignore the immediate tension, the electricity humming in the air between us, but I can't look away. I feel him leaning a little closer, I feel myself wanting to lean closer in return.

But I won't. I push those feelings further beneath the sofa and take a step back.

He clears his throat. The tension, whatever it was, dissolves.

'So,' he says. 'You'd live in this cottage, and you'd have a dog. Something universally lovable.'

'A labrador?'

'Too big. A cocker spaniel. The two of you'd go running along the beach each day.'

'Wow. I'm pretty fit in this cottage-coastline-cocker-spaniel fantasy.'

'You run.'

'I don't run. I jog. Slowly and occasionally.'

He grins. 'Your house would be filled with books and vintage candlesticks and plants. So many plants.'

I'm smiling again. I shouldn't care that he's spent time wondering about me, but I do. 'You've really thought about this,' I say, and I can feel him gearing up to say something important.

'I've really thought about a lot of things, lately,' Luke says. 'We haven't talked in a long while. You haven't replied to my messages.'

'I've been busy,' I hedge, not wanting to rub Henry in his face. 'So, where've you been travelling?'

'Norway. Look—'

'What was it like?'

'Great. Cold. Zara—'

'I hear there's a magnificent Viking Museum in Oslo.'

He sighs, exasperated. I don't want to hear whatever he is desperate to tell me because I have a feeling he's about to ruin everything.

He keeps trying. 'I've been thinking about moving—'

'There you are.' Henry is suddenly at my side, pressing his lips to my cheek, and even though I haven't done anything wrong, I jump like I've been caught.

'Henry, this is Luke. He's . . .' I grapple for an explanation. *The man I've been desperately in love with for fifteen years* will go down as smoothly as cyanide, so I settle on, 'We lived on the same street growing up.'

'Nice to meet you, Luke,' says Henry.

Luke looks surprised. 'You, too.'

I see the puzzle pieces falling into place as Luke realises that the reason I'm not with Ivy is because I'm with Henry. I stare at him, hoping he can see the apology on my face even though I'm not sure, exactly, what I'm apologising for.

Henry kisses the top of my head and says, 'There are actually a couple more people I'd like you to meet.'

'Oh.' I glance at Luke. 'Sure.'

'You're welcome to join us, Luke,' says Henry kindly.

Luke nods his head once in polite acknowledgement. 'No, no, that's fine. You go. Enjoy your night.'

'Thanks,' says Henry. 'And you.'

As Henry leads me across the room, an arm slung around my shoulders, I glance back at Luke. There's so much sadness in his face, I have to avert my gaze.

Henry kisses my cheek then growls into my ear, 'Can't let you out of my sight for a moment without someone trying to steal you away.'

'Am I yours to steal?' I grin up at him.

He stops right there in the middle of the crowded room. 'From the second we met.'

We kiss. It is an adult kiss. One which promises bedsheets and bare skin. But the *need* to have him naked beneath me is gone. Frustrated with myself, I kiss him harder, chasing that feeling, wanting it to return with feverish brilliance. It doesn't.

He introduces me to some more of his friends. I nod and smile but when they inevitably fall into reminiscence of a shared gap year in Africa, where they held lion cubs but also helped build a well out of the goodness of their hearts and not for the purpose of CVs or party-talk fodder, I check my phone. There is a message from Luke.

I'm happy for you, Zara. Leaving for Croatia tomorrow. I don't want to ruin anything for you.

Henry squeezes my arm and I quickly drop my phone to my side. 'Are you alright?'

'Yep. I'm just going to get another drink,' I tell him.

He frowns. I turn on my heel without waiting for a response and start walking away, my chest tight. What was Luke going to tell me earlier? I didn't want to know before but now, it's bothering me. I haven't thought about him in weeks. Not since Henry.

Replace a bad habit with a good one.

If he hadn't been invited to this party . . .

Then I see her. She is enjoying the attention of the petite blonde girl, leaning into her as the girl stares up at her indulgently. Oh, how she loves to be the centre of someone's world. This thought is razor-laced and surprises me. Then Ivy reaches out and runs her fingers through the blonde girl's hair.

Like fire. Like the sun coming up.

As though sensing my eyes on her, she looks up and our gazes meet. There's a moment of something strange, a crackle of meaning, and my heart canters.

She leans into the girl and whispers. The girl glances my way, smiles, then disappears into the crowd. By the time I am face-to-face with Ivy, my blood runs red-hot through my veins.

'You invited Luke?' I snap.

'Why wouldn't I?' She smiles a small, private smile. 'He's our friend, isn't he?'

'Yes, he is but—'

'So then there's no problem, is there? You and Luke are over. You said you wanted to remain friends. And now you're with Henry.'

'Yes, I'm with Henry, but—'

'But what, Zara?' she asks archly. Silence.

I stare at her, seething, because we both know she's used Luke. He is merely the sledgehammer with which she is swinging at the newly-laid foundations of me and Henry. I will not let her bait me. I take a breath. 'It's fine that you invited him.'

She's smiling that private little smile again. Like she knows something I don't. Like she has won. But she hasn't won. I won't let her. Spinning on my heel, I cast around for Henry. He's watching us, standing only a few metres away. Soon, I am in front of him. I grab him and kiss him, and I know she is watching. I *like* that she is watching. My tongue is in his mouth, my arms are around his neck and my chest is pressed firmly against his.

Without saying a word, I take his hand and lead him upstairs. All the while, I feel the blistering heat of her gaze burning into my back.

As we near my bedroom door, doubt creeps in. What am I doing? *Why* am I doing this? I don't want to have sex, not really. Not now. She and Luke have spoiled it.

'Is this your room?' asks Henry.

We've stopped right outside my door, my fingers curled around the knob. But I don't make a move to open it.

'Is everything OK?' he asks.

I nod, though I'm not sure it is.

Henry moves closer, slips his fingers beneath my chin, and tilts my face up to his so that all I can see are his hazel eyes and the tiny flecks of gold in them. 'You are so beautiful.' He traces the shape of my mouth with his thumb and my lips part. 'Can I kiss you?'

I smile at the gentleness of him and nod.

Then his mouth is on mine again. Sweet. Soft. Then harder. More urgent. He presses me up against my door, then reaches around me, his tongue in my mouth, and pushes the door open. We spill into my room in a tangle of breath and groping hands and laughter. Henry bashes into my dresser and groans.

'Killed the mood?' I ask, flipping on a lamp for him.

'Not even for a second,' he says. I grin and move to turn off the light again, but he catches my wrist. 'Leave it on.' He straightens. His eyes on me. All over my body. I take this opportunity to drink him in, too. His slim but strong frame. His thick eyebrows and straight nose. His long legs and narrow hips.

'Take off your dress.'

I hesitate only for a second before doing as he says.

He circles me. I feel his hot, steady breath on the nape of my neck and his hot steady gaze on my body. Then his hands are on my shoulders. Slowly, so slowly, his fingers trail down my arms, raising goosebumps in their wake. I am thrumming. Waiting. Then his hands travel up the centre of my back and I inhale deeply. He takes his time, his fingers tracing the inky rivers beneath my skin. He expertly unclips my bra. It hits the floor and I shiver. A moment later, my knickers follow.

'Turn around.'

Without thinking, I obey.

He takes a step back and very slowly appraises me. He swallows hard, and a sharp thrill ripples through me. Never before have I stood naked in front of a fully-clothed man. There should be an imbalance of power here: I am exposed, and he is not. But I don't feel vulnerable. I feel powerful. I feel as though I can reduce the most assertive, composed man I know into a pining, wanting animal.

'Come here.'

I do.

He is so close now that he fills the air around me until there's nothing but him and his body heat, and beneath the smell of soap and his spicy, woody cologne is *him*. He kisses me again. And I am no longer merely miming passion. There's a roughness to it, to the way he grips the back of my neck, that I'm afraid to admit I like. I am pressed firmly against the soft linen of his shirt and the toughness of his jeans.

It isn't long before he's naked, too. He settles himself between my legs. 'Put your hands above your head.'

When I don't immediately do as I'm told, he grins as though he's been waiting for me to disobey. He catches my mouth again. Tasting me. Devouring me. Deftly, he flips me over. Every inch of my body is coiled in anticipation. Just for a second, I think of Ivy. Then he's inside me. And all thoughts of her burn away.

In the morning, Henry goes to our kitchen to make me breakfast: eggs Benedict. Smiling, I reach for my phone to build bridges, to dispel the awkwardness between us last night, and ask what it means when, the morning after, he makes me eggs Benedict. But an email in my work inbox from an address I've never seen before seizes me. It's from an address I don't recognise: HTH@gmail.com

Don't let him ruin your life.

Chapter Eleven

Now

I'm not fond of my lawyer and I'm pretty sure he isn't fond of me, either. Tammingworth is as broad as he is wide, with a receding hairline and glasses that are too small for his round head. He reminds me of a cartoon mole. And he's a golfer. I can just tell. He is one of those men who will argue with you until they're blue in the face that golf is not just a competition, but a sport, and he is, therefore, a sportsman, despite getting out of breath simply walking up the stairs of his million-pound home.

He has returned to the holding room with two cups of weak tea. He slides one across the table to me, and I curl my hands around the plastic, closing my eyes as the tea warms my fingers. If I try, I can pretend I'm sitting on the plush, velvet sofa in our old flat, rain lashing against the windows, a book resting on the sofa, waiting to be read.

'Miss Barton, are you listening?' snaps Tammingworth. I jump, eyes flying open.

Before I can lie and tell him I heard every word, he sighs and says, 'Do you understand what is happening here, Miss Barton? Do you comprehend the severity of the charges you're facing if the police have any reason to believe you're guilty of murder? My advice when questioned is to repeat "no comment",' he tells me firmly. 'Anything you say now will be held against you later in a court of law.'

Panic licks up my throat and out of my mouth. 'You mean a trial . . . There's going to be a trial?'

For hours I have tried to compartmentalise what's happening, breaking down events and placing them into neat little boxes: the death, the heated, desperate conversation that followed, being put into the back of a police car and arriving here at the station. I stacked the boxes so high, it was impossible to see beyond them, to wonder what might be coming next. But Tammingworth's earnest insistence that I look to the future is so sobering and bleak, I feel sick.

'A life has been lost in extremely violent circumstances. You were present at the scene of the crime, and your fingerprints have been found on the weapon. Of course there will be a trial.'

Humiliation colours my cheeks at having asked such an idiotic question.

'They haven't charged me, though, have they?'

'Not yet.'

Yet. There's inevitability in his tone. In his choice of words. In the granite line of his mouth. There's no escaping the facts: I am going to be charged with murder.

'Your version of events is rife with inconsistencies,' he says curtly. 'We don't have time to go over your story before your next interview, so do as I advise and answer every question with "no comment".'

I lick my dry lips. 'But then they'll think I have something to hide.'

He lowers his chin and fixes me with a hard, meaningful stare. 'Don't you, Miss Barton?'

Chapter Twelve

Before

I see my father twice a year – a week or so before my birthday in September, and then again in January, to exchange Christmas presents. Our relationship is a carousel of transactions. My twenty-ninth birthday is just around the corner, so we're having dinner in the garden of his family home. It's early September and still warm enough to eat outside. Ivy sits to my right. With things between us feeling strained lately, I worried that this year, she wouldn't come. But I need her with me, because when I'm in the company of my father's new family, it feels like I've walked in halfway through a cosy dinner, and though I'm starving, there isn't enough food and there's nowhere left for me to sit down.

Julia chats away to us. She is all fuchsia-pink lipstick and Lola Rose necklaces. When I was a child, I wanted desperately to hate her, hissing my disdain as though she were a fairy-tale stepmother, complete with warts and sweeping cloak, but she's only ever tried to make me feel welcome. Meanwhile, my father sits at the other end of the table, nursing a glass of red and not saying very much. We haven't spoken since he called and interrupted my first date with Henry all those weeks ago.

Soon, Polly, her husband Matthew and their two-year-old daughter Bonnie arrive.

I stoop to kiss my niece's cheek, remembering the first time I saw her. She was already three months old, gorgeous with her feathery blonde hair and teeny cream onesie. The love was pin-sharp and instantaneous. I'd never felt anything like it. Before Bonnie, love was something I had to nurture over time – like with Luke – starting off as a seed that slowly blossoms. But it was different with my niece, immediate and instinctive – a love with deep, thick roots. If it's like this with a niece, how much more powerfully would I love my own child?

'Zara, *you're* here!' Polly exclaims. She says this every time I come to my father's house, as though I'm a homeless person who's wandered in off the street.

I'm not sure most people would guess we're half-sisters; we don't look much alike. We share the same heart-shaped face and our father's wide blue eyes, but my lashes are longer, my skin paler, my build taller and leaner. And where my hair is auburn, hers is buttercup blonde. Then my gaze drops to her stomach and I gasp.

'Polly – you're pregnant!'

Her hands move to her blooming belly, and she smiles. 'Six months.'

'Congratulations!' I hug her, bashing my hip on the table. 'Wow. This is so . . . wow!'

Another child. Another niece or nephew. Another person in my life who is happy and settled and moving forward and . . . and . . . she's so young. At twenty-five, she's so young. Or, she isn't and I'm just old, and childless and—

'Polly, sweetheart, didn't you tell your sister?' asks Julia, coming up behind her with two jugs of iced water.

She shrugs as though the thing she'd forgotten to share was as mundane as a haircut and not the impending arrival of my blood relative. 'I thought I did.'

She knows she didn't. We aren't exactly chatty. In fact, I talk more regularly to my DPD driver than I do my half-sister. She chooses to keep me at arm's length, drawing a line down the centre of our lives, putting herself, Julia and my father on one side, and me firmly on the other.

'We're delighted!' says Polly. 'Daddy is over the moon.'

Ivy leans into me and whispers, 'There's something truly disturbing about a grown woman using "Daddy" outside of amateur porn.'

I bite my lip to stop from laughing and feel another rush of gratitude that she's here.

Dad pulls Polly close, kissing the top of her head. 'Hello, darling.'

I try not to think about how, when I arrived, he merely bestowed upon me the same nondescript smile he'd give a shop assistant as they handed him back his change. This one small act reinforces that I will never simply be Rupert Ellery's daughter. I will always be Rupert Ellery's *daughter from his previous relationship.* Whenever I think this, I think of pancakes. Everyone knows the first pancake never turns out the way you hoped. It's a warmup. A trial run. Disposable. The second pancake is better. The one you savour. Take photographs of. Enjoy. I am my father's first pancake and Polly is his second.

When Bonnie starts to fuss, Matthew gets to his feet and whisks her upstairs for a nap. I like that he is not the kind of man who refers to taking care of his own children as 'babysitting.'

My father and Julia go inside to fetch the food and silence descends on the three of us, until Polly pipes up with, 'How's your mother?' with just a little more emphasis on the word 'your' than necessary.

'She's fine. Thanks for asking.'

She furrows her brow. 'She's not drinking, then?'

Before I can form a reply, Ivy, too, furrows her brow in an equal show of concern. 'How's your perineum, Polly?' she asks. 'I hear those post-birth stitches are a bitch.'

Polly glares, the quip going down like a bag of rusty nails.

We eat homemade pie and roasted vegetables around a beautifully decorated table: wildflowers in glass jugs, white pillar candles and fresh linen napkins. Fairy lights zigzag in tree branches above our heads, and smooth jazz drifts in from the kitchen, carried on a light autumn breeze.

Julia tops up my glass and asks if I'm seeing anyone.

'I am actually,' I say, my lips curling into a smile like they always do when I think about Henry.

On my dad's face, I see a mix of surprise and relief. Though he's never the one to ask the question, I get the impression he's interested in the answer. He's fairly traditional in his beliefs, and I wonder if he's eager for me to be married off so he can rid himself of whatever responsibility he thinks he has to me, as though I'm a baton in a relay race, and he can finally relax once I change hands.

'His name's Henry,' I continue. 'He's . . . well . . . he's brilliant.' I don't look at Ivy as I say this, but I feel her stiffen in disagreement.

'Oh, Zara, we are so happy for you,' says Julia.

I smile at her. Grateful she takes an interest in my love life when my own mother never has. Mum is staunchly against me building a life with a man, telling me men are the poison that slowly kills you, while at the same time swinging from one relationship to the next. Maybe she's afraid I'll withdraw from her once I have my own family, or maybe she's just jealous, embittered with thoughts of *if I can't have it, neither can you.*

'Didn't your boyfriend want to join us?' asks Polly. The way she slowly drags out the word 'boyfriend' feels like an attempt to draw attention to the sad, tragic affair that he hasn't yet taken the title of fiancé or husband.

'Obviously, he wanted to,' I say. 'But he had to work.' I need Henry to meet the Ellerys, if only to prove to him that one half of my family is sober and relatively normal. But when I mentioned this dinner and told him I'd love to introduce him to my dad soon, he smiled and said 'I'd like that' before kissing my cheek and returning his attention to his phone. I mean, it's probably too early to meet each other's loved ones and I'm only pushing for it because I don't want his lasting impression of my family to be my mum drunkenly wailing into the petunias.

'Work on a Saturday?' She scrunches up her button nose in disbelief.

'He's the managing director of Henrietta's House,' Ivy announces, her voice ringing out, clear and authoritative. 'So, he's fairly busy, you know, running an empire.' Apparently, her instinct to put Polly in her place momentarily outweighs her disapproval of Henry. Everyone except my sister looks impressed.

Matthew helps Julia clear away and fetch dessert. He really is perfect; even Amira's Nathan doesn't help clean up unless he's asked. I'd never tell Ivy I'm impressed by Matthew because she'd say no one is impressed when a woman gets up to help, why should it be any different if a man does? And she's right, of course.

We're tucking into apple crumble when Julia asks about the new house.

Polly frowns. 'You're not in the flat anymore?'

'No,' I say. 'We moved into Holt House in the summer.'

'Holt House?' Polly rolls this around her tongue, tasting the grandeur, and I know it sours in her mouth, because Polly has always enjoyed that while she owns her own house, I merely rent a flat. She insists on calling her three-bed end of terrace a 'semi-detached' even though it isn't. Still, I'm proud of her. Deposits aren't cheap and not many people can afford to buy in their twenties.

'Would you like to see some photographs?' Ivy asks her, dangling this real estate carrot above Polly's head. It's cruel, really, because we both know Polly's desperate to see them. She can't be certain what she has is shinier if she doesn't have a visual comparison.

'Sure,' she says with a little I'm-not-that-bothered-either-way shrug. Ivy slides me a knowing smile as she hands over her phone. Polly falls on the images as though she is starving and they are steak. She flicks through photographs of stone staircases and exposed beams and open fireplaces, lingering on the one of my favourite room, the first-floor lounge. It has a high, vaulted ceiling and wall-to-wall windows, with views over the garden.

'Wow,' breathes Julia who is looking over Polly's shoulder. 'Girls, it's stunning.'

'You own this?' Polly asks Ivy, and it sounds like more of an accusation than a question.

In response, she glows with pride. Since receiving her inheritance, she walks around with a renewed sense of purpose. And power. And Chanel handbags.

Matthew takes the phone from Polly. He lets out a low, impressed whistle. 'Makes our place look like a matchbox.'

The look Polly throws him promises a stern talking-to on the car ride home. 'How did this happen then?' she asks, thrusting the phone back at Ivy. 'Did you rob a bank?'

'No.' She pauses, making sure she has everyone's attention as her eyes start to mist expertly. Even though she hadn't had contact with her grandfather in the years before he died, I know his death hit her hard; but the grief she's displaying now is all for show. 'My grandfather died.'

'Polly!' scolds Julia before turning to my friend. 'Oh, Ivy, love. I'm sorry to hear that.'

'It's fine,' she says quietly, squeezing my thigh under the table as she shoots Polly a hurt little look. 'Living in the family home makes me feel close to him.'

Him, and Louis Vuitton, I think, but don't say.

Even my father is frowning at Polly for her rudeness, and she forces a contrite expression. But she doesn't stay cowed for long.

'Well, we can't all inherit a mansion,' she says archly. 'I suppose I can't complain, Daddy did give us the deposit for our house.' She looks at me, then, to see if her words, like poison-tipped arrows, have met their target. She can tell by the hurt on my face that they have, and takes a satisfied sip of her tea.

Silence ping-pongs around the table. Even the breeze has dropped, as though the entire evening is holding its breath, waiting for me to react. Under the table, Ivy squeezes my thigh again, harder this time. It feels like my chair is heating beneath me, until it's too hot to stay put.

'I'm just going to nip to the loo,' I say.

But I don't go to the bathroom, I only get as far as the dining room before tears threaten. My dad gave Polly the deposit for her house? Just gave it to her. Like it's a loaf of bread and not financial security, a step onto the property ladder that so many people my age can't make. All these years I've felt inadequate because, while my younger sister has managed to buy her own home, I've never been able to save enough money. Not even close.

I swing into the kitchen to make more tea, grabbing the kettle and thrusting it beneath the gushing tap.

All the times Polly has said things, like, 'Oh, Zara, don't you want to have a place to call your own? Buying was the best thing we ever did,' as though my inability to drum up thousands for a deposit was due to a lack of effort rather than a lack of possibility. Of course I could buy a house, if someone handed me the fucking money for the deposit.

The kettle comes to the boil, and I cast around for a mug.

My dad isn't wealthy enough to make sure that two of his children can buy a house, but did he think, even for a second, that it might be fairer to split whatever money he did have between Polly and me, so that we were on equal footing?

I wrench open another cupboard, but it's full of tinned food and pasta.

It's not even about the amount of money he's chosen to give to her and not to me. It's keeping it a secret that hurts most. A secret Polly has kept in her back pocket, to throw in my face like a splash of acid whenever the urge struck.

And where the fuck do they keep their fucking mugs? Shouldn't I know where my father keeps his tossing mugs?

I am a stranger in this house. I don't belong here. I never have.

'Are you OK?'

I jump at the sound of Ivy's voice. She is standing in the doorway, eyes searching my face. I swallow hard and blink back tears. 'I'm fine.'

'Zara . . .'

How can she stand there all innocence and sympathy when she was the one to sweep through my life like a natural disaster? Devastation quickly bubbles into anger. 'Did you have to fucking bait her like that?'

'Ignorance isn't always bliss. At least now you know what kind of people they are.'

'So, what, you want a written fucking "thank you" note?' I hold my breath, waiting for her to snap back. Instead, she issues me with a warning.

'That tone really doesn't suit you, Zara.'

I take a deep breath and look out the window. It's getting dark. Dad bounces Bonnie on his knee. She's older now than I was when he abandoned me.

I'm with my family, Zara.

And then I am livid all over again and I turn on her once more, because being angry is better than being unloved. 'If you didn't want to come, you shouldn't have bothered.'

'I came because I care about you. I spoke up against Polly because you never do. No one does. She isn't allowed to talk to you like that and get away with it. Would you let someone treat me the way she treats you?'

'No.' I take several deep breaths to calm myself. My anger is misdirected. She's not the one I've been hurt by. 'I'm sorry.'

She presses a kiss to my cheek.

'Can we leave soon?' I ask.

'Great idea.'

When we return to the garden, it's just Polly. 'Matthew is on nappy-changing duty. Mum and Dad have gone to the study to send an email or something.'

'Or something,' I say, sure they've retreated to discuss damage control. How will my father spin this one in his favour? Maybe he'll claim he *thought* he'd written me a cheque, too. Just as Polly claimed she *thought* she'd told me she was having another baby.

'So,' she says. 'We've talked about Zara's *wonderful* Henry. What about you, Ivy? Is there a man in your life? Somebody special?'

'Many men. None of them special,' Ivy says coolly.

Polly doesn't like this answer. It's honest and flies in the face of her habitual monogamy, which makes her feel uncomfortable. She thinks Ivy's a slut. It's written all over her face, but she isn't brave enough to say it. Instead, she says, 'Oh, so no children on the cards for you?' as though this is a fate worse than death.

'Unlikely. I've become pretty fond of sneezing without worrying about pissing my Agent Provocateur knickers.'

I bite my lip to stop the laughter that gurgles up. I'm not sure which is funnier, Ivy's deadpan delivery, or Polly's furious, ashen face. I have to give it to her, though, she recovers quickly.

'Well, we just had to have a second. Bonnie is such a happy little girl as she is, but I've always wanted her to have a sibling. Growing up an only child has its benefits, I was so close to my parents, but I suppose you always want for your own children what you didn't have.'

Her words are another back-handed slap to my face, and I recoil. The laughter that rose just seconds before is gone, replaced again by anguish.

Beside me, I feel Ivy unsheathe her claws. 'Are you sure?' she asks, her smile full of bitch. 'Because, in my experience, younger siblings are usually malicious, self-involved little wankers.'

We leave shortly after that.

In the car on the way home, I check my work emails to distract myself from thinking about that disastrous dinner. I haven't had another from HTH@gmail.com since the one the morning after the housewarming party a week ago. I open it up again, now.

Don't let him ruin your life.

At first, I was convinced it was in reference to Luke, because he'd sent me a message that night about not wanting to ruin anything for me. The more I thought about it, though, the more unsure I became. After all, everyone loves Luke. Even Ivy. Besides, my email address is on the Hillington Wedding Planners' website for anyone to access, so, having not received another once since, I reason that the email was inconsequential spam.

She sleeps in my bed. We curl up against one another. It's dark and warm. She whispers, 'Sorry about your dad.'

I shrug.

'My father was meant to call me today,' she says.

'Did he?'

'No.'

Sometimes, I think of us as two strays that have been rescued and rehomed together. 'Love you,' I tell her.

'How much?'

'Too much.'

'Impossible.'

Chapter Thirteen

Yesterday, I turned twenty-nine, and tomorrow, Ivy turns twenty-nine too. With our birthdays only two days apart, we celebrate them both in the no man's land. And today is the day.

I'm woken by her climbing into my bed. She slips beneath the covers. Our bare legs touch and her skin is so warm. 'I'm taking us to a spa.' She presses her nose against mine so all I see is the green of her eyes, and when she speaks, I taste her minty breath. 'Are you excited?'

I cover my mouth with my hand. 'I have morning breath.' I make to roll out of bed, but she snatches my wrist and then she's on top of me, straddling my thighs. She pins my hands above my head and showers my face with kisses. I giggle and kick but it's a half-hearted attempt to dislodge her.

Then we still, our hearts racing, our chests rising and falling fast. She plants one final kiss on my nose and then she hops from the bed, and it suddenly feels too big. 'Get showered, get dressed, we leave in half an hour.' As she slinks from the room, she calls, 'And brush your teeth. You're right about the morning breath.'

At the spa, I get a facial. I've never had one before, but I'm twenty-nine now and worry my skin will end up looking like a scrunched-up piece of paper if I don't start looking after it.

The facialist's fingers deftly stroke upwards, moving across the tops of my cheekbones. She tells me I am an 'English rose', but what she really means is that I have the complexion of a Victorian ghost child. She covers my face with a warm flannel. It's meant to be relaxing, but instead it feels as though I'm about to be water-boarded into a confession, like I only use sunscreen in the height of summer. 'I don't smoke or anything,' I tell the flannel, as though this fact will absolve me of all past sunscreen-related transgressions.

I know growing old is a privilege, but I don't want to look like a wrinkly walnut in the next ten years. Botox isn't an option – not only is it expensive and risky, everyone knows it's cheating. I want to grow old gracefully, like Olivia Colman.

Whale music fills the room and I'm told to relax. I *want* to relax, but I start thinking about the dozen missed calls and messages I have from my mum, and how I haven't answered a single one for weeks. Things in my life are finally going well. OK, so I don't have my own home, a husband and two children, like I hoped I would by this age. But I do live in a beautiful house, even if it isn't mine. I'm saving more money each month thanks to living with Ivy, practically rent-free, and I have Henry. I have a shot at the life I want with a man I want it with. I worry my mother's failings are contagious, so I've pulled away from her. Just a little. But I promise myself I will call her back. Soon. Next week.

At the end of the facial, my skin is so glowy and *clean* looking. I buy skin products I can't afford, including a serum with vitamin C in it, even though I'm pretty sure you're meant to ingest vitamin C, not slather it on your face. I think about how all the men I've dated have gotten by with only a bar of soap and tap water.

When we have been sufficiently polished and waxed and massaged, we sit in fluffy white robes by the pool. I'm just coming to the end of a chapter in my book when I glance up and my heart stops. I'm convinced the woman in the red swimsuit disappearing into the changing room is the dark-haired woman I keep seeing. I am so sure, I almost get up and go after her – but what would I say to her? How can I be sure she's following me? It's not a crime to walk down the street or make a reservation at a restaurant or come to a spa. Still, if she is following me, I want to know why . . . Don't I?

'You OK?' Ivy asks, taking out an earbud and peering at me over the top of her complimentary mimosa.

I nod, my eyes wandering back to the changing-room door. 'I mean . . . Yes, but . . .'

It was the same woman; it has to be. The long, waist-length hair, the lean figure of a ballerina.

'Are you waiting for a drum roll . . .'

I give her a look. 'No. I just thought I saw someone I know.'

She returns my look with one of her own. 'OK?'

'Well, not that I know her exactly. I keep seeing her around.'

'OK?'

'Everywhere.'

She stares at me.

'What if she's following me?'

'Maybe she likes your coat. I once followed a woman through Oldfield Park just to find out where her coat was from.'

'I'm not wearing a coat.'

She laughs.

'Ivy, I'm serious.'

'I think you'll find the woman-on-woman stalking statistics are pretty low. But, if you're worried, why don't you just confront her?'

'And if she's a nutter with a knife?'

'Then it's better you confront her in broad daylight in a public place, than wait for her to break into our house and stab you to death in your sleep.'

I roll my eyes. 'Thanks for the advice.'

She grins. 'Any time.'

I glance at the door again, but the woman doesn't come back. I reach for my book, but I can't concentrate, I am still thinking about her. Thanks to Ivy, I'm imagining her looming over my bed, long, inky hair matted and wild as she swings a knife, aiming for my throat.

Ivy's watching me, brows drawn in concern. 'Still upset about your dad?'

She's mistaken my fear of that woman for lingering sadness over my father, but I don't correct her since she isn't taking my concerns very seriously at all.

'I did offer to help you out with a deposit for your own house,' she says.

She said she *would* offer, but she knew I wouldn't accept. And she seemed more keen that I move into Holt House with her. But maybe I'm splitting hairs. 'I don't want to take your money. And it's not the point.'

'I know.'

We fall quiet and I remember I'm not the only one with a

disappointing father. Though it may be cruel, this brings me some comfort. 'Have you heard from Hugo?'

'He's coming for brunch tomorrow.' Feigning indifference, she starts scrolling through her phone, but I see hope in her expression and I worry for her, because Hugo Holt only ever lets her down, and hope, Ivy, breeds everlasting misery.

I open my mouth to press her again, but she beats me to it. 'I used to want a sister,' she says. 'Mum struggled to conceive me, so a second child was out of the question. But actually, being around Polly makes me grateful I'm an only child.'

'She isn't *that* bad.'

'Yes, and Hitler was just misunderstood.'

'Ivy!'

'Polly is a power-hungry bitch. She has all the power, and she knows it. She lords it over you.'

I wrinkle my nose. 'What power?'

'She bought her house just before Bonnie was born.'

'So?'

'So, your dad and Julia wanted their child-bearing daughter to have a home for her family. Like a reward for following the same well-trodden path they did.'

I pull a face at this, but she is undeterred.

'Polly has children, so to them she's fundamentally more important than you. They will do anything to keep her happy so that they don't lose access to their only grandchild. It's a competition you can't win.'

'It's not a competition.'

'Isn't it?' Silence sinks and surrounds us like quicksand. 'Anyway, they don't love you like I do,' she says softly. I feel the truth of this. No one loves me like she does. And that's OK. Like the tide, lovers and everyone else come and go, but she is the moon. Whether I see her or not, she is there, always. 'And you know the best part?'

'No?'

Her face splits into an impish grin. 'You don't even have to stretch your vagina to earn it.'

After the spa, she takes us to a bar. We stay out later than planned. Our phones become these forgotten things that lie in the bottom of our bags, and each time we say we're having one last drink, Ivy orders us another round. So we drink Russian vodka, we make friends with women in toilets, we sing loudly and happily, we make to stumble home holding our heels, but then Ivy calls a taxi because we can afford it now. On the ride back to Holt House, we shout '*privet!*' at one another which the bartender taught us is 'hello' in Russian.

'Come inside with me,' she whines as we pull up outside the manor.

'Can't. I promised Henry I'd stay with him tonight.'

She glowers. 'You're *always* with Henry.'

'That's simply not true, is it? I've been with you all day.'

I make sure she gets into the house safely before I hop back into the taxi and head for Henry's. Before I'd ever been to his house, I imagined him living in central Bath, but he chooses instead to live on the outskirts, in a little village called Freshford. He likes his privacy, so his three-bedroom home is set back from the road, hidden by a copse. Unlike a lot of men I've dated, Henry's place isn't all black flat-pack furniture, sports memorabilia and a week's worth of dishes in the sink. It is glossy dark wood and artwork and alphabetised vinyl. The first time he showed me around his house, I wondered again if he'd ever been married or lived with a partner because most straight bachelors don't deal in candles and cushions.

I knock on the door – twice – but he doesn't answer. I pull my phone from my bag to call him and I'm surprised by how late it is. I should've been here almost two hours ago. The only saving grace is that we didn't plan a date, not one with reservations or tickets or anything. We agreed on a cosy night in, which usually means too much wine and a lot of toe-curling sex. Then I see all the missed calls and messages – not from my mother, but from Henry – and realise my phone is set to silent. Didn't I put it back on vibrate after the spa? I call Henry, but he doesn't answer. I'm considering phoning for a taxi and going home when the door opens.

Henry looks not in the mood. 'You're here.'

He doesn't welcome me inside. 'Yes . . . I thought I was staying with you tonight.'

Without a word, he holds the door open for me to pass, then he shuts it behind me a little harder than necessary before marching into the kitchen. Confused, I take off my shoes and coat then follow. And I can't believe it. There are candles everywhere, on the kitchen island, the windowsills, the dining table. A huge vase of roses is nestled between two plates of delicious-looking food. 'You cooked for me?'

'I did,' he says, pouring himself a glass of red. 'Hours ago.'

The guilt is piercing and instant. 'I'm so sorry, I didn't know.'

'I told Ivy.'

'When?'

'When I picked you up for our theatre date last week, she was leaving Holt House as I arrived.'

'She didn't tell me.'

'Of course she didn't.'

'What's that supposed to mean?'

'She doesn't like me.'

I close the distance between us, walking around the kitchen island to be by his side. 'She doesn't dislike you . . . She doesn't know you.'

'She doesn't *want* to know me.' He downs his wine then pours himself another.

I've never seen him upset before. 'I'm so sorry I missed dinner.'

He stares down into his glass and I desperately want to know what he's thinking. He's gone to a lot of effort tonight. This entire thing is so romantic, and I ruined it. 'I really am sorry.'

He shrugs one shoulder. 'It's not your fault.'

'But it is. I should've checked my phone. I didn't think.'

Finally, he looks at me. 'If I'd known what time you were coming, I'd have waited to start dinner.'

'I'm sorry.'

'Zara, I've already told you this isn't your fault. You didn't know what I was planning.'

But *you* did, Ivy, I think. *Why didn't you tell me?* Frustration with myself hardens into anger towards her as I recall that every time I said we should leave, she ordered another round of drinks.

'I was just trying to surprise you,' says Henry.

'I am surprised.'

I rest my chin on his shoulder and look up into his hazel eyes; he's still smarting from his wrecked evening. I imagine him in the kitchen, stirring and sautéing and sipping wine between tasks, anticipation building as he pictures my face when I walk in through the front door. Then the agonising wait as time winds on, him frantically calling me as the dinner grows cold and his mood darkens, disappointment dispelling anticipation. All that effort, all that time, wasted.

'This won't happen again. I promise.' I kiss his cheek and his lips quirk up in a half-smile.

'There's an app my friend and his wife use. It's called Friend Finder.'

'Is that what we are now?' I tease. 'Just friends? Am I being demoted?'

'Never.' His turns so he is facing me, his hand sliding round to my waist and I'm glad he's touching me again.

'OK, so what is this *friend* app?'

'It allows us both to know where the other is. Say we've arranged to meet at a restaurant, I'm working late, stuck in traffic, can't use my phone to update you, you just tap into the app and you can see how far away I am. It'll even give you my ETA. Or, like tonight, if you're out with a friend and I don't want to resort to calling you five times—'

'Six,' I correct.

'*Six* times,' he says. 'I can simply open up the app and see how far away you are. It means fewer steak-dinner casualties.'

I'm quiet, digesting this. I mean, he is right. It's a practical solution. This entire terrible evening could've been avoided if we were using the app. Still, is it a little weird?

'I know.' I swallow. 'I know, but . . .'

'It's a stupid idea.' His hand drops from my waist and he turns away from me and grabs a cloth to start wiping down the already-gleaming countertop.

'No,' I say to his back. I move towards him, close enough that I can feel the heat from his body again. I lay a hand on his shoulder and after a beat, he turns to me again.

'It's not stupid. It's logical. I just . . .' I trail off, not sure what I want to say. I don't have a solid reason not to download this app onto my phone, so why am I hesitating?

Henry cups my face. 'I worry when you're out alone. You travel so much for your job. Anything could happen – an accident, a mugger, God forbid, a rapist.'

It's on the tip of my tongue to tell him not to worry, that he's being dramatic, but the sad reality is that the streets are so much more dangerous for me, as a woman, than they'll ever be for him.

'I worry,' he says again, his eyes searching mine.

'I know.'

'I worry because I love you, Zara.'

My breath catches. 'You love me?'

'I know it's fast but the first night we met, I knew you were the one I've been waiting for. I wanted to tell you over a romantic dinner but—'

'You're right,' I tease, gabbling nervously because I can't quite believe this is happening. 'There should be a hundred yellow roses and a band playing and—'

'I'm in love with you, Zara.'

'I love you too.' How many times in the last few weeks have those words flirted on the tip of my tongue? It feels so good to finally give in to them, I do it again. 'I love you.'

Then there are no more words.

Later, as I lie naked in his bed, I feel lucky to have a man who worries about me, who cares, who loves me. And before I fall into a deep, blissful sleep in the safety of his arms, I download the app.

Chapter Fourteen

Once again, I am all alone in bed on a Friday night. Henry is visiting his grandmother in York and Ivy isn't talking to me. So, instead of wallowing in the silence that spreads like a frost throughout Holt House, she's out again. I'm not sure where: another five-star restaurant, another spa, another champagne-fuelled night at an exclusive bar in the city. She has slipped back into this world where power is everything because money means nothing, and she's done it with startling ease.

I replay our argument over again, remembering how I was bounce and bliss as I came home the morning after Henry declared he was in love with me. I couldn't wait to tell her, and when I saw her at the breakfast bar, nursing a coffee and scrolling through her phone, that's exactly what I did.

I wasn't prepared for her carefully blank expression, and I wasn't going to settle for it, either. I pushed for a reaction.

'Well?' I asked. 'What do you think? Don't just shrug. Say something. Isn't this exciting?'

'It's . . . fast.'

'We've been seeing each other for a couple of months.'

'Yes. That's fast. I'm surprised you don't have whiplash.'

I'd whacked the hornet's nest and I should've expected to be stung. But she's my best friend, more of a sister to me than Polly has ever been, so I was hurt by her cynicism.

'Why can't you just be happy for me?' I said, firing the words at her like bullets.

'Why are you so desperate for my approval?'

I opened my mouth. Closed it again. I didn't have an answer, so asked another question.

'Did you know about Henry's dinner plans?'

'No.'

'He said he told you.'

'He's lying.' Seemingly bored of our conversation, she returned her attention to her phone.

But I was so angry she'd dismissed me I grabbed her phone from her hand. I could hardly believe I'd done it. Slowly, she raised her eyes to mine, and I saw the livid flash of fury. Still, I'd committed now.

'You're seriously calling Henry a liar?'

'He didn't tell me about his *fucking* dinner plans.'

'So, you didn't see him the evening he came here to take me to the theatre?'

'I don't know, I can't remember.'

'Convenient.'

'I really don't give a fuck, Zara,' she snapped, surging to her feet. 'Do whatever or *whoever* the fuck you want. It'll end in tears. It always does.' Then she snatched her phone back and was gone.

Now, I listen to the cold October wind rattle the bones of this house. Things haven't been right between us since we moved here. It's like the house is a Venus flytrap: pretty, until you're caught between its teeth. I feel so alone. How is it possible to be in a relationship *and* live with your closest friend, but still feel so consumed by loneliness? I have deliberately left my phone downstairs to stop myself from sending her grovelling messages, because as I lie awake, imagining all the fun she is having with people that aren't me, I sink even deeper into my loneliness. Until, eventually, I sink into sleep too.

I wake in the night, my heart beating hard against my ribs. Something woke me. I don't dare move. Don't dare breathe. What woke me? A nightmare? A noise? Then I realise: there's someone in the house. Adrenaline whips my heart into a frenzy. I tell myself that it's all in my head. Just a bad dream. But I know with dreadful certainty that I am fooling myself because someone *is* here. I lie in a state of near-paralysis, unable to get out of bed. I imagine the woman with the long, dark hair creeping into the house, rummaging around in the kitchen for a knife, and I think I might be sick.

Get up, I think, *move.*

There's no light near me, the nearest lamp is across the room on my dresser, but I'm too terrified to move. My eyes dart around in the dark. Where is she? I am statue-still as I listen. I think I can hear someone moving between rooms downstairs. I wait for my heart rate to slow a little before stretching my arm out towards my side table where my phone rests, only to remember I left it in the kitchen.

Fuck.

Heart racing so fast I am dizzy, I move my legs from under the covers. The wooden floor is cold against my bare feet. The door is slightly ajar, and I can't remember whether or not I closed it before going to sleep. I'm about to call for Ivy, then stop because I know instinctively it isn't her. She comes home loud and drunk and eats KitKats in her underwear on the countertop. Whoever lurks in Holt House now is trying to be quiet.

I run over the layout of the ground floor, planning my escape route. The front door is opposite the stairs. To the right is the lounge, to the left is the dining room, which leads into the kitchen and then out into the garden. At the back of the house is the snug and the study. From the top of the stairs, I listen, trying to work out where the intruder is. I stare down into the dark. If I flip on a light, it'll alert whoever is in the house that I'm awake.

When I hear a drawer slam shut in the lounge, I jump, my hand flying to my mouth to cut off my scream. I shift to the left a little. From here, I can see the front door, moonlight filtering in through the stained-glass panel. Do I creep down the stairs quietly or make a run for it? If the intruder is faster than me, I'll never make it. Swallowing hard, I decide to go down as quietly and as quickly as possible. My pulse races even faster with each step. I am shaking so hard, my legs feel like violin strings being pulled too tight.

I hear heavy footfalls on the wooden floor of the lounge. Too heavy to be a woman. Who is in this house with me? I am halfway down the stairs, but the front door feels a million miles away. As I get closer to the bottom, I hear the angry, ragged rhythm of his breath. I try not to think about him tackling me, his crushing weight bearing down, pinning me to the ground as his hands wrap around my throat and squeeze until—

The stair beneath my foot creaks. I still. And listen. Silence. Broken only by the rush of my pulse in my ears.

The urge to run is almost overwhelming.

I hold my position, barely breathing, waiting for him to spring from the lounge and attack.

I count to five and when he still hasn't emerged, I carefully slide my foot onto the next step and the next and the next until I am finally standing on the foyer floor. I glance in the direction of the lounge, into the yawning dark, then I move quickly towards the front door. I try the handle. It's locked.

Fuck. *Fuck!*

My keys are on the kitchen countertop. Maybe I could—

But I don't finish the thought because I can *feel* him behind me. Close. The hairs on the back of my neck lift. Slowly, very slowly, I turn around. He is cast in shadow, standing in the lounge doorway. A scream rips its way up my throat. He lunges but I swing left, smashing into the side table. I slip-slide on the wooden floor, scrambling to get up. To run. Then, in the shaft of light from the front door, the letter opener glints. I scoop it up and sprint. In my panic, I race back up the stairs, automatically fleeing to the safety of my bedroom. He pursues me, his footfalls steady and measured against the fumbling, frantic cadence of my own.

Still clutching the thin, silver blade, I throw myself into my bedroom and slam the door shut.

'I'm calling the police,' I warn, but it is nothing more than a whistle of fear. I try again, louder this time, 'I'm calling the police.' I pray he doesn't know I'm without my phone.

I wait for him to kick down the door, but I am greeted by nothing but the dizzying thump of my own heart. I wait and wait and wait until the tension is so unbearable, I move away from the door to my window, wondering if I can climb out. But all I can see is a swell of darkness. I'm obviously not going to sleep again tonight, and I can't just sit and wait in painful trepidation for him to burst into my room. I move back across the room and, clutching the letter opener so hard my hand aches, I slowly open the door. As soon as I do though, I know he is gone. I can't feel him in Holt House anymore.

I flip on the hallway light. My weapon will only be dangerous if I thrust it deep into someone. Which I could never do. Nevertheless, it gives me a feeble sense of confidence as I move quickly and quietly through the house, switching on lights as I go. Soon, the entire place is lit up like a jack-o'-lantern. No windows have been broken and the front door is still locked. The only room I haven't been into is the study. Heart racing, I push open the door and snap on the light. It's empty, just like the other rooms. Only, the desk drawers and filing cabinets are open. Whoever broke in was looking for something. But *how* did he get in?

I rush to the kitchen to grab my keys and my phone. I'm dialling the police when I hear a car pull up outside. I run for the front door. I'm still clutching my phone and the letter opener when it swings open and there she is.

Her champagne grin falls away when she sees my face. 'Zara? What's wrong? What's happened?'

Then I let out a sob and I crumble in her arms, fear and relief making my knees give way. I babble hysterically. We call the police. Hours later, once they've taken my statement and, telling us not to touch anything, promise to dust for fingerprints in the morning, we retire to her room, though neither of us can sleep. We lock the door from the inside and keep the lamp on.

'Who do you think it was?' she asks.

'I didn't see his face.'

'You had a letter opener.'

'I just grabbed it. I wasn't going to use it.'

'You could have.'

Silence.

'I don't think so.'

'Everyone is capable of killing when pushed, Zara.' Her voice carries so much authority, I don't argue. 'It would've been self-defence.'

'That doesn't make it right.'

'Doesn't it?'

Soon, she is asleep, but sleep cannot find me, so, desperate for a distraction, I reach for my phone and start scrolling through my emails. That's when I see it. Another anonymous message from HTH@gmail.com, sent at midnight, two hours before the break-in.

You aren't safe, Zara.

Chapter Fifteen

'I'm fine, Mum. You don't need to worry,' I say into the phone. I am sitting in the window seat in Henry's bedroom, overlooking the garden. It's the first week of October and already the leaves are bright bursts of ruby and gold.

'Someone broke into your house.'

'I'm not hurt.'

'I'm worried for you.'

'Don't be. I'm fine. Really,' I reassure her even as I secretly enjoy her motherly concern, which feels like tucking into a hearty, homecooked meal after weeks of just water and stale bread.

'Come and stay with me, Zara. There's room.'

Now, living in a space as large as Holt House, it seems impossible that I ever squeezed myself into my mother's teeny, two-bed terrace. As much as I enjoy my mother's sober periods, they only last a few weeks – at best, a few months. Maybe I should be seizing each stretch of time and savouring it, but, as always, it will soon sour, and I don't want to be trapped in that house with her when it does. I've worked so hard not to be like her that moving in with her now, even for the short term, would feel like taking a giant leap backwards into a life I've fought to break free from. 'Thanks, Mum, but I'm OK.'

'You shouldn't be alone.'

'I'm not.'

'I know you have Ivy, but really, Zara, if he breaks in again, you could both get hurt.'

I glance over my shoulder at the four-poster bed and then down at the shirt I'm wearing. It still smells of Henry. 'I'm not staying at Holt House. I'm . . .' I hesitate, not sure I want to snap off a piece of my happiness and share it with her in case she keeps gnawing at it until there's nothing left. 'I'm staying with my boyfriend.'

She doesn't hesitate. 'Luke?'

'No, not Luke.' Given my on-again, off-again history with him, her assumption isn't a surprise. Still, it irks a little because I don't want Mum, or anyone else, thinking of Luke and me as star-crossed lovers, destined for one another. Though my mum has spent my entire life warning me off men, she's always liked Luke. Everyone does. 'Actually, I'm seeing someone else,' I say. 'He's called Henry. You . . .' I pause, hoping I don't have to remind her, tell her, that it was Henry who helped me take care of her in her last drunken meltdown.

'I see. How long?'

'Nearly three months.'

'Oh.' She sounds wounded and I wonder if it's because she's embarrassed that I'm still with the man who has seen the ugliest parts of her life. Then she adds, 'Well, I should meet him.'

So she doesn't remember Henry. I guess it wasn't like she was fit for a proper introduction that day. I knew she was drunk. Obviously. But I didn't realise she was drunk enough to have no recollection of me coming to her house, the wailing, the vomiting, the *assault*. The man who scooped her up and put her to bed. It's baffling to me that what is a momentous disaster for one, is just another Saturday night for another.

'Yes,' I manage. 'Great idea.'

She clicks her tongue in annoyance. A noise that acts as a warning; the heavy, greying clouds right before the storm rolls in. I brace myself. 'It's been a long while since we saw each other, Zara,' she says, a thick layer of ice in her tone. And just like that, the cosy blanket of motherly concern is whipped away, leaving me cold. 'I offer for you to stay with me, you refuse. I call, you don't answer. I send text messages, you send back one-word responses. You're my only daughter; it would be nice if you could make a little effort.'

I take a breath, trying to force down the bubbling, boiling indignation that surges like heartburn. I could remind her that the last time I was in her company, she *slapped* me and declared I'd ruined her life and maybe, just maybe, *that's* why I've been avoiding her. But what would be the point? She doesn't remember, and even if she does, she'll only insist that I'm being dramatic or, worse, making it up completely. Just as she's done dozens of times before.

Instead, I promise to see her soon and ring off.

'Who was that?' asks Henry, coming into the bedroom.

He's wearing the softest pair of navy joggers and a plain white T-shirt. Every weekday morning, he runs, getting out of bed at the crack of dawn to jog around the local park.

'Who even does that?' I teased him once. 'No one in their right mind wants to go running before 6 am.'

He'd kissed my cheek. 'Just call me a masochist.'

Now, he comes up behind me, his hair still damp from his shower, and wraps his arms around my waist, resting his chin on the top of my head and I get that feeling, like I fit. Like *we* fit. 'My mum. She's worried about me.'

'That's what mothers do best.'

In the four days since the break-in, I've been living with Henry. I couldn't sleep in Holt House. I wish Ivy had agreed to leave with me, but she insisted it was her home and she wasn't being scared out of it. Maybe she'd have felt differently if she'd been there when it happened, rather than on the fringes of it.

I am so lucky to have Henry and so grateful he's taken time away from work to be with me. I lean back into him, into the rush of love I feel for him. 'Any more peculiar emails?' he asks.

'No, none,' I say, 'and the police haven't had any success, either.' I'd mentioned the emails to the police when they'd come round the night of the intruder, but so far they've come up empty-handed.

'Great use of tax-payers' money,' says Henry.

After that last email, it was obvious the messages weren't spam because they'd used my name and warned me about the break-in. I don't understand. If the email and the intruder are connected, and it seems likely, why allude to the crime before it took place? Henry thinks it's all some elaborate game, probably some of Ivy's old boarding-school friends trying to scare us. And when I asked him why, he said that's what boarding schools were like, pranks and dares, and I wouldn't understand because I've never been a part of one. I tried not to take his comment personally. I mean, he's right, isn't he? But if boarding-school culture leads you to send creepy emails and break into someone's house for fun, years after you've graduated, I'm glad of my state-school education.

I also told the police about the woman I suspect has been following me, but, as I've never seen her watching Holt House, they don't think she has anything to do with the break-in. They didn't seem in the least bit concerned about her, but I am. There's something *off* about the dark-haired woman.

'It's been nice having you around,' says Henry. 'Keeping an eye on you.' He nips my ear lobe. 'I've been thinking.'

'Mmm?' I ask, enjoying his hands on me, his warm breath on my neck.

'You should move in here.'

I still. 'What?'

'It makes sense,' he says, as I turn in his arms and peer up at him, trying to work out if he's serious. 'We both work a lot. We'd see each other more. You'd be safe here.'

My heart flutters in my chest. He's asking me to move in with him. This is serious. This is romantic. This is—

'It's practical,' he supplies.

I frown. Practical. OK. Is that a good-enough reason to ask someone to move in with you? Because it will save on water bills? Shouldn't you ask someone to move in with you because you're excited to wake up beside them each morning?

'What's wrong?' he asks.

'It's just . . .' I wrinkle my nose, trying to choose my words carefully so that I don't upset him. 'It's not how I imagined being asked to move in.'

He grins. 'And how did you imagine it? What was it you said when I told you I loved you? A hundred yellow roses and a band?'

I roll my eyes. 'I was joking.'

He kisses my nose. 'Well, I'm serious. Move in.'

I don't know why I am hesitating. I want this life with him. But then I hear her voice telling me I am moving at breakneck speed, and I can *feel* the truth in it.

'We've only been together three months . . .'

'It's been the best three months of my life. Hasn't it been that way for you?'

'Yes, but—'

'So, let's do it. Let's move in together.'

I bite my lip. 'What about Ivy?'

He pulls back, his hands still on my waist. 'You want her to move in, too?'

'No. Of course not. I just . . . I . . .' I'm not sure what I'm trying to say so I trail off into silence.

Henry's hands drop from my waist. Cold air rushes to fill the gap between us. 'Aren't you ready for a change? Don't you think it's time to . . . grow up?'

'Grow up?' I say, not bothering to hide my sudden flare of anger.

'Yes. Move on, close that chapter to start a new one. You and Ivy have been living together for how long? Since university? You aren't students anymore. Do you want to be almost thirty and still living with a friend?'

The answer is, no, I don't. I thought by this age I'd have a husband and a family, but I'm frustrated he can't seem to understand that not everyone was born with a nifty little trust fund so they can buy their own half-a-million-pound property in their mid-twenties. Still, I am careful to water down my words like weak coffee, so they're not quite so bitter.

'Bath is expensive. You know I don't come from money, Henry.'

Weak or not, they don't go down sweetly; he glowers at me. 'You're twisting what I'm saying.'

'No. That's not—'

'I've asked you to move in with me, I'm offering to share my home with you, my whole *life* with you, and you're wittering on about Ivy and making excuses.'

I look away, across the garden. *How* did we go from kissing one moment to sniping the next? Is he right – did I twist his words? Is this fight my fault? I *love* Henry. He's my perfect match and he has just asked me to move in with him, so why am I so reluctant? But I already know the answer, don't I?

It's because of Ivy.

'She isn't a penniless PR assistant anymore, Zara,' Henry says. 'Ivy has money. She doesn't *need* you. Maybe it's *you* who needs *her* and I'm just a spare fucking part.'

I am stunned into silence.

Henry yanks open his wardrobe doors, snatches up a suit and chucks it onto the bed.

'Are you going out?' I ask gently, wanting to diffuse the tension.

'Work.'

'Oh.'

'If I leave in the next hour, I can make up the time I lost this morning.'

I stand awkwardly on the fringes of the room, still wearing his shirt, my face colouring with shame. I want to make this better, but I don't know how.

'I take it you're going home,' he says coldly, with an emphasis on *home*.

I cast around for words that will soothe things between us, a cooling balm to whatever part of our relationship I have managed to singe, but I can't think of a single thing to say, so instead I find myself agreeing. 'Fine. I'll go back today.'

He nods curtly, before marching over to his bedside table and pulling out his wallet. He slaps a few notes onto the side table.

'For the taxi back,' is all he says, before disappearing into the en suite.

It's only then, as the door slams shut behind him, that I wonder how he knows Ivy worked in PR, because I can't remember having ever mentioned it.

Chapter Sixteen

By mid-morning, I am on my way to Holt House, feeling miserable and anxious about my confrontation with Henry, and sick at the very thought of returning to the stage in which I was forced to play victim. As I pull up outside, the churning in my stomach worsens.

Once I've paid the driver and exited the taxi, I hesitate on the pathway and stare up at the house. It seems to lean forward in anticipation. My breath catches at the memory of being chased, the palpable terror that an intruder was coming for me, that I was alone and fleeing for my life. The knowledge that he is still out there somewhere sits like lead in my stomach.

As much as I don't want to go inside, standing on the steps all day isn't an option. And neither is returning to Henry's. So, I force thoughts of strangers and Venus flytraps and letter openers to the very back of my mind, and bring all my courage to the forefront, before entering Holt House for the first time since the attack.

In the hallway, I take off my shoes. I hear her before I see her.

'Get the fuck out.' Her voice rises from the kitchen, furious and spitting. '*Now.*'

I freeze, but she isn't talking to me.

'Did you really think I wouldn't come back?'

A man's voice rolls through the house like thunder across a darkening sky. I move quickly towards the commotion, stopping in the adjoining dining room, just out of sight.

'Don't get too settled, Ivy,' he says. 'The second your secret is out, so are you.'

Staying close to the wall, I peer into the room. The man, who has his back to me, is tall and slim with thick, sandy hair. She's positioned herself across from him, keeping the kitchen island between them, and although her face is drawn in anger, I see beneath it an undercurrent of very real fear. This person, whoever he is, frightens her.

'Don't threaten me,' she tells him.

'It's not a threat.'

'GET OUT!' Her screamed command reminds me of cornered prey, desperate to make itself appear bigger and wilder to scare off a predator.

'There's no doubt you're Hugo Holt's daughter,' he growls, placing his palms flat on the island and leaning forward with malice. 'The apple doesn't fall far from the scheming, rotten tree.'

At the mention of her father, there is an immediate change of air pressure; it's as though the room grows hotter with her rage. And with fury replacing fear, she straightens and glide around the kitchen island until they are face-to-face, toe-to-toe. She tilts her mouth towards his, and I'm not sure whether she's about to kiss him or spit in his face. Then her lips curve into an insidious, saccharine smile.

'It's obvious to me now why Mummy Dearest killed herself,' she purrs. 'Though, if you were *my* son, I'd have slit *your* wrists instead of my own.'

It happens so fast. One moment we all hang in charged silence, the next there is a brilliant burst of noise. Heart galloping, I stare at the shattered bowl which lies in pieces by the pantry door.

'You fucking bitch,' he snarls. Chest heaving, he steps towards her, and she stumbles back.

Before he can throw her at the wall the same way he did the bowl, I surge into the kitchen.

'She told you to get out,' I say with a confidence I don't feel.

He rounds on me. For the first time, I get a good look at him; his mouth is thin and mean, his face all harsh angles and arrogance, and there's a little scar on his cleft chin. At first, he appears surprised by my arrival, but then his surprise bleeds into indifference and, deciding I am not a threat, he turns his attention back to Ivy.

'I'll call the police,' I warn, sliding my phone from my pocket.

Abruptly, he spins on his heel. The sudden movement makes me jump. He grins, amused by my skittishness.

'That's getting rather old,' he says in an apathetic, boarding-school drawl. 'Sing me another one, love.'

Then, like a flash of lightning across the night, everything is illuminated and there's a moment of frightening clarity. 'It was you who broke into our house,' I say.

He cocks his head. 'It isn't breaking in if I have a key, and it isn't *your* house.'

Shaking with adrenaline, I take a step back, prepared to bolt if I have to.

'I'm calling the police,' I warn him again.

'Do it.' He advances on me. 'Then I can tell them how you pulled a knife on me.'

'It was a letter opener.' My back hits the wall. 'You chased me. You—'

'It was dark. You ran. I thought you were Ivy. As soon as I heard you whickering about the police, I knew you weren't *her*, and I left.'

My mind is still racing when she appears by my side, taking the phone from my hand. 'No one is calling the police.'

She turns to him.

'You need to leave.'

He squares up to her and for a second, I think he might lash out. Then he brings his face close to hers.

'Gladly.'

I hold my breath and keep holding it until the front door slams shut. Feeling shaky, I sag against the wall. For now, we are safe, but I *know* he will come back. Whatever is between them isn't dead and buried yet.

She slaps my phone onto the worktop before grabbing a dustpan and brush from under the sink.

'Who is he?' I ask.

Across the room, she starts clearing up the shattered bowl. 'No one.'

'Why does he have a key to our house?'

'I'll change the locks.'

I stare at the back of her head, dumbfounded by her secrecy. Clearly, this man terrifies her, and they know each other – pretty well, judging by the calculated insults about one another's parents. Then I realise.

'Ivy, are you two . . . together? Is he married? Or—'

Her laughter is hollow. With the punchline a mystery, I don't join in.

'Another married man, Ivy, seriously?' I snap, incensed.

Quinn was the last one she got involved with. His wife found out. She spray-painted obscenities on the walls of our rented house share and, with the backing of the two girls we lived with, our landlord kicked us out. Quinn didn't tell Ivy he and his wife had a young son, layering more lies on top of his cheating.

'You promised you'd never go near a married man again, Ivy. Fucking hell, what is wrong with you? How can you be so—'

'Just drop it, Zara,' she bites back. She strides towards the bin and I follow.

'Why won't you tell me who he is? What does he want? What secret does he—'

'Like you even care!' She wheels on me so fast, pieces of shattered pottery fly from the dustpan clutched in her hand and skitter across the flagstone floor. 'You've been gone for days. You left me here alone for *days*.'

It's now that I notice the purple crescent moons under her eyes, and I wonder if she's slept at all. Remorse and guilt curdle in my stomach and rush up my throat and out of my mouth in a torrent of explanation.

'I thought someone broke in and attacked me. I couldn't be in Holt House. I—'

'So you just left me here, all by myself?'

'You wanted to stay.'

'I thought you'd stay with me.' She is defiant and wounded. 'Like I would for you.'

I am desperate and sorry, but she never forgives easily, and I don't have the words to make this right.

We stare down at the mess between us, the shards of broken pottery. She kneels and starts picking up the pieces, chucking them into the bin. Even though it's obvious the bowl can never be fixed, the suggestion to save the pieces, just in case, sits on the tip of my tongue.

I crouch down opposite her to help.

'Just leave it.'

'Ivy, you're right, I should've stayed with you.'

'But you didn't. You chose to hole up at Henry's house and busy yourself *fucking* him. Was he worth it? Does he make you come?'

I recoil from the venom in her voice and the crassness of her words.

'You really don't like him, do you? Why? Do you know him?' I ask, remembering his comment about her working in PR.

'I know exactly what kind of man he is,' she says sourly.

'Look, things between you and me haven't been great since we moved here, but—'

'You're honestly going to blame the house?'

Silence.

I feel a wall is rising between us and I must be careful what I say, or we could end up trapped on opposite sides. 'Let me help you.' I pick up the largest broken piece, but she snatches it from my hand, then yelps when it slices her palm. We watch in silence as blood pools and drips onto the flagstones.

I reach for her, but she flinches away. 'Please.' The pain on her face has nothing to do with the cut on her hand. She feels abandoned by me, just as she has been by everyone else in her life that she's loved. I am sick with guilt that I thought only of myself, of what I needed, and left her here by herself.

'Ivy . . .'

'Please.' There are unshed tears in her eyes and a bite to her voice. 'Just leave me alone, Zara.'

Chapter Seventeen

The morning after our fight, I woke up to a note from Ivy: she was taking a break in Greece with some friends. She didn't say when she'd be back. She's avoiding me and my questions. She doesn't want to tell me who our intruder is and how she knows him, or tell me what he has over her. It hurts to think she's keeping secrets from me. Yes, there are bigger things to worry about, but this is us. Why won't she tell me?

I have thought a lot about who the intruder might be, and I am convinced he's in her rotation of lovers. It's not unusual for her playthings to become obsessed with her; possessive, maybe even a little dangerous, because she tends to get bored of them long before they are bored of her. She's like a siren, luring men to sink their ships on the rocks of her.

Anyway, she's gone, and I am alone. Henry and I are barely speaking: his messages are short and cold, and mine are much the same. I want to reconcile but I'm not sure how. Not without agreeing to move in with him. I mean, we've only been together a matter of months. Is it too soon? She'd say it was too soon. And if I do move in with him, what will that mean for me and her? She'll feel abandoned, just as she did by her mother when she chose to end treatment, just as she did by her grandfather when the invitations to Christmas parties stopped coming, and just as she did by her father when he remarried. But then, I *do* want a husband and children. How long can I put my life on hold for fear of hurting Ivy?

After the break-in, the owner of Hillington Wedding Planners insisted I take some time off to 'rest and recover' from my 'traumatic ordeal.' At first, this seemed like a good idea, but without Ivy and without Henry, the days stretched on, long and lonely, and the solitude of Holt House was too much to bear, so I returned to work earlier than planned, busying myself with brides and grooms and their queries about outdoor ceremonies and string quartets. I hoped that upping my in-office days this week would help with the suffocating loneliness, but Hillington's is a family-run business, and even though I adore everyone I work with and they're so welcoming, they are blood, and I am not.

Determined not to let my melancholy seep into the weekend, I called Amira.

Now, as I wait for her in a tapas bar, I make the mistake of scrolling through Ivy's socials. They shine with all the photographs of her having glorious, enviable fun. I've never had a group of girlfriends, the kind you go away with, the kind you brunch with, ones you're so close to that any one of them could be your Maid of Honour; and you're all such great friends that no one will mind who's chosen. Of course, I *have* friends – I have her, I have Amira and the girls from work – but as I've gotten older, my social circle has shrunk. I tell myself my relationships are quality over quantity but sometimes, I suspect my lack of a giggling gaggle of girls is another piece of evidence that I'm unlovable. Testimony to the fact that I don't really fit in anywhere. Not in my broken family, not at work and not out in the world. And now, maybe not even with Ivy. Beneath the surface of me, I worry there are dark, festering waters where any meaningful connection I make is drowned, and that immersing myself in big groups of people long enough will mean exposure. They'll smell the rot in me, the rot that drove away my father and wrecked my parents' marriage, the rot that is driving Ivy and Henry away, too.

'You're here already!' says Amira, ripping me away from the darkness of my own thoughts. She looks incredible: her inky-black hair is thicker and glossier than ever and she's wearing a mustard-coloured woollen coat that's stunning against her dark skin. 'Am I late?'

I put my phone face down on the table and stand to greet her. 'Nope, I'm early.' I do not admit I've been awake since 5 am because I couldn't take one more minute in the treacle-thick silence of Holt House.

'How're you doing?' she asks. 'You look . . . tired.' A polite way of saying I look like shit. 'Struggling to sleep because of the break-in?'

I don't know what to say to this. Since discovering Ivy knows our intruder, I feel like a fraud. I'm pretty sure you aren't meant to be quite so familiar with the person who breaks into your house in the middle of the night. Not that I can admit this to anyone. Too many questions I can't answer.

'Kind of.'

'I hope they find him,' she says, and I smile weakly in return.

The waitress takes our order and I start to relax. Maybe I should talk to Amira about my fight with Ivy . . . But then, she doesn't need another reason to dislike her. For just a second, I consider telling her about my fight with Henry, but I want people to love him, and I want people to love us together, which means only speaking positively of him. But maybe I could confide my fear about being supremely unlovable instead – open up about my relationship with my father, which, really, only Ivy knows anything about. Amira is one of my closest friends, she's wise and direct and the kind of together that makes me think she owns one of those rubber caps that keep your cucumbers fresh in the fridge. Still, I don't want her to pity me – she has such a good relationship with her parents.

I'm still deciding what to do when she says, 'I have some news.' Her eyes are big and bright, her cheeks flushed with excitement. I wrack my brains, trying to work out what it might be. A promotion! She's wanted it for so long. It's all she talks about. It's in The Plan.

This *is* exciting. I'll have to order her a card and some flowers. The fancy kind from Bramble & Wild and—

'I'm pregnant!'

For a moment, I am so shocked, all I can do is stare. I swallow. 'You're pregnant?'

She nods, grinning like a Cheshire cat.

'Oh, my God,' I say. Then I am on my feet, and we are hugging. 'Congratulations!'

The food arrives. And I still can't believe it. Polly, now Amira; is there something in the water? Soon, I'll be the only person in the world who isn't housing a foetus. 'How?'

'You want a diagram?'

My laughter is thin. 'No, I mean, I thought . . . What about your promotion? What about The Plan?'

'I know, I know! It just happened, I missed a couple of my pills and, I don't know, maybe I did it subconsciously. It's like, I'm one of five, and I want a big family too – if we're going to fill our house then we need to start now.' She laughs. 'We aren't getting any younger.'

This is not meant as a dig, I know that, but it feels like one. She's right, we aren't getting any younger, *I'm* not getting any younger. The panic that I am missing out sets in and my heart batters my ribs. I sip my water.

She digs into the *patatas bravas*. 'The promotion can wait. I'll pick it all back up after the baby comes.'

I wonder how many women think this when they're pregnant? As though a career is a Netflix box set that you can just dip in and out of when you fancy without losing your place. Babies are blessings to everyone but employers. Maternity leave is a swear word in most companies. For Amira, the gender pay-gap starts now.

The waiter comes over and I order a glass of wine because I can. It doesn't matter that I am not starting a family with my husband in the house we bought together, because I can drink wine.

God, I want to be where she is, happy and glowing, stomach blooming with socially-celebrated bliss. I want it so intensely; I could press my face up against the glass of that life hard enough that I fall through it and tumble, Alice in Wonderland-style, down the rabbit hole into a burrow of rompers and late-night feeds and a teeny little human looking up at me with all that unconditional love.

'Gosh,' I say, 'the child of a lawyer and a surgeon, your baby will do amazing things.'

'Or it'll stack shelves in Asda. I don't mind. As long as little one is happy, so am I.'

She'll make a good mother. She's pragmatic and thoughtful and kind. I've never stopped to wonder if I'll be a good mother. If being unlovable means I am therefore incapable of loving a child the way it needs to be loved. I push this new fear to one side and focus on being happy for Amira. Because I *am* happy for her. She deserves this.

'Are you worried about the birth?' I ask. I worry about birth and I'm not even pregnant. My palms go clammy just at the thought of a torn perineum and mucus plugs and stitches.

She rests a hand on her stomach, and even though there's no significant bump she looks like a serene earth mother. 'No. I think it will be the greatest day of my life.'

We talk all things baby. There's a script to these conversations and we know our lines off by heart. We spend some time poring over the blurry image on the scan she shows me, and I coo, even though I have no idea which bit is baby and which bit is uterus.

This is it now, where her life is neat and settled, while mine is messy and open-ended. She can spend the rest of her days coasting on her own domestic bliss, all the way to the care-home gates where she'll be met by the smiling faces of her children and her children's children. Unlike me, Amira will never lie awake in bed, panicking that The One doesn't exist and that her inability to be loved will mean she'll never have a family of her own.

'Sorry,' she says, finishing off her dessert. 'We haven't even begun to talk about you. What's new? How's Henry?'

I don't want to tell her that I have no idea if we're still a couple. She's so happy and I am so miserable. I don't want to take the shine off her joy, I don't want to have another conversation about my withering eggs, and I don't want her pity either. I'm flustered and floundering and before I know what I'm doing, I hear myself say, 'Oh, well, he asked me to move in actually.'

This is not a lie.

Her mouth falls open. 'No!'

I nod.

She beams at me. 'This is amazing, Zara. *Amazing!* Such a relief. You've been so hung up on Luke for so many years, I worried you'd never settle down with anyone.' She inhales sharply, her eyes sparkling as a new, exciting idea occurs to her. 'Maybe you'll be pregnant soon, too.'

I nod, and smile so wide I'm worried my face will split. We cheers to our success – me with a glass of wine, her with a glass of fizzy water; my success entirely fabricated, hers totally genuine – and I think about how, if there isn't a word for feeling joy for someone even as their joy makes you feel sad for yourself, there should be.

Chapter Eighteen

Henry misses me, wants to see me. The text comes moments after Amira and I have left the restaurant. Hope beats its wings fiercely in my chest as I arrive back at Holt House, and spend the next couple of hours getting ready. I shave and shampoo and moisturise. I highlight and blend and apply lip tint. I am smooth and polished and, despite the biting October wind, I'm wearing a silk dress liberated from Ivy's wardrobe. I knock on Henry's door. And there he is, in a shirt and jeans, his hair artfully swept off his face.

I think about the last night we spent together, how he kissed the insides of my thighs and tugged on my hair to expose my throat. My entire body is gnawing for him. There is a feral, clawing, writhing desire to have him. To be with him. To have with Henry what Amira has with Nathan.

'Come in,' he says, stepping to one side.

In the hallway, I take off my coat and feel his eyes on me, drinking in the silky cream dress and my hair tumbling around my shoulders in auburn curls. When our eyes meet, I know he feels that burning itch as keenly as I do.

'I don't want to fight,' he tells me. 'I love you.'

We are barely two feet apart; I can practically swirl the spiciness of his cologne on my tongue.

'I love you too,' I say. 'And you're right, it doesn't matter *how* you ask me to move in, the point is, you want us to live together.'

'I do. I want to wake up next to you every day.'

'You might get sick of me.'

'Never.'

'I leave wet towels on the bed.'

'Don't care.'

'There will be half-drunk glasses of water all over the house.'

'Fine.'

'You'll find hairbands everywhere. It'll be like they're breeding and—'

He kisses me.

For days, every time I've eaten, it's like I'm chewing on a handful of lint. I thought loneliness was making food taste like nothing, but now, with his tongue in my mouth and the burn of whisky on his lips, I know it was the bone-deep hunger of wanting Henry Frith. I'm reaching for the button of his jeans when he catches my wrist and breaks away. His eyes shine with a secret.

'I've got something to show you.' He takes my hand and leads me along the hallway, and when he pushes open the door to the kitchen my breath catches.

On every available surface are vases of flowers with thick petals and glossy stems. 'A hundred yellow roses,' I whisper.

My head is still spinning as he tugs me around the kitchen island, past the dining table, and throws open the French doors. There's music and more roses. Roses on the stone steps, roses on benches, roses crowding across the patio. A trail of yellow roses leading to a fire pit. Just like the night we met. Right at the very bottom of the garden is a three-piece jazz band.

I cannot believe the sweeping grandeur of this gesture. The roses, the band, the candlelight: it's all so silly and brilliant, romantic and cheesy, ostentatious yet thoughtful.

'Zara Annabel Barton.' He gets down on one knee and pulls from his pocket a brass key attached to a yellow ribbon. 'Will you do me the honour of moving in with me?'

'Yes!' I say, playing up to this mock proposal. 'A thousand times, yes!'

In this moment, I don't examine too closely whether I am agreeing to live with Henry in order to keep up with Amira, in a race that exists only in my head. In this moment, I refuse to think about what this means for me and Ivy, and how she'll take the news. Instead, I let him kiss away the fear that I am unlovable and take me up to bed.

Hours later, naked and satisfied, I lie on Henry's chest and listen to the steady drum of his heartbeat. Sometimes, I think these post-sex moments are more intimate than all the heat and skin and groping fingers that came just minutes before. I'm getting to know Henry's body well, the scar on the back of his left knee, the mole on his thigh, the crescent moon birthmark on his forearm, but I know very little about his family, his childhood.

'Does it bother you that we're moving in together and I haven't even met your parents yet?' I ask.

'No. Does it bother you?'

'A little.'

'I barely see them myself. They moved to the south of France six years ago and left me in charge of the business. My father steps in every now and again to flex those corporate muscles.'

'I didn't know your parents weren't even in the country.'

'That's because I didn't tell you.'

'So, when will I meet them?'

I feel him shrug.

'Are you worried they won't like me?'

'What's not to like?' He kisses the top of my head. 'Even if they don't, it doesn't bother me. I don't need their blessing.'

This is an attitude I admire but can't quite harness. I am a people-pleaser by nature. 'Are they still together?'

'They are.'

What was it Henry once said? *A happy couple a long marriage doth not necessarily make.*

'And they're happy?'

'They appear to be.'

I shift so I can see his face. His gaze is tense and fixed. He feels my eyes on him and glances down. Whatever he sees in my face makes him uncoil. 'There were rumours, years ago, that my mother was unfaithful.'

'I'm sorry.'

He pushes his fingers back through his hair. 'Don't be. They're still together. It all worked out in the end.'

'I look forward to meeting them one day.' I'm grateful he's opened up to me, if only a little, so I decide to open up to him too. 'I mean, whatever happens, it can't be worse than the first time you came across my mum. I'm surprised that didn't put you off completely.'

'Quite the opposite. I met your mother and it made me want you even more.' Before I can ask him to elaborate, he kisses me, swallowing my question. When he breaks off the kiss he says, 'I get the impression you're not close to your father.'

His words aren't intended to sting, but they do, like the slap of January wind as you step out into the winter. 'He's a university lecturer, he has a house, a wife, a granddaughter and another on the way.' Now it's my turn to shrug. 'He's busy.'

'If he's too busy for you, he's a fool.'

I kiss him, submerged by a wave of love for him. I will never tire of Henry Frith's mouth on mine.

We order dinner but his house is so rural, he has to drive into the city to pick it up. I stretch out on his king-size bed and, propped up on one elbow, I watch him dress in soft joggers and softer T-shirt. With a crooked smile, he scoops Ivy's silk dress from the floor and holds it up. 'Did you wear this to seduce me?'

'I've been wearing it all day,' I lie.

It's then I realise his smile doesn't reach his eyes. 'You wore this to Tapas House?'

'Absolutely.'

His smile slips as I amp up the teasing.

'In fact, I often slip into a sequin dress to take out the bins and I usually do the washing up in a ballgown and evening gloves. Amira loves it when I dress up for her.'

'Amira?'

I nod.

This time, his smile is genuine. He's turning away from me, dropping the dress on the armchair in the corner when it hits me. Did I mention the restaurant to him? I don't think I did.

'How do you know I was at Tapas House?'

He looks guilty, like a schoolboy caught peering into the girls' changing room. 'You still have Friend Finder on your phone.'

Slowly, I raise an eyebrow. 'So you're stalking me?' I tease.

Maybe I should mind that he's been checking on my whereabouts, but I'm secretly delighted. I may not be married with a baby on the way, but I have a man who loves me, who sources one hundred yellow roses and a band just to ask me to move in with him, who cares enough about me to look up where I am even though we're in a fight.

'You make it sound like I was lurking in the shadows.' He sits on the edge of the bed and strokes my bare arm. 'After the break-in, I worry more.'

I look away quickly. Like Amira, Henry doesn't know the intruder is one of Ivy's ex-lovers, or that we fought because of it. All the fear and upset and staying with Henry in the days that followed the break-in seem so dramatic now – like when you're in bed at night and convince yourself there's someone in the corner of the room, only to flick on the light to discover it's just a dressing gown hanging on the back of the door, the cocktail of relief and foolishness potent. Though I don't know *why* that man broke in, I know it wasn't to hurt me. It was to talk to Ivy, to wave in her face whatever dirt he has on her. By keeping this a secret, I'm not sure whether I'm protecting myself, or protecting her.

'Well, the break-in is in the past now. I want to move on. Can we just put it behind us, please?'

His brow furrows but he agrees. 'Sure.'

Feeling guilty for omitting the full truth, I decide I can at least share a little bit of it with him. 'I had a fight with Ivy.'

He stops stroking my arm. 'Why do all our conversations come back around to Ivy?'

'They don't.' His lips thin, but I ignore his disapproval and plough on because I am suddenly desperate to talk to someone about her. 'She's keeping something from me. I walked in on her arguing with a man in our kitchen. It got . . . heated. I stepped in, told him to leave. He was threatening her.'

At this, he sits up straight. 'With what?'

'Don't know. She refused to tell me who he is.'

'What did he look like?'

'Tall, slim, sandy-coloured hair.' Then, remembering, I add, 'He has a tiny scar on his chin.'

Henry glances away.

'You know him?'

He shakes his head. 'I'm sure if Ivy wants to talk about it, she will. For now, leave her to it,' he says.

'But I live there, too, shouldn't I know who he is?'

'You'll be moving out soon,' he says. 'When will you tell her?'

'Well.' I sit up, pulling the bedsheet around me, playing for time. 'It depends when we decide I'm moving in here.'

'Tomorrow.' Clothed, he climbs on top of me, sliding the sheet down my naked body. His grin is wolfish. 'No, tonight.'

I giggle and slap him away. 'Be serious, Henry. Moving takes time. I work, you work. We need to plan, get organised. There's no rush.'

He sits back on his haunches. 'Are you worried about what she'll say?'

'No,' I lie.

He surges to his feet, startling me. 'Don't treat me like an idiot.' There's so much anger in his voice where just seconds ago there had only been playful flirtation, but it's justified because we both know I'm not being honest.

'I don't want to hurt her.'

'Because she's in love with you.' His gaze is unwavering. He isn't joking. The silence has spikes and edges.

'No.'

'You really don't think she's in love with you?'

I don't like that he is standing, fully dressed, and I am lying down, completely naked. I get out of bed and search for my underwear. 'Of course not.'

'She acts like a jealous lover, and you treat her like an ex to be handled with care.'

I am shaking as I snap on my bra and step into my knickers. His take on my relationship with Ivy makes me feel exposed, as though he's just knocked down one of the walls to our home and is touching things that aren't his.

'You live with her rent-free. Nobody lives rent-free. She's just trying to keep you close.'

'No. You're wrong . . .'

'She deliberately didn't tell you about the birthday meal I cooked for you, she refuses for the three of us to spend time together – because she can't stand the sight of you with someone else – and now you're too scared to tell her you're moving on with your life.'

'I'm not scared. I'm . . . I'm . . .' What am I? I don't want to talk about this anymore, but I don't know how to stop the conversation, how to start over – how to press pause and rewind.

'She's in love with you, Zara.' He steps into my path, so close I am forced to look up at him. 'Are you in love with her?'

'Don't be ridiculous.'

He shakes his head, angrily. 'I'm airing my concerns and you're just standing there, belittling how I feel.'

'I'm not. I . . .'

Remorse spreads through my chest like a cold fog; he's right. I take a deep breath and choose my words carefully, squeezing them like I would a supermarket avocado to make sure it's ripe and without any bruising.

'I'm sorry, Henry. Look, even if she was in love with me, which I really don't think she is, I'm with you. That's not going to change. I will tell her I'm moving out, but I need a little time. Ivy's like a sister to me. With her family gone and her dad out of the picture, I'm all she has.'

He studies me. I hold his gaze to prove I have nothing to hide. Slowly, he nods then takes me in his arms. I exhale, relieved this fight was just a graze and not a gaping, gushing wound that could kill my relationship. But, as he pulls back, I can see in his face my relief is premature.

'Zara,' he says, severe and commanding. He chews on his words, deciding whether to tell me whatever it is he's thinking. 'Ivy is possessive. Territorial. I'm concerned for your safety.'

I want to laugh this off, but he's so grave, the laughter withers in my throat. He squeezes my arms. The concern and conviction in his expression makes fear slide down my spine.

'This kind of toxic obsession can become very dangerous. If you're all she has, and she truly believes she's losing you, what will she do? How far will she go to stop you from leaving?'

Chapter Nineteen

I'm just about to put my key in the Holt House door when it swings open. Only, it's not Ivy who greets me. It's her father. He's dressed in a midnight-blue pea coat over a grey suit and he's wearing shiny, expensive shoes. When our eyes meet, nerves swill in my stomach. The grin that curls his lips is smooth and charming. He has the same intensity about him that she does. When we were at uni, I had the biggest crush on her father. Everyone did.

'Zara, you look lovely,' he says.

I smile, but before I can speak, she appears behind him.

'You're home,' she says, voice bouncy with surprise and what I think is happiness. It seems the frostiness she felt towards me has thawed in the Greek sun.

Hugo was just on his way out, and when he's gone, she and I sit together in the living room on the burnt-orange sofa from our old flat – the only thing from our previous life she didn't throw away and replace – and share a bottle of wine. I don't normally drink this early, but I am tense and nervous, and the alcohol will help.

At first, it's awkward; neither of us knows how to begin because we've never fought like this before. 'I missed you,' she says eventually.

I hesitate. Henry's warnings that she is in love with me, obsessed with me, a danger to me, crowd my thoughts and make words jam in my throat. But I *have* missed her. Without her, I've been painfully alone. She is the giddy thrill in my stomach, the whisper in my ear that challenges me to be bolder, braver, wilder. I bat away Henry's concerns and smile at her.

'Me, too.'

'Greece wasn't the same without you.'

'Looked like you were having tons of fun.' I think of the photos of all those girls, ones I'm sure, alongside their shiny, private-school hair and accomplished tennis backhand, have names like Fifi and Allegra and Beatrice.

'Don't believe everything you see on social media.'

And I feel a childish sense of relief that I am still the main friend. Knowing this gives me the confidence to push just once more. 'Are you going to tell me who that guy is and why he broke into our house?'

She sips her wine, playing for time. 'You don't need to worry about him anymore. It's . . . over.'

I wish that when I saw him arguing with her in the kitchen, I'd checked his left hand for a ring or, at the very least, an indent where one had been hastily pocketed before entering our house. I'm convinced her unwillingness to talk about him is because he's married.

'Anyway,' she says. 'I changed the locks. Your new set of keys are on the dining table.'

I feel a sharp pang of guilt. This is the perfect moment to tell her I'm moving out, but I can't. It will ruin us beyond repair. This is fact: fire is hot, we are born and then we die, Ivy will disown me if I leave her to be with Henry.

'Zara.' The urgency of her tone snaps me from my thoughts. I study her face, wondering if, somehow, she already knows. 'Can we just forget all about him?'

It takes me a second to realise she's talking about the intruder. 'New lock, fresh start,' she adds.

If I wasn't already keeping secrets from her, I'd have pushed for a name, at least. But guilt acts as duct tape over my mouth. I nod.

She smiles, relieved.

But there's another niggling question I must ask. 'Why was your father here?'

'Just visiting.'

This is a lie. In all the years we've lived together, Hugo has never popped by for a visit – not at the house we rented and not at the flat either. He's always expected her to go to him, to a restaurant or to his home, and always with his latest wife or girlfriend in attendance. He uses these women as a barrier, a filter to stop Ivy from having a meaningful exchange or honest conversation with him, as though he is afraid that she will say out loud what they both already know: he has never loved her the way she deserved to be loved.

I stay quiet, waiting for her to volunteer the truth. She'll tell me, she always does, because I understand what it is to have a father who can't give you what you need.

She sighs and picks at the hem of her dress. 'He wants to buy a restaurant.'

'OK...'

'He needs funding.'

I stare at her, dumbfounded. 'He's after your money? Tell me you refused.'

She looks past me and out of the window. There's an unfamiliar slope to her shoulders and a sombre downturn to her smart mouth. 'Right before he asked, he whipped out a photograph of me that he claims he always carries in his wallet.'

'Jesus Christ.'

'I know, right?' She rolls her eyes but it's half-hearted, devoid of her trademark snark. 'It's one that was taken at my ninth birthday party. I'd spent the whole morning in tears because when I woke up, he'd taken himself off on a work trip without telling me. My mum had me pose with my birthday cake and told me to smile. I was miserable, but I did as she asked because I knew she was upset with him, too, and I didn't want to make her feel worse.' Her laugh is paper-thin. 'It's tragic, isn't it, that the picture he's chosen to carry around with him is one where I have a fake smile.'

'Maybe he didn't know it was fake.'

'But isn't that so much worse?' She stares at me, daring me or maybe even *needing* me to disagree. But I can't. As painful as it is, she's right.

'Will you give him the money?'

'Don't know.' She sips her wine.

I think she'll give in to him because even though she won't admit it, his attention, no matter how she gets it, is exactly what she craves. 'So, what's new?' she asks, deciding on a swift change of subject.

And here it is, another opportunity to be honest with her about Henry, but I'm a coward so instead I say, 'Amira is pregnant.'

She scoffs. 'Of course she is. How painfully predictable.'

'Ivy! You're meant to be happy for her.'

'Why? Has she always longed for genital stitches and stretch marks?'

'She's literally created the miracle of life.'

'And today, I literally pissed in peace. That's a luxury she's about to lose.' Then she does something unexpected: she reaches out, squeezes my hand and says softly, 'Seriously though, are you OK? I know you want what Polly and Amira have – the husband, the house, the baby.'

Since agreeing to move in with Henry, that panicky feeling of falling behind has eased, allowing me more room to feel truly happy for Amira. Taking this next step with Henry means I'm finally on the brink of having it all, and part of me thinks once a person is set – the house, the marriage, the children – it will be impossible to feel the smothering weight of thick, black misery ever again. Surely, when you've got everything you always wanted, you'll spend the rest of your life coasting on your own contentment.

But, not wanting her to debunk my hope, I say instead, 'You mean the boring, obvious paint-by-numbers life that is literally your idea of hell?'

She shakes her head. 'It's not that I think it's boring, it's just . . . my parents had what you want, and they weren't happy, so I don't strive for it. I want to choose differently.'

Which is exactly what I'm doing, trying to put as much distance as possible between my mother's life and my own. Maybe, deep down, all women are afraid of living their mother's lives. Even if the life in question is a happy and fulfilled one. 'OK, so you don't want that life. Fine. But, say you're old and grey, without a husband or children, don't you worry you'll be lonely?'

'Nope.' She grins. 'Can't rely on people, but you *can* rely on cold, hard cash, and I have plenty of that.'

'Money doesn't keep you warm at night.'

'Does. If you've got enough, you can burn it. Make a mini money-bonfire.'

She gives me her most brilliant smile and it's impossible not to smile back. Then we fall quiet again, and in the stillness she gives my hand another squeeze.

'Besides, I have you. We'll grow old together. We'll be those biddies who unapologetically push in at the post office and talk too loudly at the cinema. We'll knit each other matching cardigans and have half a dozen cats, all named after our ex-lovers.'

'I read about Cat Island in Japan, and even *that* place doesn't have enough cats for you to name each one after an ex-lover.'

She gives me a mock-scowl. 'Judgey bitch. You should be nicer to me, or you won't get your present.'

'Present?'

She leans over the back of the sofa and produces a glossy white bag. 'I know you don't like me spending money on you, but I couldn't resist.' I take it and lift silk from thick tissue paper. 'They're from this gorgeous little boutique in Greece.'

It's a pair of ruby-red pyjamas – shorts and a camisole. The kind men imagine women wearing at sleepovers as they hit each other with feather pillows. The kind you'd choose for a lover and look forward to taking off later.

'A pair for me and a pair for you,' she sing-songs. 'So, how much do you love me?'

I feel my pulse quicken and my skin prickle and I cannot look at her, because if Henry knew she'd bought me these it would only reinforce the idea that she wants us to be more than just friends.

I try to remind myself that he doesn't know her, that his assertion that she's obsessed and in love is ill-informed, when other memories bubble to the surface.

Your relationship with Ivy is claustrophobic. No one will ever be good enough for Ivy's Zara.

Not Henry's words this time: Amira's. She didn't explicitly say she thought that Ivy was in love with me, but she implied it. And unlike Henry, she *does* know Ivy. I'm guilty of discarding Amira's opinion, putting it down to how jealous she is of our friendship, but what if there's more to it than that?

'Well?' she asks, impatient.

'They're beautiful,' I manage. Then she is on her feet, unbuttoning her dark-green dress. 'What're you doing?'

'Changing. Let's have a lazy Sunday: Netflix, takeaway and wine.'

I lick my dry lips. 'Like those boring couples you complain about?'

Her dress drops to the floor and pools at her feet. She isn't wearing a bra.

'It's not boring if it's with you.'

She stares at me through powerful green eyes and long, long lashes. She has a way of making me feel like everything is dangerous. A risk. Like I am the centre of her world, and keeping up with her is imperative. It's a feeling that unnerves and excites me. One I'm sure no one else understands because they've never felt the sun on their skin.

'Come on,' she purrs. 'Strip.'

And I do.

We lounge around in our new pyjamas and drink wine. The wine makes me brave. My head is in lap. I roll over to look up at her. 'Ivy, why do you hate Henry?'

She stops stroking my hair. 'I don't hate him.'

'Liar.'

She inhales slowly and loudly to let me know this topic is deathly boring.

'Just get to know him,' I say. 'Just try. *Please*.'

'You think I don't already know him? All those old rugby-playing Oxbridge alumni are the same: entitled, ruthless—'

'That's not who he is.' I'm surprised by her cutting assessment of the people she seems to pride herself on spending time with. 'I don't want you to hate him when you don't even know him.'

'I *don't* hate him.'

'Then why—'

'I don't want to lose you to him.'

Silence. I sit up so I am facing her, giving this pearl of truth the attention it deserves.

At first, she won't meet my eye, staring down at the hands resting in the lap of her crossed legs. She looks sad and worried and terribly young.

'It's not a war, Ivy. I'm not a territory to be claimed.'

She nods, but still won't meet my eye.

Unbidden, Henry's words find me again, insistent and furious: *she's in love with you.* 'And that's the only reason?'

Silence. Silence that feels hot and alive. Slowly, she raises her eyes to mine and when our gazes lock, tiny fireflies dance at the very core of me. 'What other reason would there be?'

I reach out and stroke a lock of her glossy, dark hair. 'You won't lose me.'

Her hand catches my wrist. Her skin is so soft. 'Promise?'

I nod.

Maybe you are in love with me, I think. *Maybe, sometimes, I'm a little in love with you too.*

Maybe, when you have a connection like we do, something that is rare and forged from a bone-deep need to belong, it's expected that you hand that person a piece of yourself.

'I just want you to get to know him. He's important to me.'

'But not as important as I am?'

I smile, but don't reply because how can I? If I want a husband and a family of my own, she can't always be the most important thing in my life, and I can't keep folding my needs away into drawers, like unworn jumpers, just to please her.

She sighs. 'Fine. We'll set up a dinner or something.'

I smile, relieved and excited all at once. 'Actually, Henry's throwing a Halloween party. Come.'

She glares. 'But we always spend Halloween together.'

'And this year won't be any different, we'll still be together. Besides, you and Henry know a lot of the same people. It'll be your regular crowd, but we won't have to worry about the post-party clean-up.' She's shaking her head. I squeeze her bare thigh. 'Come on, Holt, where's your sense of adventure?'

Her eyes search my face. I look up at her from beneath my lashes. I'm remembering her once telling me that the secret to life is letting men believe they have a chance of fucking you. So I plead and I beg and I pout, until she smiles and say, 'OK. *Fine.*'

I go back to lying in her lap. 'I promise it's going to be an evening we'll never forget.'

Chapter Twenty

Now

That was the moment that sent my life spiralling out of control. The moment that led me here, to this police station. It is the lynchpin that resulted in the bloodied corpse and inked fingers, and a fear so vicious it devours. It is the reason officers are asking me the same question, over and over, but I can't bring myself to answer because the more I find out, the more uncertain of the truth I become. As I sit alone in the holding room, waiting for another round of interrogation to begin, the realisation that I can't tap the heels of my ruby slippers to return home, to the comfort of a life that feels like it happened to someone else, rips through me like a tornado, and I can't catch my breath. If I had known what was going to happen at that party, I'd never have pushed for you to come, Ivy. On repeat, I replay how I flirted and cajoled and coaxed. But it's a moment fixed in time that I cannot change, and going over it is a kind of delicious torture, a relentless picking at a self-inflicted wound, like peeling off a scab to find the flesh beneath still raw and bloody. And while the truth is a complex mistress to which I can't commit, hindsight, as it turns out, is a cruel and taunting bitch.

Chapter Twenty-One

Before

It's a masquerade ball. Nothing like the Halloween parties we threw at university in our student houses, where a black bodycon dress from Topshop, eyeliner whiskers and a pair of cat ears would suffice. No, this is far more sophisticated: men in tailored suits and tailcoats, women in ball gowns and evening gloves. Everyone wears intricate, beautiful masks. Mine is gold, Venetian lace, and the dress Henry laid out for me on the bed this morning is a rich indigo blue with a full, sweeping skirt, a Bardot neckline and tiny gold stars handsewn into the fabric. When I move, the stars catch the light, and I am a glittering night sky. I'm sure it's the most expensive thing I've ever owned. A thank you, he said, for taking time off work to help organise the party.

Henry pulls me to him and whispers, 'I can't wait to get you out of that dress.'

'You're the one who put me in it.'

'What a fool I am.'

'You look so handsome,' I tell him.

In his navy suit and bronze mask, Henry is dashing, all square jawline and Cupid's bow.

We move through the party, my hand in the crook of his arm. For once, I don't feel awkward and cheap and out of my depth among his friends. For the first time, I feel grand and elegant, as though confidence has been stitched into the dress alongside the stars. But I'm distracted as I make small talk with unfamiliar people, wondering where Ivy is. She promised she'd come. Why isn't she here? Eventually, Henry is called away to deal with a catering crisis.

The party is packed, yet somehow, Henry's house seems even bigger for it. Except for the hallway, the entire bottom floor is open plan which makes it perfect for big gatherings like this. It really is unlike any Halloween party I've organised or attended before. There isn't a fake cobweb or plastic skeleton in sight. But there are pumpkins and candles and a string quartet. In the garden is a huge, heated tent, lit inside and out with strings of golden lights.

I hover in the lounge with no one to talk to. The confidence and sense of belonging I felt just seconds ago starts to melt away. I cast around for Henry. For Ivy. For anyone I know.

'Zara?'

I swivel towards the voice and stare blankly at a woman in a black, glossy mask.

'Zara, is everything alright?' she asks.

'Erm . . .' I trail off, trying to work out who the masked woman is.

'Oh, how stupid of me,' she says and lowers her mask for just a second. Where mine is secured with navy ribbon, hers sits atop a long, black stick reminiscent of a riding crop.

Even then, it takes me a beat; I am still lost in a fog of wondering about Ivy.

'Hazel!'

She's one of my relatively new clients. I like her a lot. She's super low-maintenance and really friendly. 'I didn't know you knew Henry.'

'Oh, I don't, not really. Only through an old friend. You look wonderful.'

'Thank you, so do you. Love your dress.' It's black and slinky, with a square neckline. I don't think I've ever seen her in anything other than yoga leggings and hoodies. Tonight, she's even holding a glass of wine instead of her KeepCup.

'Thanks, it has pockets,' she declares, and promptly slips one hand inside a discreet pouch to demonstrate. '*Great* party. At least now I know what's been keeping you so busy! I was starting to think you'd abandoned me.'

I feel my cheeks heat. 'Did I forget to set up an out-of-office email?'

She laughs. 'Too excited for some time away?'

'I was only meant to take leave for a couple of days and then the party took on a life of its own and two days turned into a whole week.' In the years I've worked for Hillington's, I almost never take an entire week's worth of leave. Not since I went to London with Luke all those months ago. I've enjoyed the break, though. Henry booked us a surprise trip to Oxford for a couple of nights where we ordered room service and drank the entire minibar. I'd never stayed in a hotel so luxurious.

'Is your fiancé here?' I ask Hazel. 'I should probably meet him before the wedding.'

She pulls a face. 'Unfortunately not. He had to work. *Again.* I swear, he's all work and no play. Still, if it means we can afford the dessert table at the reception, I'll forgive him.'

She smiles warmly and touches a hand to her jade stone necklace – I think it's sentimental because I've never seen her without it, and I wonder if she'll wear it on her wedding day. She'll make a gorgeous bride, she has amazing skin: clear and smooth and tanned, in a healthy time-spent-hiking-at-weekends sort of way.

'Right, I think I need another drink,' she says, and briefly, her hand grazes mine. 'Take care of yourself, Zara.'

Just as she's swallowed up by the crowd, a voice whispers into my ear. 'Was she hitting on you?'

Startled, I jump and spin on my heel. 'You're here.'

'And you're surprised? I said I'd come.'

And come she has. Ivy is magnificent in her blood-red gown, with its low neckline and lower back, the straps so thin, it seems I could score them with my thumbnail and the dress would simply slide to the floor.

'So,' she says. 'Was she?'

'What?'

'Flirting with you.'

I roll my eyes. 'Not everyone is trying to sleep with me.'

Her lips, painted the same shade of opulent crimson as her dress, curl into a smile. 'It's all about sex, Zara.'

'What is?'

'Everything.'

Later, we're enjoying our second glass of champagne, heads bent close together, the party swirling unnoticed around us, when Henry enters the kitchen with Jonty. And even though we weren't doing anything wrong, cheeks flushing, I shift away from her.

On approach, Henry smiles but his gaze is cold and assessing. 'Ivy, good to see you again.' He leans in to kiss her cheeks and I'm grateful she lets him.

'And you, Henry. Marvellous party.'

He wraps an arm around my waist and presses me firmly to his side.

Her eyes don't leave mine, her gaze so intense I have to look away.

Jonty, Henry's closest friend, is dressed in a dark-green suit, crisp black shirt and a gold mask with a long, beak-like nose. It should be grotesque, but on blond, blue-eyed, chiselled Jonty, it's strangely attractive. I'm fond of him; he has a guileless charm and a buoyancy about him that puts me at ease.

'Zara, you look exquisite, as usual.' He swoops down and plants a kiss on my cheek, but it's her he can't keep his baby blues off.

'Ivy.' She holds out her slender, manicured hand.

He takes it. 'Jonty.'

'Jonty,' she says, and then again, slowly, as if she is holding his name in her mouth and waiting for it to dissolve like candyfloss. And that's all it takes; he'll lose himself to her now, if that's what she wants.

'Have we met before?' he asks her.

'I don't believe so.'

'Maybe you know Ivy's father,' offers Henry. 'Hugo Holt.'

His eyes glimmer darkly. 'Only by wicked reputation.' Whether he's referring to the embezzlement, the affairs or both is unclear. 'It's nice to meet you, Ivy.'

'The pleasure's all yours, I'm sure.' The words leave my mouth before I can stop them.

Henry's fingers momentarily tighten around my waist, but I don't care because I'm worrying about her and whether she's stung by Jonty alluding to her father's transgressions. When I glance at her though, she's smiling at him. Then, without taking her eyes from his, she says admonishingly to me, 'That's not very kind, Zara.'

'Yes, Zara, that's not very kind,' Jonty says, in the same tone she used.

And from the tips of his thick blond hair to the square toes of his expensive shoes, I'm suddenly struggling to remember what it was I ever liked about Jonty Farlow.

'Share your secret, Henry.' Jonty grins conspiratorially at him, then slides his gaze over me. 'Where do you keep finding all these pretty, smart-mouthed women?'

Henry sips his beer and smiles.

Then a bearded man in a top hat who's hovered on the fringes of our conversation slaps Henry on the back and bellows, 'You know Henry, forever digging for flowers in a field of weeds.'

The other men with top hats throw their heads back and laugh until I can see the fillings at the backs of their mouths.

Ivy's lips thin into a severe red slash, her good humour snuffed out by the snide little dig aimed my way. She is on the brink of rushing to my defence. But, not wanting to cause any more of a scene at Henry's party, I break away from him and grab her wrist.

'Drink?'

I don't wait for her to answer before I am leading her away from the chortling men and out into lounge. I'm trying to steer her towards the downstairs bathroom, when she whirls on me and says, 'Are you really going to let them talk about you like that?'

'It was only a joke.'

'I don't think so.'

'Please, just leave it, Ivy. It's been such a good night.'

'Henry didn't even bother to defend you.'

I'm hurt by what was said, but I can't admit this to her without stoking the flames, so I say, 'It wasn't Henry who made that silly little comment. This is his party, I don't expect him to stand there telling off his guests for every stupid joke they make. Besides, it's unlike you to champion a man riding in like a white knight on a woman's behalf.' I've won, I think, as I fling feminism back in her face. 'And if I felt the need, I can defend myself.'

'So can I.' Her eyes narrow. 'What was all that about with Jonty?'

I swallow. 'What?'

Her lips part and I can just glimpse her white teeth as she leans in, so close I can taste her Wild Bluebell perfume. There's a rushing in my ears, from the alcohol in my blood and the music all around and the warmth of her breath on my bare skin as she whispers, 'Be careful, Zara, your jealousy is showing.'

And after all these years, it should be obvious to me that she will always wield an ace.

The night slips away. My throat tells me I'm laughing too hard, and my giddiness is a solid indicator that I'm drinking too much. Still, I down every glass of wine that appears in front of me. Sometimes, Henry is sitting with me; sometimes it's her. More and more it's her. I notice, as the evening wears on, that she is tiring of Jonty. She's had less and less to say to him, but more and more to say to me.

Henry doesn't like it. From across the room, he sips his drink and watches us with a sullen expression. Sometimes, I think men struggle to understand what women mean to each other. Struggle to understand the intensity of our feelings. Struggle to understand that in a world made by and for men, our friendships with other women are as vital to our survival as the water we drink. But not Luke. He appreciates what Ivy is to me, always encouraging me to nurture our relationship. He has never felt threatened by her. By us. He's been like a big brother to her for almost a decade. I wish Henry wanted to be that for Ivy, too. I wish she'd let him.

I tell her I'm going to find us another drink, then force myself to my feet and make my way over to Henry. He's mid-conversation with Jonty and despite having spent the last hour staring sulkily at me, he doesn't even glance in my direction as I hover beside him.

'Ah,' says Jonty brightly. 'The lovely, smart-mouthed Zara is joining our lowly ranks.'

I give him a polite smile, but my attention remains fixed on Henry who sips his whisky, still without acknowledging me. I remember the first night he and I met, when we sat by the firepit and talked about distilleries with so much vigour. It's one of the things I loved about him – *love* about him – that he's passionate. Our relationship, mine and Ivy's, only threatens him because he values me as something worth losing. I can count on one hand the number of people that feel that way about me. I'm not sure my own parents are on that very short list.

Jonty talks animatedly about his trip to Mykonos with Henry last year, but I am only half-listening. Gently but confidently, I slip my hand into Henry's. He doesn't pull away. When I look up, he's staring down at me, the morose expression softening. I give him a smile. He smiles back at me; forgiven, forgotten.

Jonty raises his glass and says, 'To another year of shared excellence.'

'And many more to come,' says Henry, raising his glass, too.

I follow suit.

'The next party to be thrown here will be our housewarming celebration,' he says.

'Ah yes, I hear you're moving in, Zara?' Jonty grins. I'm surprised he knows; Henry and I agreed to keep it quiet until I have the discussion with Ivy. I even called Amira and asked her not to mention it. 'You know Henry here is a certified psychopath.'

'And you should know she likes pineapple on her pizza,' Henry interjects.

Jonty's eyes widen in mock-horror. 'I see. *You're* the psychopath.'

I smile. 'So I've been told.'

'Can't be long until you two psychopaths are deliriously blissful in your domestic haven,' says Jonty. 'When do you move in, Zara?'

'Yes, Zara, when exactly *do* you move in?' Ivy's voice rings out behind me, sharp and precise as cut glass.

Heart slamming against my ribs, I turn to her and it's all there on her face: devastation and rage and, worst of all, betrayal. She's looking at me like I've spat in the face of us. I'm not sure what has hurt more: the thought of me leaving her, or me lying about it. I don't get to ask because she turns her back on me and disappears into the crowd. For a moment, I am too much of a coward to chase after her; I'm afraid of the inevitable laboured confrontation. And even though I am an adult who deserves to be happy in whichever way I choose, I'm in the wrong because this isn't how she deserved to find out: from a virtual stranger at a party. I take a breath and start after her, but Henry catches my forearm and gently tugs me back.

'Leave her,' he tells me.

It's only then I realise, that although I had my back to her, Henry and Jonty didn't. They'd have seen her approaching or, as I suspect, standing right behind me. Fury bubbles to the surface of me. I spin to face him. 'How could you do that to her?'

Henry glares down at me and just briefly, his fingers tighten hard around my arm.

In my peripheral vision, I see Jonty raise his hands as if in surrender. 'Good luck,' he says to Henry. And then he's gone too.

Henry lowers his voice so as not to alert his guests to our spat. 'I thought you'd told her.'

'You knew I hadn't. Don't you think I'd have mentioned it to you if I'd told her? We agreed not to tell anyone until I'd spoken to Ivy.'

'You told Amira.'

'And I specifically requested she keep it to herself.'

'So it's fine for you to share the news with your friend, but I can't share it with mine? Is that fair, Zara? Why do you get to control who I do and don't talk to?'

'I'm not controlling anything,' I say but my heart races just a little faster because he's right, it isn't fair. While I was happy to share the news with Amira, I told him not to.

'I didn't think to ask Jonty to keep quiet, because unlike you, my entire existence doesn't revolve around Ivy Holt,' he says. I open my mouth to argue but he goes on, 'Why does it matter if she finds out now or finds out in two weeks' time? Christ, I was just excited we're starting our life together, so I mentioned it to Jonty. Once. How could I predict what would happen?'

'You couldn't,' I admit. I think about telling him that if he'd just warned Jonty not to bring it up this all could have been avoided, but that's not entirely accurate. If I'd been brave enough to be honest with her before the party, maybe she wouldn't be so hurt right now. This is my fault, not Jonty's or even Henry's.

'Aren't you excited to move in?' he asks but he's staring into his glass as though he's afraid to hear the answer, and I feel a stab of guilt that I haven't made this the carefree, celebratory experience that moving in with someone should be.

I wish I could say to Henry that I'm over the moon to live with him, but the truth is I've spent most of the time worrying about how she'll take the news. Instinct tells me I can't divulge this to Henry without making everything so much worse, so I lie and say, 'Yes.'

Some of the tension eases from him. Setting his glass down, he rewards me by cupping my face and tilting my head back. His mouth is just a breath away from mine. I feel my lips parting, an invitation. My world has shrunk until it's just me and him. 'I feel like I've been waiting for you for as long as I can remember, and now I've found you, I don't want to share you.' He brings my face close to his. 'But if you're not totally in this with me, Zara, don't be in it at all.'

There's a finality in his tone that makes panic tighten my chest. I can't lose Henry. I can't. What is wrong with me? I wasted years pining after Luke and now I have a man who wants me, *really* wants me, I'm ruining it. If I'm not careful, I'll end up like my mother; alone and wrecked and drinking my regrets. 'I *am* in this with you,' I say in a rush. 'Of course I am. I'm in this with you.'

Then he kisses me and, just for a second, I let myself forget all about Ivy.

Henry advises that I let her cool off, so I do. I stay far enough away that I don't crowd her, but close enough that I can watch her. She finds a band of admirers quickly, spinning and drinking and laughing at the centre of this new group. I've always envied this about her, the ease with which she makes people fall in love with her. Right from the beginning, I was aware that if she chose to, she could ditch our party of two in favour of a large circle of friends, and it made it that much more special when she didn't. And though recently being at the heart of her world has felt like a burden, before Henry, it was everything.

As the night winds on, the party amps up. The string quartet disassemble, along with the civilities of the evening, as people get drunker and louder. A man in a black bull mask and metallic bronze suit shakes up a hundred-pound bottle of champagne and sprays the crowd. Dirty drum and bass thuds from speakers. Soon, I am surrounded by heat and sweat and skin, and a mass of bodies in ballgowns and suits moving in a grinding pulse.

I lost sight of Ivy a while ago, but now I am on my tiptoes surveying the crowd, trying to catch a glimpse of her. I do a couple of loops before I find her, off to one side in the corner of the lounge. She's talking to a man in a purple velvet suit and a gold wolf mask that obscures half his face. Though it won't be obvious to anyone who doesn't know her, I can tell this conversation is heated from the way she deliberately averts her face from him, looking out of the window. Frustration or anger curls his hands into claws as he gestures at her. She laughs, then, her mouth wide and her chin high, mocking him. This winds him up even more. He steps to the right, and ducks his head to get her attention.

Arms encircle my waist from behind and Henry rests his chin on my head. 'What're you—'

'Who's that?' I ask, cutting him off. 'Who's the man Ivy's talking to?'

'Roman.'

I frown. 'Roman?'

'Roman Holt.'

'You didn't tell me you know her cousin.' On the rare occasions she's talked about Roman, she's described him as arrogant and ruthless, charmless and snide, doted on as an only child and favoured by her late grandmother.

I feel Henry shrug. 'Everyone knows everyone.'

'Did you know Ivy?' I ask, remembering how the first night I met Henry, there was a flash of recognition when I mentioned her; then how later, he knew she'd worked in PR. 'Before I introduced you to her, did you two know each other?'

'I knew *of* her.'

'How did you know she worked in PR?'

'Like I said, I knew of her. Bath is small and I'm friendly with Roman.'

Roman, frustrated with her, rips off his mask and brings his face close to hers, forcing her to look at him. From this angle, I can only see the back of his head. But something about him is familiar. Then he shifts and I see his face.

My breath catches.

Roman is the man who broke into our house, the one she rowed with in our kitchen. All this time, I was convinced he was a married ex. She gave Quinn a key to our house because when they weren't meeting in expensive hotels, it made it easier for him to slip inside, away from prying eyes, and wait for her. It didn't even cross my mind that the person with a key to our home was family, not since Theo's had nothing to do with the Holts in thirteen years and Roman is meant to be in New Zealand. He didn't even return to England for Alfred's funeral.

'What's wrong?' asks Henry.

'Nothing.'

'You're tense.'

'I'm fine.'

I never did tell him that she knew the man who broke in. How can I explain all of it to Henry now, weeks after it's happened?

'The fireworks are about to begin,' says Henry.

'Fireworks?' I ask absently.

She walks away from Roman, vanishing out into the hallway, and he stalks after her. I'm about to follow when Henry says, 'Zara, Ivy is catching up with her cousin. They're family and Roman's been in New Zealand for seven years. Give them some quality time together.'

He doesn't realise they're arguing because he doesn't know her like I do, and he doesn't know how visceral her last confrontation with Roman was.

Henry turns down the music and instructs everyone to follow him out into the garden for the display. People swarm for the open French doors and spill out onto the patio. I glance back at the hallway. Then, reflected in the mirror above the sideboard, I glimpse the dark-haired woman in a crimson dress and feathered mask, her hair flowing down her back in an inky stream. I spin towards the French doors and catch sight of her disappearing through them.

I can't be absolutely sure it's my dark-haired stalker, but instinct tells me it is.

I go after her, hurrying across the room and out onto the patio. Everyone is clustered together, staring up at the sky, waiting for the fireworks to begin. I search for her, but the crowd is so thick, it's impossible.

What is she doing here?

She's following me. I know she is. I am sure of it now. But why?

Maybe if she *is* following me, she's the person behind the emails, too. The emails started appearing not long after she did. I turn on my heel and race back into the house. It takes me a couple of minutes to find my phone, the front of it sticky where a drink has been spilled over it. With shaking fingers, I enter my PIN and click into my emails to see if my theory is correct. Because if she's followed me here, maybe she's sent a cryptic message, too. After all, that first email came after the last party. What if she'd been there the night of the Holt housewarming and I just didn't see her? And maybe she was outside the night Roman broke in as well.

My stomach drops.

Get out. Get out. Get out. Run. Run. Run.

There it is, just as I suspected, another obscure email from HTH@ gmail.com.

It *has* to be her, the dark-haired woman.

With an idea of who is behind the account, I feel more confident in taking some control and decide to engage. But what do I say?

There's a loud bang and I jump. I'm so tense, the fireworks sound like gunshots and set my teeth on edge. Wanting to get some distance, I head through the lounge, into the hallway and out the front door. The October evening is frigid. Since I saw the dark-haired woman, I haven't been able to slow my heart or catch my breath, and the cold helps sober me up. I start typing a reply to her, demanding to know what she wants from me, when a movement above my head catches my eye.

I glance up. There's a scream. A whoosh of air.

I throw myself back, out of the way.

The scream is cut short by a wet, bone-shattering thud. Something hot splatters onto my face.

I cannot breathe. Cannot move. Cannot scream for help. I can only stare down at the body on the concrete paving.

At arms and legs splayed at unnatural angles. At bone that has shattered and come loose, scattered across the slabs like broken chips of porcelain. At the blood snaking across the ground. At the lifeless, unblinking face of someone I know.

Chapter Twenty-Two

There's a twisting, clawing, burning in my throat. But I can't make a noise. Can't move. Can't look away.

On the ground are teeth. Human teeth. Ones that were smashed from his mouth when his face struck the pavement. It is this detail that sends nausea rolling through me. It is imagining the raw bloodied flesh of his toothless gums that makes me turn from the body and double over.

I'm still retching onto the grass when I see a blur of red silk to my right. It's Ivy, racing from the house, wild and panicked. When she sees me, she stops, her eyes wide with terror as she drinks in the grotesque scene. Slowly, she makes her way to me, and her gaze settles on his broken body. Blood creeps towards the round toes of her heels. She takes a step back. It trickles into the divot between the paving slabs like a morbid crimson moat.

I dry heave again. Then she is kneeling in front of me in the damp grass, hands cool against my face as she pushes back my hair. When it's apparent I have nothing left in me, I straighten slowly. Everything sways.

She's talking to me. I see the fierce, angry red of her open mouth, but I can't hear her over the ringing in my ears. I can't breathe or move or think. She grabs me by my shoulders, her fingers digging in, and like a plug being pulled from a sink, noises come rushing: the popping of fireworks overhead, our panted breaths, the wild drum of my heart in my ears. And at last, I find my voice, cutting her off.

'He's dead,' I say. Then I say it again and again because my entire world has been reduced to the sound of his body breaking against concrete slabs. 'He's dead.'

'Zara, listen—'

'He's dead.'

'*Concentrate.*'

'Roman is dead.' I swallow. My throat is so dry, it feels like my tongue will crack and split in my mouth. It's just me and her and him. Everyone else is watching the firework display in the back garden. But why is she here? Why was she running from the house? And finally, I meet her eyes and it's as though I am seeing her properly for the first time. 'Ivy, what did you do?'

We stare at each other.

Over her shoulder, I see Henry and Jonty coming out of the open front door. Henry's phone is pressed to his ear – he looks worried, and I'm vaguely aware of my phone vibrating urgently on the pavement where I dropped it. Jonty is the first to see us. His mouth is a round tunnel of horror. He puts a hand on Henry's shoulder. Henry's frown deepens, then he follows Jonty's gaze. He takes it all in: her and me and the dead man at our feet. His shock is a pale imitation of my own.

Jonty breaks into a run, dropping to his knees as he reaches Roman. He rolls him over to check for a pulse. There isn't one. Obviously, there isn't one. We gape at the brutality of Roman's injuries, illuminated by the light spilling out of the house and splashing across the front garden. His face is a wet, toothless mess of blood and split flesh.

My mouth fills with spit. Then I am bent double again, turning away and vomiting a fresh puddle onto the grass. I'm sweating and shivering, my throat sore.

Henry rubs a soothing circle on my back. 'Are you OK? Are you hurt?'

I shake my head. My words are lost and I'm afraid if I open my mouth, I'll scream.

After that, Henry is in charge. I am an extra in this drama, being told where to stand, what to say. The three of them discuss options while I tremble uncontrollably on the outskirts of it all. Then Henry's face appears again, lined with concern. 'You're going with Jonty.'

'Where?'

'Holt House.'

'But the police. We have to—'

'I'll call them. I'll take care of everything.'

'I need to give a statement,' I gabble. 'Or—'

'No. You didn't find the body. You and Ivy left before the firework display. Jonty drove you both home. *That's* what you tell people. You understand?'

'The fireworks will be over in a couple of minutes,' says Jonty urgently. 'We don't have long before people come wandering.'

Henry squeezes my arm. 'Understand?'

I nod, even though I don't understand any of it, but I can't make myself move. Shock anchors me to the spot.

'Zara,' Ivy says. 'We need to go. Now.'

For once, she and Henry are in agreement.

'Go,' commands Henry. When I still don't move, he looks to Jonty. 'Get her out of here.'

Then hands are around my waist, and I am being half-carried, half-dragged towards an unfamiliar car and folded inside. The journey back to Holt House is a tense, silent blur.

Jonty escorts us to the front door and makes sure we go inside. He tells us not to leave until we hear from Henry. We stand in treacle-thick silence in the foyer. With the front door closed, and distance between me and Roman's broken corpse, I can *think* again. And I have questions for Ivy, so many questions. I turn on her. 'What happened?'

She leans back against the front door and stares up at the ceiling. 'I don't know.'

'At the party, I saw you arguing with Roman. Then you vanished. Where did you go?'

'Why does it matter?'

I grit my teeth, frustrated she won't answer. 'Where did you go?'

'Upstairs. To talk privately.'

I'd assumed she'd left the house, continued the argument outside, but she must've gone to the spare room. It's the only bedroom with floor-to-ceiling windows that slide open onto a narrow Juliet balcony. 'Why did you choose that room?'

'I didn't. *He* did.'

'But—'

'Why does it even matter?' She pushes away from the door. 'Jesus, Zara. He's dead.'

'I know. Don't you think I know that? I saw him hit the ground. I was there. I . . .' I trail off, remembering. Nausea curdles in my gut again and my heart slams against my ribs. I grip the console table to steady myself. The wine and champagne mix with the trauma of the evening.

'He was drunk. He fell.'

'Were you with him when he . . .' I swallow. 'When he fell?'

She stares at me, hard and unflinching. 'Just *fucking* ask me, Zara.'

For a moment, I'm not sure I'm brave enough, but even if I don't like the answer, I have to know. 'Did you push him?'

Silence. The kind that burns like acid against your skin. The kind that is so unbearable, you want to scream just to break it. Her eyes narrow, furious and cold. 'Fuck you.'

She starts walking past me, but I step in her way, blocking her path to the stairs. 'He had something over you. I heard him that day in our kitchen, threatening to expose your secret. What secret?'

'I'm not doing this right now.'

She steps to the right, but I reach out and grab her shoulders. 'What secret, Ivy?' She tries to pull away, but I grip harder, fingernails biting into her skin. I am desperate and terrified, and she is hoarding all the answers. 'What secret?'

'Let go of me!' she shrieks, shoving me away hard enough to send me tumbling backwards.

I hit the ground, cracking my head on the hardwood floor.

I lie there, not quite able to believe what just happened. My head throbs and I swallow another rush of bile. Slowly, I sit up. Our eyes lock. We are suspended here, across the room from each other, and for the first time, I'm wondering if I know her at all.

'Zara . . .' There are tears in her eyes. She lifts a trembling hand to her mouth.

Using the console table, I get unsteadily to my feet.

'I'm sorry,' she whispers. Then she snatches her evening bag from the floor and bolts up the stairs. A few seconds later, her bedroom door slams shut.

I touch my hand to my temple, and I'm surprised when my fingertips come away scarlet with my blood.

* * *

I thought I wouldn't sleep, but I must've because I jolt awake, sure I dreamt of falling. I'm still wearing my ballgown, stiff and sticky against my skin. Silently, I get out of bed and change into pyjamas. My curtains are open; watery, blue early-morning light filters in through the window. Then I hear her moving around downstairs. Silently, I make my way to the ground floor. I taste the smoke before I see the warm, flickering glow coming from the living room. I edge towards the door and press myself flat against the wall so I can't be seen.

But I see Ivy. I see her standing in front of the fire in a long white nightgown, her back to me. I see her take papers from her evening bag. I see her toss them into the fire and watch as they crackle and burn.

Chapter Twenty-Three

'Everything is fine,' soothes Henry down the line.

It's the morning after Roman's death. I'm gripping the phone so hard, my knuckles ache. 'How can it be? How can anything ever be fine again?'

'The police came. They interviewed enough people to know Roman was drunk. As far as they're concerned, he wandered upstairs to find a bathroom, ended up in the bedroom and he fell. A tragic accident.'

'That's what Ivy said it was. An accident.' Silence bristles down the line. Though neither he nor I have said it out loud, I feel Henry is as suspicious of her as I am. But if he thought she was responsible for Roman's death, why did he have her escorted home? 'Henry, I don't understand why you wanted me and Ivy away from the party before the police were called.'

He sighs. 'I didn't know if you'd been there when he...' He grapples for the right word. Clears his throat, '... when he fell. I didn't want you getting stuck in the middle of anything.'

'And Ivy?'

'She's important to you, so she's important to me, too.'

I love Henry. I love him so much. Even though Ivy's been spiky and difficult with him, he's protecting her to protect me.

'Thank you, Henry. I don't know what would have happened if you hadn't found us when you did.'

'Doesn't bear thinking about.'

The idea of being held and questioned by police fills me with terror. 'And are you OK?' I ask, remembering that Henry and Roman were friends.

'It's a shock. Roman moved to New Zealand years ago so we hadn't spoken in a long time. I'm just glad I got to see him again before...' He trails off and, in the silence, I hear again the wet, bone-shattering thud of Roman's body hitting the pavement. 'I think you should move in here sooner,' Henry says.

The swift change of subject catches me off guard. 'How soon?'

'This week.'

After last night, the idea of getting away from Holt House, away from her, is more appealing.

'Roman's death made me think,' he says. 'I'm not willing to spend another second apart from you, Zara. I can't. Life's too short.'

He wants me. Even after my mother, after this dreadful mess with Ivy and Roman, he still wants me. I feel as though I am watching Ivy tumble into the dark and there's nothing I can do to help. As my relationship with her starts to wither, my relationship with Henry continues to grow. I must lean into that. Into the sun.

'OK. This week,' I tell him. His delight sizzles down the line.

And when I ring off, decision made, there is a thorny knot in my stomach because I know she won't take the news well. I go to her room and stand outside, arm raised, ready to knock. Then stop. She isn't here. I listen to the silence of Holt House. It doesn't feel the same without her; it's as though the blood that runs through the veins of it chills in her absence, leaving the bones of it cold. I push the door open, and it swings into creaking darkness. Her bed is empty. If I check the wardrobe, her suitcase will be gone, along with some of her clothes. There's no note and when I ring her, it goes to voicemail.

Later, as I'm stepping out of the shower, my phone rings. It's Luke.

'Are you free?' he asks, urgent and concerned. 'Can we meet?'

'You're here? In the UK?' I ask dumbly.

'For a few days. Can we meet?'

Normally, I wouldn't hesitate, especially when he sounds the way he does now. But after last night, my head pounds and I'm exhausted.

'I'm not sure. I've got a lot on today and—'

'It's about Ivy.'

We meet around midday at Bellflower Park. This late in autumn, when the wind starts to bite and the trees are bare, the Sunday crowd is made up of dog walkers and families on their post-roast-dinner stroll, wrapped up warm in coats and hats.

Luke is already waiting for me, two steaming cups of chai latte in hand. He's dressed in a burgundy beanie, a tan coat unbuttoned to reveal a soft, dove-grey cable knit underneath, dark jeans and black boots. And when he sees me, his face splits into a smile; it's all warmth and comfort, and for just a few glorious seconds, all thoughts of Ivy and toothless corpses and police dissolve.

We hug. I forgot how perfectly we fit together. As I breathe him in, some of the tension eases. Being around Luke is like finally being able to strip out of something that doesn't quite fit, something clingy and too tight, and slip into a favourite, well-worn sweatshirt.

We exchange pleasantries, but it's half-hearted because he has something to say and I need to hear him say it. The urgency I sensed earlier is evident in the creases of his face and the way he brings his takeaway cup to his lips over and over without ever taking a sip.

'So, you wanted to talk about Ivy,' I venture. 'You've heard from her?'

'She came to see me this morning.' I shouldn't be surprised she ran to Luke. After all, he's like a brother to her. Besides me, he knows her best. She lets him see beneath the snark and bite and reckless abandon. 'I'm worried about her.'

'What did she say?'

Looking down at his cup, he shakes his head, as though he can't quite believe what he is about to repeat. 'She told me about the party.' He lowers his voice as a woman and her two children on push bikes pass us. 'About Roman.' He scrubs a hand over his face. 'Are you OK?'

'No. I'm not. I'm not OK.' We come to a stop in the middle of the path. 'It was horrific. Terrifying.' I close my eyes against the memory of Roman's wrecked, toothless face. 'There was so much blood.'

'It's alright,' murmurs Luke, gently pulling me against his chest. 'It's going to be alright.'

He sounds so sure, I almost believe him. But it isn't alright, is it? Ivy's cousin is dead, and she is gone. I have to move out of Holt House and in with Henry because I'm starting to believe he's right: Ivy is dangerous. Being around her is dangerous.

'I think she killed him,' I say out loud for the first time. I'm astonished that the words have left my lips and the moment they do, I feel them crystallise into a truth so absolute, it is a diamond I can hold in my hand.

Luke doesn't agree; his arms stiffen around me. Reluctantly, I pull away and try to make him understand.

'Roman had something over her. A secret. He was threatening to expose her. What if she killed him to keep whatever it is buried?' I think about the papers she burned last night. Maybe she thinks her secret burned with them. I can't imagine anything so ugly it's worth killing for, but I'm determined to find out. And when I do, could she hurt me, too?

'Ten years, Zara. You and Ivy have been like sisters for ten years. You really believe she's capable of murder?'

The reminder of our bond stings like alcohol on an open wound. For so long, she's made me feel loved and wanted in ways my own family haven't. But that doesn't change what she's done.

'Isn't it a little convenient that Roman shows up brandishing a secret and a few weeks later he's dead? She told me once that everyone is capable of killing when pushed,' I throw at him, remembering the comment she made the night of the break-in.

Luke stares across the park. I think I might be getting through to him, but when he focuses on me again, he's as adamant in his conviction as I am in mine. 'She told me it was an accident. They had an argument, he got aggressive, he fell.'

'Why do you believe her?'

'Because I know her,' he snaps. 'And I thought you did, too.'

I'm shaking my head. 'Well, maybe you can't ever truly know someone.'

'I know you,' he says, closing the gap between us, the heat from his body warding off the icy chill.

I glance up at him. His gaze is powerful and there's an undercurrent of longing beneath it, one that would usually sweep us into familiar waters – ones I've drowned in again and again. But things are different now. I start walking again. Luke keeps pace easily, lurching us back into our debate.

'Ivy has bruises on her neck, her arms. Isn't it possible that Roman was aggressive with her?' he says.

I cast my mind back to the confrontation in the kitchen, how he smashed the bowl, crowded her, how his hands curled into fists, and I was sure he'd hurt her.

Luke senses the chink in my resolve and asks, 'If you really believe she murdered someone in cold blood, why haven't you gone to the police?'

'Because I love her.'

He wasn't expecting me to be so honest when things between she and I are so fraught, but denying it would be like claiming the sky is scarlet instead of blue.

'She loves you, too,' he says softly. 'But is that enough of a reason to protect someone you think is guilty of murder?'

'It's not just about Ivy. Henry got us out of there last night. He told the police we left long before Roman died. To go to the police now would mean getting Henry in trouble. I can't do that to him when he went out of his way to help us.'

'Ivy isn't as capable or as cold as she makes out. She comes from money but that doesn't mean her life has been easy. With her mum dying and her dad being so emotionally distant—'

'I know, Luke. Don't you think I know all this?'

'We aren't always right about the things we think will make us happy,' he says evenly. 'Ivy thinks money is the key. It isn't. She wants the unconditional love her family never gave her. The love *you* give her. No matter what Roman had over her, she wouldn't kill him and risk losing you. She isn't a murderer.'

He's confident and rational. So rational, doubt creeps in. Roman *did* have a violent streak, I saw it, and she feared him. Henry told me Roman was drunk, so it's plausible that they argued and, intoxicated, he fell. But what about the papers she was burning? If they had anything to do with the secret, maybe she saw her chance and took them which, at worst, makes her an opportunist. Maybe I've been letting Henry's aspersions about her being obsessed and dangerous colour my judgement. The fact is, Luke knows her almost as well as I do, and Henry doesn't know her at all.

'But if she's innocent, why didn't she tell the police what happened? Innocent people don't run and hide.'

'You did,' he retorts.

This is true. Without a counter argument, we walk along in silence for a minute. Then Luke says, 'She ran because she was terrified, and Henry offered her a way out of a nightmare situation. I'm not saying that running was the right thing to do . . .'

'It isn't.'

'Then why did you go along with it? Why didn't you call the police?'

I bite my lip, guilt swirling in my gut. 'Because I was in shock. It happened so fast and now I can't say anything because Henry will be charged with perverting the course of justice. He was just trying to help. But Ivy is out of control, Luke.'

'When she came to me this morning, she said she'd hurt you,' he says quietly. 'She feels sick about it.'

I'm surprised she admitted this to him. 'It was an accident,' I say. After hanging her out to dry, I'm now rushing to her defence.

'So, can you believe what happened with Roman was an accident, too?'

A little way ahead of us, two women walk side by side, heads bent close together, deep in conversation. Nostalgia grips me; that used to be us when things were easy. Simple.

Luke takes my hand and tugs me to a stop. 'Can I see?' he asks, gesturing towards my head.

I nod.

Slowly, he removes my hat and tilts my chin up towards the autumn light. Then his fingers brush my hair back from my face, his touch gentle and familiar. He examines the cut at my temple.

'Will I live?' I ask.

'I think you'll make it.'

His eyes are on mine, his fingers still in my hair. I feel myself leaning into him, into his warmth, it's instinctual, like a flower leaning towards the sun. He's always taken care of me. Taken care of her, too. Being near him, this close, is like a salve. A barrier between me and the horrors of that night. But whatever relief he offers to the fear and anxiety, it is only temporary, because though he is here now, he will be gone soon.

I turn my face away.

He clears his throat and drops his hand.

We start walking again and I slip my hat back on. 'How long are you staying in the UK?'

'For now, the plan is to stick around.'

I frown. 'Stick around?'

'Yeah, I'm thirty-one. I can't live a nomadic existence indefinitely. I miss home, miss my parents, my friends, miss—' He stops so abruptly that I glance at him, but his gaze is fixed on the path ahead. 'So, yeah, I'm staying.'

Staying. He's *staying*. It's almost laughable, isn't it? I waited for him for years, treating other men as detours, holding them at a distance and as soon as I've beckoned one close, decided he is more than just a pitstop, Luke swoops in. Beneath my disbelief is resentment – why couldn't he have made this decision a year ago? 'But travelling is your job,' I say, trying to keep the accusation out of my voice.

'I've got a new job. It's an editorial position which means I don't need to travel all over to write.' He sighs. 'I've been running for a long time. After Edward died, I felt this immense pressure to be the perfect son, secure the career in finance that my parents wanted for Edward, settle down, give them grandchildren – without me, they'll never have them – and I couldn't do it. Worried I'd fail them. Worried that whenever they looked at me, they didn't really see me, just saw the ghost of my brother. So, I packed a bag, and I went. Days turned into weeks turned into months turned into . . .' He shrugs. 'Well, you know.'

I sometimes wonder what life would look like if Edward hadn't died. Luke probably wouldn't have left Somerset. Maybe, by now, he and I would have the house and the marriage and a family of our own. I can't believe he's moved back.

'This just seems really sudden,' I say.

'Not for me. I've been thinking about it for a long while.'

'Since when?'

He presses his lips together, for whatever reason he's reluctant to say. 'Since London.'

The last time we were naked together. When I told him I was done because watching him leave was too hard. We wanted different things. Were in different places. But now . . . 'And you decided not to tell me?'

He narrows his eyes at the sharpness of my tone. 'I wanted to. I was going to, at the housewarming party.'

Until he saw me with Henry and sent me that message about not wanting to ruin anything.

'I want you to be happy, Zara. I've always wanted you to be happy. Your parents haven't made anything easy for you. You *deserve* to have everything you want from life.'

The anger eases because I know Luke and he isn't calculated. He wasn't aware I was with Henry until the housewarming, and by then he'd already decided to move back. He really isn't trying to cause friction. 'So do you.'

Our eyes lock. Something passes between us – it isn't just sex and heat and searing tension between two people who've been naked together; it is a past shared and a future lost and the bone-deep affection of first love.

'Zara?' someone says, and I jump like I've been scalded.

Henry is standing right behind us, head-to-toe in black: soft black boots, black jeans and a thick, black wool coat.

'Henry, what are you doing here?'

'I need to speak to you,' he says. 'I can wait in the car if you're not done talking?'

'No, I think we're done.' My gaze flits briefly to Luke. 'Are we done?'

He nods, eyes trained on Henry. I give Luke a stilted farewell. As I walk away with Henry, I feel Luke's eyes on my back.

'I've been calling you,' Henry says once we're in the car.

'I was talking to Luke. I didn't even look at my phone.'

'Why were you having a secret meeting with your ex-boyfriend?'

'It wasn't a secret,' I splutter.

'You didn't tell me about it.' Though his voice is calm and even, he's driving too fast down residential streets, hands clamped around the steering wheel so hard, the veins on the backs of his hands bulge.

'He called this morning wanting to talk about Ivy and I came straight out to meet him. I would've told you about it afterwards. And how do you know Luke is an ex?'

'You think I'm stupid enough to believe he's just some childhood friend who grew up on the same street? Come on, Zara.'

I feel my face colour with shame. I should've been honest with Henry, just as I'd want him to be honest with me.

'I put everything on the line, I lied to the police for you. For her,' he says, a sharp edge to his voice now. 'Why am I risking it all if you're still in love with him?'

'I'm not! We're just friends.'

'Well, it's obvious the poor bastard's in love with you. It isn't fair to lead him on the way you are.'

'I'm *not* leading him on,' I insist, indignant he's even suggested it. 'First you think Ivy's in love with me, now Luke.'

'It's not as though I'm accusing the milkman of an imminent proposal, Zara. But it's blatantly obvious that Ivy is obsessed with you and Luke isn't over you. Do you disagree?'

I look away because there may be some truth to what he's saying. The silence in the car is pitted. But in the silence, I question how Henry found me. 'I didn't tell you I was coming to Bellflower Park,' I say. He presses his mouth into a thin line. 'How did you know, Henry?' But, of course, it's clear. 'You used the app. I thought it was about safety, not tracking my every move.'

'I was worried. I *called* but you didn't pick up. Roman is dead and as far as I was aware, you were missing in the presence of the person who could be responsible for shoving him out a fucking window.' He takes a corner too fast, and I'm thrust against the passenger door.

'Slow down.'

He does as I ask.

'I'm deleting that stupid app,' I say, defiant. I understand he's using it to find me out of concern for my safety, so perhaps deleting it is punitive, but the feeling that my privacy is being invaded makes me feel uncomfortable.

'Fine. That's not really what this is about. Ivy killed someone, Zara. I was going out of my mind wondering what she might've done to you.'

'Don't be so dramatic.'

Henry slams on the brakes. I'm thrown forward but my seatbelt snaps me back.

'What the hell are you doing?' I snap.

If we weren't on a country lane, I'd get out of the car and start walking. I don't know what's got into him, but I have very little patience for the soap opera he's created. He reaches into his coat pocket and produces a folded brown envelope. We both stare down at it. 'I didn't want to do this,' he says, pulling out a grainy black-and-white image. He hands it to me, and I get this feeling that once I look at it, *really* look at it, things will be irrevocably changed.

'It's a still image from the camera positioned above the balcony,' Henry says. 'I had it installed a couple of years ago after someone climbed up there and broke in. I deleted the footage in case the police wanted to see it, but kept this to show you.'

I gape at the photograph.

I cannot believe what I am seeing.

I cannot.

But it's all there, right in front of me. I'm consumed by an agony so wretched; my chest tightens, and I can't catch my breath. In it Roman is mid-air as he hurtles towards the ground, falling to his death. And there *she* is, standing on the balcony, arms outstretched, suspended in time, in the moment she thrust him from that ledge.

Henry's voice comes, low and dangerous in my ear, 'Tell me again not to be so dramatic.'

Chapter Twenty-Four

Three days later, save for a couple of boxes, all my things are out of Holt House. It's incredible, really, how at twenty-nine my entire life fits into only three car journeys. And then there's Ivy and Holt House and all that she has. More than I could ever dream of owning. But Luke was right, her parents left her with an emptiness inside, so black and vast and insatiable that no matter how many stately homes and Vivienne Westwood shoes she throws at it, it'll never be enough.

I'm carrying a box of books to my car and locking the front door behind me when I sense her. She's standing beside my little green Peugeot, chin held high, expression carved from marble. 'You're moving out?'

I place the box in the boot before I answer. 'Yes.'

'And you weren't going to tell me?'

'You've been missing for three days.'

'I needed to clear my head.'

Silence. I'm calm. I didn't think I'd be so calm.

'So, this is it,' she says flatly. 'You're leaving?'

'Yes.'

She looks away. Her hands are shaking so she thrusts them into the pockets of her cream coat. The marble veneer is cracking and crumbling to dust at her feet. When her eyes find mine again, they are desperate. 'I didn't mean to hurt you. The last time I saw you, I didn't mean to push you.'

'You think that's why I'm going? Because you shoved me?' I shake my head, my laughter brittle. I slam the boot shut.

'Then, why?'

I round on her. 'Because I'm in love with Henry and I want to live with him. I'm going because wanting a fiancé, a husband, a house, a baby, are all normal things to want, and I am *sick* of you making me feel obvious and tragic and painfully fucking boring for wanting them.'

Her face hardens into ugly defiance. 'I have *never* said you were any of those things, Zara. Not once. If you feel obvious and tragic and painfully fucking boring, that's down to you.'

The calm shatters. 'Fuck you, Ivy.' I stride to the driver's side door. When I yank it open, her hand comes down and slaps it shut.

'I let you move in here rent-free so you could save for a house. If it wasn't for me, you'd have ended up in Trowbridge with your alcoholic mother, spending Saturday evenings scraping vomit off the kitchen lino and pining after Luke.'

Her words are like razors across soft flesh. I feel myself split open, exposed, vulnerable. She's never used my mother to hurt me. Until now. And I realise how she sees us, how she sees herself: as an heiress generously pulling a peasant from the gutter.

'I've supported you,' she goes on. 'I've *always* supported you.'

'You think that's fair?' I squeeze my car keys hard, so they dig into my palm. 'If I had a stately home going spare, of course I'd let you live in it rent-free, but as you're gleefully aware, I don't. After all, I'm just the daughter of an alcoholic. You win, Ivy.' I yank the door open again but she's fast, slamming it shut once more.

'It isn't about winning.'

'No, it's about you not wanting to share me. You don't like Henry. You only want me to be happy on *your* terms.'

'I want you to be happy, Zara. That's why I told you to make things work with Luke.'

'But you knew they never would, because he spends most of his time an ocean away,' I say, remembering Amira's words.

'You're wrong.'

'About everything? About how much you dislike Henry?'

'I don't dislike him.' She lifts her chin. 'I fucking despise Henry Frith.'

The ferocity of the poison in her voice, her expression, makes spit hitch in my throat. 'Why?'

'He invited Roman to that party on purpose. To hurt me. To force us together.'

'Henry didn't even know you and Roman were fighting.'

'Roman said Henry called to invite him to the party and told him I'd be there.'

'You're seriously going to attack him after everything he's done for you?' I am seething. 'He got us away from that party before the police showed up. He *lied* for us.'

'I didn't ask him to.'

'But you *needed* him to.' My heart races and I watch closely for her reaction because we both know the truth: if it wasn't for Henry, the police would have questioned her for a murder I am sure she committed. Still, I can't bring myself to accuse her out loud. Can't bring myself to tell her what I have seen, because when I do, it will be out in the open and it will be the end of us. It will have to be. 'He did it because he's a good person.'

'How much do you really know about him, Zara? Has he ever talked to you about past girlfriends, fiancées . . . wives?' At my answering silence, she raises one dark eyebrow. 'There are rumours his last fiancée, Tabitha, is missing.'

And even though this can't be true, my heart beats faster still. 'You're lying.'

'He's dangerous.'

'*You're* dangerous,' I spit. 'You'll say anything to get me away from Henry. You're obsessed with me.'

Even as the words leave my lips, they don't feel like mine. But they're out there now, hanging in the space between us. She reaches out and pops each one in her mouth, where they sour on her tongue before she spits them back at me.

'Obsessed with you?' She takes a step, so close I can smell her Wild Bluebell perfume and count each one of the gold flecks in her green eyes. 'It's *you* who gets off on watching *me*, Zara.' She tilts her mouth up to mine. If I pucker my lips, we'd kiss. 'You *wish* I was obsessed with you.'

My cheeks flame. 'Just stay away from me.'

'This was inevitable.' She shakes her head mournfully. 'I lost you the day you met him. You love him more than you've ever loved me. Years of friendship thrown away because of him.'

'BECAUSE OF YOU!' I yell. 'Because you're secretive. A liar. A . . .'

I stumble into silence before 'murderer' is flung from my mouth. I've always imagined that we are tethered together by a gossamer thread and no matter how far we stray from one another, we'll always be pulled back together. But in the months since I met Henry and we moved into Holt House, that once perfect, unbreakable thread has become frayed. What will happen to it if I admit to Ivy that I think she's responsible for Roman's death?

'What're you talking about?'

I take some scissors and score them along our bond. 'Are we really going to pretend your cousin fell from that window weeks after threatening you?'

'It was an accident.'

'YOU PUSHED HIM!'

She recoils as though I've struck her. Her denial comes out a broken whistle.

'I didn't.'

'Henry has a security camera facing the balcony. Ivy, I saw the still images from the video footage.'

I pause to give this revelation the silence it deserves, and colour drains from her face, as though someone's fiddled with her contrast button.

'Cameras?'

'*Yes*,' I hiss.

She's shaking her head. 'I didn't push him. I was reaching for him. To save him.'

'If that's true, why didn't you say so the night it happened?'

'Because you'd already decided I was a murderer. I thought you knew me, Zara. I thought you loved me.'

I want to believe her, but I don't. I remember that night: how, back at Holt House, she was defensive, angry . . . and violent with me. I saw her burning those papers in the fire. She was covering something up: a secret she still won't share. I don't say any of this to her because if I do, we will only keep arguing and I am too tired.

Tears of grief blur my vision, because this is the end. It has to be. Because I can't do this anymore. I won't. So I take the scissors and I snip the thread.

'We're done.'

I can't believe I've said it. I'm in as much shock as she is. Her eyes are damp, too. She feels this ending as keenly as I do. We stare at one another, suspended in the wretched agony of what I've just said.

Finally, she lets me open my car door and I slip inside.

'Zara,' she pleads. 'Please don't leave me here. Zara. *Please*.' She's crying now, tears streaming down her cheeks. 'I love you.'

And I can't answer the way we always do, I can't ask her how much because I already know: not enough to tell me the truth.

'I love you too,' I say, because I do.

People spend years building a relationship. Giving it foundations and walls of infallible concrete. Then in just one moment, the truth crests on a wave and the relationship is washed away, because in reality, it was never made of concrete, but sand. Now it's scattered into a hundred billion tiny granules. Years of careful construction. One conversation to destroy it all.

I get back out of the car. I take her hands in mine, and I'm remembering her singing to me in the bathroom that first night we met; I'm remembering her clinging to me in her big bed as her mother lay dying down the hall; I'm remembering her dancing like a flame on ice in an empty rink while I looked on, too scared to let go of the rail. Now, her eyes search my face, trying to work me out. For once, I have the power. The control. I don't revel in it like she does. I don't want it, but I have it now, and I need to do the right thing. So I kiss her. Her mouth is soft, and I taste her tears. 'Goodbye, Ivy.'

This time, she lets me go.

As I drive away, I decide not to look back.

Chapter Twenty-Five

At home, I am in my loungewear, pairing socks fresh out of the tumble-dryer as though they are long-lost lovers. It's been busy at work, and I've had no time for domestic chores, so Henry and I are enjoying the kind of quiet Saturday that Ivy would describe as deathly boring.

Spare moments, in between replying to emails and liaising with florists and visiting wedding venues, have been spent scrolling through her socials. In the four weeks since I drove away from Holt House for the final time, she has been partying and travelling and redecorating. She's thrust herself into the Balenciaga-clad arms of Lollie and Thea. Even though I shouldn't care, when I look at photographs of her with them, it feels as though her attention is like a flask of water in the desert; without it, I'll perish. For the longest while, everyone else was parched. Now, though, they are guzzling, and there isn't a drop left for me.

Even though I should concentrate on the laundry, I feel that pull to see if she's posted since the last time I checked. I hold out for only a few more minutes of tedious sock-pairing before I grab my phone from the bedside table.

This is when I notice the email from HTH@gmail.com. Two words: *Tabitha Gates*

Tabitha. Ivy said Henry's ex-fiancée was called Tabitha. Missing Tabitha. Missing Tabitha Gates. Just for a second, I wonder if Ivy's been behind these emails the entire time, but it isn't her style. She's forthright and blunt and argumentative, she wouldn't hide behind an anonymous email. This is someone who knows me, but it isn't her. I consider Amira, but decide she's more likely to slam *Ivy* in a cryptic message. At one time or another, I've suspected everyone I know. Even Luke or Polly. And those I don't know, like the dark-haired woman. Maybe she's an ex of Henry's. Maybe she is missing Tabitha Gates.

Adamant that Ivy's claims about Henry being involved in the supposed disappearance of his supposed ex-fiancée were nothing more than wild fallacy to bait me into a confrontation with him, I decided not to bring it up. When I came back to his house – *my* house, too, now – after she and I parted ways, Henry kissed me and told me this was a new chapter, and that we were putting Ivy Holt firmly behind us. He doesn't want to hear about her again. Fine by me. If I'm not talking about her, I'm not thinking about her either. Or, at least, that was the theory.

Now, though, as I stand in the bedroom reading this email, what she said about Henry's missing ex-fiancée rises to the surface like a bloated corpse. When I met Henry, I was determined to unwrap each of his secrets and devour them like champagne truffles. But I haven't, have I? Henry doesn't talk much about himself, and certainly not about his ex-partners. Before we moved in together, I looked him up online but there wasn't much to find besides articles that described him as a behemoth of the industry, as a retail giant, as a winner. All these articles are penned as though he were leading men onto a bloody battlefield, wielding swords and shields, and not into boardrooms, toting laptops and Starbucks coffee. There certainly wasn't any mention of a fiancée. He's a private person, so I wasn't surprised. But now I have a full name, and my fingers itch to google Tabitha Gates. I stop myself. It isn't the right way to go about finding information. I shouldn't have to skulk around, secretly internet stalking my boyfriend's ex-fiancée.

I go downstairs where Henry is making dinner. There's a joint of lamb in the oven and vegetables on the chopping board. He listens to music as he cooks, humming along. He doesn't hear me approach. I stand back, watching him, trying to imagine him hurting someone. When we met, he swept in and saved me from that intimidating, persistent wedding guest. Then, on our first date, he came to the rescue again, helping me take care of my mother. Henry's a good person. He's only ever protected me. I can't picture him wrapping his hands around a woman's throat or raising his fist. Ivy's wrong. I know she is. Still, I'm curious about the women who came before.

She wouldn't be, though. Ivy would feel confident enough in her own skin to know the women who'd previously warmed her lover's bed were as disposable and unimportant as used cotton buds.

Sensing me, Henry looks up and grins. Lines crinkle around his warm hazel eyes. I go to him, running my hands beneath his soft, cotton T-shirt. He captures my wrists and kisses me hard. I get a flash of him with his mouth on another woman's, standing in this kitchen as we are now, his fingers sliding around her waist and tugging on her knickers. I pull away but smile playfully up at him to soften the rejection. His grin is wolfish. Thinking this is a game, he pushes me up against the counter, but I can't have sex while I'm picturing him with other women. I turn my face away and say, 'You never talk about your exes.'

'No need,' he breathes into my neck. 'Placeholders. Fodder. Trial runs.'

'I don't mind hearing about them. Everyone has baggage.'

'I prefer to keep my baggage at the door.' He nips the soft place between neck and shoulder.

'Henry.' I press my palms firmly against his shoulders.

Realising I'm serious, he pulls back, frowning. 'Are you OK?'

'I'm fine,' I assure him. 'We just never talk about our past relationships.'

'We don't need to.'

'But I want to.'

He shakes his head. 'Why are you prying?'

'I'm not prying. I'm asking.'

'Well *don't*,' he warns.

'Henry,' I say, stung by his tone.

Closing his eyes, he pinches the bridge of his nose with his thumb and forefinger, as though he's getting a headache. 'It isn't important.'

'Well, maybe it is to me . . .'

I trail off, hoping to invoke our motto, the one he started, but he's unmoved. He snatches up the knife and starts chopping carrots. The sound of the blade hitting the wooden board makes me tense. But I can't slink away with my tail between my legs when I still need answers. Ivy wouldn't.

'What about Tabitha?'

He whirls on me, and I jump back, away from the knife clutched in his right hand. 'Where did you hear that name?'

'Ivy,' I say, because it's true and easier to explain than an anonymous email.

'Of course.' My eyes are trained on the knife. He follows my gaze. Then turns and slaps it onto the counter. 'Of course she fucking did.'

'Is she . . .' I swallow, tiptoeing further into this conversation. 'Were you and Tabitha together?'

'Yes.'

'And?'

'And now we're not.' He glares at me, chest heaving, and I see in his face that he is daring me to shine a torch on the elephant in this room.

I lift my chin. 'Ivy said Tabitha is missing.'

'And you believe her?' he asks, expression hardening.

'I didn't say that.'

'You want to dig up the fucking patio?' He raises his voice. 'Make sure I haven't buried her beneath it?'

I hate that we are arguing. I want to do something, say something to ease the crease of rage from his brow. 'There's no need—'

'Why is that fucking bitch *still* meddling in our relationship?' He throws his arms wide, knocking his wine glass from the counter.

It shatters. Red wine pools on the wooden floor like blood. I spent so many years clearing up after my mother drunkenly smashed something, that I automatically bend to tidy the mess.

'Just leave it,' he commands. 'LEAVE IT.'

Startled, I stumble back, knocking into the kitchen island. I watch in breathless silence as he sweeps the glass into a corner and mops up the wine. Then he stands very still, staring down at the floor, his back to me.

I'm about to go to him, to smooth things over, apologise for bringing Tabitha up, for doubting him, when he says, 'I'm going out.'

A few minutes later, he leaves the house, slamming doors.

Chapter Twenty-Six

The night of our fight, Henry disappeared and didn't come home until late afternoon the next day. Every one of my phone calls and messages to him went unanswered. I was going out of my mind, wondering where he was, worrying I'd overstepped, hating Ivy for putting ideas into my head, hating my anonymous emailer even more. I'd deleted the Friend Finder app after Henry used it to locate me in Bellflower Park with Luke, and even after downloading it again, my account was no longer linked to Henry's.

By the time he rolled in the next day, I was furious and relieved. 'Where have you been?'

I was met with stony silence as he hung up his coat and took off his shoes.

'A party with Jonty.'

'And you couldn't have messaged to tell me?' I said, struggling to hide my irritation. 'I've been up all night worrying about you. Worrying that something awful had happened.'

His lips curled into a smirk. 'Don't be so dramatic.'

He was parroting what I'd said to him in his car right before he showed me the still image from that night. I opened my mouth, but no retort came. He walked past me, up the stairs. Moments later, I heard the shower.

It's been six days since then and he's still ignoring me. When he comes into a room, he is armed with his phone. He sits and silently scrolls and scrolls and scrolls. Trying to engage him in conversation is pointless – his clipped, one-word responses make me feel like a mother trying to draw small talk from her sulky teenage son. I swing between feeling guilty for even asking about Tabitha, and feeling justified that I did. His reaction to me wanting to know about his ex-fiancée was so extreme. If he had nothing to hide, why did mentioning her make him so angry? There are so many things I want to say – words that bang at the door to my mouth, demanding to be let through – but I can't risk any more arguments with Henry. My relationship with him is the only tick I have in the right box, and, at my age, there should be many more.

Work becomes my distraction. I meet with Hazel at a little coffee shop in Frome. Out of the slinky black evening dress, Hazel is back in her usual yoga leggings and sweatshirt combo: today, her leggings are olive green, and her oversized sweatshirt is the colour of custard creams. We drink gingerbread lattes and nibble on mince pies as we pore over wedding plans. It's the start of December, and everywhere there are twinkling fairy lights and Christmas trees, festive bunting and the sweet smell of cinnamon filling the air.

'You still need to decide on the flowers,' I tell her. 'And I need you to sign off on the vintage candlestick centrepieces.'

'Zara, I trust you implicitly. If you think the candlesticks look good, we'll have them.'

'I think they'll be stunning.'

She smiles. 'Great. Consider them signed off.' I make a note on my laptop.

'So, how about you?' asks Hazel. 'Are you married?'

'No, not yet.'

'Is it on the cards?'

'One day,' I say, even though it might be a lie because things between Henry and me are so strained.

'Are you OK? You seem . . .' she watches me thoughtfully, searching for a word that won't offend '. . . tired.'

'I'm fine,' I lie, because although I like Hazel and I'm desperate to confide in someone about it all – the murder, the missing fiancée, the fight – she is still a client and I want to keep things professional. 'Your necklace is so pretty,' I say to distract her. 'Where's it from?'

She lifts a hand to the jade stone on a dainty gold chain. 'My soulmate.'

'And when do I get to meet the fiancé?' I ask. 'We've been planning this wedding for months and I still haven't set eyes on your future husband.'

'He's wonderful, but his job's so demanding. I promise I'll drag him to one of these meetings soon.'

Hazel goes to the counter and orders us another round of coffees. I check my work email and see a new message ping into my inbox from HTH@gmail.com:

He made sure she'd never be found.

Shaken, I end the meeting earlier than planned and walk around the quaint town, down the cobbled high street with the little stream, and duck into the gorgeous Hunting Raven bookshop, but I can't concentrate. I googled Tabitha Gates the night Henry stormed out of the house, but I couldn't find anything. As it happens, around twenty people are reported missing in the UK every day, and a fraction of those ever make it onto the news. I even considered calling Ivy to ask how she knows about Henry's Tabitha. But I couldn't. I can't. That chapter is closed.

When I saw the dark-haired woman at the masquerade ball and that same night another cryptic email from HTH@gmail.com landed in my inbox, I was sure the two were connected. In fact, I was about to reply when Roman's body plummeted from the Juliet balcony. After witnessing the horror of his death, all thoughts of emails and dark-haired women were blown from my mind. When the next cryptic message arrived, with Tabitha's full name, I didn't bother to send a response. Instead, I went straight to Henry to talk to him about his alleged missing fiancée. Now, though, there is no broken corpse at my feet, no disappeared women as a distraction, so I type out an email.

Who are you? What do you want?

I check my phone and check my phone and check my phone. But after an hour, there's still no reply.

I go home. As soon as I open the front door, I hear voices coming from the kitchen: Henry's, and alongside his, another, softer voice. A woman's laughter glitters down the hall. I walk slowly towards the noise, wondering who's here.

Henry is sitting at the kitchen island with Jonty and a woman I've never seen before. Her lipstick is a bold watermelon-pink. She's my age, maybe a couple of years older. Her blonde hair is braided in a fishtail plait and she's wearing a pair of denim dungarees over a lilac jumper. She smiles warmly at me, as though we are old friends. 'Zara,' she says, hopping off the stool and pulling me into an embrace.

'I'm sorry,' I say, inhaling her sweet floral perfume. 'I don't think we've met?'

'Oh, of course. Silly me.' She glances at Henry with a self-conscious little laugh. 'He's told me so much about you, I feel like I know you.'

'Oh.' I look to him. He's relaxed, sipping his tea, watching us over the rim of his steaming mug. But he offers no explanation.

'It's nice to finally meet you,' she says. 'I'm Tabitha.'

'*Tabitha*,' I repeat, agog. I look between her and Henry, confused and in shock.

Missing Tabitha Gates.

The vanished, presumed dead, ex-fiancée that Ivy flung in my face is standing in my kitchen.

'Right, I best be off,' says Jonty, getting to his feet. 'Sorry I can't stay, Zara.' Then he turns to Tabitha. 'Nice to see you again.'

'It was good to catch up.'

They hug.

I stare at Henry, still reeling. So his fiancée isn't missing. She never was. Ivy and this anonymous emailer, who could be one and the same after all, were weaving some elaborate, twisted little web of deceit. No wonder I couldn't find anything about her disappearance online. I've pulled away from Henry, dented our relationship, for nothing. Rage blisters beneath my skin. Rage at her for this ridiculous stunt and rage at myself for entertaining it.

Jonty leaves. It is just the three of us. Henry pours me a peppermint tea.

'So,' I begin, trying to keep my voice casual and breezy. 'The two of you are friends. You keep in touch?'

'Henry and I were friends before we were anything more.' She looks to him with an affectionate smile. 'We haven't seen each other in years. When he called and told me all about you, said we'd get along like a house on fire, as I was planning a trip to Somerset anyway, I thought, why not?'

I'm nodding and smiling even as my mind spins with revelations. 'Are you staying for dinner?'

'I wish I could, but I'm meeting an old friend in Bristol. I haven't been to the UK in so long and it's only a short trip. Such a rush to fit everyone in.'

'Oh, where do you live now?'

She sips her tea. 'Ireland. I moved back to Terryglass a few years ago. It's remote, off the beaten track, but it's the perfect place to paint. Quiet. Beautiful.'

'You're an artist?'

She nods. 'I paint under a different name: Rosemary Layton.'

'Why a different name?'

She shrugs one slender shoulder. 'I like my privacy.'

'I thought . . .' My gaze flits to Henry. His expression is unreadable. If I ask the question I want to ask, will it upset him? Probably.

But I need clarity.

'Someone told me you vanished? That you're missing,' I say.

She laughs. I'm not sure what kind of reaction I was expecting, but it wasn't that.

'Missing? Who told you that?'

My cheeks flame. I dart a glance at Henry before I answer. 'Ivy Holt.'

Tabitha's button nose wrinkles. 'Don't think I know an Ivy Holt.' She sighs. 'You move away and come off social media and it's as though you've died. Missing. Moved away. Truth in one, drama and mystery in the other. In my experience, people choose to believe the morbid over the mundane. But I suppose it keeps things interesting.' She twists in her seat so she's facing me and lays one cool hand over mine. 'I hear you're a wedding planner. How wonderful. Tell me all about it.'

Once we close the door behind Tabitha, I turn to Henry. I don't know what to say. This man has loved me and protected me, and I let Ivy poison me against him. I can't believe I thought, even for one second, that he'd hurt anyone.

'I'm so sorry,' I tell him.

But the apology has barely left my lips before Henry turns on his heel and walks back into the kitchen. I prepare myself for what I know will be a difficult conversation, one in which I will have to be humble and repentant, because of course Henry is going to be fuming that I let Ivy come between us.

In the kitchen, Henry is loading our used mugs into the dishwasher, his back to me.

'I really am so sorry,' I say again. 'The last few days things between us have been uncomfortable, and that's my fault.'

'Uncomfortable?' he muses. 'You thought I'd murdered my ex and stowed her body beneath the hydrangeas. Things have been a little bit more than *uncomfortable*.'

'I didn't think that . . . *exactly*.' I'm wringing my hands, feeling like a schoolgirl being admonished by her headmaster, desperately trying to worm her way out of detention. 'It's just . . . you never talk about your exes. Then I hear this rumour . . .'

'No.' He shuts the dishwasher with a little more force than necessary. 'You didn't just hear it. You were fed it.'

'I know.' I stare down at my feet, wondering how I can ever make it up to him. If Henry chose to believe lies about me, especially ones so brutal, I'd be appalled, too.

'She's nice. Pretty. I can't imagine why you even broke up.'

'I wanted children. She didn't.'

'I wasn't fishing,' I say quickly. This is one of the things I love most about Henry: he wants a family as much as I do. 'I didn't realise you were still friends.'

'We aren't. I called her hoping she'd come to the house so you could see for yourself she's alive and well.'

This is what I've pushed him to: calling ex-fiancées and getting them to travel to a different country just to make me see sense. I cover my face with my hands and mumble into my palms. 'I feel like such an idiot.'

He exhales, and all the tension that's settled in this house like dust since the fight is swept away. 'You're not an idiot,' he says, gently taking ahold of my wrists. 'I'm just disappointed that you thought so little of me when I think so highly of you.'

I groan. 'That's not helping with the crippling guilt.'

He wraps his arms around me, and it feels so good. The icy frost of loneliness and tension and confusion of the last few days starts to thaw and, in its place, appreciation and love for this man blossoms anew.

'From now on,' he says, '*please* believe what I tell you.'

In the bathroom, I pull out my phone. It's been hours since I responded to my anonymous emailer and still there's no reply. In the months I'd been receiving them, I'd sometimes wondered if this person was trying to be helpful. Like when they attempted to warn me about the break-in. Now though, I feel stupid for wondering if this person has good intentions. Tabitha is alive. This emailer, whoever they are, is trying to ruin my life and make me look like a lunatic. Angry and tired of playing games, I fire off a second reply. *LEAVE ME ALONE. If you contact me again, I will go to the police.*

Chapter Twenty-Seven

It's a week until Christmas. I was hoping work would slow down, December isn't a popular time for weddings, but today I drove to Gloucester to meet a client because my colleague has the flu, and the wedding is only two days away.

Henry planned a dinner date tonight, but I had to cancel. By the time I get home, it's gone 8 pm. He's waiting for me in the hallway, sullen between two huge wheelie suitcases.

'What's going on?' I ask, slowly setting my bag down. He shakes his head and my stomach slides to my ankles. 'Are you going somewhere?'

'No,' he says. '*We* were going somewhere.'

'What do you mean?'

'I'd booked flights for us to spend Christmas in New York.'

My excitement is instantaneous. 'Oh, my God. Henry—'

'We missed those flights,' he tells me. He's upset. Really upset. 'You weren't meant to be working today.'

The thrill I felt just seconds ago is swallowed by a dark, churning cloud of guilt.

'I had to. Margot is ill and—'

'You could've said no.'

'I hadn't a clue you'd planned a trip. We can still go. Maybe we can change our flight or—'

'All flights are full now,' he says. 'I booked this *months* ago. I wanted to surprise you. I got to fly all over the world growing up. Your family didn't have the money to take you abroad. I just wanted to make our first Christmas together special.'

That's not what I told him. I told him the first time I set foot in an airport was after university, when Ivy and I went to Italy. He's *inferred* the reason I didn't go until then is due to my parents' lack of cash. That isn't exactly true. My father had the money to go abroad, but he chose to do so with his new family, not with me and Mum.

The reminder that Henry and I have such different backgrounds smarts. I didn't realise it was something he thought about. Still, his intentions are good.

'I'm really grateful,' I say, winding my arms around his neck. 'I feel terrible.'

'I thought when you moved in here, we'd see more of each other.' He rests his forehead against mine. 'We've seen less.'

'I know. I want to spend time with you. You know that. But work has been so busy. I've been stressed and miserable.'

He shrugs. 'Then don't be.'

'Meaning?'

His hands move to my waist. 'Why don't you take a break?'

'I will. I've only got a couple of things to tie up tomorrow then I can relax and start getting ready for Christmas.'

'That's not what I mean. Take a career break.' At my confused expression, he goes on, 'I have more than enough money to support us both. I've just found a new source of income. Henrietta's House is thriving. Now's a good time.'

I unwind myself from him and take off my coat, playing for time. 'I can't just quit my job.'

'You just said you're stressed and miserable.'

'At the moment, yes, but that'll change when things slow down again.'

'You've been saying things will slow down for weeks.' He squeezes me and I feel how much he misses me and how sincere his offer is. 'We hardly get any time together. You work as many hours as I do, but for a pittance.' Before I can voice my outrage, he holds up his hands. 'I'm not saying what you do is less important, it just brings in less money for the same amount of work. I earn enough that we can be more than comfortable without your monthly wage, too.'

Even though Ivy Holt doesn't work and her money was inherited rather than earned, she'd sneer at me for even *considering* taking a career break and living off a man.

'I can't be a kept woman. I've always worked.'

'But why, if you don't have to?' He tugs me against him and kisses the curve of my neck. I lean into it, glad his mood is lifting.

'What would I even do with my time?'

I close my eyes and tip my head back, enjoying the feeling of his mouth on my skin. I feel him shrug.

'Redecorate this place,' he suggests between kisses. 'Or start working towards setting up your own wedding-planning business in the future. Take up pottery or knitting or whatever you like.'

'Knitting?' I pull back, smiling. 'Shall we install a loom in the upstairs bedroom?'

He grins. 'If that's what you want.'

I go onto my tiptoes and kiss him, but when we break apart, he's frowning.

'What's wrong?'

He shakes his head. 'It doesn't matter.'

He starts towards the kitchen, but I lay a reassuring hand on his arm. 'Henry, you can talk to me.'

He stares down at my face, pensive, and I'm worried he'll close the subject. Then he sighs and sits down on the stairs. I sit beside him, the outside of my leg warm where it's pressed close to his.

'As a boy, the irony wasn't lost on me that although my parents were in the business of creating toys for children, they were never around long enough to see me play with mine. For me, growing up was a lonely affair. I don't ever want my own children, *our* children, to feel resentful and abandoned.'

For once, he is the one opening a door into his life and beckoning for me to come inside. I do, cautiously, as though afraid he will slam it shut and lock me out if I put a foot wrong.

'Neither do I.'

'If you leave Hillington's now you have time before we start a family to build your own company, and when our first baby arrives, I could be the one to take a little break and, if you want to, you can go back to work. To run your own business.'

'You'd do that?'

'Yes. Of course. I want us to be the best parents we can be and if that means stepping back from long hours at work to be with my family, that's exactly what I'll do.'

I stand up and then climb onto his lap and kiss him hard, pressing myself into him. I am lucky. So incredibly lucky. Even though it's my fault we missed our flights, and I wrecked his marvellous surprise, Henry is offering me time away from work to start my own wedding-planning business. Henry Frith, CEO of Henrietta's House, is willing to take a break from running his empire to change nappies and do bath time.

He guides my face inches from his so all I can see are those hazel eyes I love so much.

'This is important to me,' he says gravely. And there's only one way to respond.

'Then it's important to me, too.'

Chapter Twenty-Eight

I have a secret. One I am both dreading and excited to tell my mother. One I always dreamed I'd share with Ivy before anyone else.

Spiked with nerves, I sit on the new Chesterfield sofa with my mother, sipping too-hot tea. Henry insisted I put my own stamp on the house to make it feel like home. The sofa was my first big purchase, and I spent hours choosing it. It's upholstered in beautiful, buttery velvet in the deepest navy. A far cry from the worn, beige two-seater of my childhood.

'And you really think giving up your career is a sensible idea, Zara?' asks my mother, disconcerted.

I shift uncomfortably on my very comfortable sofa. I can't help but think her question is laced with jealousy. After my father left, she struggled. She never had the luxury of not working and she was constantly making resentful, snippy remarks whenever Julia took a break from her career to look after Polly, or time off while she decided what she wanted to do next.

'Henry and I talked about it, and we've decided it's for the best.'

She looks at me seriously. 'Independence is important for a woman.'

I bite my tongue to stop myself from pointing out that she's always been dependent on cheap wine and no-good men.

'I know there are worse things to be dependent on,' she says, as though reading my mind, 'but relying on someone else for your lifestyle is less than ideal. It leaves you vulnerable.' She leans forward and rests her hand on mine. 'You're capable, Zara. I always wanted you to be capable.'

It sits oddly with me, this parental concern. My mother often feels less like a mother and more like a surly, wayward little sister. Growing up, I craved a cookie-cutter parent. Now she's dishing out pearls of motherly wisdom, I feel myself crunching on them like broken teeth. Because she doesn't understand what it is to be in a healthy, loving, lasting relationship. Just like Ivy doesn't.

'Henry and I really love each other. We're building a future together.' I mean it sincerely, or at least I think I do, but it comes out of my mouth like a childish taunt.

She presses her lips together in a tight, hurt line. 'That's all very well, but you never know what might happen. You love each other now, but what if you wake up tomorrow and feel differently, or he feels differently?'

I put my mug down on the coffee table too hard, and tea sloshes over the rim. 'So what's the solution? Don't ever be with someone in case your heart gets broken?'

'Be with someone who's more in love with you than you are with them,' she says sternly. 'For heaven's sake, Zara. It's bad enough giving a man power over your heart. Does he really need power over your bank account, too?'

'I have savings,' I insist. 'Love doesn't work the way you think it does. It's not something you plonk onto a scale and weigh.'

I'm happy. Isn't that what all parents want for their children?

Unless they're jealous and bitter.

She puts her tea down next to mine. 'I thought you loved your job.'

'I do. And I can go back to it later. Whenever I want. Henry is going to help me start my own business,' I say, echoing his words. 'I'll earn for myself instead of making money for other people. That's the *sensible* thing to do. He's giving me freedom. Without working the long hours I did and worrying constantly about savings, I can focus on what matters.'

Her eyes narrow but she finally drops the subject. I glance at the clock. Henry will be home soon. I need to tell her before he comes back. I sit up a little straighter, trying to muster the joy of sharing this with my mum, but I'm worried she will take a pin to my bubble of bliss.

'So,' I begin, dispelling the tension with my widest smile. 'I have a lot more time on my hands these days. It's good. Great actually, because I've got a lot of exciting things to plan.'

She picks up her tea and sips it, raising her brows in a silent query.

Beneath the trepidation is a tiny spark of delight. 'Actually, just *one* exciting thing to plan.' I slip my left hand out of the pocket of my dress and rest it deliberately on my knee. My mother's eyes fall on the emerald ring.

'You're engaged,' she whispers, stunned.

I nod, emotion swelling in my throat at the memory. Henry took me to a cosy little cottage in Bourton-on-the-Water during the no man's land between Christmas and New Year. After a walk around the quaint village, we went back to the cottage where Henry heated two mugs of milk on the stove and gave me a spoon encased in a block of chocolate. 'Like this,' he said, dipping the spoon into the mug and swirling it around until the milk turned dark and rich. We sat down in front of the fire, and he told me how much he loved me. 'I've been waiting for you for a very long time. I never want to share you, but I do want to share my life with you, Zara.' Then he took the spoon from my mug and asked me to read the engraved message which was visible since the chocolate melted.

Zara Barton, will you marry me?

Heart racing, I raised my eyes to see that he was down on one knee, proffering a dark-green ring box. He'd wanted to propose in New York, but it didn't matter in the end. I'd have said yes, no matter where we were.

Mum takes my hand in hers and gazes down at the ring. 'You're getting married, and I haven't even met him,' she says.

Oh, but she has, she was just too drunk to remember.

'He'll be home soon.' I run a critical eye over my mother. She's wearing a black jumpsuit, her hair grazing her collarbone in loose, shining waves. No one would know the woman sitting before me was that same woman who wept into the lawn all those months ago, reeking of cheap wine and tragedy.

'It's so fast,' she says.

'Fast for who?' I shrug. 'It's right for us. And it isn't like we're getting married next month. We want a long engagement.'

She's visibly relieved.

Beneath my skin is a hot wave of irritation. Why can't she just congratulate me? Why must she treat my happiness like a scab to be picked at? So many of the decisions I've made have been ruled by the loyalty I have to her; I attended university locally because she needed me. After graduating, I didn't take a job in another city so I could remain close by. And later, when Luke asked me to travel the world with him, I turned him down because I couldn't abandon her the way my father did.

Mum's brow furrows. 'Does Luke know you're engaged?'

The mention of Luke catches me off guard, and I feel a stab of foreboding. How many of his messages and calls have I ignored since we met in Bellflower Park? But Henry's right, I don't want to lead Luke on. He's putting down roots in England and I can't be a part of it. Maybe once Henry and I are married, I'll fall back into a friendship with Luke. Maybe he'll become the same brotherly figure to me as he is to Ivy. I'm not losing Luke, not really.

'He doesn't.'

'How do you think he'll take it?'

I pick up my mug so I have something to do with my hands. 'Fine. We're friends. And anyone who cares about me will be happy that I'm happy,' I say pointedly.

She swallows and nods. 'You're right.' She brushes imaginary lint from her jumpsuit without meeting my eye. 'I just always thought that you and Luke would . . .'

So did I.

The ring on my finger suddenly feels too tight.

Behind us, shoes scuff against the tile floor. My head snaps round so fast it hurts. Henry is standing in the entrance to the living room, an enormous bouquet of flowers in each hand. Shit. How much of that did he hear? I spring to my feet. The walk around the sofa to greet him is the longest of my life. My palms are clammy with panic as I kiss him, trying to recall the entire conversation, worrying I've said something that could hurt Henry. Especially when he's already sensitive about Luke.

Mum gets up from the sofa to introduce herself. 'I'm Rebecca,' she says, and I'm surprised because she's Becky to everyone else. Maybe she thinks Rebecca is more middle class. Not that it matters when the person you're trying to impress has seen you curled up in the foetal position, chunks of vomit drying in your hair. 'It's nice to meet you, Henry.'

Confusion flickers briefly across his face, but he recovers quickly, leaning in and kissing both cheeks. 'Yes, nice to meet you.' He presents her with a bouquet. 'For you.'

She thanks him and we dawdle awkwardly in the living-room entrance for a moment before Henry suggests we sit down. I still can't tell how much of the conversation he overheard. Mum congratulates us both, her smile strained. Maybe one of the reasons she's struggling with this so much is because she's had me at her beck and call my whole life. Now though, my priorities are shifting, and I have everything she never did at my fingertips.

In the kitchen, I take the flowers Henry bought and put them in water. As I do I wonder, for the millionth time since I accepted Henry's proposal, how Ivy will react when she hears the news. We aren't talking, but she and Henry know the same people. Will she be hurt I didn't break my silence and reach out? Or will she feel stupid for thinking Henry and I would only ever be a brief fling? Will she feel the sharp bite of jealousy when Amira is my maid of honour? I'm deep in thought when Henry appears behind me.

'Can you call The Salt Block,' he says, pausing to kiss my neck, 'and amend our reservation for two, to three. I've invited your mother to join us at the restaurant.'

'Why?' I turn to face him, with a knot of unease in my chest. I don't want my mother to join us. The Salt Block is the kind of restaurant that has a dozen pieces of cutlery laid out around shiny bone china plates. But there's more to my hesitance then worrying whether my mother will know which piece of cutlery to use. It's the fear that she might somehow sabotage my relationship the way she's sabotaged all of hers.

'Zara . . .' Henry's mouth is set in a determined smile. 'We've just announced to your mother that we're engaged, and I think she's very much looking forward to celebrating with us.'

'Yes, very much.' Mum appears in the kitchen doorway, a lilt of mocking in her tone.

I look between the two of them and can't find a way out of this. 'Sure,' I say, 'I'll call them now.'

The restaurant is all thick linen tablecloths and chandeliers and dark wood, and waiters in tailored suits. Mum's eyes are wide as she browses the menu. I'm not sure which she finds more intimidating: the prices or the food. I don't think she's ever been to a place that serves 'parsnip foam' and 'puréed garlic' and 'dehydrated strawberries'. But then, before Henry, neither had I.

My mother brushes her palm against the tablecloth and looks perturbed. Probably because the material is better quality than her jumpsuit. She's uncomfortable, just as I knew she would be. I felt the same way on that first, spontaneous date with Henry, when he took me to the restaurant down by the weir and I discovered the napkins were better quality than the thin summer dress I wore. This evening, though, I am wearing a slinky midi dress in brick-red that Henry bought for me this Christmas. It's silky and soft and by a designer I'd never heard of.

After we order, we fall into clumsy silence. I wish Henry hadn't invited my mother. This dinner was meant to be just for me and him, so that I could decompress after telling Mum about our engagement. Now, I am on tenterhooks, hoping she doesn't do something to embarrass me. At the moment, she seems fine, sober and composed, but this is how it always goes. She's fine . . . until she isn't. We talk about how lovely the decor is and manage three whole minutes of discussion about how the Bath Christmas Market was wonderful, but the month-long surge of tourists made it impossible to travel across the city.

'So, have you told your dad about your engagement?' Mum asks out of the blue. Her nonchalance doesn't fool me, I can see from the hard edge in her expression that she's been dying to know.

'We have.'

'And?' Her eyes narrow; she isn't happy we told him first.

'And he congratulated us,' I say, adding at her expectant expression, 'and though he'd love to have dinner with us sometime, Polly's had another baby and they're too busy at the moment.'

'Lovely, another grandchild for Rupert and his wife,' she says bitterly. Mum has a morbid fascination with my father's new life, even though hearing how happy and settled he is without her is like sticking her hand directly onto a hot stove.

Absorbing the tension, Henry sweeps in with his smoothing-over charm and says, 'We made the call to Rupert this morning, but it was especially important to us to tell you in person, Rebecca.'

This, at least, eases the furrow from her brow. She offers Henry a smile and says, 'Zara mentioned you want a long engagement.'

'Fairly. A year or two.' He reaches across the table and takes my left hand. The ring is breathtaking. I love the way the light hits the emerald. Though I can't tell anyone it reminds me of Ivy's eyes.

'Is a year considered a long engagement?' she queries.

He squeezes my hand. 'Every day I spend not being married to her feels long.'

I still can't believe after years of wanting and waiting and hoping, I'm engaged. Only seven months ago, I was knee-deep in planning other people's perfect day and now I have my own to think about. I wake up every morning to my ring gleaming expensively on my nightstand. Then I roll over and look at Henry's smooth, freckled, sleeping back, and I'm relieved I'm getting somewhere, that my life is moving forward faster than I imagined, and finally in the right direction.

'How's Ivy?' asks Mum. 'I saw Luke the other day, he was on his way to a funeral. You didn't mention her cousin had passed away.'

The cold, clammy horror of that night seeps beneath my skin. I close my eyes against the visceral image of Roman's swollen, toothless mouth. I slip my shaking hand from Henry's and shove it beneath the table before my mother can see.

'This has become terribly morbid, ladies,' says Henry in a mock-sombre voice. 'We should be celebrating.'

Mum looks like she wants to push the subject but decides against it, pasting on a cordial smile. 'You're right.'

'Excellent.' He beckons a waiter.

While they talk, Mum leans forward and says quietly to me, 'Are you OK?'

I nod, even though I'm not.

'Sure?' she probes.

I sigh. 'Yes. Can you please just be normal and happy for me for *one* night?' I say hotly, hoping she'll drop it.

The waiter leaves and Henry starts up a conversation with Mum about her work at the school. I don't listen. I'm picturing Ivy and Luke standing together at the funeral, his arm curled around her waist, pulling her close at her victim's graveside. I'm not surprised her friendship with Luke has continued without me. They're close. But I'm the bridge that connects them. Or I used to be. It's not comfortable to search inward, to turn a flashlight on feelings I wish would stay in the dark, but when I do, I see it is coiled, ugly jealousy that, in my absence, a chasm hasn't opened between them, as it has between *us*.

Maybe it would if Luke knew what she was capable of. I considered sharing the still images from the security footage with him, but that would mean admitting to Luke that Henry was concealing evidence. If, on seeing evidence that Ivy killed her cousin, Luke demanded we hand it over to the police, Henry would face criminal charges for perverting the course of justice. So, not believing she's a danger to Luke, I decided I wouldn't risk telling him or anyone else.

Then the waiter reappears with three glasses and a bottle of champagne. Mum's eyes widen, not with the usual delight at the prospect of free alcohol, but with unease. 'Oh, none for me.'

'We hear your daughter is engaged. You must raise a glass!' exclaims the waiter. 'On the house!'

Henry looks apologetically at me.

I've never seen my mum this reluctant to drink. Maybe she really is turning a corner. I am opening my mouth to tell her she doesn't need to toast with champagne when she says, 'Of course.' And I can't help the twist of disappointment that she didn't turn it down and ask for something non-alcoholic.

The champagne is poured. We toast. We drink our drinks.

The night wears on and as it does, I realise my mother is slurring her words. She's only had two glasses. She gets louder and sloppier.

People around us are noticing. She leaves the table to use the toilet. It's her sixth trip in less than an hour. I lean into Henry and say, 'Shall we get the bill?'

'We haven't had dessert.' Then he spots someone across the restaurant that he knows and excuses himself to speak to them.

I drain my glass, trying to stifle the rising feeling of dread when my mother returns and flops into her chair. I seize her wrist to get her attention. It takes her a couple of seconds to focus on me.

'Are you drunk?'

'No,' she barks, causing a woman at a neighbouring table to stare. 'Don't be so bloody stupid. Why are you so bloody stupid?'

She's drunk. Of course she is. I need to get her out of here as soon as possible. I cast around for Henry but he's deep in conversation with the couple, whom I don't know.

Mum reaches for her glass of water but knocks it over. It spills across the table and soaks the linen tablecloth. She swears loudly. I'm dabbing at the water with a napkin when she surges to her feet, pushing her chair back.

'Mum,' I say through gritted teeth. 'Sit down. Please, just—'

She sways, gripping a fistful of tablecloth to steady herself. Then her eyes roll back, and she is falling, dragging the tablecloth with her. Crockery shatters as it hits the ground. Open-mouthed bystanders push to their feet. I run around the table and fall to my knees beside her unconscious body.

Chapter Twenty-Nine

It's almost midday by the time Mum gingerly emerges from the spare bedroom. Her black jumpsuit is crumpled and her skin is sallow, but she's finger-combed her hair, which only hours before was stuck to her face in damp-sweat clumps.

Henry and I have been sitting at the dining-room table for a while now, waiting, my hands clasped tightly in front of me. Mum hovers awkwardly; for once, she seems suitably ashamed of herself.

'Take a seat,' I say, glad my voice doesn't waver. I'm nervous and livid but grateful that Henry is by my side. Mum dithers like a contrary child before folding herself into the chair opposite. 'I got you some water and some pills,' I tell her, nodding towards them.

The silence is fraught and feels endless until finally, she says, 'What happened last night?'

I laugh. I can't help it. It's the same script as always. She's rehashing those old familiar lines, claiming she can't remember a single thing from the night before. This time at least, she hasn't tried to act as if nothing happened, making me doubt myself, question whether her drunken antics were as bad as they seemed, or if they even happened at all.

Mum slams her glass down onto the table. 'Stop laughing. Stop laughing right now.'

I bring my hand to my mouth to stifle the biting, hollow sound.

'I'm sorry,' I say, finally recovering. 'But are you really going to pretend you don't know what you did?'

Her eyes are wild and searching. 'I don't remember.'

'Stop it.'

'I don't remember. I—'

'You drank yourself into oblivion.'

She shakes her head. 'No. I haven't had a drink in months.'

'Don't treat me like an idiot. You had champagne last night. We all did.'

Caught out, she flushes. 'Well, yes, but it was only the one.'

'*Two.*'

She frowns, as though trying to recall. 'That's not enough for me to—'

'To collapse? To cause a scene? To black out in a restaurant?'

The staff wanted to phone for an ambulance, but Henry convinced them we'd take her home and look after her. She was just drunk. Again.

'I don't know what happened,' she says. 'Two glasses of champagne aren't enough to get me in such a state.'

I scoop her handbag up from beneath my chair and dump it on the table between us. She reaches for it, but I snatch it back and pull out the silver hip flask that stinks of paint-stripping vodka. She stares at it, mouth agape. 'That's not mine.'

'STOP LYING,' I shriek, bubbling over.

She lifts her chin indignantly, but her bottom lip quivers. 'Don't yell at me, Zara.'

'DON'T GIVE ME A REASON TO YELL AT YOU, THEN!'

'I brought you up better than this.'

I am blistering with rage as I stare incredulously at my mother. She didn't bring me up. I brought myself up. In fact, I looked after us both.

Henry lays a soothing hand on my arm. 'Zara. Rebecca doesn't need our anger. She needs our help.'

I take several deep breaths. He's right. We have a plan. Everything is going to be OK. Henry's hand slips beneath the table and rests on my thigh, the weight of it reassuring.

'I don't remember the flask,' says Mum quietly. 'I don't remember anything.'

'But isn't that the point?' I lean forward and keep my voice feather soft. 'Mum, you need help.'

'How dare you?' She flicks her chin up, dignified now, defiant. 'I only drank the champagne because you told me to be happy for you, to be normal.'

I feel a stab of guilt because I *did* say those things. I glance at Henry. He sees my fear and he shakes his head. 'No one forced you to have a drink, did they?' he asks firmly, but fairly.

She swallows. 'No . . . but I don't need *help*,' she insists again. 'I have a job. A house.'

'You have a problem,' I say.

'I'm not going to one of those groups, sitting in a circle like some sad sap. I'm a grown adult. I'm not going. I'm—'

'Mum.' I catch her wrist just as she pushes her chair back to leave. She stills. I take another deep breath, this one for courage. The weight of what I have to say sits like a concrete block in my gut. 'Mum, if you don't get some help, I can't see you anymore. I can't keep worrying about you. I have my own life now. And I deserve to be happy. I won't let you take that from me. I can't.'

Silence, at first. The kind of dark, lingering silence that follows a devastation: a tsunami, a forest fire, an earthquake. And in the whorl of that silence, my mother digests what I'm saying and scrutinises me to see if I'm serious. I am and she knows it.

'I see,' she says.

'There's a place in Scotland. They can help you. Here . . .'

I pull up the website on my phone and hand it to her. Henry showed it to me late last night, after we put her to bed. He said he'd done some research into rehab facilities after meeting my mother because he knew from the very start that he was in this for the long haul. God, I'd never loved him as much as I did in that moment. He had a carefully thought-out plan of action, and he was going to help me execute it. I wasn't alone anymore.

'I can't afford this,' she says, sliding the phone back to me across the table.

I glance at Henry, and he nods, encouraging me to lay it all out.

'Henry has very generously, very kindly, offered to cover the cost.'

She shakes her head vehemently. 'No. Absolutely not. No.'

'Mum.' I clasp her hand too tightly in mine and look very seriously into her eyes. 'Mum, please, don't make me walk away from you like Dad did.'

I didn't want to say it, but what choice did I have? It's a line so manipulative, so calculated and cold, that it might make even Ivy blush. But it works.

One month later, Mum is in Scotland.

Chapter Thirty

When I told people I was taking a career break, I joked about becoming a 1950s housewife. Now, as I browse the supermarket shelves for something nice to make for dinner, the gap between me and the Stepford Housewife I said I'd never be – the one who spends her time cooking and cleaning and making sure she's wearing lipstick before her bread-winning other half returns home – is laughably small. Ivy would hate who I am now. She'd never spend a morning browsing recipes online and then beetling along to the shops to fetch ingredients, all in the name of whiling away an afternoon over a stove. But I'm content in my life and the choices I'm making. Is Ivy happy in hers? I wouldn't know, not anymore. She hasn't updated her socials in months. Maybe she's ascended. She's so busy living her extraordinary, glittering life that she doesn't need to spend time posting about it to prove she has one.

I miss her.

This thought comes out of nowhere. And just like a pothole in the road, I swerve to avoid it.

It's the first week of April and all the little Easter decorations line the shop walls. Mum has been at the clinic in Scotland since January, and we weren't allowed to have direct contact for the first three months. But now I'd like to send her an Easter care package. I'm just dropping a candle into my basket when I see Hazel coming towards me. She's with a man who I assume is her fiancé.

'It's been so long,' she says, coming close and pulling me into a hug. When I sent the email to my clients informing them I was leaving Hillington Wedding Planners, Hazel was upset. I felt so guilty, but Henry reminded me we were doing this for us. For our future children.

'Great to finally meet you,' I say to her fiancé. He's tall with a friendly smile.

'You too,' he says. Something flashes across his face, but it's gone before I can place it. I wonder if he's upset that I quit before their wedding.

Hazel squeezes his arm. 'Can you grab the sourdough? I'll meet you in the bakery.'

As he disappears down the aisle, I turn to Hazel. 'How's your wedding planning going?'

She shrugs. 'On the back burner for now. Hillington handed me over to your replacement, Margot. She was really nice but . . . I don't know, it wasn't quite right.'

'I'm sorry.'

'Oh, no, don't be. It'll work itself out. I was so surprised you left, though, you seemed really happy.'

'I was. It's just . . .' I wonder how honest I can be with her. She isn't a friend exactly, but she could be. I like her. 'As much as I loved my job, it was demanding, long hours, lots of travel. It's difficult to raise children when both of you have all-consuming careers.'

She claps a hand over her mouth. 'Oh, my God, you're pregnant?'

'No. Well, not yet,' I admit. She looks relieved, though I'm not sure why since I'm no longer in charge of planning her events.

'So, if you're not pregnant . . .'

She's confused because most people don't have the means to pre-emptively leave a career for a baby that doesn't yet exist.

'I'm engaged,' I offer, as though it explains everything.

There is a slight pause before she says, 'Congratulations!' But she looks puzzled.

'I need time off to plan the wedding,' I elaborate.

'You're getting married?' She smiles but it doesn't reach her eyes. 'How long have you been together?'

I don't want to tell her it's just shy of nine months, because even though it feels like I've known Henry a lifetime, it doesn't seem long to other people.

'Ages,' I say. 'I'm so happy. Really happy.'

'That's great,' she enthuses, grin fixed.

We lapse into silence. I kick myself for not better explaining why leaving Hillington is the right decision: I'm not nearly as stressed, which increases our chances of conceiving when we're ready; I have lots of time to plan the wedding; and, most importantly, I see much more of Henry.

'If I wasn't working, I'd end up eating ice cream and watching Netflix all day. I can't imagine being unemployed,' she says, then. It isn't meant snidely, that's not who Hazel is, but the word 'unemployed' nettles. Her eyes widen excitedly, like she's struck by an idea she thinks is brilliant. 'Now you've got so much free time on your hands, you should come to my dance studio. Business is hectic but I'm sure I can squeeze you in.'

'That sounds great,' I say, and find myself adding, 'but, actually, I'm starting up my own wedding-planning business. Freelance. I have more creative control and my hours are as flexible as I want them to be.'

My brain is screaming for me to shut up even as my mouth keeps moving, but now that I've said it, I realise how much I want it to be true. Because the days have started blurring, monotonously.

'Perfect!' Hazel raves. 'Are you taking clients now? I'd love your help with the wedding. It really hasn't been the same without you. I mean, no pressure, but why don't you give me your number?'

I type it into her phone, excited and horrified all at once. Maybe I *could* start my own wedding-planning business. I have time, and Henry even suggested it. This could be the perfect opportunity. I'm remembering Luke casually mentioning he could picture me with my own company and insisting I was smart enough to do it, telling me I could do anything I wanted.

As I leave Hazel and head to the checkout, I am feeling bouncy with possibility. I can't wait to get home and tell Henry that Hazel will be my first client. I'm at the till, loading the shopping onto the conveyer belt when I see her: the dark-haired woman.

She is standing in front of the magazine rack by the door, but she isn't browsing them, she is watching me. Our eyes meet. The sharp shock of seeing her again hits my bloodstream like adrenaline. She has been tailing me for months. I'm certain. But why? Who is she? The urge to know suddenly eclipses everything else. I abandon my shopping, causing the woman behind the till to call, 'Excuse me? Excuse me?' and I march towards the dark-haired stranger.

She is dressed in thick black tights and a woollen coat the colour of icing sugar. She is all wild dark curls and wide doe eyes. She is classically beautiful and older than I thought – late forties maybe – and is now frozen mid-reach for a magazine. And even though I don't know who she is, she still feels familiar.

'Who are you?' I say with more malice than intended.

She blinks, the spell apparently broken. Then she turns and flees.

I chase her.

She's swallowed up by the crowd and I'm running up against backs and hands and shopping trolleys. People swear and swerve to avoid me. Breathless, I tumble out into the open. It's raining and the frigid air cuts like a knife. The dark-haired woman is halfway across the car park by now.

Ping-ponging off parked cars, I yell at her to stop. She doesn't.

As we near the road, I hear the roar of vehicles, the hiss of wheels on tarmac, like waves on a beach. I'm soaking wet and out of breath, but I don't slow. I need to know who she is and why she's stalking me. We're out of the car park and onto the slim strip of pavement before the A-road. She'll be forced to stop. She must or—

She doesn't.

The dark-haired woman dashes into the rows of speeding cars. My stomach plummets, expecting to hear the bone-breaking thud of her body across a bonnet. Unthinkingly, I race after her, following her into the surging traffic, sure that once she's reached the other side, I'll never see her again.

But I'm not as fast or as deft or as lucky. Car horns blare. Brakes squeal. I throw myself back onto the pavement. A van whooshes past, so close the breeze whips my hair across my face. My heart hammers.

The dark-haired woman is gone.

Chapter Thirty-One

An hour after the pursuit, once I am calm enough to drive, I arrive home. Henry isn't back yet. I go upstairs and take a shower to warm up, to scrub this horrible day off me. My jeans are torn, and my clothes are filthy and soaked. I consider calling the police, but how can I? She was at the Halloween party, most likely following me, watching me. What if the police question her in relation to her stalking, and she tells them anything and everything she saw that night? What if she saw all four of us standing around Roman after he was killed? Henry will be caught in a lie, and Ivy will be charged with murder.

When Henry comes home, he knows I'm rattled. Reluctantly, I tell him about the dark-haired woman. He makes me a hot tea and listens patiently to my garbled, rambling story.

'But she hasn't hurt you?' he asks.

'No. She's never even tried to talk to me.'

He nods slowly. Even though he's trying very hard not to show it, it's obvious he thinks this is trivial, and I feel stupid for almost getting myself killed in pursuit of answers. But I have to know why she won't leave me alone. 'Do you know her?' I ask. 'Curly dark hair; slim – late forties. Attractive.'

'Why do you think I know her?'

'She was at the Halloween party.'

'Lots of people came. Friends of friends of friends.'

But I'm not ready to give up on this theory. 'Could she be an ex, maybe?'

'An older woman?' His grin is lascivious and teasing. 'I like them young and impressionable.' He tries to kiss me, but I pull back. 'She isn't an ex of mine.' Then that grin is back, he lowers his voice conspiratorially. 'Don't forget, all my exes are buried beneath the patio.'

My smile is weak.

He moves closer and brushes damp hair from my face. 'If it's any consolation, Zara, I don't think she's dangerous. She ran from you today. Sounds like she's more scared of you than you are of her.'

'She isn't a spider lurking in a high corner, she's a person and she wants something from me.'

'You say she's been following you for months, but you've never mentioned her. If you were really afraid, wouldn't you have told me?'

But I'd already told Ivy and been mocked. Then after we were broken into, I told the police, and they were unconcerned. I came away from each interaction feeling melodramatic. If the police didn't take me seriously, why should anyone else?

'Perhaps she's as infatuated with you as I am,' Henry purrs, leaning close. This time, when he swoops down to kiss me, I let him. 'Send her to me, I'll tell her I'm not willing to share you,' he says against my lips. 'At least, not until I get bored.' Then his mouth is on mine again, hands sliding beneath my jumper. Soon, we are horizontal on the sofa. He grinds against me, and I kiss him, even though I'm not really in the mood. He fumbles for the button of his jeans and when I don't rush to take off my clothes, too, he frowns.

'Sorry,' I say, sitting up. 'It's been a strange day.'

'It's fine,' he says and laces his fingers through mine. 'Let's do something fun tonight, take your mind off it.'

We go to a dark, pricey gin bar with smooth music and red-velvet seats, the entrance to which is at the back of a flower shop. We're greeted by a ruggedly handsome man with intense eyes, whose gaze lingers on my face before he plucks a flower from a barrel and hands it to me with a smile. It's a deep, rich burgundy colour, round and large, made up of small, arrowhead petals in concentric circles.

'What is it?' I ask.

'Black dahlia,' he says in a French purr.

When we're seated, I browse the menu. Liking gin is a personality trait, one I haven't adopted. I tell this to Henry who says, 'That's because you've only ever drunk cheap gin.'

He orders us two Wylde Flower cocktails. It tastes as all gin does: bitter and citrussy and like handfuls of pine needles and earth. I wrinkle my nose but drink it, because, after Henry's comment about cheap gin I don't want him to think I'm unrefined and classless. I've barely finished my first cocktail before the second arrives, followed by three shots of straight gin served in ice-cold glasses.

In the toilets, I think of *her*: of that first night we met when she whirled into the girl's bathroom and sang to me. I think of the university nights that followed: sticky clubs, drenched in sweat and songs. The two of us dancing in a throng of grinding bodies to dirty drum and bass, pressed close against each other, her head thrown back, coloured lights spinning across her skin. When we were young and reckless and wild and carefree. When our future was uncertain and all our own. Anything we wanted it to be.

I tell Henry I want to go home. I can't drink any more. But a third cocktail arrives, and he says, 'We came here to enjoy ourselves.' Then he catches my chin between his thumb and forefinger and tilts my face up to his. I'm drunk and his face blurs, I can't tell if he's angry or turned on. He kisses me roughly, nipping my bottom lip.

By the time we leave the bar, I'm hot and dizzy and stumbling alongside him to the taxi, the black dahlia tucked inside my bag. Even as we speed away from the gin bar, the sickly-sweet perfume of gardenias and roses and lavender clings to my nose. I breathe through my mouth, but my gin-breath makes me gag. Henry laughs as he helps me from the taxi to the house.

I fall up the stairs to the bedroom. He is behind me, shepherding me up, up, up and herding me to our bed. I flop down onto it, but he grabs my wrist and yanks me to my feet, catching my yelp of surprise in his mouth and swallowing it down. Then his hands are on me, all over me, everywhere. Soon, I am naked. And he is naked, too. I smell her Wild Bluebell perfume and missing her becomes a physical pain. The room dips in and out of focus. Henry is between my legs.

The room whirls like a merry-go-round and black dahlias bloom across my vision.

The next morning, I am sick. My throat is sore, and my head is a nest of livid, stinging bees. I grip the rim of the toilet seat for strength. I can't remember the last time I was this hungover. Maybe Ivy's twenty-sixth birthday party, when we wore matching sequin dresses and got so drunk, we fell asleep in our glitter-filled bathtub?

Downstairs, Henry cooks breakfast. The smell of frying bacon makes me sick again. After brushing my teeth twice and taking a shower, I wince at my reflection in the en suite mirror. God, I look awful. My skin is so dry, like the gin has sucked the moisture from it. Then I spot the inky smudges on my neck. I lean into the mirror for a better look and raise my hand to my throat. There are three of them, evenly spaced. Bruises. I reach for memories of last night but it's like grasping at smoke.

I take my phone and scroll though my camera roll for clues. There are several photos of cocktails garnished with edible flowers and some blurry selfies I took with Henry. A web page is open. Apparently, I googled black dahlia – I have a vague memory of being handed one at the bar's entrance – and the first result says that they symbolise betrayal and death.

Dressed in some comfy, cream loungewear, I join Henry in the kitchen, but I can't stomach his breakfast offering and instead opt for dry toast.

'If I'd known you couldn't handle your gin, I'd have saved my money and dropped you off at a park with cans of Strongbow,' he says. It feels like a pointed dig at our different upbringings. I should challenge him, but the more pressing issue is how I got the marks on my neck.

'I'm covered in bruises,' I say.

He barely glances up from constructing his breakfast sandwich. 'You are?'

'Yes, look.'

He sighs, but when he sees them, he grins. He wraps a hand gently around my neck and I realise the inky smudges were caused by his fingers. 'Yes, from when I fucked you last night.' Then he kisses me hard.

'I don't remember,' I say.

'Drinking and forgetting?' He shakes his head in mock-reproval and kisses my cheek fondly. 'Maybe you're more like your mother than you think.'

Chapter Thirty-Two

Amira's house is up on a hill, barely a fifteen-minute walk into Bath. It's a Georgian semi-detached with off-street parking and three bedrooms. When we lived in the flat, I was hideously jealous of Amira's house. Now, though, as we sit in her kitchen, the French doors thrown wide on this glorious spring day, the jealousy is gone. Now, I have a home of my own, with Henry. It's grander than anything I grew up in, anything I thought I'd ever live in. Grander even than Amira's house. Not that it matters, not really. But I like that I have something worthy of envy.

Her baby son, Orion, is sleeping in the wicker bassinette beside her. I gaze down at him, already in love. He has Amira's long, long lashes and dark hair. I breathe in that calming, new-baby smell which I wish could be bottled like perfume.

'He's so gorgeous,' I tell her.

She smiles. 'If only I could say the same about me.'

'Stop it. You're gorgeous, too.'

'I'm shattered and bloated.'

'You've had a baby! I think you're doing it wrong if you're not exhausted.' There are deep-purple shadows beneath her eyes. Her hair, which has always been bouncy and thick, hangs limp and dull. Not that I'd ever tell her that. Even so, she's holding herself differently. She seems wiser and more confident, like a proper grown-up. She has it all now, everything we're told we need to be content adults.

'How's your mum?' asks Amira. 'Is she enjoying her cruise?'

'She is.' This is the story we decided to tell people. Mum isn't in rehab; she is sunning herself on the deck of an expensive ship somewhere exotic. In all honesty, I'm not sure how she is, though we've had updates from the centre and they're apparently really happy with her progress. When she comes home, I'm going to take her for afternoon tea and shopping. Bond like normal mothers and daughters. Henry will never truly know the gift he's given me and my mum; it's a chance at the relationship we should have had. I sip my tea, my stomach knotting with guilt because he is so good to me and we're in another fight. I'm ruining everything.

'And your wedding plans?' she asks, and even though I can't be honest, I'm grateful she's interested because so many of my friends who are parents can only hold a conversation about their children.

'Great,' I tell her, hoping my nose won't grow and my tongue won't turn black. 'Absolutely brilliant.'

'Good! You've set a date now, then?'

I reach for a biscuit and cram it into my mouth in a bid for time. 'Not yet. The venue we want has a waiting list,' I lie, because I don't want her to know how bad things between Henry and me have become since the drunken night of sex that I don't remember. 'Everything else is done though.'

She's watching me too closely. 'Is everything OK?'

'Yes, of course. I just . . .' I trail off and look into the steam rising from my mug. 'Henry and I had a bit of a tiff.'

'What about?'

I have to be careful what I say because it was more than a tiff – it was an all-out row.

'A couple of weeks ago, I came home, and Henry was waiting for me with a bottle of champagne. He'd lit a hundred candles and covered the floor in rose petals.'

'Sounds *terrible*,' she says in mock-horror.

I'm pretty sure my smile has all the strength of vending-machine coffee.

'He blindfolded me and took me upstairs.' I glance nervously at Orion and even though he can't understand what we're saying, I'm glad he's sleeping soundly. 'We had sex.'

She leans forward, suddenly excited now that we've got to the juicy centre of this story. 'Good sex?'

'Great sex.' I'm caught in a sticky, humid sex memory that makes me turn crimson. I remember the scratch of his newly grown stubble against the inside of my thigh and the feel of him sliding into me.

Amira sips her tea and waits for me to go on.

I hesitate, wondering if sharing this is a good idea. What if it changes her opinion of Henry forever? I don't want her to dislike him. Things between Henry and me will go back to normal. We'll have the wedding. My friends can't hate my husband. But I need to know if I'm overreacting. I take a deep breath.

'When it was over, though . . . he said he'd filmed it. But I was blindfolded, so I didn't see his phone propped up on the bedside table. I had no idea.'

I lick my dry lips, waiting for her reaction. Ivy would tell me what he did was wrong. But then, she hates Henry. Amira is impartial.

'So you come home, your fiancé has gone all out, flowers, candles, champagne, you have *great* sex and this is bad because . . .'

I bite my lip, unsure. 'Because he didn't tell me he was filming it.'

'Did you ask him to delete it?'

'Yes.'

'And did he?'

'Well, yes, he did.'

'So why are you fighting?'

Regret slithers in. Clearly, I was too quick to anger with Henry. Too close-minded, too 'boring', like he said.

'I've never been filmed before.'

Her eyes widen. '*Really?*'

'Have you and Nathan?' I ask, disbelieving.

'Yes. A couple of times. *Years* ago. It was exciting.' I stare at her, reassessing how well I know her. Ivy once joked that Amira is so organised and efficient, sex with her would come with a clipboard, schedule and feedback form. 'God, I miss sex,' she laments. 'We haven't done it in months. There's a stage in pregnancy where you have all these raging hormones, and you just want to do it all the time, but then the bump gets in the way and sex becomes awkward. Nathan was worried about poking the baby.'

I snort. 'Did you tell him that was wishful thinking?'

She grins, then she's suddenly serious. 'And now the baby's here, we're both exhausted. I'd kill for just one night of rampant, dirty sex. You're so lucky.'

Now, I feel like a complete moron for being so dramatic.

'It's fine. Like I said, just a tiff.'

'Good, I'm glad,' she says. 'Hopefully you'll be pregnant soon, too, then our children can play together . . . unless you leave it too long and there are years between them.'

'Oh, I mean . . .'

'Don't worry. We plan to have at least three. I'm sure your child will be close in age to at least one of ours.' She smiles and leans over Orion's bassinette. 'You'll catch up eventually.'

I'm glad she's so wrapped up in her son in this moment that she can't see my face. I thought I was the only one who felt like we were in a lifelong race, but maybe I'm not. And I wonder if it's normal to love your friends dearly, whilst feeling trapped in a competition with them at the same time. Still, I'm glad I spoke to her about Henry. Now I can go home and apologise to him, because they're both right – we are consenting adults who had great, consensual sex and he was only trying to do something adventurous and romantic. I just hope I can make it up to him, that he won't end things with me for being ungrateful and ridiculous. If he did, I'd be back at the starting line.

'Do you want another tea?' she asks, already getting up to boil the kettle.

'Please.' While she's making it, I check my phone.

My heart stops as I see the email. I glance up. Amira is leaning against the counter, tapping and scrolling on her own phone.

'Did you just send me an email?' I ask her.

She frowns. 'I'm standing right here, why would I email you?'

I stare at the message, this time in my personal inbox, from HTH@gmail.com. It's just over six months since the last one. Since I told whoever it is to leave me alone. It seems, though, they aren't quite done with me yet.

Be careful. Look after yourself.

Chapter Thirty-Three

On the kitchen island, my coffee cup has left two overlapping rings which makes me think of my elbow hooked through Ivy's.

Without Henry or work as a distraction, and with Amira still in her baby bubble, I've had lots of time with my thoughts. Thoughts that keep drifting back to her. Maybe I didn't sever that gossamer thread after all.

Because I miss you, Ivy.

Even after what she's done. I miss the us we were before. The pain of it is acute. Usually, I don't let myself wallow like this, but I have buckets of time now. Today isn't special. It isn't a birthday or anniversary. It's just another day that she isn't with me. I imagined the loss of her would become easier over time. It hasn't. There are just more gaps where she should be. More events she should be part of. More things I see or do that I wish I could share with her. Today, for whatever reason, the pain of her absence is a hot iron jammed up into my ribs. An agony I can't ignore. To soothe the burn, I check her socials for a glimpse into the life she's leading without me. She hasn't posted a single thing since late November. It's mid-May now. I'm starting to worry.

I stare down at those overlapping coffee rings, of my arm hooked through hers, and I *long* to call her. But the way we left things was so final. That day, six months ago outside Holt House, I slammed a door shut on us. One I didn't think I'd want to open again, and now I might, I'm not sure how.

But you killed someone, Ivy.

I try to picture it. Picture her coming at Roman, arms outstretched, palms flat as she shoves hard against his chest. The feel of his thin shirt, and the warmth of his body against her hands. Then the cold air that rushed in as he toppled away, over the Juliet balcony. Did she look him in the eyes before he plummeted? Was he terrified? Did he know he was going to die? Then, those few soaring, blistering seconds of silence before he hit the pavement. The wet, bone-crunching finality of his demise at her hands. To think about it makes me sick.

Fury whiplashes through me. Fury at her for ruining both our lives with one, wicked act. Fury at myself for missing her still. I know I shouldn't ever want to see her again. But I do. She was a sister to me. Blood. And I don't know how to be me without her.

But in all these months, she hasn't reached out. I told myself I didn't want her to. That isn't the truth. Perhaps I could've made contact sooner, but every time I was tempted I remembered it was *her* who took an instant and irrational dislike to Henry, it was *her* who kept secrets, it was *her* who killed Roman to protect that secret.

It was you, Ivy, who slowly poisoned us.

I tip my mug up so that the last few drops of coffee spill onto the counter and erase the rings. Then I take a cloth and wipe it clean.

It's Friday. Henry is working. I am not. I talked to him about starting up the wedding-planning business sooner rather than later, but he said start-ups take time and money, and with our wedding to plan first, it would make more sense to wait until after we are married. He's right. But I can't get any further with the wedding until Henry has time off work to look at venues. I don't want to be one of those brides who makes all the decisions alone. I want us to choose things together.

Bored and at a loose end, I decide to go for a walk around Bellflower Park in the sunshine. It's one of those bright spring mornings when the air is warm, and the blue sky is dotted with white cotton-wool clouds.

Everywhere I look, there are mothers chasing after chubby toddlers, or enjoying a coffee with other mothers, watching their little ones play. I want so desperately to be one of them. I want to grow a life. I want to feel that eclipsing love that mothers boast about.

There's a loneliness that makes my breath hitch, because there's no one in my life I can confide in. With my own mother in Scotland, and Ivy gone, and Amira busy with the baby, I'm left with only a handful of friends, who feel more like acquaintances. Even if Amira had time to see me, I know now that she thinks she's competing in a race with me where she is the gold medallist and I am forever trailing behind – so I can't admit to her that I've barely left the starting line.

I'm wondering what to do with the rest of my day when I see her. The dark-haired woman is paying for drinks at the little outdoor café. She doesn't see me, though. Adrenaline pumping hot through my veins, I hover close to a gaggle of women bouncing babies on their hips, and watch her. She's wearing a daffodil-yellow midi dress with brown sandals and a wicker bag, her dark hair tied loosely in a plait. Once again, I'm struck by her beauty. And her familiarity. How do I know her? How does she know me? I still suspect she is my anonymous emailer. I don't know how she got my personal address but then, I don't know how she's been keeping tabs on me for all these months, either. On this occasion, though, I'm convinced she has no idea I'm here. Watching her.

Takeaway cup in hand, she turns and heads across the courtyard. There's an easy, sloping grace to her as she weaves between tables. Not wanting to lose sight of her, I follow. The urge to pounce is a nettle beneath my skin that I will myself not to scratch. I won't chase, not after last time. I will be calm. I will approach. I will ask her who she is and what she wants and why she's been following me.

I stumble. I stop.

She isn't alone.

My stalker joins a second dark-haired woman who sits at a little white patio table with her back to me. It was nerve-wracking enough confronting the woman who's been following me when I thought she was by herself. Knowing she has company means I'm outnumbered, and it makes me want to back away. But when will I have another opportunity to confront her again?

Ivy wouldn't hesitate.

She would march up to them both.

She would be witty and cutting and in control.

And though I'm not her, it's as though I am bottling some of her confidence; I spritz it on like expensive perfume and approach.

My stalker sees me first. Her doe eyes widen and she freezes, cup halfway to mouth. In all the months she's been following me, I have never been this close to her. There are delicate laughter lines around her eyes and a few strands of silver streaming through her hair.

Sensing me behind her, the second dark-haired woman twists in her seat.

Our eyes meet.

And . . .

No.

My breath catches.

I blink, unable to believe it.

'Zara,' Ivy whispers, as stunned as I am.

Heart slamming, mind whirring I say, 'You know her?'

Ivy doesn't answer. She just stares up at me with a mixture of surprise and fear and something else, an aching, longing relief. The ghost of which echoes within me, dulled only by the discovery that she's somehow involved with my dark-haired stalker. Ivy is thin, thinner than the last time I saw her, and wearing a green polka-dot dress which must be new. Her hair, which once flowed to her waist, now hangs just below her shoulders. No wonder I didn't recognise her from the back. Looking at her makes my eyes sting, as though I'm gazing into the whorl of the sun, so I shift my focus to the woman who's been haunting me, scrambling for my script.

'Why have you been stalking me?' I practically spit at her.

The couple at the next table stop mid-conversation and tune in, the way people do when their favourite TV drama blinks to life on screen.

'It's not what you think,' Ivy says, answering for her, keeping her voice low and even, wanting me to do the same.

I don't. 'Did you hire her to follow me? Are you working together? Jesus, Ivy, what twisted game are you playing?'

'It's not always about you, Zara.'

'Why?' I shoot back, stung. 'Because it's about you?'

'Yes,' she hisses, rising gracefully from her chair.

I breathe in her Wild Bluebell perfume. With it comes a thousand memories. I clear my throat.

'You really expect me to believe it's a coincidence that you just happen to be enjoying a coffee with the woman who's been following me for months? Did you put her up to this? *Why* would you put her up to this? What is wrong with you?'

'I didn't ask her to follow you.'

'You're lying. Jesus Christ, Ivy, Henry was right – you're a psychopath.'

She flinches, as though I've burnt her with the end of a lit cigarette. The dark-haired woman comes around the table and rests a soothing hand on Ivy's arm. A look passes between them. A silent question Ivy answers with a nod.

Frustrated, I snipe at the woman, 'Who *are* you?'

She glances nervously at Ivy. I wait, my patience stretching far too thin, on the verge of snapping when Ivy sighs wearily and says, 'This is Jennifer.'

'Jennifer?'

Ivy lifts her chin, in that heartbreakingly familiar way. 'My mother.'

Chapter Thirty-Four

Mother?

I am stunned into a stomach-churning silence. In the park, we're surrounded by the rise and fall of conversation, the giddy squeal of playing children, but it's dulled by the fierce rushing of blood through my ears.

'No.' I shake my head. 'I knew your mother. I knew Odette...'

Not to mention that her mother is dead.

'Odette wasn't my mother.'

Shock ricochets through me. 'What? What do you mean? Of course Odette was your mother!'

'Not my birth mother,' she says.

I'm stunned into silence. I stare at her, trying to work out if she's lying, but I can tell from her face she's serious.

'But *how*?' My mind turns over and over. 'There are photographs of Odette when she was pregnant with you. I've seen them.'

'They were staged. After all the miscarriages, she told the family she was going to a fertility clinic in Sweden. Months later, when she came back, she had a baby. No one suspected the truth. That I wasn't hers.'

'So, you're telling me you're adopted? That's the big secret?'

Indignation creeps across her cheeks and out of her mouth on a furious breath. 'You don't get to drop back into my life after six months, like a fucking summer cold, and interrogate me, Zara.'

'I don't believe you,' I say. 'How did you even find out? How can you be sure this woman is your mother?' But as I take in the dark-haired woman again, I can see the resemblance. They share the same lustrous hair and high cheekbones, the same ski-slope nose and petite frame. She looks like Ivy. Or, more accurately, Ivy looks like her. *That's* why she feels so familiar. The dark-haired woman – Jennifer – is Ivy twenty years from now.

'She isn't lying to you,' says Jennifer, speaking for the first time. Her voice is clear and musical, like a spoon chinking against the side of a wine glass before a toast. 'Ivy's father and I, we got together while he was married.' She blushes shamefacedly.

I glance at Ivy. A penchant for married men. Like mother, like daughter. It's not a kind thought, but it's one that creeps up on me anyway.

'I thought we were in love,' says Jennifer. 'But when I told Hugo I was pregnant, he ended our affair. I was angry and hurt . . .' The colour in her cheeks deepens. 'I went to Odette.'

And I always thought Ivy's lust for revenge came from her father. Two for two. It seems she and her birth mother share far more than just their looks.

'I couldn't afford to raise a baby alone. I was barely twenty-one, working as a waitress. I didn't have any close family. No one to help. But I couldn't go through with an abortion either.'

I glance at Ivy, checking for a reaction. Though she's carefully guarding her feelings, I see a flash of pain, quicksilver, like lightning across a darkening sky. It will hurt her to know she was an inconvenience even before she was born.

'Odette was kind,' says Jennifer. 'Kinder than I deserved. She told me about the failed pregnancies and how desperately she wanted a child. She asked if I'd be willing to keep the pregnancy a secret and hand the baby over to her and Hugo when it arrived. I didn't think Hugo would agree, but apparently he'd do anything to save his marriage.'

Only to make sure he didn't lose his hold on the Holt family fortune, I thought, cynically. If Odette mattered to him at all, Hugo would never have cheated on her. I look at Ivy, wondering if she can now see her father in this uglier, more exposing light. I want to talk to her about it, I have so many questions, but stop myself because that's not the relationship we have anymore. Pushing the sting of that truth aside, I fire another question at Jennifer.

'But why did you agree to just hand her over?'

Her fingers knot nervously in her necklace. 'I had a deal with the Holts. They gave me financial compensation and—'

'You sold them your baby?' I ask, disgusted.

'You, of all people, should know how hard it is for a mother to raise a child alone,' Ivy says archly, and though it's deserved, her reference to my alcoholic mother wounds.

'I wasn't ready to be a mother, Odette was,' Jennifer continues. 'The Holts had money. I knew my baby would be taken care of. In exchange, I couldn't talk about the pregnancy, I couldn't have contact with Ivy or the Holts, ever again.'

'Why?'

'My grandfather didn't believe in adoption,' Ivy says bitterly. 'The Holt name, the bloodline, it was everything to him.'

'And why have you been following me all these months?' I ask Jennifer, because while this is all very compelling, I don't see what it has to do with me.

'With Odette and Alfred gone, and Hugo cut off from the family, there was nothing left to stop me reaching out to Ivy. But I worried she'd reject me or resent me for giving her up. So, I kept to myself and I observed. I knew the two of you were . . . very close.' She sighs. 'I thought I could talk to you, Zara, before approaching Ivy. Thought maybe you could help soften the news. But every time I tried to speak to you, I lost my nerve.'

'What changed?'

'That day in the supermarket when I ran,' she says, and I think of the blaring car horn, the whoosh of traffic as it narrowly missed me. 'You were nearly hit. It was getting dangerous. I realised then how unfair it was to drag you into all this. So I resolved to speak to my daughter myself.'

There's a sliver of relief as some of the puzzle pieces fall into place. Still, I don't have the entire picture. 'And why the cryptic emails?'

She frowns. 'Emails?'

'Yes, anonymous emails. The ones you've been sending me.'

'I . . .' She opens and closes her mouth, dark brows knitted together in confusion. 'I haven't sent you any emails.'

This throws me because I was *sure* the emails were linked to my dark-haired stalker – to Jennifer – but she looks genuinely perplexed. There's no reason for her to lie about being the sender.

In my desperation to tie off loose ends, to put this all to bed, I fire the question at Ivy. 'Have you?'

She snorts. 'I'd never cower behind an anonymous email, Zara. I thought you knew me better than that.'

'Given all the secrets and lies, I don't think I know you at all.'

I don't mean for what I've said to hurt her, but I see that it has. It hurts me, too. The sudden wave of wanting things between us to go back to the way they were hits me viscerally, making my chest ache and my eyes water.

'You girls need to talk,' Jennifer says softly. 'I'll go.'

'No,' Ivy protests. 'Don't. Just—'

'Talk to her, Ivy,' Jennifer insists, and another look passes between them. Then she is gone, walking across the park in the May sunshine.

It's only now, as I stand feet apart from Ivy, that I really take her in; the shadows like faded bruises beneath her eyes, the jut of her collarbones and the sharp angle of her cheeks. She's different. The change isn't simply her shorter hair or how thin and tired she looks. It's something else. Something haunted and earnest. The news of her heritage and the lie she's unknowingly lived has taken its toll.

'I'm sorry I wasn't there when you found out about Jennifer,' I say sincerely. 'I wish I had been.'

She looks past me, uncomfortable, caught between not wanting to leave and wanting to get as far away as possible.

'You really had no idea?' I ask.

She shakes her head.

'I can't believe no one knew. I mean, you never did look like your blonde, blue-eyed mother, but you were so obviously Hugo's daughter, I never doubted they were your parents. I suppose no one did.'

She presses her lips together and looks away. A prickle of unease whispers across my skin; she is hiding something. I can tell. I . . . the realisation arrives like a slap to the face.

'Roman,' I breathe, and her eyes snap to mine. 'He knew. This is the secret he was holding over you.'

I think of her grandfather's will. The inheritance that was meant only for Alfred's blood-related grandchildren. How she shrugged it off as a technicality with the aim of making sure Theo, her aunt's stepson, didn't receive anything because he isn't a Holt. But *she* isn't a Holt either.

Not in the way it mattered to Alfred. That clause in his will was never about Theo. It was about her.

'The papers you burned in the fire the morning after Roman died – what were they?'

'I'm not doing this,' she says. Then she spins on her heel, snatches up her bag hanging on the back of the chair, and walks quickly across the park. I follow, rushing forward to step in her path. We're off to the side, halfway between the outdoor café and the path that loops around the park, away from the crowds.

'After everything, after years of us, can't you finally be honest with me, Ivy? Don't you owe me that?'

'No.'

She tries to move around me, but I snatch her wrist. 'Ivy. *Please.*'

Her eyes search my face. Can she feel it, too, in the bright red of our blood, that although we aren't sisters, we are family? She does. Because then she sighs softly, and I feel her uncoil just a little.

'Odette wrote me a letter every year on my birthday,' she says. 'She loved to write. Apparently, she wrote letters to my father, too. The summer before I went to university, she found out he'd started things up with Jennifer again and poured her heart out onto paper, ranting about how she'd taken him back over and over, raised a child that wasn't hers, tried to love him.' She shrugs. 'After she died, my grandfather found the letter. He must've told my aunt and she told Roman. That's why he let himself into Holt House that night.'

'The break-in?'

She nods.

I take a second to digest this. 'So, Alfred found the letter and knew you weren't a Holt?'

'Yes. That's why he cut me off after my mother's death. He didn't want any more to do with me.'

She looks away, her eyes filling with unshed tears. In turn, each member of her family has rejected her. Jennifer and Odette, Hugo and Alfred – not one of them loved her enough to hold on to her.

'Roman found the letter in our grandfather's study, it was the reason he broke in that night. That room was the only one in Holt House I left untouched when we moved in. I wasn't ready to sift through his things. If I'd known about the letter . . .' She closes her eyes. 'Roman wanted everything. He had his half of our grandfather's money, but he wanted all of it *and* the house.'

'Why not just leave everything to Roman in the first place, though?' I frowned. 'If he was the only blood-related grandchild, why bother with that wording in the will?'

'Because although Alfred knew the truth about my parentage, my grandmother didn't. He didn't want to upset her with all the unpleasantness about my father and Jennifer. So he was careful not to give anything away – while still cutting me out.' She takes a deep breath to steady the tremor in her voice, then goes on. 'The day you walked in on me and Roman arguing in the kitchen, he'd told me about this letter. He said he had it and if I didn't hand everything over to him, he'd take it to the lawyers.'

'Why not go to the lawyers right away?'

'He was hoping I'd leave immediately so he could save himself the legal battle and the possible attention from the newspapers, too.'

I wish I could press pause on this conversation and give myself a second to catch up, to compose myself. I sift through all that I've been told, trying to sort truth from lies, like I'm panning for gold.

'But why did he bring the letter to the party?'

'I told him I didn't believe he had any such letter.'

'So you manipulated him into proving he did.' Of course. Ivy Holt is made of flesh and bone. Sex and confidence. Manipulation and cunning. 'And that's what you were burning in the fireplace? How do you know that was an original and not a copy? What if there are more copies?'

'It doesn't matter. Original letter or copy, they aren't any good to him now that he's dead.'

I blanch at her cool detachment.

'Don't look at me like that, Zara. He was cruel. He always was. After his mother's suicide, he inherited everything she had and he didn't even shed a tear at her funeral. I mean, her death was ruled a suicide, but my father always wondered . . .'

The hairs on the back of my neck stand to attention. I always assumed her aunt was taken by cancer like her mother. I didn't know she killed herself, or that there was a possibility that her son killed her for the inheritance. I'm wary that this is a means to justify her pushing her cousin that night. People care a lot less about a dead villain than a dead hero.

'Anyway,' she says, 'Roman did as I asked and brought that letter to the party, all too eagerly. He wanted to prove to me it was real and, I suspect, watch my face as I read it. He wanted me to know why it was so easy for the woman I knew as my mother to refuse treatment when the cancer came back. And there it was, in black and white. In her own words. Her husband was cheating again and she had a daughter who wasn't even hers. I was just a reminder that the supposed love of her life treated her no better than a used carton of milk. And I wasn't worth staying alive for. So, she left me here, alone.'

'You weren't alone,' I say gently, remembering how I often thought of us as strays that had been rehomed together. 'You had me.'

'And now I don't.'

I reach for her, but she pulls back. The rejection smarts so I lash out. 'Whose fault is that?'

'Henry's!'

'Henry has *nothing* to do with this,' I shout, angry that she can't let this ridiculous and irrational hatred of him go. I step close to her and lower my voice. 'You killed your cousin to keep your inheritance. *You're* the reason we're ruined.'

'Is that really what you believe?'

'It's what I know.'

She laughs. 'What do you want me to say, Zara? That I pushed Roman from that ledge and watched, unfeeling, as his head split open like a watermelon on the concrete below?' She tilts her face up to mine. I feel her breath on my mouth. 'That I'd have pushed you, too, if you'd come between me and my inheritance?'

I am barely breathing. 'Would you?'

She is pained, she makes a noise of frustration or hurt, and spins away from me.

'I love you.' She throws her arms wide. 'You know how much I

223

love you, but now I'm wondering if you even know me at all.' She sounds wild and furious. 'I thought Luke had gotten through to you, but obviously not.'

I don't like that she has brought him up. He isn't hers to bring up. 'I'm not as gullible as Luke.'

She laughs again, shaking her head. 'You have no idea, do you?' she taunts. 'You're blind to it all, Zara. Blind to Henry, blind to Luke.'

'What has Luke got to do with any of this?'

'He's been paying your mother's rent for years.' She's pausing for effect, giving this statement the stage it deserves, but I am an unwilling audience.

'What? Luke doesn't pay for—'

'How do you think a drunk, part-time receptionist could possibly afford to live in that house alone? She can't. Luke has been paying so you wouldn't have to. He's been buying your freedom for years.'

The denial surges like a wave. 'No.'

'*Yes*,' she hisses. 'And you gave him up. Luke who is kind and loyal and good. *So* good. You gave him up, and for what? Children that don't even exist. That aren't born. That you don't even know you can have. That bullshit, white-picket-fence life you've forced yourself to want because you never had it. You gave him up for nothing and what do you have now?'

I am breathing hard as my world tilts off its axis. I am overwhelmed with revelations and unearthed secrets. It's too much. Too much.

'I gave him up for you too, Ivy. I couldn't go travelling with him and leave you in that overpriced little flat all alone.'

'I never asked you *not* to go with him. Not once. You just assumed, Zara. I didn't like any of the men you half-heartedly dated in the interludes between Luke, because *you* didn't like them either. Luke was who you wanted. And I wanted that for you. No matter what. But instead, you have a prison. A gilded cage. With *him*.' There's so much venom in her voice, I recoil.

'I have a relationship with someone I love. Not that I'd expect you to know anything about being in love, Ivy.'

'I know what it is to love someone from afar who will never love you back, because they're so wrapped up in someone else.'

It's as though the words have been ripped from her. She's trembling and wide-eyed, surprised by her own confession.

For a moment, I am speechless. Breathless. All these years we've played the How Much Do You Love Me? game. But now, I realise, it was never a game to her. Henry was right.

'Is this why you hate Henry? Because he has me and you don't? You can't possibly still hate him after everything he's done. He rescued us from that party after you killed Roman. He had video footage of you doing it, which he destroyed to protect you. Photographs, all gone – to protect you.'

She laughs again and the mocking arrogance of it sets my teeth on edge.

'Grainy stills. Clever angles. That's all it was. And you're more naive than I thought if you believe, even for a second, that he destroyed any of it.'

Riled, I spit, 'You killed Roman to protect your money and you targeted Henry, and you ruined us. *You.*'

'*I* didn't ruin us. *He* did—'

'My God, Ivy, you can't take responsibility for any of it, can you?'

'Stop it.'

'You're wild and reckless and selfish.'

'*Stop!*'

'Henry is chivalrous and kind and thoughtful and—'

'He raped me.'

Silence.

Her fingers fly to her lips, as if checking that she's really just said that. Her words are neon-lit, suspended in the warm spring air between us, and she is as shocked by them as I am. But she can't petal-pluck them free and stuff them back into her mouth now.

Indignation and disbelief and roiling rage rise up and out of my mouth on a breath. 'No.' There's a writhing, twisting, burning fear in my chest. 'He didn't.'

Her eyes fill with tears. For a second, I think she is going to apologise for the lie, but she swallows and swallows and holds my gaze and says, 'I'm sorry, Zara. He did. At a party months ago.' Her gaze holds mine captive. 'He raped me.'

Chapter Thirty-Five

I don't go home straight away. I can't. So I walk instead. I walk without knowing where I am going. I am struggling to breathe beneath the landslide of revelations. It's possible Ivy is lying about the rape so that I leave Henry and come back to her. Maybe her accusation is a tactic to detract from Roman's death. Now I know the secret he had over her, there's a solid motive for his murder. Maybe this is an attempt to discredit Henry, in case he has held on to evidence and gives it to the police. This could all be an elaborate game. A manipulation. She is so used to wrapping people around her little finger that when they prove to be immune to her magic, she loses her temper. Just as I imagine she did with Roman as he brandished her mother's letter in her face, threatening to expose her and take everything.

But what if she's telling the truth?

If she is, I've been sharing a bed with a rapist. Having sex with the man who assaulted my best friend. Wanting children with a monster. If she is telling the truth, my life with Henry has been a lie and my future nothing more than smoke. If she's telling the truth, I pointlessly burned our friendship and watched as it turned to ash, leaving her alone in the soot to cope with a brutal wound that will never truly heal.

I should've asked her questions. When *exactly* it happened. Where. But a numbness spread from my heart to my lips and for the longest time, I couldn't speak. Could only stare, my ribs cracking and splintering beneath the heavy, crushing weight of despair. I felt faint. I *had* to get away. I stumbled out of the park, and now I am wandering aimlessly, regretting that I didn't stay to ask more questions.

It's late afternoon, the air is cooler and I'm shivering. How do I confront Henry? What if she's lying, and he is so devastated that I'd even entertain this accusation that he ends things right there and then, and throws me out of the house? Where will I go? Do I seriously think my fiancé might be a sex offender?

I think of the sex I can't remember that night Henry took me to the gin bar. And the sex he filmed without my knowledge. But that's different. We're a couple. It was consensual. Drunk sex and a penchant for sex tapes doesn't make him a rapist.

I need to find more information. I go through her socials again. She posted almost every day after I left, then, in late November, she stopped. I take a closer look at her last post. In it, she is at a party, wearing a black velvet dress and holding up a glass of champagne. She's smiling widely into the camera, her arm slung around the waist of a pretty blonde. In the background, there is a fuchsia-pink sofa and a gold bar cart. It's a house I don't recognise, filled with people I don't know. I stare harder at the image, searching for clues, sure there must be one. I think about calling her, but I can't. I'm still processing our last conversation and after I left her in the park like that, I'm not sure she'd even answer.

I check my calendar to see where I was on the date she last posted. When that brings up nothing of note, I scroll back through my messages to Henry. My stomach lurches. My messages are desperate, pleading for him to return home. It was the evening Henry and I fought, after I confronted him about his missing ex. He'd been furious that I'd dared to mention Tabitha, angrier still when I told him it was Ivy who'd let me in on the rumour. He'd snarled, 'Why is that fucking bitch *still* meddling in our relationship?' before storming out of the house. And he hadn't come back until late afternoon the next day, claiming he'd been at a party with Jonty. Henry doesn't have social media. But Jonty does. I take a look, scrolling through photographs, all the way back to November.

Oh, my God.

I go hot and cold, clammy with dread.

I'm staring at a photograph of Jonty and Henry and two other men I don't know. Henry is handsome in his jeans and shirt, his dark hair artfully pushed back from his face. Jonty and Henry and the two strangers are laughing and drinking. And sitting on a fuchsia-pink sofa. The one in the background of her last post. She was at the same party that night. Is that when he did it?

I must speak to Henry. If he's guilty, he's not going to tell me. The clues will be in what he doesn't say. I'll find the truth in his initial reaction. He won't expect Ivy and me to have talked. He'll be caught off guard.

Gathering my nerve, I call a taxi and head to Henry's office.

Henrietta's House is marketed as a family-run affair, which conjures images of a small team conducting business from a cosy Victorian house, with vintage gold frames on the walls and thick tapestry curtains. It isn't. The Frith & Sons offices are located in the centre of Bath, in a building that is all large windows, corrugated ceilings and concrete floors. It's vast and industrial and modern. The receptionist lets me up to the top floor to see Henry. He's between meetings. I've visited a couple of times, usually with boxes of doughnuts from the bakery down the street, stopping for a chat with the team. Today, though, I am steely and determined as I march down the corridor. I feel eyes on me as I pass rows of desks, catch glimpses of people taking out their headphones and turning to watch as I barge into Henry's glass-walled office.

He is sitting behind his desk, tapping away at his computer. He looks up and smiles, all straight white teeth and dimples, his hazel eyes crinkling at their corners, happy to see me.

I'm remembering the first time we had sex. How he tilted my face up to his outside my bedroom door and told me I was beautiful. How he *asked* if he could kiss me. How I'd smiled at the gentleness of him. That man can't be the same person who Ivy is claiming raped her.

Seeing my face, the wretched devastation, Henry pushes to his feet and then he's in front of me, taking me gently by the shoulders. 'What's wrong?' he's asking. 'What's happened?'

I look down at his hands. Ones that stroke my hair back from my face in the morning to kiss me as I wake. Hands that chop vegetables in the kitchen then slide playfully beneath my top. Hands that reach for me at night. The same hands that she claims held her down as he forced himself into her. But that isn't the man I know. It isn't. It can't be.

'What is it?' he demands.

I don't know how to ask what I need to ask. I don't know if I want the answer. It would be so easy to ignore her accusation, to never mention it to Henry, to put it in a box at the back of my mind and leave it to collect dust while I walk merrily into a piece of happily ever after with the man I love. Only, it isn't easy, is it? I will think about it every minute of every day, wondering if what she said was true.

'Did you rape Ivy?' I blurt. I watch. I wait for the gravity of my question to hit him. I don't blink in case I miss a second of his reaction. He pales and pulls back. He swallows. I watch his Adam's apple bob in his throat. Then his expression hardens, as though carved from stone. 'What did you just say?'

'Did you rape Ivy?' I ask again, louder this time, slower.

Silence.

A clock somewhere in the room ticks off the seconds. I am tense and still, muscles coiled in trepidation.

'No,' he says finally, the word as sharp and decisive as a knife.

I wait for the relief to come, treacle-thick and twice as sweet. It doesn't. 'No' isn't good enough. He was at a party with her all those months ago and he failed to mention it. *Why* wouldn't he mention it?

'She said you raped her, Henry.'

He glances up, his gaze travelling over my right shoulder. We have an audience. He moves swiftly to the interior floor-to-ceiling windows and closes the blinds so we're safe from the prying eyes of his employees. Once he draws the last one, he doesn't turn immediately. The tension rises, hot and thick and difficult to breathe. And when he finally swivels so we are face to face, he is apoplectic. Fury emanates from him like heat from a bonfire. His hand grips the edge of his bookcase, as though using it to hold himself still.

'She's lying.' His voice is tightly controlled, but I hear the light, dangerous lilt beneath.

I choose my next words carefully because I'm sure if I don't, I'll be met with a snakebite. 'When was the last time you saw her?'

His gaze slides away from my face and he clenches his teeth. 'Don't know.'

'*Think.*'

His expression darkens. 'I can't remember.'

It's not usually this early on in a show that the magician pulls the rabbit out of the hat, but we are both agitated, ready for it to be over, so I say, 'You saw her at a party, the last Saturday in November.'

'That's very specific.'

'I've seen the photographs on Jonty's socials. Why didn't you tell me you saw Ivy at the party the night we fought?'

It's as if I'm looking at a pressure gauge and the needle is trembling precariously at the farthest edge of the dial. At any moment, he could blow. I'm glad I've confronted him here, in the office. I can't decide whether his anger at being asked if he sexually assaulted her is a sign that he did or didn't do it. I suppose if such a serious allegation was levelled at me and I knew I was innocent, I'd be incensed too. But I don't like this side of Henry, how quick he is to anger. I've only glimpsed it a couple of times and almost always when Ivy's involved. It's true, there is a fine line between love and obsession, but can't the same be said of hatred and obsession too? Does he hate her so much that he's become infatuated? Infatuated enough to have her, no matter the cost?

Henry steps towards me and I stumble back into his desk. At first, he's surprised, then his face falls and I feel his pain. 'You're scared of me.'

'Wary,' I say, voice trembling. 'I've just been told my fiancé raped my best friend.'

'Stop saying that. It's an ugly word.'

'Ugly word? Henry, it's a hideous thing to do.'

'AND I DIDN'T DO IT!' he bellows.

The silence that follows is absolute. Everyone outside this room will have heard. I want to run from him, from it all, but I stand my ground. I need him to admit what he's done. 'If you ever loved me, Henry, even for one moment, just tell me the truth.'

His eyes flit around my face for a few seconds before he makes a decision. 'Fine.' He marches forward and snatches his phone up from his desk. A moment later, he is thrusting it at me. It takes me a few seconds to realise what I'm looking at: a conversation between her and Henry.

The tears come immediately as I read and scroll and read and scroll. Hot, fat tears of humiliation and betrayal. Messages from her to him, flirting and propositioning and asking him to meet her at a hotel.

'I didn't want to tell you because I knew how hurt you'd be. She meant so much to you,' he says softly and his sudden switch in demeanour brings with it a release in pressure that makes my ears ring. 'She'd been hassling me for a while when you admitted it was her who told you the rumour about Tabitha. I was enraged. I'd warned her to leave us alone and she was still interfering. I'd had enough. After weeks of her begging to see me, I agreed. I went to the party with Jonty. She offered herself to me on a plate and I rejected her. Demanded she stay away and if she didn't, I promised I'd take the footage from the masked ball to the police. But that's it. That's all.' He shakes his head. 'I never thought she'd take the rejection or the threat so badly that she'd concoct such a twisted narrative.'

But why did she want to sleep with him in the first place? She *hates* Henry. Or maybe she doesn't. Maybe she always wanted him, which is why she was so disparaging that first time she realised he was interested in me – the daughter of a drunk part-time receptionist from Trowbridge – over her. Over well-bred, well-educated, well-monied Ivy Holt.

'She lied about not being involved in Roman's murder,' Henry says. 'She lied about my fiancée being missing. This is what Ivy Holt does, she deceives, and you're letting her do it again. I've never lied to you, Zara. Never. Why is it you're so ready to believe the worst in me?'

'I'm not.'

Oh, but I am.

'It's as though you don't really believe you deserve happiness, so you let this woman poison you against any opportunity you have to take it.'

Without even meaning to, I am nodding.

'Your father left. He was a fool to leave. But, Zara, from the moment we met, I planned to stay.'

I struggle to stop myself from unravelling completely in his office. Ivy is the scissors that have been snip, snip, snipping at the seams of my life until I am scraps on the floor she can scoop up and lock away. Not anymore.

'But if you continue down this path, believing whatever terrible thing it is you hear about me, we aren't going to work,' he says earnestly, and my stomach slides to the floor; I love him, I don't want to lose him. 'I want to be with someone who sees the best in me, not digs for the worst without question.'

Later that night, when Henry is sleeping, I creep from the bed and down the stairs. She picks up on the third ring. 'Zara? Are you alright? Do you—'

'Listen to me,' I seethe quietly, cutting her off. 'Don't you ever come near me or Henry or anyone else I love ever again, you twisted, lying psychopath.'

'Zara, I didn't lie—'

'He showed me the messages,' I interrupt again.

Silence. She is caught, and she knows it. 'Yes, I did send those messages but—'

'I finally understand why Odette chose death over being a mother to you. Lucky her, Ivy, at least she's rid of you now.'

Then I hang up and I join my fiancé in our bed.

Chapter Thirty-Six

The next couple of weeks go by in a whirr of trying to make it up to Henry and hating Ivy in equal measure. I cook for him most nights, and while I chop carrots or sauté onions, I think about how her false accusation spits in the face of everyone who's ever been sexually assaulted. I slide into expensive silk lingerie and while Henry and I are halfway naked, I close my eyes against thoughts of her sending my fiancé lusty messages, wishing he was between her legs instead of mine.

Despite her attempts to destroy us, Henry and I are happy together.

Still, there are other things she said in Bellflower Park that I can't shrug off. Like the one about Luke paying my mother's rent. At this stage in her recovery, I am allowed a once-fortnightly call with her, for thirty minutes. But I don't risk asking her about the money in case it stunts her treatment at the clinic. I have tried to dismiss Ivy's claim as another lie. But why would she make that up? If I can't find a motive, then maybe this, at least, is true. To find out, I decide to visit Luke myself and ask.

When his older brother died, Luke inherited his house. He's never lived in it, choosing instead to rent it out while he travels. Now he's back, though, I can only assume that's where I'll find him.

Late afternoon, I knock. I'm nervous to see him again. The sky above is white and grey. It's drizzling. I pull my coat close and catch the woody, spicy scent of Henry's cologne. He doesn't know I'm here. He wouldn't be happy about it if he did.

The door opens.

Luke, tall and broad and stubbled, stands in front of me, wearing a white, ribbed jumper and a pair of faded blue jeans. In his hand is a beaten paperback, in his eyes is surprise that I'm here.

'Can I come in?'

We sit at the oak dining table and I wrap my hands around a mug of peppermint tea to warm them. I don't have time for small talk – Henry could be home soon and wondering where I am – so I cut right to it. 'Have you been paying my mother's rent?'

He stills. 'What?'

'Have you?'

He glances down.

I exhale. 'Why?'

'So you wouldn't have to,' he says, echoing what Ivy said exactly. So she *was* telling the truth about this, at least.

'Luke, I *never* expected you to give me or my family any financial help.' Guilt rushes through me. 'I didn't ask for this. How will I ever pay you back?'

'I didn't give something to get something. I did it because your mother was struggling and I knew it would fall to you to help her. It always has. Zara, you fought for so long to get out of that house, and even when the chance came with university, you stayed local, never wanting to stray too far. I didn't want you to end up back in that house with her, sacrificing your future to help pay her rent.'

The enormity of what he has done sits like oil on water, unable to sink in. He gained nothing by helping my mother all these years. If it wasn't for Ivy, I'd probably never have found out. It's not a jazz band and a hundred yellow roses, it's more. So much more. An emotion too big to name has sewn up my throat.

'How did you know—'

'Ivy told me.'

'Are you two back in contact?' he asks, seemingly surprised.

'Not really, no.'

He looks away. Opens his mouth. Closes it again.

'Zara, I don't know what exactly the two of you have fought about. I thought all the business with Roman was sorted after we talked.' He doesn't know about the still images Henry showed me. As much as I want to tell him, to smear her, I can't without admitting Henry concealed evidence from the police. So I bite my tongue. 'I never thought anything or anyone could come between you,' Luke says.

He's talking about Henry. What has she told Luke? She's probably tried to spread her poison there, too. Not that it would require much heavy lifting on her part. I suppose it was silly of me to think exes and new lovers could ever truly be friends.

'When did you and Ivy last speak?' he asks gently. I swallow at my parting words to her.

I finally understand why Odette chose death over being a mother to you. Lucky her, Ivy, at least she's rid of you now.

Shame seeps into my bones and knots my stomach. I can't believe I said that to her, and with so much venom, too. Yes, she tried to elicit an affair with my fiancé, and yes, when he rejected her, she accused him of the unthinkable. I haven't forgotten that. But what I said was so cruel. So cutting. I'm disgusted with myself. What would Luke say if he knew? Why hasn't she told him what I said? It would be the best kind of revenge.

'I don't want to talk about Ivy,' I say, firmly.

And even though he looks like he wants to say more, he nods once.

'I'll find a way to repay the money,' I promise, even though I have no idea how that will be possible without going to Henry to ask for help. Though admitting to Henry that my ex has been paying my mother's rent will only feed into his theory that Luke is still wildly in love with me, and since things are finally back on track, I don't want to ruin it now by telling him something I know will rattle him.

'I don't want it back. I don't even need it back.'

'Luke, I can't let you do this. I'll find a way. I don't have a job right now but—'

'What? *Why?*'

I try not to squirm under the scrutiny of his stare. 'I decided to make a change.' *Why* did I tell him I'm jobless? He's quiet, unsatisfied with my vague response and waiting for me to go on. 'Working for someone else, putting money in other people's pockets, it didn't make sense anymore.'

He smiles widely. 'So, you're starting your own wedding-planning business?'

'Eventually.' Luke frowns and I start to babble, regurgitating Henry's reason for *not* starting the business right now. 'Start-ups are a lot of work for little profit in the first few years. It just isn't a good time.'

'Well, yes,' he says, choosing his words carefully. 'But you're smart and capable, Zara . . . What's stopping you?'

Involuntarily, I glance down at my engagement ring. He does, too.

'Oh.' He clears his throat. 'Right. Of course. You're busy planning your own wedding. That makes sense.'

'I'm sorry I didn't tell you . . .'

'No, it's fine. Ivy mentioned it.'

I didn't realise she was aware of my engagement. Perhaps in the months we haven't spoken, she looked me up online or heard about it from friends of friends. Or maybe she saw the ring that day in Bellflower Park. I shouldn't be surprised she told Luke. After all, even without me, the two of them have remained close.

'Are you happy?' he asks.

'I am.'

He nods. I see a flicker of something – sadness maybe, or relief. 'We were both going to move on eventually, weren't we?'

'Yes,' I manage, even as my stomach twists at the thought of him with someone else. It's irrational and hypocritical, since I'm happily engaged. Still, imagining him with another woman, *permanently* with another woman, makes me feel as though something precious has been stolen from me and stuffed into another's back pocket. But Amira was right to encourage me to move on fast. This way, by the time Luke has fallen in love with someone else, I'll be married and maybe I'll be pregnant, too. By then, any leftover feelings I have towards him will be swept into the ocean of my happily-ever-after and drowned.

Before I leave, I nip to the bathroom. It's only when I'm washing my hands that I notice the tube of lipstick on the shelf next to the sink.

I pick it up. It's a very dark red. I feel a little sick. I wonder what she looks like, what her name is, how long they've been together. Long enough, I guess. I put the lipstick back and scan the room for any more clues about this woman, the one who has Luke stowed away in her back pocket. On the side of the bath, I find a necklace, a lone ruby on a long gold chain. I imagine the woman unclipping the necklace and discarding it before climbing into the hot bath with Luke. The two of them skin-to-skin. The necklace forgotten as his hands slide over her wet body. In the mirror I see myself, white-faced and miserable. I smile at myself. My reflection grimaces back at me.

I leave without saying goodbye.

Chapter Thirty-Seven

When I leave Luke's, I check my phone. There's an email from HTH@gmail.com.

You don't have to be alone.

This time, I'm not unnerved by the message. I'm comforted by it. It feels like it's written by a friend. Who though, I don't know. It isn't Ivy or Jennifer or Luke or Amira. Maybe it's me. Is it possible I'm writing them to myself without realising?

Henry rings, but I decline the call and turn off my phone. I'm restless, too agitated to talk to him. I drive around for a while, thinking about the lipstick in Luke's bathroom. The more I dwell, the more bothered I become. Why didn't he mention he was seeing someone? He could've told me, rather than have me stumble across her things in his bathroom. I don't like how riled I am by my ex dating someone new. This doesn't mean I don't love Henry. It doesn't mean I'm not happy with him. But Luke was my very first love, and up until last year, I clung to the possibility we'd end up together. First and last. It's not as though I feel I have some claim over him. Except that's exactly how I feel, which is ridiculous and petulant. I've never considered myself possessive, not like Ivy is.

I'm so distracted by Luke and his new lover, that I don't see the car in front coming to a stop. I grip the wheel. Slam on my brakes. I whip forward then snap back as my seatbelt locks. My car is millimetres from the other driver's red bumper. A near miss. I'm shaking all over. I can't go home to Henry like this, wound up like a violin string being yanked too tight.

I make a snap decision to drive into the town centre and see a film at the Little Theatre. It's a charming vintage-style cinema with plush velvet seats and gold wall sconces. I don't browse the film listings, I just buy a ticket for the next thing showing. It's cosy and quiet in here.

* * *

The film is nearly over. I'm not sure what I'm watching, and even with a gun to my head I couldn't tell you anything about it. From the laughter of those around me, I assume it's a comedy. Despite that, there are tears streaming down my face and an ache in my chest.

I have lost Luke. He is with someone else. Maybe that's why he's stopped globe-hopping and finally settled here. Because of her. Torturously, I wonder what's so special about this woman. Or, rather, what's so wrong with me that he never even considered living in the UK full-time while we were together.

Even though Luke moving on with someone else was inevitable, it's shaken me. After fifteen years of our on-again, off-again relationship, the permanent splintering of our lives in different directions was always going to be an adjustment.

Then there's Ivy.

I have lost her, too. But maybe that is for the best. Just because she was telling the truth about Luke paying my mother's rent, it doesn't mean she was telling the truth about anything else.

The film ends. Patrons file out. I don't. Then forty-five minutes later, the film blinks to life again and I stay to watch it a second time.

Hours later, I emerge, stepping out into the cold evening air. The drizzling rain from earlier is a torrent now. It's dark and I have no idea what time it is. When I turn my phone on, it buzzes incessantly, notifications streaming in. I have several missed calls from Henry and half a dozen messages, each more urgent than the last. I fumble to call him back when Jonty's name flashes on screen.

I answer.

'Zara? Thank God,' he says. 'Where are you?'

'In town. What's going on?'

He is somewhere loud and echoey. 'You need to come to the hospital.'

My stomach flips. 'Why?'

'It's Henry. He's been stabbed.'

Chapter Thirty-Eight

The sting of antiseptic hits me as I spill into the hospital. Jonty meets me in the foyer and walks me to Henry's room. It's the longest walk of my life, and I can't concentrate on a single thing Jonty is saying, even though I'm sure it's important.

Henry is sitting topless on the edge of a bed, a large, square gauze on his left side. He is ravaged and grey. His cream joggers are blood-splattered. It is this detail that makes it real and has my trembling hands flying to my mouth.

A nurse with wide hips is scribbling something onto a pad at Henry's bedside. She looks up, concerned, and clocks the ring on my left hand. 'He's been stitched up, but he'll be fine.' She smiles at Henry. 'Just needs to rest.'

I nod my thanks then turn to my fiancé. 'What happened?'

He glances at the nurse. 'I was mugged.'

'Mugged?' I say, aghast.

He nods.

'Where?'

'Mells.'

I frown. That's out by Wickerycombe, just over from Holt House. Mells is a friendly little village half an hour from Bath. It's all hanging baskets and horse paddocks. 'What were you doing there?'

'Jogging.'

This doesn't make any sense. Henry has routes near our house. He doesn't drive to another village to go for a run. I stare hard at him. 'Who did this?'

His gaze flicks to Jonty. 'A young lad. Didn't see his face.'

'What did he take?'

'Nothing. I refused to hand over my phone and keys. We scuffled. He got me and ran.'

Something isn't right. Jonty stuffs his hands into his pockets and says, 'I picked Henry up after it happened and brought him here.'

'Why didn't you just call an ambulance?' I ask Henry.

'Quicker for me to drive him,' says Jonty. 'He's going to be fine.'

Henry watches me, his expression stormy. I think of all those missed calls and my stomach swirls.

The nurse scoops up a metal tray that had been resting beside Henry, and gives me a small, sympathetic smile as she leaves.

'Where were you?' Henry asks darkly.

'I'll leave you to it,' says Jonty, making his exit.

'I was . . .'

I stumble into silence because how can I tell him that I spent late afternoon drinking tea with my ex, and then the entire evening in the cinema, while he was being mugged?

'I'm sorry. I turned my phone off. I had no idea,' I say, but the apology does nothing to assuage him. 'I met up with Amira and we decided to see a film. I forgot to turn my phone back on. I'm so sorry, I didn't think.'

'Amira?' he says, turning her name over in his mouth.

The silence is tense. It hangs between us like a noose that I am foolish enough to dip my head into. 'Yes, she needed an evening away from the baby so—'

His hand shoots out and he clutches my wrist. The sudden movement and the shock of contact makes me jump. 'Are you lying?'

'*No.*' I try to pull away, but he only tightens his grip. Pain shoots up my arm.

He blinks, then drops his gaze to his fingers digging into my skin and bone, and he lets go, as though he can't believe what he's just done. I rub my wrist, trying to soothe the ache.

'I'm sorry,' he whispers. Then he pinches the bridge of his nose between his thumb and forefinger, like he's trying to stave off a headache. 'I'm sorry. Of course you aren't lying.' When he looks at me again, he's remorseful and sheepish.

I feel guilty for lying. But how could I tell him I was with Luke? 'It's fine. I'm sorry I wasn't here for you.'

He tries to stand, then winces and clutches his side.

I rush forward, laying one hand on his bare chest and the other on his back to steady him. 'Do you need me to get someone?'

He shakes his head and grits his teeth. Slowly, he rights himself. I sit beside him on the clean white sheets and then pull a pillow, soft and thin with use, onto my lap.

I imagine him sprawled on a country lane in the wet and cold and dark, his blood mingling with rainwater and dirt as he fumbles for his phone, desperate and terrified, and the guilt curdles like sour milk in my gut. He's always been there for me, right from the start. And I failed him.

'I'm so sorry, Henry.' I hop off the bed and stand in front of him so that he can see how sincere my apology is. He pulls me close so I'm nestled between his knees. I cup his face and he rests his forehead against mine. All I can see are his hazel eyes. Moss and earth and autumn leaves. In this moment, I'm sure I don't need stone and steel and winter skies. Or light hitting water. We kiss, softly at first. Then harder as I imagine I could've lost him tonight. All thoughts of Ivy and Luke are blown from my mind like grains of sand.

'There's something I should tell you,' Henry murmurs against my mouth. I pull back but he keeps his hands, warm and reassuring, on my waist. I wait for him to go on. 'I wasn't mugged,' he confesses. 'I was attacked.'

He inhales deeply, as though what he's about to tell me is already exhausting him. At his tentative, grave expression, foreboding creeps icy fingers up my spine.

'It was Ivy. Ivy stabbed me.'

Chapter Thirty-Nine

Now

Rape accusations, stabbings. It was all becoming wildly unbelievable. Which makes sense, since not all of it was to be believed. Somebody was lying. As I sit here, being questioned about a murder, being interrogated for my involvement in it, the truth still isn't crystal clear. What I do know, is that if you put a frog in a scalding pan of water it will jump right out. But if you put a frog in a tepid pan and gradually increase the temperature, the frog won't notice. It will sit in that pan even as its skin blisters and bursts. It will boil alive. If I was the frog, Ivy, was it you or Henry who turned the dial?

Chapter Forty

Before

Henry tells me that the morning after Ivy and I saw each other in Bellflower Park, he woke to dozens of messages and missed calls from her. He thinks us seeing one another is the reason she started harassing him again. But I know it was the phone call I made that night, when I spat poison at her about Odette and her death. I whacked the hornets' nest, but it was Henry who got stung.

'I was determined to ignore her, but she wouldn't stop,' he says in the calm of our bedroom. We are back from the hospital. Only the soft glow of my bedside lamp lights the room. 'She came to my office yesterday and made a scene, ranting and raving, accusing me of turning you against her. Then she started shrieking about rape. I don't know if she believes her own lies or if she's trying to drive me out of business.'

Henry goes on to say that the only way he could make her leave quietly was to agree to meet her in Freshford that evening after work.

'I went there to warn her for the last time that if she didn't stay away from us, I'd go to the police about Roman's death. She lost it, started screaming that I'd ruined her life. Stolen you.' He scoffs. 'She threatened to tell the police I raped her.'

This surprises me. It's one thing to lie to me but to lie to the police, too? I keep quiet, not wanting to interrupt him.

'There was no reasoning with her,' he says. 'I told her as much, and when I tried to leave she attacked me. Throwing punches, shrieking. She was out of control. Feral.' He pushes his fingers back through his hair. 'I pushed her. She hit her head. I should never have reacted. Never.' His gaze slides to mine, trying to gauge my reaction.

I'm not thrilled he hurt her. It's not OK. But he knows that. I've experienced first-hand Ivy's violent outbursts, like the night we returned to Holt House after the masked ball and she lashed out. I take Henry's hand and squeeze it reassuringly. He exhales a sigh of relief. 'I panicked. I turned and started walking away. She came after me. I didn't even see the knife. It felt like a hard punch to the side. Then I saw the blood.'

I picture her getting up from the cold, wet ground. Humiliated and burning with rage as she glowers at his retreating back. Reaching into her pocket for the pen knife. Feeling the reassuring weight of it in her hand. Then she darts forward and swings into his path. In my mind, her hair is wild, *she* is wild, and terrifying but beautiful: a banshee from the pages of a myth, fuelled by hate and the overwhelming lust for revenge. She's amazed that the blade slides in so easily. It's not unlike cutting meat for a Sunday roast.

'Then what happened?' I ask.

'It's a blur. I was shocked. She was, too, as though she couldn't believe she'd actually done it. She ran.' He shakes his head. 'I should've seen it coming. I've been telling you for months she's dangerous. I mean, she killed her own cousin.'

And now she's tried to kill Henry. 'We need to call the police.'

'No,' he says swiftly. 'She'll tell them that I . . .' he's struggling to say the word, 'that I raped her.'

'But there's no evidence, because she's lying. However, there *is* evidence she stabbed you.'

'Yes, but there's also evidence that I pushed her.' He looks at his fists, clenching and unclenching them on the clean white sheets. 'I shouldn't have pushed her.'

'No, you shouldn't. But you wouldn't have done it if she hadn't been attacking you.'

'The police won't see it that way. I'm bigger. Stronger. They'll see a man who lured an attractive young woman to a rural country road and shoved her. God knows what else she'll claim happened.' There's a tremor of fear in his voice. 'I need to think about the business, Zara. I can't risk her dragging my family's name through the dirt in a messy public trial. Besides, she's mentally ill. It isn't a prison sentence she needs, it's psychiatric help.'

I've never thought of Ivy as mentally ill. Despite what she did to Roman and what she tried to do to Henry, the idea that she is deranged doesn't ring true. But maybe I am clinging to the vestiges of the woman I thought I knew. Of the friendship I thought we had.

'I'm exhausted,' says Henry. 'Can we just go to sleep?'

But he doesn't sleep. Not really. He is anxious, waking with a jolt, the bedsheets damp with sweat, twisted around his legs. In the morning, he talks about moving. 'I want to get out of Bath,' he tells me. 'Go somewhere new, where no one knows us and she can't follow.'

But the business is an anchor that holds him here.

Three weeks later, Jonty calls to ask if he can stay with us while his place is renovated. I gladly agree, hoping it will be a distraction for Henry. And it is. They go out to pubs and dinners and parties. The night terrors stop.

One evening, I am in the kitchen making dinner for the three of us. The boys are in the lounge, enjoying pre-dinner drinks. The sound of Henry's laughter makes me grateful Jonty is here.

I'm just putting the meat into the oven when Henry comes up behind me, winding his arms around my waist. His fingers move beneath my top. 'I want you.'

'We can't,' I whisper. 'Jonty is practically in the room with us.'

Henry laughs into my neck. 'He likes to listen. He'll probably come in and try to join us.' I think he's joking, but on more than one occasion since Jonty arrived, I've felt his eyes on me, lingering a little longer than is appropriate. It's flattering, I suppose, to capture the attention of someone so attractive. I still remember the way Ivy made him fall in love with her the night of the masquerade ball. 'You know,' he says, 'I think Jonty has a crush on you.'

I turn in Henry's embrace. 'Well, *I* have a crush on *you*.'

We kiss. It's heated and indulgent. When we break apart, I jump. Jonty is in the doorway, eyes trained on us both, lips curved into a crooked smile. 'Don't stop on my account.'

'I told you,' Henry calls to him without taking his eyes off me. His grin is mischievous. 'Not sharing.'

'Not *yet*,' jokes Jonty.

Chapter Forty-One

I am jolted awake by insistent banging. Henry throws the duvet back and climbs out of bed.

'Who the hell is that?' he mumbles, irritated to have been woken so abruptly. Six weeks ago, right after the stabbing, he struggled to dress himself. But now the stitches are out and he's left with only a scar and full mobility. He angrily pulls on a pair of joggers without so much as a grimace.

The light filtering in through the shutters casts the room in a gold sunrise glow.

I get out of bed, too, taking my silk robe from the back of the door and following Henry onto the landing. Jonty is at the top of the stairs, bleary-eyed, his hair sleep-mussed, wearing nothing but a pair of boxers.

Henry thunders down the stairs.

'I'm coming!' he bellows as someone hammers on the door again.

'Who is it?' asks Jonty around a yawn.

I shrug, and head downstairs. I'm only halfway, when Henry yanks open the front door. A moment later, he is flung backwards. He hits the wood with a dull thud. On his back, he gasps for breath. Looming over him is Luke, rubbing the knuckles of his right hand. Vaguely, I register Jonty swivelling towards the spare room, but I am already rushing down the stairs. Luke steps inside and grabs fistfuls of Henry's T-shirt.

'YOU BASTARD!' he screams.

Then he hauls Henry to his feet and tosses him outside.

I stumble after them.

Luke is enraged.

'You raped her,' he yells, and swings for Henry again.

Henry ducks and staggers back.

I race down the steps and onto the drive. 'He didn't do it!'

Luke whips around and glowers.

'He didn't do it,' I insist again. 'Henry didn't hurt her. But she *stabbed* him. She isn't stable.'

'She didn't stab him.' He's disgusted by the idea, aghast. 'She met with him to give him an ultimatum: admit to you he assaulted her, or she'd go to the police with evidence of the rape.'

Evidence. What evidence? I glance uncertainly at Henry who is red-faced and seething. Then I turn my attention back to Luke. 'Does she have evidence?'

In my peripheral vision, Henry stiffens. The question feels like a betrayal, but I had to ask it.

'No,' says Luke. 'Rape isn't easy to prove and he knew it. Called her bluff. *Hit* her. Left her on some country fucking road in the dark.' He stalks towards Henry and I rush to stand between them. 'She told me everything last night. All of it.'

'Did she tell you she tried to start up some sordid affair with Henry? For weeks, she was harassing him. When he turned her down, she lost it. She lied about the rape for revenge and then she stabbed him.'

His laughter is biting and so unlike him. 'Is that what he told you?' he says to me. Then he scowls at Henry. 'That's how you spun it?'

I look between the two of them. 'What do you mean?'

'He propositioned her at a PR event years ago, when he was engaged to someone else.'

My gaze slides to Henry. 'Is that true?'

'No,' he growls. 'I'd never touch that mad bitch.'

Luke dives around me and hits him. The force of the blow knocks Henry off his feet. Then Luke is on him, all rage and flying fists. I am screaming at them to stop. A blur flies past me. It's Jonty, now dressed in joggers and a T-shirt. He tackles Luke around the waist and the two of them tumble to the left. Henry staggers to his feet, spitting blood onto the paving. Then he piles in, kicking Luke over and over.

'STOP IT!' I howl. 'STOP!'

I stand aside like a flailing *useless* spare part. I listen to the dull thud of flesh on flesh and then I am hurling myself forward, trying to tear the two of them off Luke. Henry flings his arm out, catching me in the chest. I topple to the ground.

'Get her out of here,' barks Henry to Jonty.

He gets in one last kick. Luke curls into the foetal position, spluttering. Jonty hauls me to my feet and tries to drag me away. I fight him. But he's too strong. He lifts me easily and starts marching towards the house.

I see Luke pushing himself up. He swings for Henry again, but misses and loses his balance. Luke's bleary, bloodshot eyes land on mine. I kick wildly, trying to get away from Jonty.

'Let her go!' bellows Luke.

Jonty doesn't slow. He jogs up the steps. Luke staggers towards us. Too late.

Jonty carries me over the threshold and kicks the door shut.

Chapter Forty-Two

Kicking and screaming, I am dragged upstairs. Jonty tells me to calm down, to stop struggling, but I am desperate to make sure that Luke and Henry don't tear each other apart. Jonty holds me against the wall outside the spare bedroom door and puts a hand over my mouth, cutting me off mid-scream. He brings his face close to mine.

'Relax,' he commands. 'Everything is fine. You're safe.'

But it's not my safety I'm worried about.

He takes his hand away from my mouth and his gaze drops to my lips. I am pinned between the wall and the hardness of his body. His breath is warm on my cheek. My heart quickens beneath the heat of his gaze. He pushes away from me abruptly, and opens the door. Before I can run, he takes my wrist and leads me inside.

He positions himself in front of the exit. He's built like a sturdy, antique wardrobe. There's no way I can get past him. He crouches, rifling through his duffle bag.

'We need to go out there,' I babble. 'We need to stop them before—'

'Drink this,' he insists, handing me a hip flask. 'It'll help.'

I slam the flask down on the chest of drawers and step forward to go around him, but he blocks my path.

'Henry can handle himself,' he says reassuringly.

But it's not just Henry I'm concerned about. I'm trembling with adrenaline.

'Two on one, Jonty, you really think that was fair?'

He eyes me. 'What would you prefer? I stand by and let that lunatic attack your fiancé?'

I look away guiltily, because obviously I didn't want Henry to get hurt, but I didn't want the two of them going in on Luke like that either. Luke, who is gentle and curious and kind, was a torrent of fury.

He who has always run away from his problems, came here to

stand his ground. For Ivy. He believes her. Every word. She's the sister he never had and as far as he's concerned, Henry has committed the unthinkable against her. I don't blame Luke for his rage. For this violent chaos. I blame *her*.

I can't just stand here. I try again to go around Jonty but he lifts his finger and tuts. 'I don't think so.'

'Jonty—'

'They haven't drawn muskets at dawn, Zara. Let them talk it out. Meanwhile . . .' he picks up the flask and hands it to me again.

He isn't going to let me leave this room, but my nerves are shredded. Desperate to dull the stomach-churning anxiety, I take a swig. The burn of whisky scorches my throat. Then I take another, longer sip. I pace the length of the room, pleading with Jonty to let me leave.

Soon though, my tongue feels foreign in my mouth and I'm slurring my words. Jonty's face blurs and the floor becomes sinking sand. Arms go around my waist and suddenly I am floating. A moment later, I feel the cool press of sheets against my fevered cheek, and then everything goes black.

I wake. There's a thunderstorm raging in my head and a drought in my mouth. I am alone. I struggle to remember where I am and why. Then it all comes flooding back. I sit up and the room spins. Then I am off the bed, staggering for the door on quaking legs.

I move quickly down the stairs, fighting wave after wave of nausea. I pull open the front door and the sun momentarily blinds me. I tumble outside, almost falling down the stone steps. Jonty is in the driveway, jet-washing the slabs. He grins when he sees me.

'You're up,' he calls, too cheerily, over the roar of the machine.

'Where's Henry?' I croak as he turns it off. 'Luke?'

'After Henry sent Luke packing, he took himself off for a walk to calm down.'

I hover, not sure what to do. My head hurts and the nausea relentlessly batters me. 'How long was I out?'

He shrugs. 'Couple of hours.'

How much did I drink? Not enough to make me pass out.

Jonty appears in front of me. 'You alright?'

'What was in that flask?'

'Whisky, tequila, probably a bit of everything. It's my party mix.' He pulls a face. 'Sorry, I should've warned you. Took the edge off though, didn't it?'

I only remember taking a couple of swigs from the flask. Large swigs, admittedly but still, something doesn't feel right. *I* don't feel right. Not that I have time to dwell: I need to speak to Luke, get hold of Henry, make sure they're both OK.

Back in my bedroom, I snatch up my phone and call Luke. It goes straight to voicemail. Over and over. Then I call Henry, but his is switched off too. I stare helplessly at my phone. What am I to do? Do I call the police? Or—

The bedroom door swings open. Henry storms through the room. He doesn't even look at me, just starts yanking open drawers and pulling out fresh clothes.

'Are you OK?' I ask. 'Where have you been?'

He doesn't look up or acknowledge I've spoken. It's as though I'm not even here.

'Henry?'

I approach and lay a hand on his back.

He spins around, knocking my arm aside. 'Don't fucking touch me,' he bellows. I spring back, shocked by the outburst. His left eye is swelling and bruised. Veins stand out in cords on his wrists and his eyes are alive with so much wrath. 'First your drunk mother, then that possessive, deranged *bitch* and now your violent, unhinged ex. Since I met you, all I've done is put out fires.'

The tears are immediate. 'I'm so sorry. I'm—'

He grips my chin and brings his face close to mine.

'You,' he snarls, 'are turning out to be more trouble than you're fucking worth.'

For days afterwards, Henry barely looks at me. He refuses to talk about the altercation with Luke or the confrontation between him and me that followed. All my calls and messages to Luke go unanswered. Three days after the fight, desperate to make sure Luke's OK, I drive to his house, but he doesn't come to the door. He'll be fuming with me for staying with Henry after what she claims he's done. Just like Henry, he probably thinks I'm too much hassle to bother with anymore. When I moved in with Henry, I distanced myself from Luke – that's what I had to do to ensure my relationship with Henry was more than just another pitstop. But I never planned for Luke and me to lose contact completely. I decide I'll give Luke more time to cool off and if I haven't heard back from him by the end of the week, I'll reach out to his parents to make sure he's OK. Henry won't like it, but things between us are strained anyway, and it's the right thing to do.

At the supermarket, I wander the aisles, not really paying attention to what I'm putting in my trolley. Instead I'm longing for the man who snuck me into an empty ice rink, who filled his house with a hundred yellow roses, who engraved his proposal onto a silver spoon. When I return home, I smell bonfire smoke. I ask Henry what he's been burning.

'Nothing,' he says shortly.

'But—'

'I haven't burned anything,' he says with barely-contained hostility. 'We had a barbecue. What? You think I *killed* Luke? Just as you thought I killed Tabitha?' Then he gives me a look that makes my gut wrench: it is pure undiluted disappointment, as though he'd discovered gold, only to be told it was cheap, tacky nickel. 'You're beginning to seem just as mad as Ivy.'

That evening, though, when Jonty and Henry leave the house for a drink at the local pub, I go out into the garden and find a patch of scorched earth.

Chapter Forty-Three

Now

I am still in the tiny, cramped interrogation room. My lawyer, Tammingworth, is on my right. Opposite is Detective Blackburn, who sports a cheap suit and a pin-sharp gaze, and Detective Perkins, who, with her long lashes and dark hair, reminds me of you, Ivy. Her clothes are tailored, expensive, but her nails are bitten to the quick.

'We appreciate your cooperation,' says Blackburn, in a tone that warns me my cooperation is an expectation and not a choice.

Tammingworth gives me a look; a sharp reminder to respond only with 'no comment'.

'There's one particular question we have asked you a few times this evening that you've refused to answer,' says Blackburn.

I keep my expression blank.

He frowns. 'So, would you like to answer it now you've had some time to think?'

I glance at Tammingworth and then back at Blackburn. 'No comment.'

While Tammingworth gives me a small, approving smile, as though I'm a remarkably slow student who's finally mastered a simple maths equation, Blackburn shakes his head, disappointed. In that moment, he reminds me of my father. And, in these last few weeks, of Henry too.

Perkins is watching me carefully. She gives me a kind smile and says, 'Let's move on.'

Blackburn produces a cardboard folder from a pile beside him and pulls out a selection of photographs. 'We'd like you to identify these men.'

'If you can,' says Perkins.

I do as they say, trying hard to hide the burbling anxiety in my gut. Blackburn jabs a finger at one of the photographs. 'This person is dead. And this one,' he says, sliding it across the table, 'is missing. Now, do you really expect me to believe that you have nothing to do with either of these two incidents?'

'No comment,' I whisper.

'Do you know where this man is?' asks Perkins. 'His parents are extremely worried. You know his parents, don't you?'

I nod, tears brimming as I stare down at the photograph of Luke.

'I'm not a mother, but I'm sure if my son disappeared, I'd be beside myself,' she says gently. I glance at her nails again. Then at my own, crusted with blood.

'He travels,' I offer. 'Maybe he's on another trip . . .'

Blackburn scoffs. 'On a trip for two weeks without so much as a goodbye to anyone?'

I think of Henry and Luke fighting on the driveway. Of the scorched earth. Of how Henry later explained it away, claiming he'd knocked over the barbecue. Of the calls and emails and messages to Luke that have gone unanswered since. But how do I tell them this without confessing to it all? You can't break off a piece of the truth and feed it to a person without them wanting another and another and another, until they've devoured the whole lot. And I don't know which version of events I am going to tell.

'You were involved with Luke Northman for quite some time, is that right?' asks Perkins.

I nod. Beside me, Tammingworth stiffens. I forgot my 'no comment' soundbite. Once again, I am the failing student. Perkins exchanges a meaningful look with Blackburn. He clears his throat and pulls another photograph from the file. 'We suspect this woman had something to do with Mr Northman's disappearance.'

I frown, staring at the photograph he's slid in front of me. 'Why?'

Then my gaze zeroes in on the necklace: a lone ruby on a long gold chain. The one I found in Luke's bathroom. The one I knew could only have been worn by the woman he was in a relationship with.

I pick up the photograph. As I stare at it, my stomach roils and twists. When the agony becomes too much to bear, I slam it onto the desk, facedown. And clamp my mouth shut around a scream.

Everyone in the room tenses.

I force myself to breathe deeply.

Blackburn and Perkins exchange another look. 'Let's put Mr Northman's disappearing act to one side,' Blackburn instructs gruffly.

Perkins leans in close to me, as though we are old girlfriends sharing secrets over a cup of coffee. 'There's a body in the morgue. We need to know how it got there.'

Then she asks the question I have been asked a thousand times since entering the station. The one they are most desperate for me to answer.

'Zara, was the death self-defence or murder?'

Chapter Forty-Four

Before

It has been almost two weeks since the fight between Henry and Luke. I went to Luke's house again this morning while Henry was out, but if he was there, he didn't answer. With Luke still giving me the silent treatment, I have vowed to visit his parents' house tomorrow and ask if he's OK. I haven't had a contact number for them for years but they still live on the same street we grew up on. It's harrowing to think, after knowing Luke for most of my life, he may want nothing more to do with me. Still, I must find out how he is. *Where* he is. I imagine he is globe-hopping again, or holed up somewhere with the owner of the ruby necklace.

Things with Henry aren't much better. After living with us for a month, Jonty moved out last week. Henry spends most nights at Jonty's newly-renovated penthouse flat, or entertaining clients or having drinks with his team. When he's home, he whiles away time in his study, the door firmly locked, or at the kitchen island scrolling through his phone. I've apologised a thousand times for bringing so much trouble to his door, and though he insists it's fine, he won't touch me or look at me or exchange more than a few words. And there's no one I can turn to. Ivy is gone, Luke is AWOL, my mother is still in rehab and Amira is enjoying her family. I am alone.

I cry in the shower, so that Henry won't see my blotchy face. I pick at the flesh around my fingernails until it is red-raw and peeling. The hideous truth is that I can only hold a man's attention for so long before they tire of me, abandoning me like a pair of worn socks, forgotten at the bottom of a washing basket. My father, Luke and now Henry.

Be with someone who's more in love with you than you are with them. My mother's words, cynical, but perhaps true. I cry harder in the shower, realising that if Henry leaves me, I will be without a job, without money, without anywhere to go and any way to pay for my mother's treatment.

As I emerge wrapped in a towel, Henry is waiting for me in our bedroom. There is a stiff, glossy bag from a boutique at the foot of the bed.

'What's that?' I ask.

He picks it up and holds it out to me. 'This is what you're going to wear to Jonty's flat-warming party tonight.'

After how strained things have been for the last couple of weeks, the invitation surprises me. Maybe he's finally forgiven me. Maybe he's realised I am more than just my alcoholic mother, my protective ex-lover, or Ivy. Feral, conniving Ivy. I don't blame him for his stony treatment since Luke stormed the house. I haven't made Henry's life easy. Especially recently. I'd be in turmoil too, if one of Henry's exes came to my house and attacked me.

Now, though, he smiles at me. Properly. His hazel eyes crinkling at their corners. I find myself smiling back, so widely my cheeks ache. I haven't smiled like this in weeks. He kisses me and I dissolve into it, relieved that he still wants me. Being loved by Henry Frith was like having the brightest, most dazzling light shone on you after too long in the dark.

That evening, at Jonty's party, I am wearing the dress Henry bought for me. It is scarlet silk. Expensive silk. With a low neck and lower back. It's slinky, like a second skin. I am determined to drink only one glass of red wine so I don't do anything else to upset Henry. He curls an arm around my waist and kisses the top of my head. I beam up at him, grateful things between us feel as though they are getting back to normal.

Jonty's penthouse apartment is in one of those beautiful limestone buildings in the heart of Bath. The decor is clean and simple and expensive. The main part of the apartment is an enormous open room. In one half are three plush grey sofas around a wood and glass coffee table, and on the wall is a ginormous cinema-style TV. The second half is a dining room complete with a modern mid-century table and chairs, and adjoining kitchen. At the back is a utility room and toilet. Everything is in shades of grey and white. The only colour comes from a few hanging William Morris prints and the guests that mill around with drinks. Beyond the sofa area is the hallway, and off that are the two bedrooms and a bathroom.

Beside me, Henry is humming with electric excitement, like someone waiting for the fireworks to start. When he isn't laughing and talking with friends, he is kissing me.

'I can't wait to have you,' he murmurs against my mouth.

Usually at these events, Henry will disappear and leave me alone to mingle with people I don't know, or recognise only vaguely from other, similar parties, but tonight, he keeps me close. I think he's making up for the distance between us the last couple of weeks.

Jonty joins us, carrying two bottles of beer and a glass of something pale and sparkling for me. 'Wow,' he says when he sees me. 'You look . . .'

'Edible?' offers Henry.

Jonty grins. 'Delicious.'

I get that feeling again, as though I'm standing too close to an open fire. My cheeks are hot. I'm getting the kind of intense attention Ivy's used to receiving. I was never jealous though, I didn't need to be, because of everyone in my life, it was *her* who made me feel beautiful. This is the first kind thought I've had about her in a long while.

I push her aside and say to Jonty, 'The apartment is fantastic.'

He nods and sips his beer, eyes never leaving mine. He hands a bottle to Henry and holds a glass of bubbles out to me.

'Oh no, thank you,' I say. 'I'm just sticking to the one tonight.'

Jonty looks at Henry uncertainly, who says, 'Darling, it's rude to turn down the host.'

And because I don't want to be difficult, I smile graciously at Jonty and take the glass from him.

'It's not your party mix, is it?' I ask, remembering the last time I took a drink from him.

He gives me a crooked, boyish grin. 'You'll have to drink to find out.'

'A toast,' says Henry in good cheer.

'To?'

Jonty gives Henry a private smile. 'To shared experiences and making memories!'

'I'll cheers to that,' he says.

We clink bottles and glasses. They take a swing from their bottles and, with their eyes unwaveringly on me, I take my first sip.

The party moves around me like a carousel. I am rarely alone. Arms snake around my waist, but I can't keep track of whether it is Jonty or Henry at my side.

I lose focus. I want to go home. I tell Henry but my tongue feels too thick in my mouth and I don't think he understands.

Time slips through my fingers and I get that feeling again, as though the floor is sinking sand. Then I am in the hallway. Henry is at one shoulder, Jonty at the other. They are holding me up. They carry me into a bedroom, the toes of my heels barely skimming the floor.

Jonty lays me down on a big, soft bed that smells of him.

'Let us take care of you,' I hear him say.

The sheets are cool against my clammy skin.

I think of her. Of us huddled beneath the covers of her bed, when she whispered those magic words for the first time: 'How much do you love me?'

This memory mingles with the present and I struggle to distinguish between the two.

'To the moon and round the stars.'

I hear the sound of a zipper.

'Not enough,' she breathed. 'How much do you love me?'

One of my heels is gone.

'As much as you want me to and even more.'

And then the other.

Through the silky blackness, I feel her smile.

Only now, it isn't her face next to mine, it's Jonty's. He climbs on top of me, his chest bare, and kisses me. I turn my face away. He grabs my chin roughly in his large hand.

'Henry said I could.'

The room cartwheels.

Henry appears on my other side and unbuttons his shirt. Jonty's hands travel up my legs and slide beneath my dress.

'Ivy,' I hear myself mumble.

Then Jonty is gone, and fingers curl around my throat, as though trying to squeeze the word out of me. For a few seconds, I can't breathe. Henry's nose is pressed against mine, his warm, beer-soaked breath on my face. 'Don't say her name,' he warns. 'Look at *me*.'

Then he forces his tongue into my mouth and bites my bottom lip hard enough to draw blood.

My limbs are concrete-filled as the two of them lift my arms to remove my dress.

Then comes a piercing shriek over and over. Too shrill in the darkness of this room. Footsteps outside the bedroom door, frantic and relentless, like rain on a windowpane.

'Fire alarm.' Jonty's voice is somewhere above my head.

The door is flung open and light floods in.

I taste blood. I am still on the bed, shivering. Too hot. Too cold. I am being pulled to my feet, but the floor dips and slides out from under me. My head rolls back and I stare up into the blur of a woman's face and reach out to touch her dark hair.

Ivy?

Then I am swallowed up by the dark.

Chapter Forty-Five

The room I wake up in is bright. My head pounds but the world has stopped spinning. I'm still wearing the scarlet dress but one of the straps is broken. I groan into my arm as my stomach cramps and nausea rushes through me. I lie very still, urging myself not to vomit.

I concentrate on the room. The walls are a soft white, the bedding is white, too, and smells faintly of lemons. Above my head is an arched window. It's open. The summer breeze makes the curtains flutter. On the wall opposite the bed are two floor-to-ceiling bookcases, paperbacks arranged meticulously by colour, and nestled in between is a desk. Clean and tidy, with a vase of yellow sunflowers. To my left is a chest of drawers with a gold mirror above it. It's flanked by two doors. And to my right is a bedside table. This is where I find the water, the painkillers and the pink Post-it note:

Gone to fetch breakfast.
Be careful. Look after yourself.

I pick it up and turn it over in my hands. I don't know whose bedroom I'm in or who the author of the note is, but that last part feels familiar: *Be careful. Look after yourself.*

I should be panicking that I am in a stranger's bedroom, but I wear calm like a thick, welcome blanket on a winter's night. I feel safe. I don't know how I got here, though. I search for the memory but it's a blank tape. Static.

What happened last night? I remember the party. A glass of wine. A glass of champagne. And then . . .

My stomach lurches.

I can still feel their hands on me. Fingers digging into my thighs, pulling at my hair, sliding beneath my dress. It rewinds and replays on a loop. The calm falls away, leaving me trembling. I sit up. The room tilts, threatening to slide away from me. I climb off the bed and grab the drawers to steady myself. In the mirror, I catch sight of my reflection.

There is make-up smeared under my red eyes. My hair is a tangled mess. On my cheeks, my chin, my chest, there is a rash. Stubble burn. My skin smells of men's cologne.

I had two drinks. Only two. Not enough to end up in the state I did. Was I . . . I can barely bring myself to think it, but what other explanation is there? Jonty drugged me. Everything started to dim around the edges a short while after the champagne. I felt out of control, just as I did when I drank from Jonty's hip flask. Did he drug me that day, too? Because I was hysterical. Because Jonty had been given orders to keep me away. Because he wanted me subdued and compliant.

Last night, the reason for drugging me is obvious.

Panicked, I reach down between my legs, checking for torn flesh or dried semen. I'm relieved to find neither. That, at least, I am still wearing my knickers. Like a stone over a lake, my mind skims across all the comments Henry and Jonty have made about sharing me. Henry told me once, after I'd confided in him about my dark-haired stalker, that he wouldn't share me with her, or with anyone – not until he got bored. And he had got bored, hadn't he? That's what the stony silence in our house has proven these last two weeks. I'd brought too much trouble to his door and now I am no more than a thing to him. One of the dolls his company sells to be passed around at will. What was it Jonty had us toast to? *Shared experiences and making memories.* I see it in slow motion, their private smiles, the clink of glass on glass on glass, ringing out, too loud in my memory.

I am furious and sick and betrayed. My breaths come fast. The shock of it, of what could've happened, repeating on me like reflux.

I need air. I need to get out of here.

My heels are gone. Frantic, I open one of the two doors flanking the drawers. The first is a closet filled with women's clothes. I take a pair of white trainers from the floor and slip them on. They're a little too small but I can't leave barefoot. I don't have my phone or keys or purse so I take the tenner on the dresser too. Then I hurry out of the room, fumble for the front door and soon I am outside.

Grief fills me slowly, like sand running through an hourglass. I feel the pressing weight of it in my gut, rising to encompass my lungs until I can't breathe. With every second, I edge closer to full-blown hysterics, right here on the street, in the middle of the day. I reach out and press my palms against the hard brick. Then I turn so my back is pressed against the wall. My chest heaves as sobs break through my ribs and expel themselves in gasps. How could Henry do this to me? How could he do it to anyone?

It's only now that I am slammed by the most excruciating realisation: Ivy was telling the truth when she said Henry raped her.

Chapter Forty-Six

I'm angry at myself for not believing Ivy. For letting Henry lie and manipulate me. And when I think about how I spoke to her on the phone, I feel sick. Maybe it's the guilt or the shock or the drug leaving my system, but my stomach roils and I retch, still clutching the wall, and vomit pours out of me, though the betrayal and the regret do not. Across the road, a woman lifts her chin in disgust, and I realise what I must look like to her, hungover, wearing last night's clothes, puking in the street. I quickly push away from the wall and start walking. I look around. At first, I'm not familiar with this residential area but soon I am on a street I know. I'm still in Bath.

I have to go back to Henry's for my bank cards, some clothes, my car. After that, though, I'm not sure where I'll go. Mum's house isn't an option, since it's been rented out to new tenants. She's due to leave rehab in two months and plans to stay with a friend while she gets back on her feet. I could go to Amira's, but it doesn't seem fair to drag her into this while she has a three-month-old baby to take care of. With Luke missing and my friendship with Ivy in tatters, I have no one to turn to. For a moment, I think about returning to the safety of the house I just left. But I don't know who it belongs to.

I consider going to the police about the attempted rape, but worry I won't be believed. I was with my fiancé at a party. I drank. And I wasn't actually raped. The two men involved are white and educated and wealthy, and what evidence of an attempted assault do I actually have? Yes, I could take a drugs test but anything in my system could've been taken willingly. I'd have to relive what happened last night in excruciating detail and to what end? A suspended sentence? A warning? And then there's Ivy. I don't know exactly what happened between her and Roman, but I do know Henry had photographs that made it seem like she pushed her cousin. If she was telling the truth about the rape then she was probably telling the truth about Roman, and about Henry still having copies. Those photographs were enough to convince me of her guilt. They'll be enough to convince the police and a jury, too. If I go to the authorities about last night, Henry could turn her in as punishment.

On foot, the journey to Henry's will take a couple of hours, so I walk the twenty-five minutes to the taxi rank where I use my stolen ten-pound note. My heart races as we arrive in Freshford. I thank the driver and ask him to drop me off a little way from the house. I don't want Henry to hear me arrive. The walk up the driveway feels long, and I am light-headed with anxiety. The open sky above feels like a hand pressing down on me and I stop just before the house comes into view. If he's home, I'll turn around and get my things another time.

I'm relieved to see his car isn't here. I don't have my bag which contained my phone and house keys. I imagine it was left at the party along with my heels. Luckily, Henry keeps a spare key hidden in a plant pot at the back of the house. I climb over the locked gate and soon I am inside, entering through the back door. I return the key and push into the house.

It's still. Quiet. I breathe in the last nine months of my life: yellow roses; red wine; that unidentifiable scent which is unique to each home and, underneath it all, the woody, spicy scent of Henry's cologne. I allow myself one moment to mourn the future I've lost and the man I thought I loved. The intensity of it is visceral. I put my hand over my mouth to stop the sob I can feel catching in the back of my throat. Then I think of what might happen if Henry returns home before I leave. I can't face him. So I force my grief aside and propel myself into action. Upstairs, I grab a bag and start shoving things inside. I wash my face quickly and change into clean clothes: jeans and a T-shirt. I'm zipping up the bag, ready to go, when I hear his key in the front door.

I freeze.

Fuck.

I can't charge downstairs and out of the front door without risking a physical confrontation. Even on my best day I'm not sure I would win. Silently, I place my leather holdall under the bed. As I hear footsteps coming up the stairs, I hurry to the en suite and leave the door open by a hair's breadth in case he hears the click of it closing completely. I press myself against the wall beside the door.

He enters the bedroom. My heart pounds so fast, I'm surprised he can't hear it. I listen to the sounds of him pulling clothes from drawers. I am tense, ready to fight my way out of here if he enters the en suite.

He hums to himself and I feel him close by, right outside the door.

What will he do to me if he finds me in here? Will he finish what he started? I squeeze my eyes shut and hold my breath.

Then the humming stops.

I count to ten before turning and pressing my ear against the wall to listen. Silence. I can't hide in here all day. I need to get my bag and get out. Then I hear running water. It's coming from the main bathroom down the hall. I don't stop to wonder why he isn't using the en suite. I release my breath and hope mingles with terror as I slowly open the en-suite door. The bedroom is empty. Carefully, I pull my holdall out from under the bed and hurry to the door. I'll go out the front, it will be quicker, if louder, but—

Henry swings into my path as I step onto the landing. His hand wraps around my throat, cutting off my scream. He thrusts me back into the bedroom. I stumble, my heel catching the bed frame. I lose my balance and hit the floor.

He towers over me. 'Where have you been?'

I can't speak. Terror locks my voice inside my throat. He notices the holdall, which is beside me on the ground.

'Or, more pressingly, where is it you *think* you're going?'

Shaking, I get to my feet. I have no idea where I'm going, but wherever it is, I'm not coming back.

'I'm leaving, Henry.' I'm grateful my voice doesn't quiver. 'We're done.'

He stares at me. I hold my breath, feeling as though I am facing off against a rabid dog. I glance at the door behind him and I think about running. Then he laughs. He *laughs*. I flinch, unnerved by the quicksilver of his mood. And even as he is showing all of those perfect white teeth, the sound leaving his mouth is taunting.

Anger surges through me. 'What's so funny?'

He shakes his head, his smile condescending. 'Where are you going to go?'

'Anywhere I want.'

'You don't know what you want. Women like you never do.'

Outrage burns in my chest. 'Women like me?'

'Broken home. Daddy issues. You're all the same. Needy. Erratic. Fucking *pathetic*.'

'Excuse me?' He's never spoken to me with such vitriol, and though I now know what he's capable of, it still shocks me. The beautiful, charming veneer falls away. It's like watching Michelangelo's David crack and crumble to reveal a gargoyle beneath.

'Most men would've turned and run a mile after meeting your mother. Even your father couldn't stand to be around the both of you. *I* stuck around and this is how you act? Trying to sneak out of here without so much as a goodbye?'

The tears come, then. Fat, furious, dreadful tears. I *loved* this man. I thought he loved me. The future we planned has been torn to shreds. The remnants of it are scattering. Lost. I grab my bag and shove past. I move quickly down the hall. He follows, snatching my wrist and yanking me around to face him. I struggle, trying to break his hold but he doesn't let go.

'Zara, I'm sorry.'

'Let go of me.'

His grip tightens. 'I said, I'm sorry. Come back and let's talk—'

'Sorry for what?' I cry. 'For the things you said? Or for what you tried to do to me last night?'

His eyes narrow. 'What?'

'At the party. You or Jonty drugged me,' I say, voice trembling. 'You took me into the bedroom . . . the two of you . . .' I swallow back the ebbing nausea at the memory. 'You were all over me.'

'You were drunk. It was *you* who was all over *us*.'

How dare he? How *dare* he?

'That's a lie.'

'Jonty suggested we go somewhere more private, and to my shame, you were more than up for it. Don't start throwing around accusations now, just because you're worried people will think you're a *slut*.'

The air is too hot and thick to breathe.

'You raped Ivy and you tried to rape me, too.'

His fist tightens around my wrist, grinding my bones. I cry out. His anger blisters. He hauls me into his study. I twist and turn in his grip, but it doesn't loosen. I scream. He yells for me to calm down. To listen. Then he pins me against the bookcase. I wince, the hard edges digging into my spine.

'I did not!' he bellows. 'And if you *ever* tell anyone I did anything of the sort, I'll . . . I'll . . .' Spit bubbles on his lips as he grapples for a threat.

'You'll what?' I choke. 'What could you possibly take from me, Henry? You've destroyed every meaningful relationship I had.'

'I'll bury you,' he says with barely-contained rage.

I blanch, because something about the way in which he's looking at me tells me he isn't joking.

Then he blinks, as though he's as surprised as I am by the venom that has just dripped from his mouth.

'This has gone too far,' he says. 'I can't talk to you when you're like this. I'm going out and when I come back, we will sit down and we will have a civilised conversation.'

'I'm leaving you. That's it. There's nothing to discuss. This isn't one of your business negotiations.'

He lets me go and takes a step back. I don't think it's very often that Henry hears the word no. Especially from someone he clearly believes is below his station. He's entitled, like a child king, and I can't believe I didn't see it before. I'm glad he's no longer touching me, though I can already feel the bruises on my arms. I think he's calming down, starting to see reason. Then I notice his hands balling into fists.

He whips away from me and in seconds he is out the door, slamming it shut behind him.

I breathe out, relieved he's gone.

Then, to my heart-stopping horror, I hear the unmistakable click of the key turning in the study door lock. I throw myself at it but it's too late. I'm trapped.

Chapter Forty-Seven

Henry's study is the only one with a lock and with bars on the window – *that's* why he dragged me in here. He keeps a spare key in the kitchen drawer. My forearms are numb from hammering on the door, my throat raw from screaming. Henry has gone. The house is empty. Exhausted, I slump to the floor. Sobs rip through me. I'm crying because I have burned to ash every single one of my closest relationships. I'm crying because my fiancé tried to share me with his friend against my will. I'm crying because Henry raped Ivy and I was so wrapped up in chasing after this perfect life that I didn't believe her. I'm crying because the man I gave my heart to is a Venus flytrap. I cry until there are no tears left in me. Then I force myself to stand on quaking legs so I can find a way out of here before he comes back.

To no avail, I rummage in every drawer for another key, a phone, anything that will help. His laptop isn't in here; it must be in the kitchen or in his car. The bars on the window mean it wouldn't do me any good to smash it. I'm on the brink of giving up, when I realise I haven't rummaged through the inbuilt storage cupboard. With a fresh lease of hope, I get to work. Most of it proves to be useless: there's a locked filing cabinet and a few boxes of electric cables and extension leads. But, at the very bottom, I find an old tablet. My pulse kicks and I frantically search for a charging lead. It takes a while, but finally I find the right one.

I wait impatiently for it to charge enough to turn on. It's old and slow but it blinks to life. I stare at it, not sure exactly how this can help me since it isn't a phone. I remember that the Wi-Fi password is scribbled on a piece of paper in Henry's desk drawer. I find it, and then fumble to type it in. After a few minutes, I'm online. I stare at the screen, heart racing, wondering what to do next.

I consider logging on to my social media accounts and messaging a friend... But who? A public plea for help would be a disaster if Henry saw it first. Besides that, the tablet is so ancient that it doesn't even have a Facebook app which means I'd have to download everything and God knows how long that will take. I decide to log on to my email account. When I'm finally in, I wonder who to contact, what to say. I think about Ivy. But how can I ask for her help when I refused to believe her? No. It isn't fair. I dragged Henry into her life, I can't keep exposing her to him. Luke would come but I don't know where he is, and my previous messages are still unanswered.

Then I have an idea. Hoping that my anonymous emailer is a friend and not a foe, I type out a message to HTH@gmail.com.

Please help me. Henry has locked me in his study. I can't get out.

I add some more instructions, and then I wait.

Forty minutes later, I hear footsteps on the stairs. Fear winds itself around my body and I can't move, afraid that Henry has returned. For one panicked moment, I wonder if he's been behind the emails this entire time. If he's been testing me, feeding me information to see where my loyalties really lie.

A key is pushed into the lock. I hold my breath.

I watch wide-eyed as the knob twists and the door creaks open.

Then, after all these long months, my gaze finally meets that of my anonymous emailer.

Chapter Forty-Eight

'You've been emailing me this entire time?' I ask, bewildered but relieved. So relieved.

Hazel nods. 'We need to get out of here before he comes back.'

'But why?'

'I'll explain later, let's go.'

We leave quickly. Hazel followed the instructions I emailed, collecting the spare house key from the garden and then the study key from the kitchen. We put everything back as she found it, even locking up the study again.

Hazel got a taxi here, so the two of us take my car. She gives me directions to her place, and I'm not surprised when we pull up outside the house that I woke up in earlier.

'You got me out of the party?' I ask.

'Yeah, I set fire to some tea towels in Jonty's sink to set off the alarm. In all the panic, I grabbed you and brought you here.'

I remember reaching out to touch her dark hair in Jonty's bedroom, thinking it was Ivy.

As we head inside, I go back over all the emails Hazel has sent. For a while, I was certain my anonymous emailer was the dark-haired woman, Jennifer – it made sense, she was already stalking me. But now I think about it, a lot of the emails from HTH@gmail.com were either signposts – *Tabitha Gates* – or advisory: *Don't let him ruin your life. Be careful. Look after yourself. You don't have to be alone.* The only email I can't get my head around is the one she sent two hours before Roman broke in: *You aren't safe, Zara.* How did she know? I ask her, wondering if she was somehow involved with Roman and knew what he was planning.

She shakes her head. 'Coincidence. I had no idea about any of it. I was referring to Henry.'

We go into the house and as we do, I realise that the emails only switched to my personal address after I bumped into Hazel in the supermarket and gave her my phone number to discuss planning her wedding, via my non-existent start-up. My phone number and my personal email are connected: it wouldn't have taken a genius, just a quick internet search.

The house is airy and light, the colour palette neutral: creams and greys and shades of white. It's a calming space. A safe space. For the first time in days, I am able to catch my breath.

Hazel is wearing a pair of navy yoga leggings and an oversized sweater. Since she runs her own dance and aerial fitness studio, I wonder if she abandoned a class to come to my rescue for the second time in less than twenty-four hours. That is, if what she told me about owning a studio is true. How well do I really know this woman?

'Are you even engaged?' I ask as we sit down in the kitchen with two mugs of something herbal.

'No,' she confesses. 'But it was the best way to keep an eye on you. Make sure you were OK. I hoped we'd become friends. That maybe you'd open up to me, confide in me if there was something to tell.'

'But we never really spoke about Henry . . .'

'I tried,' she says. 'I asked if you were married, knowing you weren't, asked if it was on the cards. You stubbornly refused to talk about your personal life.'

She's right. At the coffee shop in December, she'd commented that I looked tired, and wanted to know how I was with the kind of care that was sincere. I'd been tempted to tell her everything, but I held back, too afraid to confide in someone I didn't know very well about murder and missing fiancées.

'I even sent you another email,' she says. 'Right there as I stood at the counter and ordered us more gingerbread lattes.'

He made sure she'd never be found. When I read it, dread flooded my body and I was too aware of the fluttery, panicked thrum of my heart.

'I thought if you got an email while we were together, it would prompt you to say something. I wanted to get it all out in the open but you took off and I knew you weren't ready to hear what I needed to say. If I went to you about Henry too soon, I risked driving you further into his arms and away from people that wanted to help.'

She isn't wrong. Just look at me and Ivy. She tried to warn me about the kind of man Henry was and I resented her for it. I feel another wrench of regret. When it subsides, I am left with more questions.

'What about the man I met in the supermarket? Your fiancé?'

She's shaking her head and as she does, I realise she never introduced him as such. I'd just assumed. There was an odd look on his face when I exclaimed I was glad to finally meet him. I put it down to residual upset I'd abandoned them pre-wedding, but now I realise he had no idea who I was.

'Sorry,' says Hazel. 'I didn't want to lie.'

'So why did you?' I ask, frostier than intended. I'm feeling like an idiot for being so easily fooled by everyone.

She arches a brow. 'Would you have believed a practical stranger if they walked up to you and slated the man you were in a relationship with?'

'No,' I say because if I didn't believe Ivy, I wasn't going to believe anyone else.

'Exactly,' she says. 'I sent those emails to warn you, hoping if I fed you information slowly, it would be easier to digest, or that you'd start to realise what he was like and leave him before the two of you got serious.'

I nod. What she's telling me makes sense, but I feel like a fool for not piecing it all together. At this moment, I have more questions than I do answers. 'What else have you lied about?'

She looks guiltily at me. 'Hazel's my middle name. Most know me as Cleo.'

'Right . . .' I say slowly, trying to get my head around everything.

'I didn't want you to mention Cleo to Henry in case he realised who I was.'

'And who are you to him?' Was she another one of his exes?

'We met through an old friend,' she says.

That's what she told me at the masquerade ball. Then a thought strikes me. 'If you were trying to conceal yourself from him, why did you turn up at the Halloween party?'

'Because you'd disappeared for a week. You didn't reply to any of my emails about the wedding. I was worried. Henry throws a Halloween gathering every year, so I went and stayed for less than twenty minutes just to check on you. His parties are always packed and since I was masked, I felt confident I could slip in and out undetected,' she says, and I see the stress of this entire saga etched on her face.

I open my mouth to thank her for putting herself in such a difficult position just to see if I was alright, when she goes on.

'I was desperate. I thought I was too late. Again. That I'd failed. Again.' Her fingers absently reach up to the jade pendant around her neck. I knew from how often she touches it that it held sentimental value. I'd wrongly assumed her fiancé had gifted it to her, but now I know she doesn't have a fiancé, I have to ask.

'Cleo,' I venture. 'Who really gave you that necklace?'

She drops her hand to her mug. Swallows. 'Tabitha,' she answers. 'Tabitha Gates.'

Shock rolls through me. 'His ex-fiancée?'

'We were best friends.'

'Soulmates?' I ask, remembering what she'd said.

She nods. 'Before Henry, we were. Things between the two of them progressed quickly. Within months, he'd moved her into his place. They were engaged. He talked about children.'

It still hurts that I wasn't special. That I wasn't The One. I was just one of many.

'At first, I liked Henry,' says Cleo. 'But he grew jealous of my friendship with Tabitha. Grew jealous of anyone she held dear. He wanted to be the centre of her universe. She didn't have any close family, she lost both her parents, but she did have close friends. Until he came along.' She blows on her tea. Takes a sip. She's angry and sad, I can feel it. 'He chooses women who wouldn't usually mix in his circles.'

It's all so familiar, isn't it? Same story, same Prince Charming, different rags-to-riches princess. Hadn't that man at the Halloween party said Henry was forever digging for flowers in fields of weeds?

'But why?'

'He's constantly surrounded by women who have power because they have money. They grew up privileged. They aren't impressed by silver spoons and exclusive restaurants. How can they be when they own them? Besides, in his circle, he isn't the richest, or the most influential, or the youngest. So he steps outside of it. Hunts for women who are excited by fancy hotel rooms and wine tastings and spontaneous weekends away. Who feel lucky to have someone like Henry pay them attention.'

A dark, shameful blush creeps across my cheeks. I've been so naive. So stupid.

'Most importantly,' she says, 'he targets women who come from difficult childhoods. Women who can be isolated easily. Women who won't be missed.'

And even though my fingers are curled around a steaming mug, my blood runs cold. He'd told me that when he met my mother it made him want me even more. That he'd been waiting for me for a long time. All the clues were there but I was blind.

It's only now that I wonder if Henry drugged my mother at the restaurant. Maybe, when he arrived at the house, he'd overheard more of my conversation with her than I thought. We'd been talking about Luke, how she believed he'd be the one I'd marry. Perhaps Henry was so jealous, he drugged her to make her seem out of control just so he could ship her off and isolate me even further.

'For your own good, Zara,' she says, 'don't ever go back to him.'

'I won't,' I assure her, feeling the truth of it.

I don't want the last year of my life with him to have been a lie. But I can't cling to the scraps of what I had with him: the conversations under the duvet late at night, the kisses in the kitchen, the contentment at knowing the future was already written whenever I was in his arms. It's gone. It was never real, no matter how much I wanted it to be.

'So, you and Tabitha, you aren't friends anymore?'

I am asking about the two of them, but I'm thinking about *us*. Me and Ivy. I can't imagine never reconciling with her. No matter what, no matter the cost, I'll find a way to show her how sorry I am.

Cleo stares at me, dumbfounded. 'We can't be. I thought you knew? I thought my emails would have prompted you to find out more. Tabitha's been missing for almost two years.'

'I did ask questions. I asked so many that Henry rang her and had her come over to the house. I met her, Cleo. Tabitha moved away from Bath but she lives in Ireland. She paints.'

Cleo is shaking her head. 'There's no way. She's a missing person. I filed the report myself.'

'Cleo.' I put my hand on hers and hold her gaze. I want her to know I'm telling the truth, and I hope it brings her some comfort. 'I met her. She isn't missing, she just relocated.'

It doesn't placate her. She whips her hand from mine and pulls out her phone. She scrolls then she slides it across to me. On the screen is a photograph of Cleo, cheek-to-cheek with a blonde, blue-eyed woman. She's striking, with a wide smile and thick, enviable brows. Only, this isn't the blonde, blue-eyed woman who drank tea in my kitchen. They're similar but they aren't the same person.

'I don't understand . . .' I scroll through a bunch of photographs of the two of them together, stopping when I come across one of Henry, Cleo and the *real* Tabitha, all together. They're in the courtyard of a restaurant with a huge fishpond and red hanging paper lanterns.

'It was Chinese New Year,' says Cleo. 'We went out to celebrate. My aunt and uncle own the restaurant. Henry paid. Of course he did. Everyone loved him which made my loathing of him look completely unreasonable. But I could see what Tabitha couldn't: he was like a black hole, swallowing everything in her universe until there was nothing left. He made it impossible for us to stay friends.'

'You fought?'

She shakes her head. 'Nothing like that. Our relationship broke down slowly. He'd start fights with Tabitha whenever she and I were together, so she spent the entire time on her phone trying to smooth things over. She anticipated he'd pick an argument when they were apart, so she either cancelled our plans or brought him along. He hacked away at our friendship until there was nothing left.' She stares down into her tea. 'But I missed her. I reached out. We met up, and she told me she was a mess. She started sobbing, telling me he was having an affair. That she'd found receipts for flowers, hotel rooms, lingerie boutiques.'

I shouldn't be as surprised as I am, not after everything I know he's done. Still, he was always adamant about Ivy and Luke being in love with me, the implication being that he didn't trust me around either of them when, this entire time, Henry was the one who'd been unfaithful to a partner.

'Did Tabitha know who the other woman was?'

'Not as far as I'm aware. She did some more digging after what she'd found. She took his phone and read their messages, but the other woman was listed under something inconspicuous like a plumbing company, so I don't think she ever got a real name.'

'Didn't she ring the number?'

'A few times, but it rang out or went straight to voicemail.'

Knowing Henry, he probably lavished his other girlfriend with a new phone. One number in the contacts. His.

'He was *infatuated* with this mystery woman,' says Cleo. 'He wanted to leave Tabitha to be with her.'

'And why didn't he?'

'From the messages it seemed this other woman suddenly grew a conscience and didn't want to break up the relationship.' Her laugh is knife-sharp. 'Can you imagine?'

I think about how enraged Henry would be at this woman's rejection and I wince.

'Anyway,' she goes on, 'when Tabitha confronted him, she thought he'd beg for her forgiveness, since his bit-on-the-side had broken things off. He didn't. He wanted Tabitha out of the house but she had nowhere to go. No job anymore.'

'No job?' It isn't really a question, but it's all I can manage. The hairs on the back of my neck start to lift. Mine and Tabitha's lives are mirror images of one another's, with Henry the glazier. So where is she now? What did he do to her? What was he planning on doing to me?

'He asked her to quit her job,' Cleo explains. 'Told her he didn't want to be with someone who worked as much as he did. She did data entry at the hospital but always wanted to paint. He told her to give up work and then he bought her an easel. It all seemed very romantic.'

'Until he got bored.'

She nods. 'Tabitha threatened to tell the papers about the affair, or post about it online to expose him. She said she wanted him to pay her off, but I think she was hoping she could buy herself more time in the house so they could work things out. She was in love with him, right up until the end. One day she just stopped answering my calls, messages. He'd already made her delete all her social media so I couldn't reach out to her there either.'

I'm nodding – this explains why there was no trace of Tabitha Gates when I googled her.

'I went to the house and Henry told me they'd broken up. That she'd moved out. I didn't believe it,' Cleo says. 'Because the week before, Tabitha and I had reconnected. She'd have told me.'

I'm quiet, thinking about Tabitha. How Henry carefully selected her. How he seduced her and made her feel like the most precious thing in the world. How he manipulated her. I think about how, when Henry had Tabitha eating out of the palm of his hand, he closed his fist and isolated her from everything. Everyone. There will be things Cleo doesn't know. The sex tapes Tabitha didn't consent to. The nights he plied her with alcohol and the intercourse that followed, which she couldn't remember. Angry, sad tears well in my eyes. I furiously blink them away. Cleo is gracious enough to avert her gaze until I collect myself.

'You said you filed a missing persons report,' I say. 'What happened after?'

'They investigated. Without Tabitha there to explain about the receipts, they found no evidence of another woman, which meant they had no motive. Apparently, Henry offered the police a handwritten letter from Tabitha to say she was leaving him. But how did they know he didn't force her to write that letter or that he'd forged it altogether? I said as much, but they thought I was a lunatic. Henry Frith. *The* Henry Frith, an abuser? A murderer? They didn't believe it. One officer even suggested Tabitha may have hurt herself. She had a history of depression. Who wouldn't, after losing both their parents? But I don't believe she'd throw herself off a bridge or whatever it was they theorised . . .'

Cleo looks away then, swallowing a potent cocktail of anger and sadness before she continues.

'Henry has three powerful advantages on his side: he's wealthy, white and well-educated. With the police proving to be useless, I decided I'd finish what she started and go to the papers . . . but the story was never printed. They contacted him for comment and he set his lawyers on me. He took out a court injunction to stop the news outlets reporting on it.'

'How?'

'Money. He argued it was slander since the police found no wrongdoing, and if I were to spread my *salacious* lies, it would damage his business. Frith & Sons has a carefully curated, family-friendly image.'

'Which an affair or a missing fiancée would ruin?'

'Exactly.'

We sip our tea in silence but the questions, the noise, in my mind is so loud, I can barely think.

'So the woman I met who said she was Tabitha . . .'

'An actress maybe? If you were getting suspicious, it was in Henry's best interests to do whatever he could to mislead you. Tabitha's story didn't even make it into the news, her social media accounts were gone. She was always a private person, she shied away from the limelight. Henry liked it that way. Liked that she didn't want to be photographed at public events. He's the jealous type, so it suited him that she was for his eyes only. If you'd looked for a photograph of her online, you'd struggle to find one.'

'But Jonty was there. He acted like he knew her.'

She looks at me over the rim of her mug. 'You know as well as I do that Jonty is his partner in crime.'

The bedroom. The two of them, their meaty hands groping and pawing. The memory rushes up like bile but I swallow it down. I thought I'd be floored by all these revelations, but after everything that's happened, I'm numb to it all.

'I'm sorry about Tabitha,' I say.

Cleo gives me a sad smile; she knows that the breakdown of a friendship bruises the heart so much worse than the breakdown of a romantic relationship. Though lovers come and go, friends are meant to be there always, weathering the storm.

'Have you saved others from him?' I ask.

'I keep a close eye. I'm not ashamed to admit I've followed him before now. I saw you together, walking through Bath in the summer. He took you to the same restaurant he took Tabitha.'

The one by the weir, that night my father called. The same night Henry met my mother and realised I was easy pickings. 'But how did you find out my name? Where I worked?'

'Henry doesn't have a social media presence, but Jonty does. The two of them don't often stray too far apart. I went through his posts, earmarked all the ones Henry was in and then did a little digging. It took time, but eventually I found photographs from a wedding tagged at Pennard House. The couple had commented on the post, thanking the venue for such a wonderful day. The bride's profile was public, and when the couple's wedding photographs went live, I spent time going through their tagged guests. I recognised you instantly as the willowy redhead I'd seen heading towards the restaurant with Henry.' She sips her tea. 'You have your place of work listed on your profile. Your public profile.'

I am stunned into silence. It was so easy to find me. Too easy. My fingers itch to privatise all my social media pages. I want to slam the doors shut on my private life and keep it that way.

'You're the first one since Tabitha that he's taken a real interest in,' she offers. 'You know, moved in with, proposed to. All that. His attention usually dwindles long before now.'

'Lucky me,' I deadpan. We fall quiet again. It's starting to rain. Softly. The sound of it against the windows is soothing. 'What do you think he did to Tabitha?' I ask, and it's Henry's voice I hear. *I'll bury you.*

She stares out of the window, across the garden. Outside, although it is raining, it is bright and beautiful.

'I don't like to imagine, but whatever it was, she isn't coming home.'

Cleo offers for me to stay the night with her. I can't. I have somewhere I need to be. I thank her for the offer and make a mental note to pay back the stolen ten-pound note and return her trainers.

But, just as I slide into my car, I think about the email address and ask, 'HTH?'

She smiles. 'Here to Help.'

Chapter Forty-Nine

When Ivy answers the door, her face is the perfect picture of shock. She is barefoot, dressed in cream pyjama shorts and matching cropped T-shirt. I hold my breath, expecting her to slam it shut. She doesn't.

'What are you doing here?'

'I've left him. It's over.'

When I said that to Henry, it was like I was playing a part in some dramatic, low-budget stage show, but saying it out loud to her makes it feel true. I'm worried she will tell me to go. That when I sided with Henry, I betrayed her, betrayed us. That crawling back to her after all these months and everything that's happened isn't an option. I'm so afraid of being rejected by her, no matter how justified, that I feel sick.

'Ivy, I'm so sorry,' I say.

Her expression is unreadable. The air hisses and spits. I wait. I want to remind her of it all. Of our lives together. Of what we had before him. I want to promise her I will never let her down again. I want to drink wine with her and lie with her under the covers of her big bed. I want to tell her how much I love her. But I don't. I wait. And wait. And—

Her face splits into a smile, eyes shining. It's as though someone has moved the clouds away from the sun. We collide, clinging to one another tightly. I bury my face in her neck and breathe in the familiar, comforting scent of her Wild Bluebell perfume. I sob with relief. With the certainty of knowing she is mine and I am hers and we were made to fit.

Inside, on our big rust-coloured velvet sofa, I tell her everything. She listens intently. Guilt is a dagger in my ribs.

'I'm so sorry,' I say again, through tears. 'I'm sorry for all of it. For bringing Henry into your life, for calling you a liar. Oh, Jesus, for what I said about Odette and—'

281

She takes my hand and squeezes it. 'No one is perfect. That's the thing about people who love you, they love you back even when you don't deserve it. It's in the past. It's behind us.'

The ease with which she's forgiving me makes the guilt that much worse. I thought she'd be angrier, that she'd make me work for it. But maybe she's felt my absence as keenly as I've felt hers, and she's as grateful as I am that we've finally found our way back.

'Are you going to report the rape to the police?' I ask softly.

Her hand slips from mine and she looks away. 'You know I can't. He'll deny it. I have no proof. He'll tell them what he told you, he'll show them the messages I sent about meeting in a hotel room.'

'Why did you send those messages?' I ask hesitantly.

She sips her tea. 'I thought if he agreed to an affair in writing, I could show you and you'd leave him. It's stupid, but I was desperate. Even if I was deluded enough to think I had a chance of getting a conviction for the assault, Henry would retaliate. He'd hand those images of me and Roman to the police without a second thought.'

'If he hands over the images, he'll have to admit to perverting the course of justice or withholding evidence.'

'The charge I'd face for murder is far more serious than the one he'd face for withholding evidence. He'd have more to gain than he would to lose. And they'll never believe I was reaching for Roman, not shoving him.'

'They might.'

'You didn't.'

Shame and remorse colour my cheeks. 'Maybe you could say it was self-defence.'

'And serve time for manslaughter?'

She's right. But I still can't bear the thought of Henry getting away with it. 'How do you know Henry still has the images?'

She won't meet my eyes. 'Because he isn't stupid.'

I get this feeling she's hiding something, but I don't know how to push it without upsetting her. That, and my track record of not believing her when she's actually telling the truth, doesn't serve me well.

'If you really don't think you can go to the police, I'll support your decision, but maybe you could go to therapy? Talk to someone about what he did?'

'They.'

A rock drops to the bottom of my stomach. 'What?'

Her eyes find mine. 'Talk to somebody about what *they* did.'

I don't need to ask who 'they' are. How many women have Henry and Jonty shared? And how many of them were willing?

'I'm so sorry,' I breathe, around the horror. The shock.

'It's not your fault. You didn't make them turn up to that party.'

But I did, didn't I? I told Henry it was Ivy who'd mentioned Tabitha, and he was so infuriated, he went hunting for her. It *is* my fault. If I hadn't thrown her under the bus, he wouldn't have come after her. He'd never have raped her. I swallow thickly. The guilt crests like a wave, sweeping me up and pulling me under until I'm drowning in it.

'Henry was fuming I'd told you about his missing ex-fiancée,' she says quietly, as though reading my mind. 'I wanted to leave the party but it was my friend's birthday and she convinced me to stay. I drank, but not enough to get drunk, I was too on edge for that.'

'What happened?'

She shrugs. 'The next thing I remember, I was in a taxi, hemmed in by Henry and Jonty. After that, everything goes black. When I woke up, Jonty was naked beside me, drinking a whisky. I couldn't remember anything, but I could smell them both all over me. I was sore. Covered in bruises.'

I am too angry, too pained to say anything. And nothing I say will change what they did to her.

'I staggered off the bed just as Henry came out of the bathroom. The way he stopped and looked at me, satisfied. Arrogant. He knew he'd stolen a piece of me I'll never get back.' Tears slide down her cheeks. He *has* stolen something. The vivid acrylic ink of who she was *before* is gone. Now, she is a watercolour. I want so much to give her back what Henry took. But I can't. When something this horrific happens, there is the person you were *before* and the person you are *after*.

We sit in silence. I fight back my tears. It isn't my place to cry, to make her pain about me. She's so small. I swallow my revulsion at the thought of two of them on her, *in* her, manoeuvring her like a plaything. A doll. I move my knee so it's touching hers, to remind her that she isn't alone.

'Why didn't you ever tell me Henry hit on you at a PR event?' I ask gently. 'At the wedding when I mentioned you, I saw this flash of recognition in his eyes, but he denied knowing you. If I'd realised he'd had a thing for you, I'd never have entertained the idea of getting involved with him.'

'Who told you about that?'

'Luke.'

She looks away quickly. 'I asked him not to say anything.'

'Then why risk telling him?'

'Luke came by the house. I wasn't coping well after . . .' She swallows and shakes her head, as though trying to dislodge the memory. 'After the assault, and then our confrontation in Bellflower Park. I broke. I told Luke everything. The PR party, the rape . . .' Her breaths are coming faster, harder. I shift a little closer to her, to let her know she isn't alone. 'I told him in confidence. I didn't think he'd charge over to Henry's like that and tell you everything I'd asked him not to.'

'Don't be mad at Luke. He didn't have a choice. He was trying *again* to make me see what kind of person Henry is.' I brace myself against another wave of regret. 'Of course Luke was going to defend your honour. You're like a little sister to him.'

She turns away from me, taking a blanket from the sofa and wrapping it tightly around herself. I can see this conversation is bringing it all back, hurting her, but there's still so much I need to know.

'Why didn't you mention Henry had hit on you while he was engaged? You know how I'd feel about that.'

'Of course I do,' she says a little briskly, as we both remember the ultimatum I issued her when she got involved with Quinn.

'You could've told me all about his character when you found out I was seeing him.'

She shrugs. 'What happened with Henry was years ago, and by

the time you told me, you were besotted. He has a reputation for getting bored easily. I hoped you'd have a fun little fling and then both move on. But that didn't happen.' She sighs. 'When you invited him to the housewarming party and I saw the two of you together, I realised things weren't fizzling out, they were getting more serious. I confronted Henry there and then but he warned me if I brought it up with you, you wouldn't believe a word.'

There was so much tension between the two of them that night. Between us as well. But there's more I need to know. Other things that happened where the lines between truth and lies are blurred. This is the ultimate game of he said/she said. I bite my lip, wondering if I can ask my next question without hurting her.

'So when Henry said you stabbed him—'

'I didn't,' she says quickly. Firmly. 'I met with him and told him I had evidence of the assault, and if he didn't admit to you what he did, I'd go to the police. He said I was lying, which I was. But he must've been worried because he injured himself, or got Jonty to, and blamed me. Whether he was hoping to discredit me in your eyes or in the eyes of the police, I don't know. When I left him, though, he was very much in good health.'

I'm nodding like this is all normal but it's outlandish. Ridiculous. Though, with the disappearance of one fiancée and the accused rape of another woman, he'd be in hot water and maybe desperate enough to hurt himself if he thought it would help him later. 'Is there anything else I need to know?'

She shakes her head but the feeling that there is more crawls up my spine. I'm about to ask if she's sure when she says, 'Look, can we please stop talking about Henry?'

There's so much anguish in her face that I agree immediately. 'Of course. Sorry.'

We lapse into silence again. It's getting dark now. Henry will have discovered I'm not where he left me. That is, if he was planning to come back to the house at all tonight. I'm glad I don't have my phone. There will be a hundred messages from him, each more furious than the last. I need to think about where I'm going to stay tonight. What my next move is. Before I go, though, I have to ask.

'Have you heard from Luke?'

She reaches for her tea. 'Why would you think I'd heard from him?'

'He and I may have stopped talking, but the two of you remained close.'

'He hasn't been in contact for a while.'

I feel myself pale.

'Zara?' She sits up straighter. 'What's wrong?'

Panic fills me slowly, like water being poured into a glass. 'Two weeks ago, Luke came to the house. He was apoplectic. He attacked Henry for what he did to you.'

I recount it all. The fight. Jonty whisking me away upstairs. How Henry and Luke were alone on that driveway for God knows how long. My chest tightens. The glass overflows and I grip the back of the sofa, struggling to draw breath. I should've just called the police. I should've done more. What if he's dead? What if Henry's made Luke vanish forever, just like he did Tabitha?

Her face appears in front of mine. She is on her knees, telling me to breathe.

'Look at me,' she says. 'Look at me.'

I do. I inhale deeply and let it out slowly, keeping my gaze fixed on her long dark lashes until my pulse stops leaping about like a rabbit caught in a trap.

'Luke isn't dead,' she says. She is so confident, it makes breathing even easier. 'He's probably on a trip. Things weren't easy for him after you and Henry got together.'

I'm nodding. Slowly, I tip the glass up, letting the anxiety drain away. When I am calm again, she sits on the sofa beside me.

'I never meant to hurt Luke,' I say. 'I loved him more than I've ever loved anyone. You were right, I was convinced if I did things in the right order, I'd be happy. But there is no *right* order. It should've been Luke. It was always Luke.'

She hesitates only a second before saying, 'Are you going to tell him that?'

'No. I mean, not yet, anyway. I can't even think about having that conversation with him at the moment.'

She falls silent, staring down at her hands folded in the lap of her crossed legs. She looks young, with her hair falling in front of her face. Something is wrong. I'm about to ask, when I realise I already know. I take her hand.

'In the future, if I tell Luke how I feel, and things between him and me fall back into place, it won't change things between me and you. I won't ever let a man change our relationship again.'

Chapter Fifty

That night, she asks me to stay. She tells me she doesn't want to be alone. We make dinner. A delicious, meaty spaghetti Bolognese, with garlic bread. We listen to music from our university days. We share wine and conversation. It's as though I never left. Tomorrow, I will make a plan. I will start over. For now, I concentrate on chopping onions with a knife that is far too big but the first one I could find. The wooden board is thick and hefty, a solid piece of oak with a live edge – H.H. carved into the wood. It's the housewarming gift from Henry.

'I'm surprised you kept this,' I say, nodding towards the board.

She takes fresh pasta from the fridge. 'It's not the board's fault the person who gave it to me is a psychopath.'

'True,' I say with a smile, and lift it to scrape the onion into the pan. 'It's heavy.'

She pushes the back door open to let in a breeze. It's the first day in August and so hot in the kitchen, I can barely breathe.

I go upstairs to shower and change before dinner. I slip into soft lounge shorts and a T-shirt, loosely braiding my wet hair. Music drifts up the stairs, louder than before. I imagine her dancing in the kitchen, a glass of wine in her hand. As I reach the bottom of the stairs though, I feel something is wrong. I stand still in the hallway and listen. The music is loud, but beneath it, I can't hear the scrape of pots and pans or the sound of her singing along.

What started off as trepidation hardens into fear as I enter the kitchen. It's empty. I stand still, scanning the scene. The sauce simmers on the stove. There's a glass of half-drunk wine on the counter. The knife I was using to chop the onions earlier rests on top of the heavy wooden board. I call for her.

Silence.

The hairs on the back of my neck lift. Something isn't right. She wouldn't leave her own house without telling me.

I turn to look for her upstairs, already knowing she isn't up there. I'd have heard her, surely? But then, with the shower running, maybe I wouldn't. I walk slowly back up the stairs, not sure why my heart flutters erratically in my chest. The only feeling worse than being alone in a big old house is sensing that you aren't.

The room that used to be mine is empty, as is the neighbouring spare room. Glancing down the hallway, I see that her bedroom door is ajar. It wasn't before. I'm sure when I went into the kitchen to look for her, the door was shut. Terrible, icy fear drips inside me. An instinct stops me from calling her name as I move silently towards her room. I stand outside and listen. There's a breeze. Beneath the roar of my pulse, I hear a muffled cry. Without thinking, I fling it open and tumble into the room.

'Stop!' thunders Henry.

He stands in front of the French doors that open out onto a small balcony overlooking the walled garden, and one arm is snaked around her shoulder, with his free hand wrapped around her throat. Her back is pinned firmly against his chest. He is holding her hostage. The moonlight casts eerie, dramatic shadows across his jaw and cheekbones, while she keeps her expression neutral. But I can see the uneven rise and fall of her chest as my heart pounds deafeningly in mine, a lump of terror in my throat.

'What are you doing?' I hear myself ask Henry.

'Taking you home.'

'She . . . *is* home,' Ivy protests, though the pressure of his hand on her throat makes her words strained and weak.

Henry squeezes and her eyes widen in fear.

'*Stop!*' I shriek. 'Have you lost your mind?'

'If I have, it's because of you two *bitches*,' he hisses back, though I see the uncertainty in his eyes, and though he is still gripping Ivy tight, I can tell his nerve is faltering.

'You're disgusting,' I spit back. 'You can't blame either of us for your behaviour. *You* drugged me. *You* tried to share me with Jonty against my will. *You—*'

'That's not what happened.'

'Stop it. Stop lying.' My voice is calm, and he looks at me briefly in surprise. No doubt he was expecting I'd be hysterical.

We stare at one another. If I thought it would make any difference, I'd tell him that if he ever loved me, he'd be honest. But appealing to someone's good side only works if they have one. Looking at him now, face contorted with hostility again, I'm not sure he does.

'Fine,' he says, surprising me. 'Yes, I slipped you something to loosen you up. You were paranoid. A nervous wreck. I was trying to help you relax.'

The way he says it, so nonchalantly, as though it's absolutely normal, expected even, to drug your fiancée, makes me wonder how many times he's done it.

'You're twisted. Sick. You were going to force me into—'

'I'm not a rapist,' he shoots back, his face hard.

Ivy opens her mouth to argue but I shoot her a warning look.

For once, she does as she's told.

'*Think*, Zara,' he tells me, as though I am an idiot child. 'At any point, did you say no? Tell us to stop?'

Words clog in my throat. I'm caught out. He's right. I didn't. But I didn't say yes, either.

'If you'd asked us to stop, we would have,' he assures me. 'I was surprised you agreed to Jonty joining us in that bedroom.'

'I didn't agree to anything!'

'Are you sure about that?'

I hesitate. My memories from that night are blurry, like I'm viewing it through frosted glass. I can't actually remember. And if I can't remember, how could I possibly have consented?

'You'd drugged me,' I said. 'You made sure I couldn't say no.'

He doesn't answer, but any vindication I feel at knowing the truth is overshadowed by his wider crimes. This isn't just about what he did to me.

'You raped Ivy.'

'No!' he snarls, sharp and irate.

Why admit to drugging me, but deny assaulting her?

I look at her. She's mouthing for me to run. But I won't. Not without her.

'Just *please* let her go, Henry,' I beg.

'You're coming with me.'

'Don't go with him,' she says boldly.

Infuriated, he crushes her throat again.

I take a step forward, but to my alarm he steps back onto the balcony.

'Wait there,' he orders me.

Fearing he will choke her right in front of me, I do as he says. Outrage balls my hands into impotent fists. I need to convince him to leave.

'You don't need me,' I tell him with feigned confidence, remembering what Cleo said. 'You'll move on quickly. There are plenty of women who'd kill for the lifestyle you offer. Who'll be excited by it. By you.'

He laughs, a short, cutting sound. 'Is that what you think this is about?'

Not sure where this is going, I keep quiet.

He glances down at her. 'Haven't you told her?'

And there's something about the way her gaze slides to mine, the look of dread on her face, that makes my heart canter. I get that feeling again, as though my world is shifting.

'Tell me what?'

He gives her a sharp shake. 'Go on, Ivy. The floor is all yours.'

Her eyes hollow with something. Regret? Sympathy? She presses her lips together, refusing to speak.

He jerks her so roughly, she cries out.

I step forward, desperate to intervene, but he barks for me to get back. 'Tell her,' he commands through gritted teeth.

She closes her eyes, as though she can't bear to look at me. 'His anger isn't about you.'

Suddenly, I don't want to hear whatever it is she has to say. I feel the enormity of it expanding, moving through the room like lava, and I know I am about to be incinerated by it.

'It's about me,' she says. 'About me and Henry.'

'You and Henry?' I repeat dumbly, rolling the words around on my tongue, *tasting* the intimacy of it. *You and Henry.*

'Yes, it's about us.' His voice is thick, like double cream. He looks down at her in a way I've never seen him do before. It is all lust and sex and breathless heat.

'*You* were his lover,' I hear myself say. 'You're the one who had an affair with him behind Tabitha's back.'

And it all makes sense. The flash of recognition I saw on his face when I mentioned her at the wedding. Her instant and irrational dislike of him. The real reason she didn't tell me that Henry had hit on her at a PR party years before is because it was so much more than that. It wasn't just a misjudged flirtation; it was a full-blown affair. She failed to warn me about Henry, because if she had, she would have had to admit that she'd broken her promise and hopped into bed with *another*, if not married, then as good as, man. When I came here tonight, she forgave me so easily. Now I know why.

'I didn't find out he was engaged until later, but I did the right thing,' she says, pleading her case. 'I broke it off with him.'

Henry's expression darkens at the memory.

'As soon as you found out he was engaged, you ended it, did you?' I ask, already knowing the answer – she only called it off once he was willing to leave his fiancée to be with her.

Shame creeps across her cheeks.

What if Tabitha *did* kill herself after her relationship broke down? Or Henry dispatched her to clear the path for him and Ivy? Seeing him now, his hand around her throat, I think he's capable of it. No matter what the scenario, *she* played a part in the vanishing of Tabitha Gates.

'Why didn't you tell me?' I ask her.

'I wanted to but I couldn't admit to the affair, not after I promised you I was done with married men. I believed you when you said if I ever got into a situation like the one with Quinn again, you'd walk away.'

'SO WHY DID YOU?' I yell.

'I'm sorry. I'm so sorry. I'm not lying. I really didn't know Henry was engaged. Not at first. I got caught up.'

Her recklessness, her ability to make everything feel dangerous, always excited me. It was intoxicating. It kept things interesting. The problem is she always takes it too far.

'I didn't want to admit to you how I really knew Henry – the affair, Tabitha – but when I found out at the masquerade ball that you were moving in with him, I knew I *had* to tell you, even if it meant losing you.'

'But you didn't . . .'

She licks her lips. 'No. I couldn't. Roman's death that night meant Henry had something to hold over me. He pulled me aside after Roman fell and warned me that if I breathed a word of our affair to you, and stopped you moving in with him, he'd tell the police I was involved in my cousin's death. He even threatened to make you vanish, just like Tab—'

Henry's hand tightens around her throat and her words are trapped in a gurgle. 'You're a vindictive bitch,' he spits at her. 'You sabotaged my relationship with Tabitha and now you want to sabotage my relationship with Zara, too. You're not going to win. Not again.'

This entire time, the two of them have been playing a game of chess and I am nothing more than an unwitting pawn. My heart races almost as fast as my mind. I look at Henry. 'Did you deliberately target me at the wedding because you knew who I was to Ivy?'

'No,' he says. 'I knew she'd be at the wedding. I saw you talking to her but I didn't realise how *involved* the two of you were until you volunteered the information.'

I wince, hearing myself tell him we were like sisters. With that one comment, I'd sealed my fate, slipping my head into the noose while he tightened it around my neck.

'And once you knew, that was it,' I say through furious tears. 'You were going to pursue me no matter what, just to get one over on her. You wanted to destroy my relationship with Ivy to punish her for destroying your engagement to Tabitha. It's all been one big game.'

'No,' he says, but it's weak. A lie.

I'm remembering that day in Mokoko's when we bumped into one another. I'd thought it fate but maybe it was by design. Henry knew my name. He could've found me on my socials. They're public. I'd posted a photograph of my coffee and tagged my location. It was barely an hour later that he turned up. I've been manipulated from the very start. Over and over. I am hot with betrayal, with humiliation and despair.

'We're done, Henry. I never want to see you again. Just leave! GET OUT!'

He glares at me like a spoiled prince. For him, rejection is like arsenic, and he won't swallow it without a fight.

'We're going home to talk about this.'

'I'm not going anywhere with you. How can I after all the lies, the games, the manipulation? You heap so much blame onto Ivy. She isn't innocent, but neither are you. She didn't put a gun to your head and force you to cheat on your fiancée, Henry. *You* made a choice. *You* ruined your own life.'

I can see his temper is boiling over, his mantle of control slipping, but I can't stop. All the fear and frustration and fury rush out of my mouth on a torrent.

'You're nothing more than a monstrous, sociopathic *rapist.*'

He bubbles over, whipping her around so she's on the balcony. He thrusts her forward, and she screams. I race across the bedroom but Henry bellows for me to stop. I stumble to a halt beside the bed. He bends her over the balcony, one hand on the back of her neck, forcing her head over the railing. If he tucks his free hand beneath her knees, he could easily flip her over it.

Her arms flail wildly and her next, panicked scream rends the night air. Desperately, she claws at the hand around the back of her neck. If he tosses her over the side, she will plummet headfirst onto the paving stones below. I'm seized by the memory of Roman's wet, toothless mouth. The pieces of brain and bone splattered across the concrete.

I cling to the four-poster bed as terror steals the strength from my legs.

'Henry, please.'

'Tell her I didn't fucking rape you,' he yells at her. 'Tell her. Fucking tell her.'

But she doesn't. She refuses. She screams, but she will not do as he asks.

I see his patience running out fast, like a match burning down to the end, only it is her who will be snuffed out.

Do it, Ivy, just say it. Please just say it.

She doesn't.

He reaches for her legs, preparing to toss her to her death. 'I'LL LEAVE WITH YOU!' I shriek.

He glances back at me.

'You win, Henry. I'll leave with you.'

He is breathing hard. He looks down at her and for a moment I think he'll toss her over the railing, just to see her fall.

Slowly, he lets her up. But he doesn't release her. She stares at me, hair wild, tears streaming.

'Don't go,' she mouths.

But what choice do I have?

Henry alters his grip, capturing both her wrists and pinning them behind her back. He walks her into the bedroom and I am thankful she's away from the balcony's edge.

'We need to tie her up,' he says.

'Why?'

'So she can't follow.'

He clicks on her bedside lamp and looks about the room for something to secure her with. I glance around the room too, looking for a weapon, but even as I do, I can't imagine using it. I remember what she said to me after Roman broke in: *Everyone is capable of killing when pushed.* But I'm not sure I could.

He spots her dressing gown on the bed and leans forward to take the tie from it. Seizing her opportunity, she flings herself forward, onto the floor. The sudden shift in weight throws him off balance and she slips free. Scrambling to her feet, she races towards me and grabs my hand.

Then we're running. Along the hall, down the stairs. My hand squeezed tightly in hers. I hear him behind us, his boots echoing as he gives chase. I hit the bottom step just as arms go around my waist. Then he is lifting me, spinning me away. My hand is wrenched from hers. I kick and scream. He sets me down in the kitchen but catches my plait. He winds it around his hand and wrenches my head back. Hair rips from my scalp and I scream again. He loosens his grip, but I am panicked, struggling to be free. His hand slips from my hair but he shoves me forward. I round on him, too terrified to speak.

She is on the other side of the kitchen, beyond the island. I am on the side closest to Henry who stands in front of the door. On the stove, the water for the spaghetti is nearly boiled dry, steam pumping into the air. We ignore it. I scramble back, away from the island until I hit the counter. His gaze lands on the knife I was using earlier and he snatches it up, advancing on me.

I throw my hands out to fend him off. 'Henry! Henry, stop!'

And he does. He looks down at the blade in his hand and blinks at it as though he can't remember picking it up. The rage is slowly burning off and what's left is confusion. I think he's almost as shocked by his actions as I am. It's only now that I realise how strongly he smells of alcohol.

'What're you going to do, Henry?' I ask, voice quivering. 'Kill us both? Is this vendetta really worth throwing your freedom away for?'

It's like I am trying to extinguish a forest fire with a cup of water, but still, I can see him thinking, weighing up his options.

'If you walk away now, it's over. We put it behind us.' I keep my gaze locked with his, imploring him to listen. 'Jonty isn't here to cover for you. If you do this, Henry, you do it alone.'

We are breathless and exhausted. I wait, shaking all over. Too terrified to blink in case he lunges. Then his expression shifts and he looks suddenly much older than he is. Finally, he slaps the knife down onto the island.

I feel some of the tension dissolve.

He steps forward until we are barely two feet apart, then he shakes his head, as though I am his deepest disappointment.

'You're going to end up just like your mother; a tragic, baying, fucking waste of air,' he says, his words dripping with acid. 'Fuck all of you.'

Then he turns slightly in the direction of the back door, making to leave.

There is a crack, gun-shot loud. It makes me jump. His eyes bulge.

Then there is another crack and another. Something wet and warm splatters across my face.

The shock drains from his eyes. The disappointment and the fury and the life drains from them, too. He drops to his knees, and I see a flash of crimson. Then he crumples to his left. I stare down at his body, fallen at an odd angle. He looks small. Blood pours from the back of his head and across the floor in a thick, dark stream.

I don't need to check for a pulse to know he's dead. There's a hole in his skull big enough to fit my fist.

Slowly, I raise my gaze. Ivy stands pale and still, the thick, hefty chopping board still clutched in her hand, coated in a sticky, hot film of his blood.

'Ivy,' I breathe. 'What have you done?'

Chapter Fifty-One

Now

I dress in something respectable and black. I do my make-up and brush my hair, leaving it to fall in waves around my shoulders. Just how you like it, Ivy.

Like fire. Like the sun coming up.

I scrutinise my reflection in the mirror of my studio flat, knowing my photograph will once more be plastered all over the news by this afternoon.

The media will wait for me outside the courtroom, as they always do. We're nearing the end of the trial and the media attention, the public interest, is insatiable. They have gobbled up every gory detail, sucked the meat from each juicy tidbit, picking over the corpse of our story, and still they aren't satiated. There's something delicious about a millionaire's killing, especially when it involves two attractive young women. The worst reporters aren't the ones that shriek my name or shove microphones in my face, they're the ones who grab me, who leave red welts on my arms from their greedy, desperate fingers.

In the nine months since Henry's death, I haven't become used to the media frenzy. My face sells papers. Millions of them. It makes people click on their notifications whenever my name or a photograph of me pops up on their phone. What you did that night has made me famous, Ivy. You've made the entire world fall in love with me. And I hate it.

I'm grateful the studio flat I rent is tucked away in a gated community. It's small and lacks the luxury of Henry's home, or the grandeur of Holt House, but I'm comfortable here. It's cosy. It isn't the cottage by the sea Luke predicted, but it is filled with books and vintage candlesticks and plants. No golden cocker spaniel yet, though my therapist has encouraged me to get a dog to help with my anxiety. If it weren't for Hillington Wedding Planners taking me back, I wouldn't have been able to afford to rent anything at all. They've been so generous. Celia, the founder of Hillington, has even been advising me on how to start my own business. And I will. Not now. But one day.

I glance at the clock. It's seven in the morning. I don't have to be in court until just before nine, but I have a visitor coming. He'll be here soon.

I sit on our rust-coloured velvet sofa, which I rescued after the police tape was taken down, and I sip chamomile tea to calm my nerves. I drink a lot of soothing tea these days. It doesn't stop the night terrors. When I close my eyes, I see men falling from the sky, splitting open like watermelons at my feet. Or I am trapped in dreams of a kitchen without doors, where I slip-slide across a blood-slick floor and crunch over pieces of fractured skull. Because of you. Because of what you did, Ivy, I can't sleep at night. And when I do, I wake with a jolt, my breath locked in my chest.

The intercom buzzes, telling me he's arrived. I inhale deeply, readying myself, and let him in.

I offer tea. He takes cold water instead. He sits at my little table, so tall and broad, he makes it look like something from a child's playhouse. He's cut his hair, but kept the stubble. The pale grey suit is new, but like me he's dressed for court. And though he looks different, more refined, his eyes still make me think of stone and steel and winter skies.

'Thanks for coming, Luke.'

The day Henry and Luke fought, Henry warned him to stay out of his business, threatening to hurt the both of us – me *and* you – if he didn't. Luke's attempt to defend you and rescue me had been catastrophic. So he retreated to a friend's holiday home in the New Forest to regroup, leaving civilisation and his phone behind. He wanted space to clear his head. He was in a bar when the story hit the news. He returned to Bath immediately.

After I was released from police custody without charge, he tried over and over to reach out. I never reciprocated. Until now. He doesn't know why. He doesn't realise I know his secret. Still, I don't have all the information. He's here because I have questions I need answered before I go on the stand today. I could dilly-dally with small talk, but we don't have time, so I cut right to the heart of it.

'Are you in love with her?'

He frowns. 'Who?'

'Ivy.'

Silence.

'What?'

'It wasn't just sex, was it? It was more than that.'

I think of you in that study with your grandfather, popping stolen chocolates onto your tongue as a young girl. Was that the first time you were told you were special, Ivy, above everyone else, entitled to things you aren't allowed? All those married men. Then Henry. Then Luke.

He thrusts his fingers back through his hair. 'Did she tell you about us?'

'She doesn't even know I know.'

His frown deepens. 'Then how . . .'

'I saw a necklace in your bathroom. A ruby on a gold chain. After Ivy and I were arrested, the police showed me photographs of people they believed were involved in the events leading up to Henry's death. In the one they had of Ivy she was wearing that same necklace. It didn't take a genius.'

There were other clues too, ones I'm not willing to share with Luke. When I rake back over everything, it's plainly obvious to me that you were in love with him, Ivy; that you had been for years. He was the only man you ever approved of, ever complimented, who shared in your anguish and rage at losing someone. Besides me, he was the only other person in the world you let past your acerbic wall. And that day in the park, right before you told me Henry assaulted you, you said you knew what it was to love someone from afar who will never love you back because they're wrapped up in someone else. I'd wrongly assumed *I* was the object of that love. But it wasn't me, was it? It was Luke.

'Did you go to her after Henry hurt you?' I ask.

He nods. 'I stayed with her a few days before going to the New Forest.'

It makes sense now, why you were so confident that Luke was OK after the confrontation.

'How did it start?' I ask.

'Zara—'

'I want to know.'

'Let's not do this.'

'Please.'

He looks away. 'You were with Henry,' he says finally. 'You and Ivy weren't speaking. *We* weren't speaking. I felt like I'd lost you. And so did she. One night, she asked me to come over. We stayed up talking about you. We ate. We drank.' He sighs. 'It just happened.'

'And kept on happening?' I say with more accusation and hurt than intended. After all this time, it still stings. I battle the image of the two of you together, sharing a bottle of red. The little looks that turned into more. I can see you now, taking a dessert from the fridge, something thick and rich and dark. One dessert. Two spoons. The perfect recipe for the beginnings of a mouth-watering affair.

He puts his head in his hands. 'I'm sorry.'

'I loved you,' I whisper through the burn of betrayal. 'I loved her.'

His eyes are remorseful but there's fire in them, too. 'You were gone. You were off with *him*.'

Silence.

'I know.'

I lean against the kitchen counter and stare at the patch of spring sunshine splashing across the wooden floor. It's bright today, but the forecast promises rain. Unbidden, an image of you and Luke unfurls in my mind; you are naked and on top of him, your head thrown back as he moves inside you, your nails digging into the taut muscle of his bare chest. Then the image changes and it's me beneath you, Ivy. My skin against yours.

'You didn't answer my question,' I say. 'Do you love her? Are you in love with her?'

'Does it matter?'

'Yes.'

Silence. This time it is thick and expectant. 'I think I was.'

Something inside me breaks, and I suck in a breath as the pain takes hold. I go back to looking out the window. Somewhere in this colossal betrayal, I recognise that you encouraging me to be with Luke while you were secretly in love with him is the most selfless thing you've ever done. Let's be honest, you could have had him whenever you wanted. Like me, like all men, he was in thrall to your siren song.

He gets to his feet. 'I waited for you.'

'I know.'

'I didn't think you'd ever leave him.'

'I know.'

He stands in front of me, forcing me to meet his eye, but I can't without remembering what it was like to be loved by him. He taught me what it was to feel safe. You both did. Without him, without you, will I ever feel truly safe again?

'Before Henry, I thought you and I would eventually start a life together,' he tells me. 'It was you, Zara. It was always you.'

'Until it was her.'

He doesn't deny it.

The pain in my chest returns, visceral and not to be ignored. The tears come, even though I try and stop them. His face is so close to mine that I breathe in the scent of him: cedarwood and pepper, heat and skin. He wants to touch me, but he can't. And I'll never let him touch me again.

'Look,' he says imploringly. 'Don't let what happened between me and Ivy affect what you say on that stand today.'

'And what do you think I'll say?'

'Honestly? I don't know.'

'What do you want me to say? Do I tell them it was self-defence or murder? Because that's the magic question. That's what everyone so desperately wants to know. Will I save her or condemn her?'

He turns towards the window. Beyond the gate, the media and the rest of the world await. They are salivating to hear my story. I am the key witness. My testimony is the main course.

'What will you say?'

'I have no idea.'

'Henry could've made you disappear, like he did Tabitha.'

The prosecution deemed the situation with Tabitha inadmissible in court, claiming it has no bearing on you being tried for Henry's murder. No one really knows what happened to Tabitha, and thanks to Henry chipping away at her relationships, there aren't many people left who care. Except for Cleo. She has worked tirelessly to prove Henry's involvement in Tabitha's disappearance, but to no avail. I thought she'd be bitter and twisted about it. I would be. But she says she's glad, that at the very least she played a part in saving me from him. Now he's dead, he can't hurt anyone else. Can't make them disappear, either. Cleo is a friend I think I'll have for life.

'He was a monster,' Luke says vehemently.

'But it wasn't Ivy's place to decide whether he lived or died, Luke. What he did wrong doesn't make what she did right.'

'Doesn't it?'

'Henry was leaving. I talked him down, he was unarmed and ready to go before she picked up that chopping board.' I close my eyes against the memory, counting back from ten until I open them again, and when I do, he is watching me carefully, trying to make me understand.

'She did it for you. She said you'd never be free of him, so she did what she had to do to save you.'

'I DIDN'T ASK TO BE SAVED!' I yell. The air between us is tension-filled and electric. I have to tell him what I know. I'm not doing it to be spiteful, or that's how I justify it to myself. 'Did you know Henry was blackmailing her? She was paying him to keep things hidden.'

He stills. 'What?'

I think back to you sitting on that sofa the night Henry died, how you were so certain he still had the images, but you wouldn't say how you knew. And Henry telling me after we missed the flights to New York for Christmas that he'd found a new source of income: it was you, Ivy. The money you were paying him to keep the photographs a secret. 'Thousands every month. The police have no idea *why* and she obviously won't tell them it's because Henry had photographs of her with Roman before he died.'

'Henry had more money than sense. Why would he need to take anything from Ivy?'

'It was never about money. It was about power and punishment. He got a kick out of making her submit. Did you know? Did she tell you?'

He shakes his head. 'No.'

'Of course not. I love her, Luke, but I also know she's secretive and manipulative. The two people who came between her and her money are dead.'

He looks up sharply. 'So what – you think she'd always planned to murder Henry?'

'He claimed she stabbed him. Sometimes I believe it. Maybe that was her first attempt to rid the world of him. *Herself* of him. Other times, though, knowing what Henry was capable of, I'm sure he did it to himself just to discredit her. But one thing I know for certain: two can only keep a secret if one of them is dead.'

He snorts, angry with me now. 'By your logic, we were next because we knew about Roman, too.'

'No. Of all the people who knew, Henry was the only one with actual evidence. Even if we'd wanted to tell the police she killed Roman, his death was already ruled an accident. He was drunk, there were class A drugs in his system when he died.'

The police have never found the evidence that Henry had against you. I assume it was left with Jonty. Now Henry's dead, Jonty has nothing to gain by coming forward. He'll open himself up to an investigation which, knowing what he did to you and tried to do to me, wouldn't be in his best interests.

'Ivy never told me about the blackmail,' I say. 'Or about her affair with Henry – or about the two of you. She withholds information. She always has an agenda. She's told you and anyone else who will listen that she killed Henry to protect me, but what if she was just protecting herself? What if she saw an opportunity to silence Henry for good? And in cold blood, she took it?'

He shakes his head. 'I don't think Henry Frith's death is much of a loss. He was a rapist. Maybe Ivy's reason for killing him had nothing to do with money and everything to do with the fact he raped her. Maybe, Zara, you feel guilty for bringing him back into her life after she warned you to steer clear, after those emails tried to warn you, after *I* tried to warn you. And now you need everything in this situation to be black and white so it's easier for you to navigate, because what happened has made you question your own judgement.'

I can't speak. There's some truth in what he's said. More than I'd like to admit.

'You need to be sure about what it is you're going to say today, Zara. Once it's out there, that's it,' Luke tells me evenly. 'The truth isn't black and white and no one is ever completely innocent.'

He leaves shortly after that. He has to get to court, too.

I am so overwhelmed by it all, so confused and lost, not knowing what to do, that I stuff my fist into my mouth to stop myself from screaming.

For so long, I thought I needed a husband and a baby to complete me. *You* to complete me. Now, I am trying to complete myself. But I'm adrift and I miss you, Ivy. Sometimes, the agony of missing you feels like a weight that will crush me to dust and carry me off on a breeze. Sometimes, I wish it would.

When I am calmer, I go to the window and open it. A cloud passes over the sun. I can feel you, somewhere in Bath, not too far away. We are still tethered by that gossamer thread. I wonder if you are thinking about me too. I shut my eyes and try to imagine what it will be like to see you again with the entire British legal system between us.

I still don't know what I will say when I take the stand. There are two possible outcomes, but it will start the same way. When I am called forth, the room will fall silent. Waiting. There will be eyes on me. But yours will be the only pair I long to meet. Though I must avoid them until I have said my piece. I'll hear the scratch of pencil on paper as the court artist draws my face.

They will ask all the boring questions people are desperate to skim over quickly. My name, my age, my address. Then they will dig into the meat of it. They'll ask me how I know you.

I'll tell them how I was heartbroken and in pieces on a sticky bathroom floor when you burst into my life and sang to me, putting me back together with confident, manicured hands. This part of my story, at least, will remain the same.

But then I have a choice.

In the first instance, I'll tell them what they expect to hear. I'll confirm all the things the papers write about you, weaving a tale of sex and power and money and obsession. I'll tell them how you were the life and soul of every party. The glittering disco ball at the centre of every social event. That you ensnared married men. That you set your sights on Henry even though he was taken, engaged to Tabitha Gates. That when he realised the mistake he'd made, he broke things off with you. I'll tell them I was the object of your next infatuation – which aligns with the smear story Amira sold to the tabloids. That you were bitter and furious when Henry, the man you'd wanted for yourself, took an interest in me, your new obsession. The prosecution speculate you were so jealous of my relationship with Henry, you viciously butchered him. The papers speculate you may have viciously butchered Tabitha, too, hoping Henry would return your feelings once she was gone.

Maybe I will lay it all bare. How you inherited Holt House. How your cousin wanted to claim the estate and everything with it for himself. How your aunt had told him about the letters your mother had penned to your father about his affairs and raising a child that wasn't hers. How Roman entered our home and found them. How, at the masked ball, you saw an opportunity to bury the secret, and so you did, pushing him to his death. And then, later, when Henry threatened you with images of what you'd done and blackmailed you, you were so infuriated by his audacity at coming between you and your money, that part of you was pleased when he entered through the back door of Holt House that night because you had a chance to end him, too.

How afterwards, you begged me to lie for you. To tell the police he was coming at me, fists raised, and you saved me. You didn't have a choice. How you asked me over and over as shock enveloped me, *'How much do you love me?'*

The courtroom will be enrapt.

The prosecution will ask me again, 'Was the death of Henry Frith by Ivy Holt self-defence or murder?'

I'll wait a beat, the tension will mount and then I will answer, 'Murder.'

And finally, I'll look at you. And it will break my heart to know that I will never see you again or hear your laugh or feel your soft skin, but I'll walk away knowing that, no matter what, I told the truth. I wasn't like you or Henry. I didn't lie or manipulate. It will be hard, but maybe it will be right.

The judge will sentence you to life in prison, and finally – finally – it will be over.

But there's another way.

I could tell the courtroom that you have always protected me. That it wasn't obsession like the papers say, like Amira says – it was sisterhood. I'll tell them how your mother chose to end her treatment and leave you with your father, a man she knew could never love you the way you deserved to be loved. How we lay in your big bed and listened to her dying. I'll tell them of your generosity, how you let me make Holt House a home without ever taking a penny from me. How you, alongside Luke, helped pay my mother's rent. I will tell them that we planned to grow old together, knitting each other matching cardigans and keeping half-a-dozen cats. The court will fall in love with you, just like I did.

I'll tell them how everything changed when I met Henry. Not because of you, but because of him. How he charmed me and promised me a picture-perfect future. How he manipulated me into downloading a tracking app onto my phone. I'll tell them about the sex he recorded without my consent and the sex I don't remember having. I'll tell them how he was quick to anger. I'll tell them about my suspicion that he drugged my mother and drugged me, too. How, on that last night, my life was in danger and you, Ivy, were my only hope of survival. I'll tell the court how he threatened our lives. I'll tell them your story. That he came at me. That you picked up that chopping board because there was no other choice. That I am grateful you saved me.

The prosecution will be disgruntled. Reluctantly, they'll ask, 'Was the death of Henry Frith by Ivy Holt self-defence or murder?'

Only, in this version, I will lift my chin and meet your eye and answer, 'Self-defence.'

Now my mother arrives at the house to travel with me to court, and I still don't know what I will do. But I know I will not look at you when I testify. I can't. It's too hard. In the car, Mum sits on my right and Dad on my left. Both of them take my hands. This is the only positive thing to come out of this horrendous mess; my parents are a united front, relieved their daughter survived.

Time passes until finally it is my turn to take the stand. It is exactly as I imagined. They ask the questions no one is interested in. I give them my name, my age, my address. I do not look at you. What I wasn't prepared for is how hard it would be to keep my gaze from yours. I feel myself drawn to it, like a moth to a light in the dark.

I want to know if you killed Henry to protect me or to protect yourself. It shouldn't matter because either way, you killed him when you didn't have to. But I still want the answer. I breathe deeply. The adrenaline is dizzying. I am so light-headed I have to grip the wooden rail in front of me. I do not look at you. But I feel you. I must decide. I must pick a version of whatever story I am about to tell. Luke is right, there will be no going back.

I realise, in this moment, I am angry with you. I didn't choose this, Ivy. I didn't choose any of it. That night, you made a decision for us both. And now I suffer the consequences of it, the media maelstrom, the night terrors and panic attacks, the bone-splitting agony that comes with deciding your fate. I wish you had never picked up that chopping board. Henry would have walked out of Holt House, and we wouldn't be here now. Maybe I'd never have found out about you and Luke. Maybe we could've fallen back into our lives together.

Still, Henry hurt you in the worst possible way. Perhaps he'd never have stopped coming after us both. Perhaps the decision you made was the best one, even if it was grey instead of black and white.

I do not look at you. Until I do.

Our eyes lock. And I see in them the most pressing question of all. *How much do you love me?*

Acknowledgements

Firstly, thank you to my agent, Thérèse Coen. You are a constant stream of support, wit and wisdom. And my gratitude always to everyone at Hardman & Swainson for all your hard work.

Eternal thanks to my editor, Hannah Smith. I don't have the words to explain how dramatically you have changed my life. All I ever wanted was to be a published author and you granted my most precious wish. Thank you for signing me, for believing in me, for making me a better writer. I have been exceptionally lucky to work with you.

I have infinite appreciation for everyone at Embla Books. I am confident that I have the *best* team of women around me. Emilie and Jane are wonderful and patient and kind. Jennifer Porter was instrumental in the success of my first novel, *One Small Mistake*, and I know *The Perfect Match* is safe in your capable hands. The same goes for Marina Stavropoulou who expertly brought the audiobook version of *One Small Mistake* to life. I am confident you'll weave your magic on this story too. An extra special thank you to Anna Perkins – without you, this would be a very different book. You poured so much time into this story and you understood these complex characters completely. You're supremely talented and working with you has been a gift. I think you're brilliant.

Thanks to Dr Matt Stuttard for the medical advice, and to

detective-turned-author Caroline Mitchell for answering my legal questions.

To all the wonderful people I work with, thank you for stopping me in the halls to talk about my books, for listening to half-thought-out plots, for buying and reading my first novel and for being endlessly kind in your reviews of it. And a special shout out to Andrew Chapman for your patience and suggestions.

This book is about women and the friendships we forge. It's a book that wouldn't exist without two incredible women who have been with me for more than half of my entire life. Thank you to Lucy Perkins for your kind heart, your generosity and your thoughtful nature. You are my sister. We will always find our way back to each other. Thank you to Mel Monteath, the first person to read this story, for your honest gems of feedback; I've never been more grateful for your morbid fascination with true crime. I really would not be the person or the writer I am without you. Thank you both for patiently listening to my second-book fears and for soothing each one of them.

Thank you to the friends I've been lucky enough to know for years. With special mentions to Hazel Ho and Joanne Wells who devoured my debut and have eagerly awaited my second novel. I hope it doesn't let you down. To Rachel Delahaye-Lefever who I met when I was just eighteen years old. Babysitting your two gorgeous children paid my way through my first degree, and your insistence I'd be published one day got me through years of rejection. Thank you for never letting me give up. And to Joanna Nadin, the first person who encouraged me to stop writing for children because I was too twisted and too dark, and to turn my acerbic wit and expletives to stories for grown-ups. Thank you for teaching me that difficult, wild women are fascinating and also pen-worthy.

And thank you to Jenn Bateman and Lia Anson, new friends made on dog walks and at puppy parties, for all your encouragement. And to Rachel Rowlands who understands.

To my mum for reading every page of every novel, published and left in a drawer. Your love and enthusiasm mean everything. I'm sure eighty percent of my sales is down to you. I know you are proud, and I am so grateful to have parents who always told me I could.

Many thanks to every reader who bought and reviewed *One Small Mistake*. And a very special thanks to those of you who took the time to reach out and contact me personally to express how much you loved my first book. Connecting with so many of you has been the most tremendous part of this writing journey. I hope *The Perfect Match* is loved just as dearly.

And lastly, thank you to Josh Butler-Smith. At the time of writing this, you are my fiancé but, by the time you read this, you will be my husband. We met on our very first day of university and though I never expected to find the love of my life, I am thankful every day that I did. Right from the start, we supported one another's dreams. Thirteen years on, we are published writers with two wonderful cocker spaniels, and we are living a life we love. I am so proud of how far we've come and I'm excited for our future. Thank you for being *nothing* like any of the men I write about. You are my familiar face now and always.

Dandy Smith

Dandy Smith lives in the Somerset market town of Frome with her husband and two cocker spaniels. She has an undergraduate and master's degree in Creative Writing from Bath Spa University and enjoys all things aerial fitness, Gilmore Girls and chocolate orange.

About Embla Books

Embla Books is a digital-first publisher of standout commercial adult fiction. Passionate about storytelling, the team at Embla publish books that will make you 'laugh, love, look over your shoulder and lose sleep'. Launched by Bonnier Books UK in 2021, the imprint is named after the first woman from the creation myth in Norse mythology, who was carved by the gods from a tree trunk found on the seashore – an image of the kind of creative work and crafting that writers do, and a symbol of how stories shape our lives.

Find out about some of our other books and stay in touch:

Twitter, Facebook, Instagram: @emblabooks
Newsletter: https://bit.ly/emblanewsletter